TAKEN
IN THE
COLD

BOOKS BY ROGER STELLJES

Agent Tori Hunter
Silenced Girls
The Winter Girls
The Hidden Girl
Missing Angel
The Snow Graves
Their Lost Souls

ROGER STELLJES

TAKEN IN THE COLD

bookouture

Published by Bookouture in 2024

An imprint of Storyfire Ltd.
Carmelite House
50 Victoria Embankment
London EC4Y 0DZ

www.bookouture.com

Storyfire Ltd's authorised representative in the EEA is Hachette Ireland
8 Castlecourt Centre
Castleknock Road
Castleknock
Dublin 15 D15 YF6A
Ireland

Copyright © Roger Stelljes, 2024

Roger Stelljes has asserted his right to be identified
as the author of this work.

All rights reserved. No part of this publication may be reproduced, stored in any retrieval system, or transmitted, in any form or by any means, electronic, mechanical, photocopying, recording or otherwise, without the prior written permission of the publishers.

ISBN: 978-1-83618-090-6
eBook ISBN: 978-1-83618-089-0

This book is a work of fiction. Names, characters, businesses, organizations, places and events other than those clearly in the public domain, are either the product of the author's imagination or are used fictitiously. Any resemblance to actual persons, living or dead, events or locales is entirely coincidental.

Taken in the Cold is my fifteenth novel, a threshold I could never have ever imagined achieving when I first put pen to paper in 2002. That I have is due in no small part to my namesake, my dad, Roger Stelljes Sr.

Rog Sr. is a loving husband of Mary for sixty years, father of three boys, Roger Jr., Chad, and Matt, of which I am the oldest, grandfather of eight, a high-school social studies teacher for thirty-four years, a football and hockey coach for just as many and a friend and mentor to so, so many. The number of lives you've impacted so positively simply boggles the mind.

Without fail, Dad, you have always been there to talk, to listen, to help, to guide, to provide wisdom, to motivate, to encourage and support. You have and continue to instill in all of us a strong sense of right and wrong, a will to fight and compete, to strive and achieve, to live full and meaningful lives and to do it all with grace and humility.

It seems fitting Taken in the Cold is at its very base, a story about love, never giving up, and fighting to the very end no matter the odds. Dad, the very characteristics you have imbued our entire family with.

So, it is with immense pride and gratitude that I dedicate this book to my dad, Roger Stelljes Sr.

Chief, I couldn't have done it without you.

Thanks, Dad. I love you.

ONE

"GOOD MORNING, SPORT."

February 23rd

6:37 a.m.

There was just the beginning of light in the frosty morning sky. When the sun did ultimately rise, it would do so behind ominous dark gray clouds, a foreboding warning of the blizzard barreling down on Manchester Bay. According to the local meteorologists, snowmageddon was coming.

Jenks's winter coat, thick pants and long underwear were keeping the icy four-degree Fahrenheit air at bay. He peered around the corner and over the top of the tall woodpile, breathing through his nose, limiting the airy exhales that would hint of his presence, were anyone inside the house to look outside.

The first lights came on in the kitchen window. If inside, he no doubt would have inhaled the comforting rich smell of brewing coffee. A moment later, pulsating flashes of colored light reflected in the long bay windows of the family room. The television had been turned on, to CNBC no doubt. For the man he was watching, business never slept.

It was all part of a usual morning; one they had observed several times of late.

Routines. Rituals. Habits.

Such disciplined consistency drove success and the man certainly had plenty of that. The modern house, one of three vacation homes he owned around the Western Hemisphere, was evidence of that. For Jenks's purposes this morning, those consistencies also made him predictable, and vulnerable.

Twenty minutes later, the deep darkness of the early morning sky starting to lighten, he heard the garage's side door loudly creak open in the crisp morning air. Keeping his back tight to the house, crouched low behind the tall woodpile, he caught a glimpse of the man carefully stepping out the side door in his winter running gear. The navy-blue nylon running suit with white stripes, the bright yellow stocking cap on his head, that matched the yellow running shoes, all very color coordinated and on schedule.

He heard the man's feet speedily crunching in the snow, starting off along the side of the garage. Peeking around the corner, he glimpsed the man, the yellow stocking cap bobbing along, jogging down the driveway, taking his customary morning run. He gave the man a good minute and then checked around the corner again, this time peering up toward the bedroom window.

The curtains were closed.

He walked around the woodpile and made his way up the steep hill, weaving his way through the dense mixture of pines, spruces, oaks, elms, and hickories, stopping at the edge of the tree line and taking one more look up to the windows at the back of the house. All seemed quiet though he knew she was up and about somewhere inside, starting her day as well.

He high kneed the fifteen feet through the snow to the back

patio, and then made his way up the landscaped steps to the unlocked side door and slipped inside the garage.

He made the call.

Towne immediately answered. "He on the way?"

"Right on time."

* * *

Teddy gritted his teeth, gazing into the mirror as he brushed, getting all the way back along the side as his dentist instructed last week. "You're ten years old, Teddy. You're getting permanent teeth, you don't want cavities in them, do you?" the dentist said, playfully holding up his drill as both joke and warning. "If you do, I have to use this." The drill hissed its evil high-pitched grinding whir. He cringed, suddenly wanting out of the chair and away from all things dental.

The dentist was a funny guy, and now he knew he was just playing him, but just the same, why risk it. He brushed a little harder, one more sweep, reaching all the way back one more time, before rinsing and wiping his face. He gave his thick, wavy brown hair a quick brush as well, organizing it a bit, knowing if he didn't, Mom would and when she did it, it wasn't all that gentle. And it wasn't as if Dad gave him any sort of break on it either when he stayed at his house. A professor and a banker, neither of them let much slide.

"Teddy!" his mom called from downstairs.

"Yeah."

"Are you up?"

"Yes, Mom," he said, exasperated, and then mumbled, "of course I'm up," at the ass crack of dawn, as his dad would say.

"I'm making breakfast."

"Okay."

She would drop him off at school on her way to work at the university. The good news was he could smell breakfast. Eggs and bacon. It was for him, *and Ed*, but still, that was becoming maybe okay. He didn't like that his parents were divorced. But he was learning that Ed was nice. He was pretty chill as compared to his mom, whom they both called The Professor, but only when she wasn't able to hear them.

He was tying his tennis shoes when his mom called up again, "Teddy!"

"Yeah, Ma?"

"Dress warm, honey. Add a layer. I mean it. It's really cold out with the blizzard coming. And you're wearing a winter coat today, young man."

Yeah, yeah. He had on a T-shirt and was planning on wearing his bulky Timberwolves hoodie. But she would check, so he grabbed a black, long-sleeved crewneck and pulled it on over the T-shirt. He could take it off at school and stuff it in his backpack. Speaking of which, he better get that packed.

The backpack was downstairs. As he rushed down the stairs he looked out the window and saw Ed, who was coming up the driveway, finishing his usual morning run.

"Did you put on an extra layer?"

He held up his hoodie.

"Good boy," his mom said, kissing him on the head. "Go pack. Breakfast is almost ready."

"Any chance school gets cancelled? Or shut down early?"

"Cancelled, no. Close early? I'd say that's entirely possible, especially since it's a Friday."

"Cool." Who didn't want to get out of class early? He rushed back up the stairs.

Bap!

He spun around at the loud popping sound.

"E-E-Ed?" his mom called worriedly. "Ed?"

* * *

Jenks felt the slightest bit of perspiration as he pressed his back against the interior garage wall to the right of the door.

He heard the crunch of the footsteps.

Just about forty minutes on the run. Not bad in this frigid air.

The door swung open to his left. He waited a two count and stepped from behind the door.

Bap!

The silencer and garage muffled the gunshot, but only some. It was still plenty loud.

The man crumpled to the floor, a hole in the back of his head.

Jenks stepped over him and hustled between the vehicles to the door leading to the inside of the house, which opened as he came around the back of the Cadillac XT5.

"Ed?" The woman's eyes went wide. "Ed? Wha—" She back stepped inside the house. Jenks, his gun up, followed her inside into the kitchen. "No. No! *No!*"

Bap! Bap!

He stepped over to her body and stood over her, two wounds in her upper chest. Her mouth open, gasping, her eyes wide in shock. "This has been a long time coming, bitch," he murmured, looking her coldly in the eye, aiming, feeling the tension of the trigger as his finger pulled it back. "You won't be putting down people like me anymore."

Bap!

As he'd thought earlier, the kitchen smelled of coffee and breakfast.

"Mom?" a meek voice came from upstairs.

* * *

Barry Marist stared out the front picture window into the white expanse of his front yard and the great wide open of the new housing development beyond. There were not yet many homes, his being one of the first. Instead, he gazed upon vast piles of gravel and dirt, now covered with a light dusting of snow, soon to be covered with so much more. It was a blank canvas, much like his new house itself he thought as he turned around, the sparse furniture new, the white and gray walls blank and antiseptic, unlike his old home.

The divorce had been inevitable and ultimately vitriolic and messy. He and Lainey had not been happy as a couple for some years, yet despite it all there were times he was wistful about their home together. Unlike his new one, their old one had been warm and lived in, overflowing with pictures, paintings, and books, and a life centered around their ever-growing and active son. The only hint of that old life now was Teddy's two game controllers and stacked DVDs resting on top of the entertainment center under the brand-new large flat-screen.

In the kitchen, the steam rose out of the burbling new coffee pot, in harmony with the slices of toast popping up out of the toaster. As he spread a light layer of margarine over the toast, the local morning news played on the small kitchen television. A winter storm was barreling down on them. The meteorologist, or what a local radio personality on the Power Loon called the weather terrorist, was predicting a storm as massive as the Halloween Snowstorm of 1991 that blanketed Minnesota with nearly three feet of snow.

Barry peeked out the back kitchen window. The snow hadn't started yet, but if the weather radar was any indication, it would soon enough. His employees would be asking to close the bank branches early to get home ahead of the weather. It was supposed to really be coming down by 5:00 p.m. If he knew Elaine, she would likely close all the branches no later than noon so people could get home before it all hit.

And no doubt, schoolkids would be looking for an early release from school as well. At least that was his thought when he saw his phone light up with Teddy's face at pretty much the usual morning time, 7:42. He'd be one of those kids.

"Good morning, sport."

"D-D-Dad! *Dad!*"

"Whoa, Teddy, what's wrong?"

TWO

"BIG STORM COMING."

7:39 a.m.

"Gunshots?" Will Braddock said questioningly to the call from dispatch burping out on the police radio, looking over to Steak who was driving. They were motoring south on the H-4. "Out there? On the lake? Now?"

They had just finished up breakfast at the Halfway Highway Diner, so called because it was halfway between Manchester Bay and Holmstrand to the north. They were heading back into Manchester Bay when the radio crackled with the call.

"And with this damn storm coming in," Steak muttered.

Ahead they saw a sheriff's department deputy coming up from the south, lights, and sirens.

Braddock exhaled. "Well, I guess since we're in the neighborhood."

"Duty calls," Steak said and called into dispatch that they would be responding as well.

Steak turned right and followed the deputy down a winding

road that led out to a grouping of houses and cabins spread about a broad peninsula jutting into Northern Pine Lake, that in a way served to divide the northern and southern halves of the long southwest to northeast lake. They reached a fork in the road, though the road would simply loop around to all the homes on the peninsula. To the left was a man dressed in a camouflaged hunting jacket, orange stocking cap and snow boots waving them down. He was standing at the end of a long driveway, arms resting on the top of his snow shovel. A two-story house rested a couple of hundred feet in, perched above the lake.

The deputy, Austin Michaud, turned and drove to the man, and they followed. Steak was out quick, flashing his badge, identifying himself and Braddock. "You called it in?"

"I did."

"What is it you saw or heard?" Steak asked.

"Mostly heard. I was in my garage. I'd just gotten back from the convenience station out on the highway, you see. I was filling up the five-gallon gas tank so I could gas up my snowblower. I think I'm going to need it, don't you know."

"Big storm coming," Steak noted. "Gunshots though?"

"I hunt birds and deer. What I heard was muffled but I know the sound, Detective. You know what I'm saying? That pop?"

"I do," Steak replied, letting his gaze drift to the location. "Gunshots plural? How many?"

"Two for sure I heard when my ears perked up after I thought I heard the first one. So, maybe three. I walked out of the garage and through the gaps in the trees, I saw a big black SUV racing away. After I saw that, something just didn't seem right. I called it in not but—" he checked his watch "—five, six minutes ago. You guys got here quick."

"Which house?" Braddock asked, looking west.

"The big two-story modern squared one down on the opposite corner of the loop there. That's Ed Girard's place. That's the only other place regularly occupied down there during the week. Especially now that his lady friend moved in."

"Do you know him well?"

"Ed's neighborly enough for a rich retired Silicon Valley type. I saw him out taking his morning run earlier when I drove to get the gas. We have a call list for all the houses out here. I called him but he didn't answer. Then I called you guys."

"And you saw an SUV streaking away not long after?"

"That's right. It was a big one, black, maybe a Suburban or Excursion, though I can't be sure, the woods kind of obstructed my view, but it was big like one of those."

"You didn't recognize it?"

"No, but it was a movin' I tell ya."

Braddock looked to Steak and Michaud. "We better go take a look."

They drove over and less than a minute later Steak and Braddock were fast-walking down the left side of the long driveway leading to the house.

"The neighbor seemed on the level," Steak said.

"That's what worries me," Braddock murmured in reply, glancing back to Michaud who was parked at the end of the driveway.

The driveway opened into a wider apron in front of the three-stall garage to the right of the house. The curtains were closed on all the house's front windows as Braddock approached the front porch. He glanced back. Steak had stopped in the driveway.

"What?" Braddock asked.

"I'm just looking at these tire tracks in the snow is all," Steak replied, crouching, his nose scrunched, looking from the garage door to the far side of the driveway. "Hmpf."

"What?"

"They don't come out of the garage."

"But these come out of the house," Braddock said, pointing to the footprints in the light dusting of snow on the sidewalk leading from the front door. Keeping to the side, he took a step up and was under the front door portico and tapped the doorbell, hearing it ring inside. There was no response as he tried to peer into the narrow slit between the horizontal shade and edge of the narrow window to the right of the door. With no doorbell response he knocked on the front door.

The door pushed open.

Braddock instantly pulled his gun. "*Psst.*"

Steak looked up to see the front door cracked open, Braddock tipping his head for him to come, his gun in his right hand. Steak pulled his own gun and flashlight and quickly joined him on the front step. Braddock nudged the creaking door all the way open with his left foot.

"Sheriff's department. Anyone home?" Braddock called out, his voice echoing inside the quiet house.

No response.

He looked back to Steak, who nodded. Carefully, he stepped inside, his gun up now, on alert, Steak on his right hip doing the same as they stepped into a wide rectangular foyer.

The house smelled of bacon and coffee, yet had an eerie coldness to it.

To their right, Steak with his gun up, was scanning the open staircase up to the second floor. To the immediate left, Braddock peeked into the in-home office through glass doors. Straight ahead led into an expansive family room with a wide and tall picture window looking out to the frozen and snow-covered Northern Pine Lake. As they moved forward, the right side opened to a modern kitchen of bright-white upper and grayish-blue lower cabinets and marble countertops, and a massive kitchen island. The eating area with a long table was further to the left and overlooked the open sloping yard down to the lake.

"Will," Steak murmured, and then nodded. "Kitchen floor."

Braddock glanced right. On the floor, to the left of the long kitchen island, there was a small, dark reddish liquid pool edging out.

Blood.

He nodded and swung out further to the left while Steak went to the right.

Behind the kitchen island, lying on her back on the floor was a woman, her eyes open, her arms spread out. She'd been shot twice in the chest and once in the forehead. Not that there was any question, but Braddock checked for a pulse anyway. He took a longer look at her face. She was familiar.

"You know her?"

"I recognize her for some reason. Can't place it."

"She took two, center mass," Steak murmured.

"And then finished off to the head," Braddock said. "Executed."

"A hit? On her?"

"Don't know," Braddock said, then gestured to the floor to the right of the body. "9mm casing."

"Two back here as well."

Thud!

Steak spun quickly to his right toward an open door into the garage. Braddock backed away from the body and hustled around the island and they both moved to the garage.

Thud!

Steak peered around the corner into the garage. "It's the back door," he said, "banging from the wind."

"It's open why?"

Steak stepped down two steps into the garage, stepping around the back of an SUV, and his shoulders slumped.

"Dammit."

Braddock hopped down the steps and followed Steak between two SUVs to find a man in a navy-blue tracksuit lying face down on the garage floor. He had been shot in the back of the head. Braddock noticed another 9mm shell casing on the floor next to a tire.

"Who are these people?" Steak muttered.

"We better clear the house and then find out," Braddock ordered, and the two of them went back into the house and cleared the remaining rooms of the first floor. They were empty.

Braddock led the way up the stairs to the second floor. On the landing they saw a child's backpack lying on the floor, the contents of it spilled open with papers, pencils and markers strewn across the wood floor of the hallway, leading to a bedroom at the end of the hallway to the right.

"Oh boy," Steak murmured sullenly. He knelt to the backpack. There was a laminated name tag on it. "Teddy Marist."

Braddock slowly walked down the hallway toward what looked to be a child's bedroom, steeling himself. He peered inside the half-open bedroom door, grimacing at what he was about to see.

Or not.

The bed was unmade, and the closet doors open, but the room was otherwise empty.

Steak opened the door to another bedroom, which was dark and clean, the bed made, the shades pulled. A guest room.

"Teddy?" Braddock called out. "We're with the police. I'm Detective Braddock. Come on out if you're hiding."

There was no response.

They cleared the bathroom to the right and another spare bedroom. At the far end of the hallway was a large master bedroom. The pillows, blankets and sheets were strewn about the king-sized bed. The master bathroom and closet were empty. They made their way down to the finished walkout basement, but there was nobody down there.

"No kid," Steak said. "The black SUV maybe?"

"That's what I'm thinking," Braddock replied as they hustled up the steps and to the front foyer. "Call it in."

He took out his cell phone.

"Who are you calling?" Steak asked.

"Who do you think?"

Tori answered on the first ring. "Hey there."

"We need you."

THREE

"EXIGENT CIRCUMSTANCES."

"How do you know he's missing?" Tori asked as she rushed down to the basement two steps at a time and punched in the combination for the gun safe, retrieving her favored Glock 23 and checking the magazine.

"I don't... for sure... yet."

"Any blood?"

"Other than in the kitchen or garage, not that I see."

"Have you spoken to the boy's other parent yet? Mother or Father?"

"No. Not yet. We're still trying to figure out who he is."

"You know it's a he?"

"The boy's last name is Marist, Teddy Marist. It doesn't match the man or the woman's names. Given that, I'm thinking it's likely *her* son."

"But you haven't identified or spoken to the father yet?"

"No."

"Then how do you—"

"I just... do, Tor. Trust me."

"Got it," she said as she grabbed her duffel bag that had her

Kevlar vest and other equipment and started back up the stairs. "Anything else?"

"Steak went back to talk more to the neighbor who called it in. I've got a deputy knocking on doors. More help is coming."

"And the two decedents?" Tori asked. "Who are they?"

"Well." He sighed. "I'm thinking you might know one of them. Lainey Darr."

"Lainey Darr? Professor Darr, from the university? She's in my department."

"That's her. Minnesota license, with an address in Manchester Bay, though it sure looks like she's living here based on all the women's clothes in the master bedroom closet. And there's a Central Minnesota State University ID in her wallet. Did you know her?"

"Not well but I knew her," she replied. "Who's the man then, her husband?"

"Hang on a second."

She had her gear. *What next?* It was freezing outside, and the storm was coming in a few hours. Better dress for it. She rushed upstairs. Braddock was back.

"The man is Edward Girard, age fifty-seven. He has a California license in his wallet though he also owns the house and has been living here regularly, at least according to the neighbor."

"Is it a nice house?" Tori asked as she pulled on her full body thermal underwear.

"Very."

"Maybe he's one of those Californians that have a summer place here? Here for a weekend getaway maybe, although what a terrible weekend for it with the storm coming," Tori mused as she pulled on thicker socks. "So not her husband." She thought for a moment. "You know I think I heard something about a divorce with her. Maybe he's the new man."

"Could be. Do you know who her ex-husband is?"

"No."

"Well, I think this house may be a second home for Girard given his California license, although it looks like he's settled here. Lots of clothes. Cluttered home office with papers. Neighbor said he was a retired Silicon Valley guy."

"And the missing kid?" she asked, pulling on her thick winter parka.

"Tori, I don't know a thing about the kid yet beyond his name, Teddy Marist," Braddock reported. "He might not even be missing, but everything I see here says to me he is. Until we find him, he's missing and that's where you come in."

"I'm on my way," she said, tugging on winter gloves and a black wool stocking cap. From a box on a high shelf, she grabbed a handful of hand warmers and stuffed them in her coat pockets.

"Lights and sirens all the way. You're on the payroll."

She threw her duffel bag in the back of the Audi. If there was going to be lights and sirens she needed her portable police light, which she retrieved from the storage compartment. It was six minutes from the call from Braddock to when she backed out of the garage. She would have to go around the southern end of the lake and through Manchester Bay to get to the east side.

As she accelerated away, police light and siren blaring, it hit her. The break was over.

Tori hadn't worked on a case with Braddock or the sheriff's department in eight months.

It had been a much needed and enlightening respite.

She had been feeling good, her mind as relaxed as she could remember it being—ever. Or at least since she was seventeen.

Would going back now change that?

The last two cases she'd worked on before her self-imposed exile involved college kids, good kids, senselessly murdered. One victim last July, Allison Mannion, was the daughter of their good friend Kyle Mannion. She and Braddock knew Ally. And an old friend of Tori's, while not responsible for Allison's murder, was working with the men that were, and she lied, repeatedly, to Tori about it. Tori had watched her friend, a mother with a twelve-year-old daughter, a girl the same age as Quinn, throw her life, and her life with her daughter, away.

It had all weighed on her.

Even before the last investigation started, she wasn't sleeping due to a prior case a year ago now. When she did, there were recurring dreams, bad dreams. Dreams about dead college kids, shot senselessly on the front steps of a home. Nightmares replaying a phone call with an assassin who made a credible argument, at least in Tori's mind, that she and her were very much alike, given the murders of loved ones in their teens. The assassin hadn't killed the college kids. She'd come out of hiding to kill those that had. "We're not that different, you and I," she'd said to Tori.

How could she be anything like a Mob assassin? Yet, the assassin had found a way to hit that nerve. And it lingered, long after the call.

She could just feel it. Her good friend Tracy, visiting from New York last summer, could see it. A dark cloud forming.

Did she need retirement from this kind of work?

She didn't need this. Her financial situation was secure. There were other things she could do.

But was that what she wanted? Truly wanted.

She didn't know.

What she knew then for sure was that she needed a break, some time to breathe and think and assess. Braddock said she should take whatever she needed on the proviso: "If I need you. If I truly absolutely need you, I can call."

In July, she bagged all her gear and stuffed it in a basement closet, locked her guns in the safe, forgot about them and relaxed.

There had been a leisurely month of August that included a big party to celebrate completion of their home remodel, a long weekend trip with Braddock to a resort outside of Denver for a Dave Mathews Band concert at Red Rocks, another few days away at a wedding and a last-minute Labor Day weekend girls' trip to Boston to visit friends from college. Mixed in had been a lot of long runs and swims, moments of peace where she found herself able to let her mind drift to new things. Since September she had been teaching her criminology classes at the university and it was classes, plural, her normal class and the one she took over for a professor who left CMSU for Washington State University a week before the semester was to begin. It had gone well enough that she was filling in for the spring semester as well. There was an opening for a full-time professor, with full-time pay and benefits starting next fall. The head of the College of Humanities and Social Sciences, Doctor Silby, met with her yesterday to gauge her interest in the position.

"Full-time academic?" Tori had asked skeptically.

"Why not. You're an authoritative expert on the topics at hand. The students really like you and, even more, respect you. Your FBI career, what you've done since you've been back here, all carries weight. And not just with the students, but the university too. I don't know if you know this, but there was a waiting list for your classes this spring."

"I didn't know."

"The students' actions speak. And I've observed. You're a natural teacher. Sometimes, we get professionals as adjuncts who think they can teach but what they do is tell war stories and spoon-feed the material. They don't really make the students *think*. You do. You make the kids figure it out. I've seen it, even in a one-hundred level class. You're walking that student out on the branch, getting them out of their comfort zone, making them think on their feet asking them what if this or what if that happened, and making them work through the problem. They're learning. We can always use more of that."

"I'm flattered. Truly," Tori replied honestly and then thought of Braddock. "And if I get called into a case? You know, if Braddock calls?"

Silby smiled. "It's *that* work that makes you that much more attractive to us. That practical, real-life experience and the ability to teach from it. Those are the kinds of professors we want teaching and molding students. There are always ways to work around problems like a call from Will Braddock, Tori. As long as your lectures are prepared and ready, classes only last an hour a few times per week. You can probably break free for an hour here and there to teach. If not, well, with the wonders of modern technology, we can record lectures and make them available online, so it works with your schedule, and we just tell students upfront they need to be flexible. Email lets you be more available to students. Office hours can be moved, papers and tests graded when you can." He was giving her the hard sell. "Think about it," Silby said. "It's yours if you want it."

They wanted her. It was an interesting, if unexpected offer.

Was that what she wanted? And what would Braddock think? She hadn't told him about it—yet.

She reached the left turn where a Shepard County Sheriff's Department Tahoe was parked, lights flashing. A deputy waved her through. She parked at the end of the driveway and saw Braddock and Steak jogging out to her.

Tori exhaled a long breath.

It was time to go back to work.

"Come on," Braddock said with a wave. He and Steak led her back to the house and inside. "Take a look. See if you draw any different impressions."

The first thing she saw was Lainey Darr lying on the kitchen floor. "That's her," Tori said, shaking her head. "Professor Darr."

"Was she a friend?" Steak asked warily, fully aware of why she'd been taking a break. Was she coming right back to investigate the murder of a friend?

"No... not in any real sense," Tori replied. "I knew her, exchanged pleasantries on occasion. She was a sociology professor. I spoke with her a few times in the lounge on her academic specialty, the militia and fringe group movement. She was big into studying, lecturing, and warning on it. She'd written a book on it and had something of a national profile on the topic, getting called to appear on cable networks at times to talk when there was an incident somewhere in the country."

"She was involved last year with the MN Partisans, right?"

"She was. Front and center providing analysis of the group."

The MN Partisans were a fringe political group that Lainey Darr had warned Minnesota and federal law enforcement about for the past few years. While the vitriol of their online rhetoric had increased, they had not been taken seriously until a potential plot to kill a successful class action lawyer in Minneapolis was uncovered.

The lawyer had recently won damages against a food processing plant just outside of St. Cloud for failure to allow its Muslim employees time to pray during the workday. A suspicious van was observed by one of the lawyer's partners and the police were called to investigate. Two patrol units arrived, soon followed by others.

Four men linked to the MN Partisans were found in a panel van with automatic weapons. They were arrested. That night, agents of the Minnesota Bureau of Criminal Apprehension (BCA), and the Becker County Sheriff's Department, staged raids that led to arrests of thirteen other members of the loosely affiliated group, all of whom lived around the small town of Two Coves.

Would the Partisans have actually acted against the lawyer,

as the weapons suggested they would? Or was their intent merely to scare, to send a message of protest, as they had argued in court and in media interviews? Nobody knew for certain. Perhaps answers would come at the first trial for one of the conspirators that was scheduled for next month in Minneapolis.

"Professor Darr got herself some airtime with all that. Multiple news channels had her interviewed as an expert on the case. Given how she was shot, is there any reason to think all that has something to do with this?"

"I'd have gone there first, except we have the missing child and the dead... boyfriend as well."

"That's Girard," Tori asked. "Where is he?"

"In the garage," Steak said, waving for her to follow and leading her to the back of the garage, to the body lying face down.

"He was the first one," Tori said.

"Yes," Steak said. "He's in running gear. The neighbor told me he often goes for an early morning run. I figure he goes out the side door of the garage, takes his run and when he gets back, our shooter comes from behind the door and pops him in the back of the head. Then, he goes inside and Darr is in the kitchen making breakfast, and he pops her in the chest and then finishes her off."

"Which suggests," Braddock added, "that they had knowledge of Girard's morning routine. That he went out that door and would come back in it. Then our shooter goes from here, to Darr in the kitchen."

"I buy that. What makes you think Teddy Marist was here?" Tori said.

Braddock led her up to the second floor and the backpack and its contents scattered on the floor. Then he took her down the hall to the bedroom where they found the boy's clothes, bedding, and computer. "We figure he was getting ready for school."

"There is a children's toothbrush in the bathroom there. It was damp. There was moisture in the sink," Steak noted.

"Right. He's got the backpack and then he hears the shots." Braddock walked out of the bedroom while Tori lingered behind for a moment, examining the bedroom, his dresser and closet. "Hey?"

"Sorry," Tori replied and walked into the hallway.

"We figure he comes out here when he hears the gunshots. Maybe he calls for his mom and gets to the stairs and the shooter is coming up after him. He drops the backpack, maybe runs for his room. Whatever happened, I think our shooter grabs him."

"And then what?"

"The driveway," Steak said, leading her back out the front door to the wide driveway in front of the garage. "We had snow last night; a half-inch, give or take. See the tire tracks? They don't come from the garage. You can tell it came up the driveway, turned to the right and then backed up to the sidewalk from the driveway to the front door."

"The front door wasn't locked when we got here," Braddock continued. "The shooter runs the kid to the back of the SUV, throws him inside and away they go."

"The neighbor who called it in said he saw a black SUV speeding away from the house. He said maybe a Suburban or Excursion."

"Big SUV," Tori murmured.

"The neighbor said Darr had been living there for the past few months and that meant Girard had been back here more as well."

Tori nodded. "How old is Teddy Marist?"

"Another neighbor, a woman further down the street past our witness, said he was elementary school age. She thought ten or eleven," Steak said, flipping through his notes.

"What do we know about Girard?"

"He's a wealthy retired executive from California. This was his summer place for many years when he was married, or so said the neighbor. He said then he got divorced four or five years ago and didn't come as often until..."

"He met Darr," Braddock intoned.

"Right. Darr is the new woman in his life and Girard has been here a lot ever since. The neighbor thought they'd been together a couple of years and she had been living in the house over there for the last several months. Ever since *she* got divorced."

"The plot thickens," Tori said, nodding. "Who is Teddy's father?"

"We're working on it," Steak replied. "The neighbors don't know who he is. None of them recall ever seeing him. I've got Nolan tracking that down as we speak."

"When was Darr's divorce?"

"Neighbor said it was pretty recent," Steak said, and he looked at his phone. "This is Nolan." He stepped away, answering the call from his fellow detective. "What do you got?"

"Darr and Girard had been together—" Braddock started.

"Longer than that," Tori finished. "We need to find the father."

"Barry Marist is the father's name," Steak said, hanging up his phone. "I've got a cell and a work number for him, and address. I'll try the cell first." Steak punched in the number and waited and then started shaking his head. "Voicemail." He left a message and then tried the work number. "No answer, voicemail again. He works at Lakes Community Bank, vice president and chief operating officer according to the voicemail message." He hit zero for the operator and then identified himself.

"I need to speak with the bank manager? ... The president? That would be fine. It's urgent. Right away, please. ... Hello, this is Detective Williams with the Shepard County Sheriff's Department, who am I speaking with? And, Elaine, you're the bank president? Yes, for the whole bank system. Does Barry Marist work for you? He does. Is he in today? ... No? He hasn't showed up. Would he normally be in by now? ... I see, and he's the bank vice president and chief operating officer? He oversees operations for all the branches. ... Is this unusual for him? ... No, I can't say right now other than if he does arrive, I need you to have him call me immediately. Better yet, if he arrives, call *me* immediately." Steak provided the number and hung up. "I got a bad feeling."

"Yeah," Tori said, examining the tire tracks again.

"Let's get over to Marist's house," Braddock said.

"They're making progress out here," Tori noted as she pulled to a stop in front of the new one-story walkout, the first house on the block in this section of Greyler Lake Estates. It was her first return to the area since July, back when the skies were clear, and the temperature was warm. A Hummer, long submerged in a nearby pond, had been discovered with a dead body in it. The body was Duffy Randolf, a guy she had gone to high school with. While not a close friend of hers, he was someone she knew and liked in an acquaintance sort of way. What was worse, her old friend who had lied to her repeatedly had been involved in his murder.

Another one of Braddock's crew, Detective Reese, pulled up behind them along with two Manchester Bay patrol units.

Tori took a look at the house, the snow falling lightly. "Quiet out here."

"There aren't too many places out here—yet. Only this one on this block."

Cautiously, Braddock led all the officers to the front door, each of them with their guns drawn hanging by their sides. Braddock knocked on the door, but there was no answer. He peeked in the window to the right side of the front door but couldn't see anything. "We don't have a warrant."

"Exigent circumstances," Tori blurted. "If we dick around waiting for a warrant—"

"Clock's ticking." Braddock elbowed a small windowpane on the front door and reached in and flipped the deadbolt open. "Police!" he called out as he entered, his gun drawn. The uniform officers went about quickly clearing the house, while Braddock and Tori waited in the entryway. Tori spent a moment taking in the main area, family room, kitchen, eating area. The furnishings of the house were sparse. The kitchen was clean, the countertops neat, just a few dishes in the dishwasher. Although on closer inspection, a half-pot of coffee was brewed. To the right side of the kitchen sink sat a half-drunk cup of coffee and a small plate with one piece of toast and another half-eaten piece on it. The only area that was somewhat messed up within her view was around the entertainment center underneath the flat-screen mounted on the wall in the family room. There was a video game console and joysticks coiled together, and three *Avengers* movies stacked up.

"House is clear," a uniformed officer reported.

"The dad is in the wind," Braddock muttered.

Ring! Ring! Ring! ... Ring! Ring! Ring! ...

"Phone!" Tori walked toward the ringing, which took her down the hallway toward the bedrooms. It was coming from the home office. An iPhone was sitting on a notepad in the middle of the desktop. The display showed Steak's cell number.

"This is Barry Marist's cell phone," Braddock said. "You don't leave that behind unless you don't want to be tracked." He took out his own phone and called Steak, putting it on speaker. "You can stop calling Marist's cell. I'm staring at it. He left it at his house."

"The garage is empty," Reese said, sticking his head in. "Do we know what Marist drives?"

"Black Chevy Suburban," Steak replied. "And the neighbor reported seeing a large black SUV racing out of the neighborhood just after he heard the gunshots."

"Steak, put out an alert for Barry Marist and his SUV," Braddock said. He turned to Reese. "Door knocking. At least what there is of this neighborhood, which ain't much of anything. See if anyone saw Marist this morning."

"On it, boss."

Tori stepped back and away from the desk as she took off her winter gloves and pulled on rubber ones and started looking about. The house did not give off a feeling of warmth. The furnishings were spartan. That was likely due in part to the newness of the house. There was still the faintest whiff of fresh paint and just that new house smell. The other quick impression was of cleanliness. Barry Marist was a bank vice president and COO. Likely a number's guy. They were often people of organization and order.

She walked across the hallway to his bedroom, where the bed was made. The closet doors were closed. She opened them and his clothes were organized, dress shirts, dress pants, suits, hung neatly on the hanger rod. Underneath, his dress shoes were organized on a rack as well, a gap between two pairs. There were also two suitcases and a duffel bag. When she stood up, there were empty hangers, one in the dress pant section and one for dress shirts. It struck her as characteristic of a banker or accountant. Everything at work had to add up and end up in its proper place. Same thing at home.

Back in the office she observed the desk. There was a certain level of organization to it, the pens in a cup, stapler, and tape dispenser in a row. A laptop sat on the desk, along with a keyboard and large computer monitor. The phone had been placed on a legal notepad on the desk. To the left of the desk was a file cabinet, two drawers partially open. The files in the upper drawer were ordered alphabetically. There was a void in the C section. In the lower drawer there was a void between letters N and T.

"What?" Braddock asked, coming into the room, seeing the look on her face.

"The file drawers were left open," Tori said.

"So?"

"Look around. It appears that Marist is pretty meticulous about his house out there. Clean, organized, ordered. Yet these two file drawers were left open. It's odd is all."

Braddock nodded. "Open file drawers, and—" he turned around "—partially opened... closet door. With an open cabinet inside." He knelt to the cabinet. "Oh boy."

"What?"

He pulled the drawer fully open and gestured to an open gun case. "The case says Beretta on it. The gun is gone. The two magazine cutouts are empty." He looked to her. "Not good."

"No," Tori replied with pursed lips.

"You don't sound so sure."

"Just keeping an open mind. Is it Marist or something to do with Lainey and her background or even Girard, though I'm not sure why taking the boy would have anything to do with him? I want to be careful before we shove all in on one and drop the other is all."

"Fair."

"That said, what we do know for sure is that Teddy Marist is missing, his father is unreachable, and his mom was shot and killed, executed. Marist's gun is missing. He drives a black Suburban and a black SUV was seen fleeing where his ex-wife was gunned down along with her new man. He is a person of interest. Has to be. He's in this up to his eyeballs."

"We have an Amber Alert out for Teddy. Everyone is looking for his SUV."

Braddock's phone was buzzing again. Eggleston. He put it on speaker: "What do you got?"

"Marist's SUV."

FOUR

"YOU KILLED HER FOR HER MANY SINS."

Eggs had Marist's SUV, but it was abandoned behind a warming hut for an outdoor skating rink in Holmstrand. While Braddock spoke with Eggleston about coordinating the investigation of Marist's SUV—Tori stood in Teddy Marist's bedroom at his father's house. This bedroom was not like Quinn's room in any sense other than it was for a young boy. Unlike Quinn's room, the bed was made, the floor was spotless, the desk was organized, the chair pushed in. She opened the closet to see a shelving system with what clothes the boy had at the house folded, stored, or hanging, and no dirty clothes in the laundry hamper. Either Teddy's father made him keep his room this way, or would come in after his son had gone back to his mother's and cleaned up. Perhaps a combination of the two.

Tori took another walk around the house, even making her way down to the finished basement that was as neat and orderly as the rest of the house. As she came back up the steps, Braddock was waiting for her.

"Reese and the uniforms are knocking on what few doors there are. Those that are home don't recall seeing Marist leaving this morning. But you know what I'm thinking?"

"What?"

"He left *very* early, long before anyone would have noticed." He examined her thoughtful look. He could tell she was grinding on something. "What are you thinking?"

Tori checked her watch and did some quick math. "The murders occurred roughly two hours ago. You called me nearly ninety minutes ago now. The murders of Lainey Darr and Girard occurred around thirty minutes before that, maybe a little less."

"Yes. The point."

"Marist has a roughly two-hour head start on us." She felt like time was already starting to slip away. "Where is Marist going? Where would he go? And—"

"And what?"

"He's involved in all this no doubt."

"*Involved?* I'd say yeah, he's involved."

"To what degree? Is he acting or reacting?"

"What do you mean?"

"I know what we've seen. He's missing. Left his phone behind. Ditched his truck. His ex-wife is dead and her boyfriend. What's the obvious conclusion?"

"Distraught over the divorce and the loss of his wife to Girard, he killed her and him to take Teddy and go on the run."

"Exactly," Tori replied. "I mean I've seen that play out many times, where a parent goes on the run."

"Yet you have doubts,' Braddock said, hearing it in her voice. "Why?"

"Fog of war."

"Meaning?"

"Our situation is fluid," Tori replied. "We're thinking that Marist killed his wife and lover to go on the run with his son and that very well could be the case, but it also could be—"

"Something else," Braddock said. "What do you make of us finding his Suburban? Drop vehicle, no?"

"Looks like it."

"That suggests advance planning, doesn't it?"

"It does."

"Yet you have doubts? Why?"

"Nobody saw Barry Marist this morning, either here or at Girard's, despite seeing a black SUV that might have been a Suburban racing away," Tori said. "Everyone is on the lookout for Barry Marist right now and that makes sense based upon what we've *seen* so far. But what do we really *know* about him? Or Lainey Darr and her years talking about militias? Or Girard for that matter? What do we know about Barry Marist and Lainey Darr's marriage? About their relationship? The divorce? Girard's money? Any of it?"

"And if Marist is on the run, where might he go? Or who might help him?" Braddock said. "I'd like to get a look at his phone. We need to get the BCA over here as well. But until we can do that—"

"We put out the alerts and maybe we get lucky," Tori said. "But until we do—"

"We look at all of it. You have contacts at the university, start there with Lainey Darr. I'll take Marist and go to the bank, talk to the president and work from there. I'll have Nolan go to work on Edward Girard, just in case."

"Who were their divorce lawyers?" Tori said. "If they're both from here, maybe they used people from here. Can't be that many people in town who handle matrimonial law."

* * *

Gripping the wheel tightly, his eyes flicked between the road ahead and the rearview mirror, which remained empty as light snow drifted down from the sky.

Thirty miles to go.

The call just kept whirling around in his mind. The

morning was normal. He'd been drinking his cup of coffee, about to leave for work. And then... *How the hell did this happen?*

The phone had rung, and it was Teddy. His son usually called in the morning when he was at his mom's just to check in.

"Good morning, sport."

"D-D-Dad! *Dad!*"

"Whoa, Teddy. What's wrong?"

"Dad, help me! *Help me!*"

"What's wrong? Teddy? *Teddy!*"

The line dropped for a moment and then: "I want you to listen to me very carefully, Mr. Marist," a deep voice stated very calmly. "We have your son."

"Wha-what? What?"

"Do I have your attention now, sir?"

"Why have you taken my son?"

"We want something."

"What?"

There was a deep, knowing, slow ominous laugh. "That little fortune you hid from your ex-wife. You know what I'm talking about."

"No, I don't."

"Really?" the man asked with that same knowing laugh.

There was rustling of the phone.

"Teddy, tell your dad what I am doing right now?" the man's voice said coolly.

"D-D-Dad?"

"Yeah, buddy. I'm here."

"Tell him," the deep voice insisted calmly. "Tell your dad."

"He's... pointing... a gun at me."

Oh God.

"Don't hurt him. Don't hurt my boy. Please! Please don't do that. He's done nothing to you."

"Do I have your fucking attention now?" the man said more urgently.

"Y-Y-Yes. Yes."

"I know you have it all stashed about ninety minutes away. You're going to bring it to me. *All of it.* Every little account number, password, location, record. All of it."

"It'll take me some time."

"Not that much time."

"But..."

"Three hours at most, Mr. Marist. That is all you're going to need to get to me."

"How do you—"

"Focus! What matters is I do know all this and that now it's time for you to pay for your many, many sins."

"Okay, okay, okay. Wait, his mother. Lainey. He was with his mother—"

"And she won't be joining us any longer."

"Any... longer. Oh my God. Lainey... she's dead. And Ed?"

There was no response.

"Oh my God. You killed them?"

"No, you did," the voice replied. "*You* killed her for *her* many sins."

"Her... sins." He rushed to his home office and reached for the gun case on the closet shelf. He opened it. Empty. "Oh my God." They'd killed her and Ed. With his gun.

"Bring what I want, or your son dies. I shoot him and dump him in the woods, and he never sees his eleventh birthday. It's that simple."

"No. *NO!*" he screamed, frantically pacing in his home office. "I'll do what you want. But let me speak to him again, just for a second."

"Be very quick about it."

"Teddy? Teddy?"

"Yeah, Dad," Teddy replied sniffling.

He could hear it in his son's voice, the tears, the fear. Teddy was terrified. "Hey, buddy. Um... what have I said all these months, through the divorce with Mom and everything. The rumors, all that stuff. What have I said you need to do? Do you remember?"

"Y-yes."

"What is it I said?"

"Keep my chin up."

"That's right. Put on your armor. Don't let them get to you. You remember all that."

"Yes... sir," Teddy said shakily but with more of the defiant tone he was looking for. Whatever his son was about to face, he wanted him to do it with courage.

"You do that until I see you, alright. Promise?"

"I..."

The deep voice returned. "That's enough. I have precise instructions. You will follow them to the letter and trust me, I will know if you don't."

The first instruction was to leave his cell phone where he was stood.

The second was to drive fifteen minutes north to Holmstrand to exchange his Suburban for the bland gray Mercury Mariner he was now driving. Inside the Mariner he'd find a briefcase with a cell phone inside. When he got into the Mariner, the phone rang.

"Drive straight to the bank in Akeley. Do not drive on the H-4 past Pine River. And, Marist, no calls with this phone. We're watching." And they were. There was a wireless pinhole camera mounted on the rearview mirror. "Make haste, Mr. Marist. We wouldn't want anyone to find you before we make our trade."

"Isn't that why I'm driving this rickety bucket of bolts," he replied, checking his rearview mirror as he drove north on the H-4. "Where... where do I go after I get everything? When do I get Teddy back?"

"One step at a time."

The next step was to bring the deep voice everything. Just south of the town of Backus, he turned off the H-4 and made his way west until he reached Highway 64, where he turned right and drove north. It was a drive he had made many times over the past several years. Something the voice on the other end of the phone seemed to know.

North Highway 64 took him into the southern end of the small town of Akeley. When he arrived in town he reached the main intersection. He made a left turn onto the main drag, Broadway. Two more blocks and he turned right into the small bank parking lot, taking a slot just to the right of the front door.

It had been a few weeks since he'd last visited. He reached to open the door, then stopped for a moment and looked up into the rearview mirror. Looking frazzled and pale as a ghost, he took a moment to close his eyes, exhale a breath and compose himself. He needed to get in and out without attracting any special attention.

He grabbed the briefcase, headed inside and went straight to the teller.

"Good morning, sir," the teller greeted.

"I need to access my safe deposit box, right now," he blurted and then catching himself, exhaled another breath. "Sorry, that was rude of me, but I'm in a bit of a hurry. You know, with the storm coming and all." He checked the time on the clock over the teller, 9:21 a.m.

"Oh, of course, of course, right away. Let me call up the bank manager. It'll just be a minute."

"Thank you."

He closed his eyes for a moment and let out a sigh, rubbing his face with both his hands. *Settle yourself.* He set the briefcase on the customer service counter and paced about the middle of the lobby, hands shoved in his pant pockets, until he saw a familiar face approach. She smiled, "Back on such a stormy day?"

He let out a sigh and mustered up a smile. "Yes. I didn't think the snow would be on us so fast." He held up his key and grabbed the briefcase off the customer service counter.

"Well alright. Come with me." She led him back into the safe deposit boxes, opened her lock and then let him open his.

* * *

It wasn't quite pitch-black with the pillowcase back over his head and now a thick blanket lying over him, but it was close.

He was done crying.

Be tough, it's a mindset.

His dad would say that to him all the time. If you think you're tough, you are, it's a state of mind, son. Most of the time he heard it before, during and after he'd play with the older kids on the block at their old house. There weren't any kids his age in their immediate neighborhood, only older or much younger ones. His dad would say the older kids didn't want a whiny little kid tagging along. But, if he was tough and didn't complain, they would love that and include him in everything. His dad had been right about that.

If his father was all about being tough, his mom was all about paying attention. His mom, the professor, would always ask him when he got home from school: *what did you learn?* She made him tell her, every day, which in turn made him pay attention in class because the inquisition would come without fail. It could be at dinner, after football or basketball practice, just before bed. The questions would come and if he didn't have anything, there would be a firm look of disapproval and a lecture. He hated the lecture.

If his mom was here, she'd ask: *Teddy, what have you learned?*

This was the second truck he was in. The masked monster had tackled him in his bedroom and had zip ties around his wrists and ankles in seconds before a pillowcase went over his head. He'd felt like a calf lassoed by a cowboy at a rodeo. He remembered the man carrying him over his shoulder making a call saying: *Come now!* A moment later, he remembered feeling the cold on his body before he was thrown into the back of a vehicle. They drove for just a minute or two before they stopped and called his dad.

A man in a ski mask had taken the pillowcase off and was leaning over the back seat, the phone on speaker. He could only see the one man, although he knew there were at least three in the vehicle, there had been three distinct voices.

The man ripped the tape off his mouth. And then... he'd pointed the gun at him.

"Towne, the kid is just ten," he'd heard a voice blurt from up front.

"Shut the fuck up, Jared," he'd heard another voice rumble.

"But... Jenks, the kid is... And his mom, my God!"

"Enough!"

Thwap!

He knew that sound, the hard smack of the hand on the back of the head. The older kids in the neighborhood had given him those a time or two.

"Okay, okay, okay."

"Weak ass," he'd heard the third voice mutter.

He remembered hearing his dad's voice loudly on the phone, even from a few feet away after the man had pulled the gun away.

After the man hung up the phone, the tape was back over his mouth, the pillowcase back over his head, he was covered up and the SUV started moving again.

He'd heard the man called Towne, the one who had the gun in his face, growl after the call. "Don't fucking do that again." That was directed toward the one named Jared.

"Okay, okay," Jared had apologized. He could tell that person was driving. Jared was the driver.

"Better buck up, buttercup," the third voice said, a bit less threatening. That voice was up front. *What was his name?* Jenks?

There had been no reply to that criticism.

From what he'd seen, he could tell he was in the rear compartment of an SUV. His hands were tied, but at least in front of him. He could scooch and position his body to be comfortable. He rolled onto his back and wedged his head into the corner near the passenger side seat.

* * *

Given their caution and the changing weather, it had taken nearly two hours to get this far north. There were more direct and quicker routes, but they were staying as much off the regular roads given the cargo they were carrying in the back.

The white Tahoe powered through the ever more rapidly accumulating snow easily enough. It was the rutted gravel road beneath that was proving more challenging as it wound its way through the low-lying wetland, jostling them side to side, Jared fighting to keep them on the road proper.

"Oof," Towne moaned. "This road."

"With the accumulating snow, I can't see the ruts," Jared complained.

Towne turned around and checked the back compartment. The boy was quiet, nary a peep since the call. He must have taken his father's words to heart. The phone clutched in his hand buzzed. He answered without preamble. "Where is he now?"

"He just pulled into the bank parking lot. There aren't but a couple of vehicles there and it doesn't look like there are many people inside beyond employees."

This was Marist's last exposure to the public.

"Any hostiles about?" Towne said.

"Negative. Not the entire drive up. He's getting out now and... walking inside the bank. He has the briefcase. I'll call you when he comes out."

Towne hung up as Jared made a left turn and pulled up to the locked gate. To the left of the gate was the dilapidated wood sign for the long defunct Darkwoods Resort. Jenks jumped out and trudged through the snow to the padlock connecting the chain and unlocked it, swinging the two aged aluminum gate doors open, pushing snow aside. Jared drove through before Jenks closed the gate and hooked the chain and padlock back together, though not locking it.

Darkwoods Resort had been closed and abandoned for over six years since the bankruptcy, and then the aftermath of that. The bankruptcy process had long run its course but there had been no takers for the long-dilapidated resort. The resort had eight smallish red log cabins, though the red was heavily faded. Two nights prior they had borrowed a truck from Merc's uncle and plowed out a road to the cabins.

Towne made another phone call as he turned again to check on the kid in the back, who looked to be curled up in a ball, lying still, hardly a sound out of him.

Jenks looked back to see him making another call. "Max?" he whispered.

"Yes."

Max answered on the third ring. "Where are you now?"

"We're just arriving at the resort."

"And where is Barry?"

"He'll be coming to us."

"How long do you think it will be now?"

"With the snow now, a good hour I'd say. Will you be somewhere you can monitor and listen in?"

"I'm hoping to be at the house, but I may have to be mobile. You'll call me on this number?"

"Yes. We need to make sure he's not screwing us somehow."

Max cackled loudly. "Barry doesn't have the balls to screw with you."

The road came to a T with four cabins to the left and four to the right. Jared turned right and drove to the last cabin and parked next to his own large pickup truck with lifted wheels. It would have handled the road they had just come in on much better. He got out and opened the last cabin's front door, while Jenks retrieved the kid from the back of the SUV, threw him over his shoulder and walked him inside, placing him on the floor in a corner. Jared went to the side of the cabin and started the small generator to start the heat.

"Keep watch," Jenks said, taking off his wool cap. "Leave the hood on him. Understand? He doesn't need to see anything until he does."

Jared nodded as he pulled off his wool hat and walked with Jenks to the door. "How long you think?"

"A few hours and it'll be done." Jenks handed him a walkie-talkie. "Then we move on to the next thing. After that, we go get warm."

"But what about the kid?" he whispered.

"Keep an eye on him. We may need him to motivate his dad to do what needs to be done."

"Man, Jenks," Jared said, shaking his head. "I don't want to hurt the kid. He's scared to death. He's what ten, eleven? I've got a son that age."

Jenks let his eyes slide to Towne in the SUV and then back. "It's a good thing you said that to me and not to him. You *know* what we have to do here." He poked him in the chest. "You know."

"I know, I know, it's just—"

"Jared, listen! Just bring the kid when I tell you to, alright? Just do your fucking job. We'll take care of the rest."

Jared nodded nervously, letting his eyes drift to the truck.

"Hey. It'll be fine," Jenks said, slapping him on shoulder. "Today will be done soon, then we finish this." Jenks got into the Tahoe, backed out and started driving to the one larger two-story cabin that had served as the main lodge at the other end of the resort.

"What was that all about?" Towne asked.

"Jared being Jared."

FIVE

"SHE SETTLED."

Tori drove them back into Manchester Bay, the snow getting heavier though the wind was not yet whipping it all up. That would come in the next few hours and then the fun would really start.

As they drove, Tori was quiet. Braddock slyly side-eye observed her as they drove, assessing her body language, demeanor and look.

The break away from all this had been good for her.

A born and raised New Yorker from Long Island, he had been living in Manchester Bay for five years the day Tori arrived, standing in the doorway to his office, asking, really demanding, that she be allowed into the investigation of a murder that was eerily like that of her twin sister's twenty years prior, the very reason she herself hadn't returned home in all that time. Whatever happened to Jessie Hunter? It was *the case* for Manchester Bay. It was an investigation that was bound to dredge up a lot of bad memories for the town and now she was standing there to complicate it all the more.

Admittedly, for the first microsecond of a moment, he was struck at how alluring she was in her stylish pantsuit and heels.

It was a sharp ensemble chosen to make a specific impression on her old hometown. Tori snapped him out of that initial thought with her forceful manner, the intense spark in her eyes, the confidence, if not FBI arrogance, she projected. He immediately realized that standing in that doorway was someone who was going to pose him a challenge. It gave him a jolt, a vibration, he hadn't felt in some time.

A widower, he'd lost his wife Meghan to brain cancer five years earlier. Moving to Manchester Bay so Quinn and he could be closer to the only family they had, he had drifted into something of a personal solitude, grieving the loss of Meghan, focused on raising his son and his job. While other women in and around Manchester Bay had certainly made their interest in him clear, he hadn't met anyone who stirred him in that way.

Then Tori arrived and while it took a little time, she got to him over the course of the investigation. She had, by nature, a radiant intenseness to her, in everything she did, whether it was work, fitness, chopping peppers for dinner, a conversation about the news of the day or just wrapping Christmas gifts. There was a pulse to her that in turn invigorated him. When he'd joke about it with her now, or Steak, or anyone else for that matter, he would say *The Force* was strong with her. To some *The Force* could be a bit much. And he certainly didn't lack intensity when it came to work or other parts of his life, but as someone more even-keeled by nature, he found himself drawn to the vitality she exuded. She'd awakened him from his long slumber and opened that part of him again, and as he'd learned, he'd opened much of it up for the first time in her.

That verve was still there.

That was evident at the hockey party they went to last weekend, all the parents at a long table playing a dice game where she was the last person standing and won all the money, forty-eight dollars in one-dollar bills, celebrating her victory, hands full of bills, arms thrust triumphantly in the air. "Making it rain, baby!"

Yet, despite the energy she exuded, he'd also noticed how at ease she had been the last few months, how well she was sleeping, the lightness in her mood, as if at times she'd reached a bit of a Zen state. There was a sense of contentment. He didn't want to do anything to change that.

"You're awfully quiet?" he said.

"Just thinking is all," she replied.

"Does it feel odd to be back?"

"It's just been a few months."

"Eight."

"Okay, more than a few," she said with a light smile. "I wasn't retired. I took a break. A break perhaps longer than I'd expected or necessarily intended. The break is over, for now."

Braddock nodded as she pulled up to the government center. His phone buzzed. "Steak," he said. Steak had remained at Girard's house. "What do you have?"

"The forensics people are here. I had them get into Lainey Darr's phone thinking I might find something there."

"And?"

"She and Barry Marist last spoke five days ago," Steak said. "For just over a minute."

Braddock turned to Tori. "If the theory was Lainey Darr and her ex-husband had some blow-up phone call in the past few days that triggered this—"

"It probably didn't happen over the phone," Tori said. "Anything else on canvass?"

"Not much beyond what the neighbor who called it in saw. I got a little color from a few other year-rounders living nearby on Darr moving in with her son several months back. I showed them photos of Barry Marist. Nobody recognized him."

"Not a frequent visitor then, even to pick up his son," Braddock suggested.

"Why would he be?" Tori said. "If she left him for this new wealthy man living in the big house out on prime lake real estate, he wouldn't want to have to deal with that visual. My guess is they would meet up for drop-offs or if she dropped Teddy off at school, he picked him up. They kept it on neutral ground."

"Will, for now, I think this is a dead end here unless forensics comes up with something," Steak said. "Where do you want me?"

"Holmstrand," Braddock said. "That's what's hot. Go give Eggs a hand."

"On my way."

He turned to Tori. She had a faraway look.

"What are you thinking?"

"I don't know yet. Something's... bugging me."

"What?"

"I don't know."

"Verbalize," Braddock prodded. "Talk it out."

"I've seen something that matters," Tori said, shaking her head, "but I can't tell you what it was. It's just a stray nagging thought floating around in my head. It's tormenting me."

"When you figure it out, call me. In the meantime," Braddock reached for the passenger door. "I need to go check in with Boe and then I'll go to the bank. Stay in touch."

"Will do."

Before departing, he leaned over and kissed her. Something he'd not had a chance to do this morning. "You're sure you're okay? No problem being back?"

"You ask me that one more time and there will be," she replied, her eyes narrowing.

There it was. That familiar intense glare. Braddock smiled. "Now, that's more like it."

She grabbed his collar and pulled him close for another kiss, at first forceful, but then easing, turning soft, one she held for a moment. "I do appreciate the concern, Will Braddock," she whispered to his lips before pecking him one last time. "Now stop worrying about me and go. We have work to do."

Braddock stopped at Sheriff Jeanette Boe's office. Her meeting with the U.S. Marshals Service and State Patrol was just finishing up. They were meeting about security plans for next Tuesday at the university. An event entitled: *Public Education & Private Business Partnerships, the Way to a Better Future*, would highlight the value of public education and private business partnerships to build a better workforce. The governor, the state's two United States senators, several members of the Minnesota House delegation and the headliner, the United States Secretary of Commerce Cooper Farrow were appearing to celebrate and promote the growth and expansion of the university, in part due to the programs sponsored and funded by the Mannion Foundation along with state and federal funding. The event would focus in particular on the partnership of the Mannion Companies with the Central Minnesota State University and how that relationship had allowed Manchester Bay and the surrounding areas to grow and prosper. It was an event the town's business community, and the university campus was buzzing about.

"This is a BFD, Will," Kyle Mannion had said last week when they had lunch. "You need to be there, you and Tori."

"We will be."

"What we've done here between the company and the university these last several years is a model for the country, especially for rural areas who are struggling with economic opportunities. The national recognition, for CMSU, for Mannion Companies, it's huge."

"It's legacy stuff, right."

"This will be a big part of mine, no doubt."

That and a lot of politicians would get to spend some quality time with Kyle Mannion in the hopes that their continuing support of the program at the university would allow generous campaign contributions to follow. One of those politicians was Boe.

"Busy morning," she said.

"I need to make it quick."

"A double, huh?"

"With an abduction tossed in," Braddock said, laying out what they knew. "Or at least that's sure what it looks like."

"I knew Lainey Darr," Boe said sadly. "Not well, but we ran into one another a few times over the years. She'd consult with the Marshals Service from time to time when we had to track people down affiliated with certain... groups."

"Militia types."

"More broadly fringe anti-government groups. She had a database of groups and names as part of her research. That's why we'd consult her if the Marshals Service was hunting someone in this neck of the woods who had that kind of affiliation. She might have a name or two we could use. That's why she was involved in that MN Partisans stuff. They were anti-government with a violent feel."

"I understood the arrests down in Minneapolis of those guys in the van, but did you buy the need for the follow-up raid out by Two Coves?"

Boe shrugged. "What mattered was that the governor's office, BCA, state patrol and the Becker County Sheriff thought it was necessary. They consulted with her on that."

"And that's how she ended up on television in the aftermath."

"Yeah. I liked her, smart lady," Boe said. "Any chance that's what's involved here?"

Braddock grimaced. "For thirty seconds I thought it might, but it doesn't seem like it. She's recently divorced. Her ex-husband, the boy's father, is missing. He left his cell phone behind. His gun case for a Beretta was empty. We've got 9mm shell casings at Girard's. Beretta of that size uses a nine. His Suburban was found abandoned in Holmstrand. Looks like a drop vehicle was waiting. What kind? We don't know yet. Eggs and Steak are digging on that."

"Sounds like a step-by-step plan."

"It does. The missing boy is what has our attention right now, as does his missing father."

"What's your plan?"

"Twofold. First, on Barry Marist, the search is on. It sure looks like he's on the run. We've got the entire state on alert. His name is going to be everywhere, if not now, certainly in the next hour or so. Second, we start talking to everyone we can, see if we can figure out if he's capable of this, where he might try and go, who he might reach out to for help, his relationship with Darr and Girard, anything that can point us in the right direction."

"What does Tori think?"

"She thinks Marist is involved, for sure, but everything is driving us at him, and she says we don't know him, Darr or Girard. At least not enough to say this might not be about or involve one of them as well."

"Like, for example, it has something to do with Darr's work?"

"She's counseling an… open mind."

"Say Tori's concerns are on target, with all you've told me, Marist is still involved, right? Everything says that, does it not?"

Braddock nodded. "It does. If we can find him, we have a good chance of finding the boy." The unasked question was: would he be alive?

. . .

Braddock parked in front of the Manchester Bay branch of Lakes Community Bank. He glanced inside the doors of the lobby. While some lights were on, it looked like a business that was not open for business. There were only three other vehicles in the expansive parking lot. He walked up to the front door and pulled on the handle, and it was locked. He looked inside to see a tall, thin brunette in skinny jeans and a white blouse approaching. He took out his badge and held it up.

She unlocked the door. "You're from the sheriff's department?"

Braddock identified himself. "I'm looking for Elaine Baird."

"Come on in," the woman said, leading him inside the bank. "I'm Nora Bartness, Elaine's executive assistant. I'll take you back to her."

"You already closed today?" Braddock asked as they walked back, noticing all the empty desks.

"With the storm coming, Elaine made the preemptive call to close all our branches before the day got going." Bartness led him into a corner office to a woman in a sleek brown pantsuit sitting behind a large desk and another woman in tan slacks and brown sweater standing behind her.

"Elaine. This is Chief Detective Braddock from the sheriff's department," Bartness said.

"And this is Joan Wills, one of our vice presidents," Baird said, standing up. "And you've met Nora. You're here about Barry. I spoke with a Detective Williams earlier."

"He works for me and I'm afraid so," Braddock said. "We found Mr. Marist's ex-wife and her boyfriend shot and killed this morning in their house up along the east side of Northern Pine Lake. His ten-year-old son Teddy is missing. We think he was abducted from his mother's house."

Wills gasped in horror.

"Oh no," Bartness blurted. "Oh, not Teddy. He's what? Ten."

Baird's right hand went to her throat in shock, her eyes wide, her mouth agape. "And you think Barry did it?"

"We don't know," Braddock replied calmly. "We need to speak with him, but we can't find him. We went to his house. He wasn't home. We saw signs there that suggest we need to find him and soon. Do you have any idea where we can find him?"

"Uh... My God. Um... I could... I could, try and call him," Baird replied, reaching for her cell phone on the desk.

"His cell phone was left at his house. We found his Suburban abandoned in Holmstrand."

"He took Teddy and is on the run then?" Bartness observed more calmly. "That's what I'm hearing you say, Detective."

"Oh my, this is so bad?" Baird murmured, now pacing frantically. "This is going to be so, so, bad."

"For whom exactly? The bank?" Braddock asked, eyes raised.

"Well, sorry, but... yes. I mean, he's a vice president, *the* senior vice president. He's second to me with the bank overall. He's our chief operating officer. Of course, this is going to be... bad."

Is she serious? That's the worry?

"Your P.R. problems are for later. We have a double homicide and a missing boy. It's our understanding that Barry Marist was recently divorced."

Baird's eyes stared vacantly away.

"Ms. Baird!" *Could she be more self-absorbed?*

"Oh, sorry. I'm... I'm sorry."

"Do you know, did he take it hard? The divorce?"

"You know, I... I... I'm not sure. I suppose he might have. He tried to downplay it, certainly. He's not one to show a lot of emotion, about much of anything really."

"Stoic?"

"I guess. He is, don't you think, Nora? Joan?"

"Quite," Joan Wills nodded nervously.

"Calm for sure but I'm sure the divorce hit him hard," Nora said, the least frazzled of the three. "He was married a long time, fifteen, sixteen years, so how could it not. His wife, now his ex-wife, Lainey, I know she had a lengthy affair with a wealthy man, we all know. It wasn't really a secret the last, what six or seven months."

"Agreed," Wills affirmed.

"She left Barry for him and is now living in a big house on the lake," Nora continued. "A significant step up in her lifestyle for sure."

"A shot to the ego."

"I think to any man's ego. She left him for a rich guy, a *really* rich guy here in town."

"I see," Braddock said. "How long have you known him?" he asked Baird.

"I've been with the bank system for seven years, so all that time. He was working here for nearly a decade when I was hired as president."

"How about you two?"

"I've been here eight years, so that long," Bartness said. "It's about the same for Joan, right?"

"Uh, yeah, yeah. I started a few months before Nora did. Barry taught me the bank."

"Do any of you know, does he have any family in town?"

"I don't think so. At least I don't ever remember him talking about any. Do you know?" Elaine asked Joan.

"I know he was from Park Rapids, and he had a certain pride in that," Wills said. "He was proud of the fact there was a bank branch in his hometown. If he had any family left, it would probably be up that way."

"Parents?"

"Deceased," Elaine replied.

"Any brothers or sisters?"

"Well, yes, and no," Elaine said. "He had an older sister, but she died a few years ago from cancer. She was many years older than him."

"Friends?"

"I'm sure he has them, but I don't know who they are. I was his boss and we worked very well together but we weren't necessarily close friends outside of work. We didn't socialize really, other than bank or civic events from time to time."

"How about your employees?" Braddock said. "Would any of them know?"

"Other than the three of us, most at our main branch here are new, hired in the last year or two."

"But we have seventeen other banks," Nora said. "He hired a lot of the employees at all the branches. Others could know."

"I could give them the list," Joan Wills offered.

"The list?" Braddock asked.

"I suppose," Baird muttered.

"We used it earlier. It's our full employee list, for calling tree purposes," Wills said. "Nora keeps the list current for us."

"We employ over a couple hundred people at all our branches. I used the list earlier to let people know we were closing all branches for the day." Nora handed him the list. "You are free to call them. I can send an email or text around if that would be helpful."

Braddock took the list. His phone buzzed. It was Nolan. He answered.

"Boss, you need to go see a woman named Randi Love."

"And she is?"

"Marist's divorce lawyer. Reese found her name in his files."

"Okay. And I'm having the bank email you a list."

"Of?"

"Employees to call on Marist."

"I'll go send it," Nora said, walking across the hall to her own office.

* * *

Tori called ahead to the university. She spoke directly with Anderson Berman, the university's president, informing him of Lainey Darr's death.

"What can I do?" Berman said. "How can I or the university help?"

"We need to know what's been going on with Professor Darr. Her divorce, anything else. I need to talk with people who would know."

Berman was waiting for Tori in his office. He had moved fast. Professors Gene Norwich and Greta Shmyr from the College of Humanities and Social Sciences were waiting.

"Being a fairly new adjunct, I don't... didn't know Professor Darr well," Tori said. "Other than occasional pleasantries passing in the hallway and a few professional discussions in the lounge. I need your help. What should I know?"

"Tori, I worked with Lainey for sixteen years," Norwich said. "Heck, I hired her. And she and Greta were very close personal friends."

"Is this related to Lainey's work?" Shmyr asked.

Tori stopped. "Why do you say that?"

"She did all this work researching and speaking on these fringe groups and got threats from time to time," Norwich said. "People in these groups are kind of weird and they like to issue threats."

"Any recently?"

"No. There were a few last year after the MN Partisans thing, when she was on television repeatedly for about a week, but nothing recently."

Tori shook her head. "It may not have anything to do with that. We think it has to do with her ex-husband." Tori quickly recapped the morning. "Given what we've seen, we're looking for Barry Marist, and we're thinking he has Teddy. Do either of you know him at all?"

"I've known Barry longer than I've known Lainey," Norwich said. "He and I have been friends for many years. We're in a golf league together, we've boated and go to the same Chamber of Commerce meetings. Heck I was there the night he and Lainey met."

Tori examined Shmyr and Norwich closer. "You both look very surprised by all this. Tell me why."

"Yeah, I am," Norwich said. "I know you hear this all the time from some friend or neighbor when someone snaps and shoots up a bar or something, but I'm stunned by this, by what you've told me." Norwich turned to Greta. "What do you think? You knew them well as a couple."

"Lainey and I started together at university about the same time. We were both married at the time, and my ex-husband and I went out with Lainey and Barry many times in those early years and had some fun together. I got divorced six years ago and now Lainey has, or... had." Shmyr wiped away a tear. "God, I can't believe this."

"Tell me about their divorce," Tori said.

"It was bitter, kind of like mine," Shmyr said. "We commiserated on that."

"All divorces are bitter in some way," Norwich noted.

"My ex left me for another woman. He had been having an affair for years," Shmyr said indignantly, folding her arms. "Oh, I was furious, of course."

Tori nodded. "I'm sorry, Greta. That sounds... difficult."

"It was, Tori. My ex and I went to war for a year, fought, spent money on a court battle that would have been better spent on just about anything else," Shmyr said, shaking her head. "In the end, only the lawyers benefitted from the fight."

"Go figure," President Berman cracked.

"I wanted to make him miserable," Shmyr continued. "And

I did, oh did I ever, I fought him on everything, aired every bit of dirty laundry I could."

"And made yourself miserable in the process," Norwich said.

Tori nodded. "You wanted your pound of flesh."

"I did." Shmyr nodded and then turned to Tori. "I did and said things I didn't think I was capable of."

"Greta got a little... unhinged," Norwich said.

"I was. And I was messing up here. Gene and Lainey both sat me down and helped me realize that my ex-husband and I were fighting over nothing in the sense that we were both professionals, we were both loving parents of our children and the statutes basically said we split the assets, and we would share custody. So why were we spending all this money on divorce lawyers fighting over something basically set by law? Once I realized that was what I was doing, I settled a week later for what had been put before me months earlier."

"And what did Lainey do?"

"She and Barry did much the same thing. He was more the impetus of that than she was though."

"Because of Ed Girard?"

"Yes. She met Ed and she... cheated on Barry. I mean she was like my ex-husband, I guess. And, I knew, *I knew*, she was cheating on him, but I kept quiet."

"You did?" Norwich asked, perturbed.

"Yeah, Gene, I did," Shmyr said. "I'm a hypocrite. Lainey was the one having the affair. But she and Barry weren't happy together. You know that as well as I do. Which is why she started up with Ed a few years ago. That didn't make it right. It's just that's the way it was."

"Why weren't they happy?" Tori inquired. "Lainey ever say why?"

Shmyr sighed. "She said she settled. She was thirty-five when she met Barry. There were only so many prospects around here for an educated woman then and she wanted a child and—"

"Her biological clock was ticking," Tori said. It was a thought she had wrestled with herself on occasion.

"Barry was a decent enough looking guy, had a good job with the bank, so, when he asked, she said yes. They got married, had Teddy right away, and I think it was good for a little while, but—" Shmyr shook her head "—it didn't last. They tried marital counseling, but it wasn't going well and that's when she said during a session..."

"She settled."

Shmyr nodded. "Barry got pissed."

"So would have I," Norwich observed with a snort.

"How angry?" Tori pressed.

Shmyr shrugged. "Lainey said he was hurt. She regretted saying it in one sense but not in another. I think saying it freed her. After that, she was done settling. She had already met Ed. He had let it be known he was interested if she was. She decided she was and started sneaking around, going through the counseling motions with Barry but she was done, it was not if, just when."

"Ah geez," Norwich moaned.

"Sorry, Gene. Lainey should have just divorced Barry then, but instead I think she hesitated because she wasn't sure it would work out with Ed. Would he be here enough? He lived in California much of the year and was divorced himself. She loved him, wanted him, but—"

Tori understood. She had seen it before. "She hedged her bet."

Shmyr nodded. "To Ed it was would he, or won't he? If Ed didn't, I'm not sure she wanted to end her marriage and be alone. Lainey didn't have the confidence in that sense. In a way, she liked the security of being married, even if she wasn't that happy being married, if that makes any sense. But then Ed started coming back to Manchester Bay more and committed that he would keep doing it if she left Barry. When Ed made that commitment, she filed for divorce and moved into Ed's house and that's when the affair came to light."

"And you said earlier, it was a battle?"

"It was," Norwich said, interjecting. "Barry told me that too. He hired a scorched earth lawyer."

"He was angry," Tori said.

"Yes, but I think Greta is also right. I don't think he was any happier in the marriage than Lainey was. I thought he was just more upset about the how and wanted to extract a pound of flesh because he was embarrassed his wife left him for another, far wealthier man. A Silicon Valley millionaire. Barry was the vice president and COO of a local bank. He felt some status with that, but then Lainey did *that* to him. He had to live with everyone knowing that. So, he fought to make her pay. That fight was about nothing but money and pride. Not... this. I didn't see today coming. And to Teddy?"

"Me neither," Shmyr said and turned to Norwich. "I know you and Barry are friends, Gene, but I wasn't his biggest fan. I thought he was self-centered and arrogant. But I didn't see this either. He is a good dad. Even Lainey, in the worst of it in the divorce, said that. He loves Teddy."

"Can you think of anything that happened recently? I get the background of the divorce, but was there something recently that could have triggered this? Another blowup between the two of them? Something Lainey said that might have set him off? Anything like that at all?"

"I talked to Lainey just yesterday and things seemed fine." Shmyr looked at Norwich. "Gene?"

"If there was, Lainey said nothing to me about it. I haven't spoken with Barry in a few weeks. It's always a little less this time of year. I see him more in the summer when we have golf league. Last time I spoke with him he seemed okay. I know he'd moved into his new house. From the looks of things, he was moving on."

"The divorce was nasty though," Tori asserted.

"It was until I told Lainey about my experience and being on Barry's side of the table," Shmyr said. "Being the one cheated on, how that feels, how people look at you even though you've done nothing wrong. A light bulb seemed to go off in her head. Did she apologize to him? I don't know. I just know after we talked maybe a month or two ago, the two of them settled."

"Just recently?"

"Yes," Shmyr said. "I know they met for breakfast out at the Halfway Highway Diner, talked and they came to an agreement, just the two of them. I didn't ask her, and she didn't say, but I'm thinking she apologized, not for asking for the divorce but for what she did. And I thought that was the end of it. Like Gene said, Barry had bought a new house and moved into it already. Lainey had moved in with Ed several months ago and was really happy about that. She liked it out there, of course, on the lake, in that house, it was very nice, very comfortable," Shmyr said. "I thought things were fine. I just can't believe what you're telling us." She looked to President Berman. "Is word out about this?"

Berman nodded. "Word is getting out. I'm having someone work on a message to the campus."

Tori thought for a moment. "Professor Shmyr, do you know who Professor Darr's lawyer was?"

"Jennifer Weld," Shmyr said. "She was my lawyer too."

"Ah, I know Jenny," Tori said, nodding. "She's a hockey mom."

* * *

Braddock entered the Law Offices of Anderson and Love and was immediately greeted by Randi Love.

"I saw the Amber Alert," she said and led him back to her office.

"I need to find him," Braddock asserted. "He's in the wind."

"I don't know where he is," Love said defensively. "Not a clue."

"What can you tell me?"

"I have certain ethical obligations," she said. "I'd like to help, but—"

"Counselor, I don't have time to fuck around with the legal niceties. His ex-wife was murdered, along with her boyfriend. His son is missing. Your client is on the run. Is there anything you can tell me that helps me find him before anyone else ends up dead? People in a situation like he is in might contact their lawyer. Has he contacted you?"

"No, not since he came in here to sign his final divorce papers two weeks ago."

"And how was he that day?"

Love took a moment. "He looked..."

"Frazzled? Upset? Angry? What?"

"Ready," Love said. "I've seen it so many times over the years. Couples battle it out but then it just wears them down to the point where they just want it to be over."

"And Marist was there?"

"I thought so," Love said. "He said he and Lainey talked and she apologized for the affair. For their son's sake, she'd begged him that they needed to be done. A few days later, they agreed to everything and all I had to do was work with Jenny Weld, Lainey's lawyer, to finalize the language. It didn't take long, just a few nits and nats. Pretty standard given their individual situations money and career wise."

The lawyer took a moment.

"I've had clients... snap before. I've seen it coming in my meetings and when they've left the office, I'd be worried. I called the police or your department a time or two over the years because I was concerned about a client and what they might do. It cost me a few clients, angry that I thought that of them, and I even had one come back at me once. He had me up against the wall, forearm across my throat over there until my staff rushed in." She tilted her head toward the safe behind her desk. "I've had a gun in there ever since that one."

"I see," Braddock replied warily.

"I've taken classes and I go practice," Love insisted. "But not once, ever, did Barry Marist worry me like that? He was pissed as all get out at his ex-wife, like many spouses are, but I never got the sense he wanted to harm her, not like that. I don't think he has that in him. I just don't or... didn't, but from what you've told me." She shook her head dejectedly. "I like to feel like I have something of a radar for this. I tend to represent more men than women. I'm known as the lawyer for fathers around here. He just wasn't one I was worried about."

* * *

Tori drove to the law offices of Weld, Crossman, Court & Lawrie, LLP. Jenny Weld was a little, fiery redhead whose son played hockey with Quinn. Her voice carried mightily through the din of the crowd noise at a hockey game. More than one opposing parent had taken note of the intensity of Jenny, cheering on her son or, on occasion, excoriating a referee.

Jenny had seen the Amber Alert on her phone, recognized the name and had tried to call Lainey Darr. When she saw Tori, her hand went to her mouth, her body crumpling into a guest chair in the lobby. "Oh, no."

Tori held Weld gently by the arm as they went to her office. "Tell me, Tori."

Tori told her what they knew, or thought they knew. "Jen, I have the evidence in front of me telling me one thing, and people telling me another, that this wasn't like him. I need to know what you know and think."

Jenny Weld sat down behind her desk, rubbing tears away from her cheeks. "They just settled."

"I was told it was a bitter divorce battle."

Jenny shook her head. "It wasn't anything that out of the ordinary if you ask me. She left him for another man. A rich man. Barry was angry but perhaps also... hypocritical."

"How so?" Tori asked, her brow furrowed.

"I have to be careful here, attorney-client privilege."

"Your client's dead, Jen. Her ex-husband may have killed her and taken their son and is on the run. We need to find them before something else bad happens."

Weld nodded.

"He was a hypocrite why?"

"Well, Lainey said to me, when she was sitting in the very chair you're sitting in and signed her divorce papers, that she regretted that her cheating on him had become public knowledge to people in their social circle. But then she said she thought he might be, or was, having an affair too. She was doing laundry, maybe a year ago. She was already stepping out on Barry back then, had decided she wanted a divorce, but hadn't said those words to him just yet. She was doing a small load of whites and thought to grab some of his to combine the loads."

"And?"

"She smelled perfume on one of his dress shirts, and there was a reddish smudge on the collar."

"Lipstick?"

Jenny nodded. "She thought so."

"Perfume, lipstick. She thought he had something on the side too," Tori said. "You know, it seems like more and more people do these days."

"Yes."

"Did she confront him about it?"

"No. She let it go."

"She didn't know who it was?"

"No. I don't think she even tried to find out and she was with Ed anyway. I just think it made it that much easier to decide to divorce him. It was time."

"Did Lainey Darr ever speak of her ex-husband being violent?"

"No," Weld said. "I asked, repeatedly. I always do but she said no. She said he hardly ever even yelled, even when angry with her. It kind of drove her nuts."

"He held it in," Tori murmured.

"People like that can... go off," Weld said. "Maybe that happened here. Maybe he finally just blew his top."

"But why? They settled, right?"

"Yes. That's why it doesn't make sense. She signed the papers two weeks ago. She was living with Ed. Barry bought a house. They both loved Teddy. So... I can't explain it if he did. As mad as he could be at her, I just can't see him doing this to his son. If what you say happened, he'd have killed Lainey in front of Teddy. I didn't know him well, other than sitting across the table from him at a deposition and a couple of settlement conferences. However, based on what Lainey had said about him, I'm stunned by this. I don't know what could have possibly happened since they'd settled to make him do that."

Tori sat back in her chair, two conflicting questions swirling in her mind. Despite everyone's shock, what drove Barry Marist to kill his ex-wife? Or, was something else going on here?

SIX

"IT'S NOT DONE IN A SNAP OF THE FINGERS."

Marist walked briskly out the front door of the bank and got into the Mariner, dropping the briefcase in the passenger seat, and waited on the phone. It buzzed thirty seconds later. This time it was a different voice.

"Go west on 34. Drive to Nevis."

After he'd reached Nevis, the voice on the phone had turned him north and directed him on a threading web of roads through dense woods and around small lakes. He'd driven through slews and low-lying areas. On paved and gravel roads. The old SUV he was driving, nor the phone they had provided, had a GPS, so he didn't truly know where he was other than somewhere north of Park Rapids. He knew that only because of his recognition of the occasional resort or lake signs and he had a rough familiarity with the county road as he'd driven around the north end of Big Sand Lake, though it had easily been thirty years since he had done so. Was it happenstance or intentional that they were having him drive through areas he associated with his youth?

They were keeping him off the main roads while he drove what he sensed was west, northwest. He presumed that was because law enforcement was looking for him. He tried turning on the radio, but it was disabled. He imagined that if he could listen to the radio, the stations would be reporting that Teddy was missing, his mother was dead and that his father is a person of interest. And when he had checked for his handgun in the closet at home, it was missing. He cringed.

They had done a number on him.

The phone buzzed.

"Yes."

"Take the next left."

How had it all come to this? Why him? Why set him up like this? Who hated him enough to do this to him? Who could even know?

He looked to his right, to the briefcase sitting on the passenger seat, and briefly closed his eyes.

You fool.

He always knew there was significant risk despite having what he thought was the near perfect set-up. He just never thought *this* would be the risk.

Often in the past six years, usually when he was driving to the safe deposit box in Akeley, he asked himself why he was doing it, why he was *really* doing it. At first, wrong as it was, it was for a somewhat altruistic reason. To help his father when the bank, any bank for that matter, wouldn't. Up to that point, before he crossed that line, he had been an otherwise honest person. But then, before he could truly help, his dad, despairing he would lose everything, gave up and killed himself. When that happened, that was the chance to jump off the dangerous track he was on and, for a time, he thought about putting it all back, cleaning the slate.

But looking up in the rearview mirror, seeing his own eyes, his guilty eyes, he knew that it wasn't just about getting back at the bank for his father's death anymore. He had the money.

And once he'd crossed *that* line once, he knew he might be able to do it again.

He'd gotten away with it. It was a lot of money. They say possession is nine-tenths of the law and he had the money. It was his. And then he found another hole and knew just how to exploit it. Then he did, before he himself closed the hole. And then another opportunity emerged, and he did it again, and then he found another bundle of cash and did it again and the money, always in small amounts nobody would notice, started really adding up and he started feeling... entitled to it. It was always that way, wasn't it? If you cut one corner, it becomes easier and easier to cut others, your own standards of right and wrong evolving from once firm and just to very loose and elastic.

And it wasn't just with the money. He betrayed his marriage, running around on Lainey before she did it to him. Not that she ever knew. But *he* knew. And he knew he was a hypocrite for how angry he got with her when she did the same thing, no matter how embarrassing it was that she left him for Ed and his money so publicly for all to see.

Upon reflection, he'd gotten good at rationalizing the money in his mind, becoming comfortable with it and the risk it entailed for him. But that risk was for him. Not his family. Not like this.

He glanced at the mirror again. *That, my friend, is why you are here. Why Lainey and Ed were dead. Why Teddy, the person you love more than life itself, is a hostage.*

He deserved whatever his fate was to be.

But he knew that Lainey didn't deserve hers, nor Ed. And Teddy? His boy. He had to find a way. Not him too.

One question he had was how the voice on the phone knew what he'd done.

How?

He'd told not a soul. The deep voice was right. Lainey didn't know.

How would anyone know?

It was someone at one of the banks. Either in Akeley or Manchester Bay. Someone figured it out. That's what it had to be.

The phone buzzed again.

"You're going to cross over 71 and then you're going to take a right turn."

* * *

Jared paced the floor of the cabin, his arms folded across his chest, checking his watch every thirty seconds, alternately looking out to the snow-covered lake and then to the larger lodge-like cabin at the far end of the road. Towne and Jenks were waiting there inside, and the updates from the walkie-talkie told him that Merc was, as planned, directing Marist through the web of roads, leading him here.

He exhaled a long breath through his nose, feeling as if his whole body was twitching. When he got like this normally, he'd have a drink, maybe smoke a little weed, do something to take the edge off.

Edibles.

He had them in his duffel bag. It was tempting, just to calm him, slow his heart rate. It was a thought and he stopped for a moment, staring at the black bag resting by the back door. Maybe just one. He shook his head. Towne wanted him sharp, alert. "None of that shit that you used to be on when we were down in the mountains in North Carolina," he'd said earlier.

North Carolina.

Seven years ago, he and Merc had decided they wanted something different. He wanted away from all his own mistakes, of which there had been plenty, and Merc had a sense of adventure and wanted to leave their desolate little stretch of home for something new. "There's a lot of country out there. Let's go see some of it."

They left with not much more than a plan to drift south from Minnesota, with the idea of getting warmer. He had said to Merc when they left that he wouldn't mind making their way to Florida, to the Gulf Coast. He'd read somewhere that the economy was booming down there, all kinds of building going on. He was handy enough, knew woodworking and had worked for a cabinetmaker in Park Rapids. Merc had every truck driving license there was so he could find work driving. That had been the rough plan. But first, Merc had some distant relatives who lived in the North Carolina back country. They liked to hunt their land and fish the streams and a cousin invited them to come down and stay for a stretch.

"It's nice there," Merc said.

Having never been Jared thought, why not?

They never made it to Florida.

They both liked it in North Carolina. In a good way, it reminded them of home, the outdoors, the areas to roam, but it was warmer and unlike home, there were mountains.

They'd only been in North Carolina a few months when they met Jenks through Merc's cousin. Jenks in time then introduced them to Towne and their older brothers, Warrick and Rodney.

Towne's older brother Hot Rod was someone Jared would've liked to have been but never could be. He didn't have the brains, the brawn, or remotely the courage to be like him. And rarely in life had anyone like that shown interest in someone like him, yet Rodney welcomed Merc and him to his isolated thousand-acre farm up in the mountains.

Rodney was a firebrand who often held court at his farmhouse, usually about how the federal or state government was infringing on how he could use his land or the land around him. *Hunting season? What hunting season, I can hunt whatever and whenever I want. Grazing? I ain't paying to have my cows graze on state or federal land, they'll graze wherever they damn well please.* The state and federal government would fine him, but he'd never pay, or so he said. Nobody was going to tell Hot Rod what he could or could not do. Fuck the government.

Then, he began ranting about immigration, legal, illegal, it didn't matter. Hot Rod hated all of it. It was making America dirty.

"I don't like all this illegal immigration either, but the southern border is a thousand miles from here," Jared said to Merc one time. "Why does he care so much?"

Merc had pulled him aside to make sure he was out of earshot of Rod, or Towne, or anyone else for that matter. "Do you like it here?"

"I love it here."

"Then don't let anyone else hear you ask that question, you understand?"

"Sure. But still—"

"One, it's his place, he can say and believe whatever he wants. Two, it's about more than the border, Jared. The border is a line on a map. It's about the change it signifies. That's what Rod is talking about. Do you like that change?"

"No."

"Alright then. Shut the fuck up and listen."

The rants about, and fights with the government over, land use were kind of humorous, certainly not dangerous. Kind of like a spat between a batter and an umpire over all balls and strikes. The immigration views were darker, and Rodney's language more and more violent. There was more talk of needing to send a message, to act. To do something to really get people's attention.

Rodney started publicly stating his views, writing opinion pieces, and putting them on sympathetic, albeit obscure, websites. While he hadn't created any sort of an official organized group, he talked about all of them having to be ready because someday the government would come for them. At night when they were at the apartment they were sharing, he and Merc talked about how they thought he was mostly just talk, hyperbole, Rod feeling the need to be more outrageous to keep everyone's attention, to keep them coming back to the farm to listen.

They were wrong.

They didn't know it until later, but Hot Rod and Jenks's older brother Warrick had put action into motion at a pro-immigration rally in Tennessee. They were going to send a message. That intended action led to violence in Tennessee and brought the government to his doorstep, in the form of the North Carolina State Police. They came to the farm, in force. He and Merc only learned about what Rod had truly put in motion a few days later, having been left completely in the dark. They were welcome at the farm but were not part of the inner circle.

Since they didn't know about what Rod had started, he and Merc had been at the deer hunting cabin a quarter mile up the mountain that morning with Towne, Jenks, and many others without a care in the world. Towne had suggested the two of them hike further up the mountain to bow hunt. "Get us a deer or two."

Sounded good to them, so they had. There was a deer hunting stand another thousand feet up that they'd hiked, too. It had a glorious view of the valley and farm below. It was from their perch high up that they saw the stream of police vehicles roll in, the swath of officers out with their weapons.

Jared's first inclination had been to run down the mountain to support Rod and their friends, but Merc had held him back. "There is nothing we can do and nothing good that is going to come of this. Just stay here out of sight."

"But—"

"They're my friends too," Merc said calmly. "And I believe

every word out of Rod's mouth, but he's done something, and this is not going to end well. The police don't show like this unless there is a reason. Something has happened. Something big."

Merc was right.

The standoff ended quickly.

Shots were fired and then all hell broke loose. Rod and his men and the police engaged in a fierce gun battle. They saw officers go down.

Then in the midst of the firefight, the farmhouse exploded in a massive fireball.

A thousand feet below them, they could see Towne, Jenks and more of their friends positioned on the mountain at the deer hunting cabin, a quarter mile from the farmhouse. They held their position though and not long after the explosion, more sheriff's deputies and a SWAT team arrived. With all that firepower they moved up the mountain toward Towne and Jenks and the rest of the crew. Seeing that they were outmanned and outgunned, they and the others surrendered without further incident.

"I'm surprised Towne backed down," he'd said to Merc as they watched it all go down.

"It would have been suicide not to. Towne is living to fight another day," Merc replied then and there. "But there will be another fight, Jared. You can count on it. Whatever this was, it is not over."

Towne, Jenks, and the others who surrendered up the mountain were arrested and spent some time in jail but then politics intervened. The government's actions in how it attacked the farm stirred up a lot of anti-government feeling in the state, in the region, in the country. How had things escalated so quickly? Who shot first? Turned out the government had. Towne, Jenks, and the others up the mountain hadn't fired, hadn't joined the fray and showed restraint. The charges against them were dropped and they were released.

Towne, though every bit as fervent in his beliefs as his older brother, was much less bombastic and far more calculating. For the next several years, Towne and Jenks stayed off the grid, living in the mountains, maintaining no profile. But as Merc had predicted, Towne never forgot or forgave what happened that day at the farm.

Six weeks ago, Towne showed up at Merc's RV down in North Carolina and said to them both: "Boys, we're going up to your neck of the woods for a stretch. It's time for a payday and payback. Jenks and I need you both to come with us."

Jared heard *payback* and got nervous. "And then we come back here?" he'd asked.

"Maybe, Jared," Towne said. "Or maybe not."

"We're in," Merc had replied for the both of them.

Now, with the temperature crashing, the snow falling and the wind muscling up, he wished he were back down south. He'd liked North Carolina. Never one to thrive in the city or amongst crowds, he liked living off the grid and in some ways off the land. The solitude, the quiet, the lack of outside noise, and maybe best of all, the absence of judgment. They had been some of the happiest days he'd ever lived.

He'd believed in Hot Rod's world view, and he believed in Towne's as well. He'd seen firsthand why he had it, he'd experienced part of it with him. Revenge? He wanted it too. He just thought that it was those who had wronged them that should be the ones punished. Not those that had nothing to do with what happened in North Carolina.

He turned and looked back to the lump propped up, sitting in the corner, the pillowcase over his head. He was the same age as his own son, not that he'd hardly seen the boy since he was born. But he knew enough to know what the fidgeting and squirming meant. He pulled down the mask over his face and leaned down to the kid and lifted the pillowcase from over his head.

"Do you need to pee?"

Teddy Marist didn't respond.

Jared pulled the duct tape loose from his mouth.

"Do you need to pee," he said softly.

The boy nodded. "Yes, sir."

"Come on."

Jared stood the boy up and led him slowly over to the bathroom and then examined the restraints. He had no intention of standing in the bathroom with him and watching him pee, even if that was what Towne or Jenks would have demanded he do. He was no pervert.

He stood Teddy in the doorway to the small back room. The plumbing didn't work but they weren't going to be here long enough for it to matter. "Listen to me," Jared said as he knelt and undid the zip ties around the boy's ankles and took them off. "No funny stuff. I'll be right here listening. Understand."

"Y-y-yes."

Jared let the boy go into the bathroom and pulled the door half-closed to give him a bit of privacy, hearing the stream fill the toilet and then the rattling of the handle.

"It doesn't flush."

"That's okay. Just leave it."

The boy came back out of the bathroom, his hands bound in front of him. Jared noticed that Teddy's eyes glanced about the cabin and then out the front picture window. He stepped toward him and guided him back to the corner and had him sit down, ready to put the pillowcase back over his head.

"What's going to happen to me?" Teddy asked.

Jared exhaled a breath as he pulled out the zip tie and put it back around the boy's ankles, although he left it a little looser.

No sense in cutting off the circulation to his legs. He might have to walk soon. "Your dad's coming."

"And then what happens?"

Jared thought for a moment. "I guess it depends."

"On what?"

"If he has what the others want."

"What do they want?"

He shouldn't be talking to the boy at all, let alone this. "They want something your dad has, kid, and that's all I know. The rest is above my pay grade." That was a good answer.

"What is it—"

Jared placed the duct tape back over his mouth, cutting off the question. He slid the pillowcase gently back over his head. He patted him on the shoulder. "Just sit there quiet like you did before and there won't be any trouble."

* * *

Ahead in the distance, he saw the first vehicle he'd seen in perhaps a half-hour, a black pickup truck cross over the road.

"Take your next left," the voice ordered.

You've got to be kidding.

Fifteen, twenty minutes ago he'd wondered given the area he'd crossed over into after he was west of Highway 71. There was a hint of familiarity. He was in an area he'd traveled through many times in his life. Then as the voice kept having him make turn after turn, the hint turned to suspicion, turned to almost resigned expectation. Whoever was behind this knew him and seemingly wanted to punish him.

"Turn left and then I suspect you know where to go from there."

The large horizontal wood sign marking the turn for the resort was detached from its post on the right. Having fell at a forty-five-degree angle, the sign was now mostly covered in snow but he could make out the heavily faded bottoms of the letters.

Darkwoods.

The resort.

His father Otis had been barely scraping by for years as a small independent resort owner. As he got older, the upkeep got harder. He tried to help his dad, but he only had so much time with his own job and the resort was so far away. Ten years ago, his dad put the resort up for sale but there was little interest in the property on an isolated southwest corner of the lake with a marginal swimming beach.

Then there was the bed bug infestation and the county shut him down. That was eight years ago. The cabins were old, dilapidated and needed new roofs, rebuilt decks, interior Sheetrock, and exterior siding just to pass county inspection so that he could reopen. In essence, he had to gut all eight units and the lodge. He'd tried to get financing and had failed. Otis finally came to him in Manchester Bay, hat in hand, begging for help. Otherwise, "I'll lose everything."

He had dreaded the coming of that day. One look at his dad's plan, what it would cost and what he could generate from renting the cabins given the lake he was on, he knew nobody else would remotely consider lending him the money he truly needed. His dad knew it too. His son, the bank vice president, was his only hope, his last resort.

"Son, you practically run this bank. You need to pull some strings and get this through."

"I'll try."

His dad called him daily asking if he got the loan approved. He tried slipping it through, but it ended up on Elaine's desk. She said, "I'm sorry but you know we can't. There is no chance we'd get paid back. Zero. How do I explain that to the bank board?"

"We made a bad loan. Happens sometimes."

"Yes, but at the time we processed those loans, we did so because all the paperwork was in order, the plan looked solid and, in those cases, things didn't work out for one unforeseen reason or another. Not because we know it going into it. There is next to no chance it'll be paid back."

"My dad fixes it up, someone buys it, he and we get made whole."

"It's been for sale for years. If someone wanted to buy it, now would be the time," Elaine had replied. "When you could get it for ten cents on the dollar. Anyone shown interest?"

"No."

"Then what are we talking about here?"

"Elaine, come on. I've been with the bank a long time," he pleaded. "I'm owed one, just one, look the other way. This is my dad we're talking about. He's going to lose everything."

Elaine stood her ground. "It's not even a close case. He already has debt and that's with a place that will be condemned. This is a sizable loan, and you know as well as I do that there is no way this ever gets paid. He'll default. And it's your dad. If we approved it with his balance sheet as it is, and it doesn't get paid back, we'd both have a lot to answer for. We'd probably both end up terminated and I've been on the job a year. So... no. We just can't do it. If he can get it somewhere else, he should go there."

"You know he can't."

"Exactly," Elaine said. "We can't do it here either."

He knew she was right. That didn't make it any easier. Informing his dad was even worse, facing him, telling him he failed. "I need you to hold on just a little longer," he'd pleaded with him. "I'll figure something out for you, Dad. I will. Just hang on. Please, give me some time. I'll get you the money."

He knew a way, he'd known about its availability for years, just sitting there, abandoned. He had to be careful as it took time to accumulate the money without notice. He couldn't do it in one fell swoop. And while the money he could get wouldn't have been remotely enough to fix everything, it would have been enough where he might have been able to get a loan from another bank for the rest.

His dad didn't hang on. The last time he was at the resort six years ago, he found his dad hanging from an exposed rafter in the main lodge.

At the turn ahead into the resort, there was a metal gate. Parked to the side of the gate was a dual cab pickup truck. A thinnish man, a ski mask over his head, waved him ahead.

"To the lodge," the man said as he pulled through.

He drove slowly ahead along the familiar entry drive which had been plowed, all the way through to the far cabin to the south where he saw the nose of a pickup truck parked around the side of the last cabin. To the left, he saw the lodge. A boxy, two-story cabin with an office on the main level and small living quarters on half the second floor. It's where his dad and mom had lived, where he had grown up. A white SUV was parked in front of it.

As he pulled up, he looked behind to see the other man pull up in his pickup truck behind him, boxing him in. The man from the gate was out of his truck quickly, a gun in his right hand, hanging to his side.

He held up his hands.

"Grab the briefcase and get out," the man said.

As he reached for the briefcase, he looked up and saw another masked man standing in the entry way, huskier, with a gun in his waistband.

The thinnish man waved his gun to the lodge. "Inside."

* * *

Towne sat at the table, the cell phone out in front of him, wearing a ski mask of his own.

Jenks stepped back, letting Barry Marist walk inside the lodge and over to the rectangular folding table, followed by Merc.

"Sit down, Mr. Marist," Towne said, leaning forward on his elbows.

"Who are you?" Marist asked. "Why are you doing this to me? To Lainey? To my son? What did *we* do to you?"

"The only thing that matters is whether you brought me what I want. So please, sit down."

"You didn't answer my question!" Marist barked.

Merc burst at Marist, grabbed him by the throat, shoving him down into the chair. "And he's not going to asshole. But you better answer his."

"My friend is not as patient as I am," Towne said.

"It's... in the briefcase," Marist croaked, his eyes wide, looking up at Merc. Towne chuckled.

"I know it's in the briefcase. Open it so we can get on with it. This is going to take some time."

Merc released his grip and let Marist have a moment to catch his air.

Towne looked at him, as if to say: *let's go*.

Marist opened the briefcase. Inside was a laptop, a black flash drive and small dark-brown moleskin notebook.

Merc took all three out of the briefcase. He handed the moleskin notebook to Towne, who thumbed through it. The notebook listed account numbers and deposits, small ones over nearly six years funneled into several different account numbers as best he could tell. He relayed what he was seeing over the phone. There was a total balance of $6,824,530.14 as of two weeks ago.

"And the flash drive?"

"Spreadsheets that have basically the same record," Marist said.

"Let's see it."

Marist inserted the flash drive, tapped in the password, and opened it up.

Towne turned the laptop around, scrolling through the spreadsheet for each of the accounts. Each spreadsheet showed the account number, the deposit amounts and running balances. They were all lengthy. After the money accrued in various accounts in the bank in Manchester Bay, it would then be transferred to another account at a larger bank in a major city, Minneapolis, Milwaukee, Chicago, and Kansas City, all easily within a day's drive of Manchester Bay. From that second account, the money was later transferred to three different banks in Bermuda where there were four accounts in each bank. There were records for all transfers. But it all ended up in the accounts in the Bermuda banks, adding up to the total balance of just over $6.8 million.

Max hadn't been far off in the estimate and there was actually a bit more. "And these are the only records of these accounts?"

"Yes," Marist said. "What is it you want me to do?"

"Transfer the money in the accounts to the banks of my choice."

Marist shook his head, glaring warily at Merc and then back to him. "Not until I see my son."

Towne nodded to Jenks over by the door, who reached for the radio.

* * *

Jared observed the lodge from the back door, able to see in the large picture window, Towne sitting at the table with Marist, Merc standing behind him.

"Oh," he blurted when Merc grabbed Marist by the throat shoving him down to the chair.

A few seconds later, Jenks turned to him, reaching for the walkie-talkie.

"Bring the kid outside. Take the pillowcase off so his old man can get a look at him."

Jared turned and went to the corner and lifted Teddy up, pulled the pillowcase up over his head, pulled the tape off and drag-walked him outside.

"Teddy, look to the last cabin, the bigger one. See in the window."

* * *

"Teddy," Marist murmured, his son, hands bound in front of him. His son's eyes brightened, seeing him there.

He gave Teddy a furtive nod and small wave.

"Mr. Marist." He turned away from the window back to the man with the deep voice still sitting at the table. "The sooner you deliver. The sooner you get him back."

"Straight up trade, huh?"

The man simply nodded.

He didn't believe it would be so simple. But what choice did he have, at least right now.

Turning, he took another look at his son. Teddy was shivering in the cold in his hoodie, the snow blowing around him, the masked man standing behind him, his hands resting on his son's shoulders.

The husky man leaned in. "You heard him."

He glanced at Teddy one more time, his son being dragged back into the cabin before he turned and shuffled back to the table.

"This will take some time you know. It's not done in a snap of the fingers."

"Then you best get to it. Daylight is burning."

* * *

Max sat at the desk in her home office. The laptop was plugged into the dual monitors. The bank account was open and ready to accept the first of the wire transfers.

Towne's voice popped from the speaker. "You there?"

"Yes. The first question is where is the money? Is it in domestic or international banks?" They were ready for either, but the timing of the clearance of the wire transfers would be different. Domestic took mere hours, international could take one to five days before it arrived in their accounts.

"Three international banks, all in Bermuda." He listed the banks. "It's much as you suspected. He moved it out of the country except for one account. There is also a little over $100 grand between two banks in Milwaukee."

"Okay, we need to do this in smaller chunks. Take this down."

* * *

Towne jotted down the instructions and then slid over a slip of paper to Marist. "We're going to start with transfers to this account."

Marist looked at the bank and account information. Marist's bank was in Bermuda and they were transferring the money to another Bermuda bank.

Merc walked around behind Marist to observe, while Jenks stood at the front door, keeping out a watchful eye. Into the radio he said, "He's starting."

Marist started tapping at the computer, shaking his head.

"Seeing your retirement nest egg go up in smoke?" Towne needled.

* * *

The man had not put the tape back on his mouth as he sat up, nudged into a corner. His ankles were bound, albeit a bit more loosely and while his hands were still bound, they were in front of him so he could reach up and scratch his nose through the pillowcase, which was itching his nose.

He pulled his knees up to his chest and laid his head on them, resting, his eyes closed, listening to the wind howl outside, rattling the cabin and windows. The man was pacing again, he could hear and feel it, the groaning of the creaky floors. He was walking a loop around the cabin.

"Why are we here?"

There was no response, the man just kept walking. The footsteps fading away and then louder again.

"Why are we here?"

"Quiet."

The man walked away again, making his loop slowly around the cabin. He felt his approach again from his right, stopping at what was probably the large picture window. A loud wind gust roared by, and he felt a little shake of the cabin.

He was getting uncomfortable and let his legs out a little. "What is my dad doing?" There was no response. "Hello?"

"Just keep quiet, kid."

"What is my dad doing?"

"Last I looked, he was sitting at a computer."

"Why?"

"Money. No other reason to do this."

The man began walking again, making the loop around and around. He didn't know how long he'd been sitting in the corner, but it felt like a long time that they had been at the cabin. He heard the man go into the bathroom though he didn't shut the door. Then the pacing started again.

He was feeling hungry. As much as he didn't want to, he thought about the morning, when he'd gotten up, his mom nagging him about wearing extra clothes and making breakfast.

She always said he needed a good breakfast. No sweetened cereals. It was always eggs, bacon or ham, fruit, toast, juice. He never went to school hungry. That and he'd learned Ed liked breakfast too. His mom and Ed relished the mornings. They'd drink coffee, read and talk. Often Ed would have his computer on the table, checking his investments. He'd asked Ed about it one morning. Ed started showing him a few things, explaining stocks and bonds to him and the market and what he was trying to do each day, anticipating what the market would do and making his predictions of what would happen.

"Seems like gambling," he'd said. "Like on sports. Playing the odds."

Ed had smiled at that. "In some ways, Teddy, yeah."

It was kind of interesting, then.

As he approached again, making the loop, Teddy said, "My mom is dead, isn't she? And Ed. They're both dead."

There was no response. That was an answer in and of itself. Despite his father's admonition to stay tough, his eyes welled up, thinking of her. "Why did you have to kill her?" he said, sniffling, starting to cry.

The man didn't respond.

"*Why!*"

Footsteps approached. "Don't do this, kid. Don't do it to yourself. It'll only be worse."

"But... my mom. Why did you kill my mom? What did she do to you? She never hurt anyone. She's a professor."

"I wasn't the one to do it. I wish they wouldn't have. I really wish that didn't have to happen."

"Why?"

"Just stop, okay. Otherwise, I'll put the tape back over your mouth. I don't want to do that. But I will."

"What's it matter? You're just going to kill me too."

SEVEN

"IT'S NOT AS SIMPLE AS WE THOUGHT."

Tori stepped off the elevator into the main floor lobby, having left Jenny Wells's law office. It was just before 1:00 p.m. They were just over five hours in. She was about to charge outside into the snow when she stopped, her hand firm on the door handle. Glancing right, there was a small sitting area that looked out to Lake Drive that cut downtown Manchester Bay in two. She took one of the leather chairs, looking out to the street, needing a minute or two of quiet to just think.

She opened her notebook, flipped to a clean page and wrote the question: *What's bugging you?*

She'd seen something this morning. It was gnawing at her.

What was it?

Maybe it was nothing but when something like this rolled around in her mind, it was usually for a reason and it left her feeling uneasy, like when you knew you were supposed to do something and you'd forgotten and by the time you'd remembered, it was too late.

Everything pointed to Marist. *Everything.*

His gun was missing. They found shell casings consistent for usage of a Beretta.

He had motive. The affair, the divorce, the wealthier man.

Nobody had seen him today, before, during or after the shooting.

His cell phone was left behind. He dumped his SUV in Holmstrand.

Everything, *everything*, said it was him.

Or did it? she wrote, slowly circling the question with her pen.

She'd seen something that was planting a seed of doubt. *What was it? What's nagging you, Tori? What?*

Lainey's cell phone?

Lainey Darr's cell phone showed no activity in the last few days from her ex-husband. The last call between them had been a minute in length, five days ago. So, what would have been the trigger? That bothered her. If Marist snapped there should have been a trigger. But while that was a concern, it wasn't what was nagging her.

Marist's SUV?

While he hadn't been seen at his ex-wife's house, it didn't mean he wasn't there. "But it doesn't mean he was either," Tori mumbled. Black SUV racing away was generic. The fact that his black Suburban was found, most likely abandoned for another vehicle, was indicative it was Marist. That wasn't it though.

Shock at Marist?

Was it all the people telling her they didn't see it coming from Barry Marist?

Tori shook her head. It wasn't that, though to a person, nobody seemed to see it coming, either from the bitterness of the divorce itself or just from him. "But you've heard that story before," she murmured. And then it turns out the person was absolutely capable of doing just that.

Those things were counter to all that they were seeing but it wasn't what was truly gnawing at her.

Her phone buzzed. It was Braddock. "You have something?"

"I'm conferencing everyone in," he said without preamble. When everyone was on, he said, "It's just after 1:00 p.m. Let's go around the table and see where we're at. Nolan, go."

"Two things. I've done work, one, on Marist and two, on calling the employees at the bank on the list they provided. On Marist, he's from the Park Rapids area originally. His mother is long deceased. He had a dad up there who died a little over six years ago, committed suicide. He's been employed with Lakes Community Bank the last sixteen years, currently a vice president and chief operating officer and from what Braddock learned, basically the second in command to the bank president, Elaine Baird. As we know, recently divorced from Lainey Darr. No other marriages. No criminal record and from what the bank president, Elaine Baird, said, he has a spotless employment record.

"I've spoken by phone with some employees from the Manchester Bay branch, which was where he mostly worked out of. I've only spoken with them by phone given the urgency, not to mention the weather. Nobody has heard from him. To a person they're all—"

"Shocked that he did this," Reese said. "That's what I'm getting."

"That's the same thing I've been getting," Braddock said. "Universally."

"That's right," Nolan said.

"Me too," Tori said, relating what she'd learned at the university and from Jenny Wells, Lainey Darr's lawyer.

"Of course, people always say that," Reese noted. "Any time there is one of these shootings. I never saw it coming. He never showed any signs. I didn't see a violent streak in him, yada, yada, yada."

"That's true," Tori said. "To a point. I've seen one parent kidnap the child after a bitter divorce, or before the divorce. There is shock because they're a loving parent. Great father or mother. I can't believe they did this. Except, when you dig further, you always find warning signs. Have we seen any?"

"Is that's what is bugging you?" Braddock asked. "That nobody thinks he could do it?"

"No, it's something else I think, but... and we haven't talked to everybody, but... if it's him, what triggered it because nobody says he would do it. It's not about could he do it, I think we've seen plenty to suggest he could have, but *would* he do it?"

"I'd say yes," Reese replied. "I mean, this whole thing today shows he planned this. Nobody saw him leave his house. Granted he's somewhat isolated out here, but that works to his advantage. Nobody saw him at his ex-wife's house, but it was early. He had a drop vehicle and abandoned his SUV. He left his cell phone behind."

Planned. She closed her eyes. That's what she saw.

"We've checked Darr's phone. Have we checked Marist's?" Tori asked.

"Uh," Reese started. "Yeah. I'm at Marist's house. Jennison is pulling up here now."

"That's the first thing she checks," Tori said. "I'm on my way there. But a hundred bucks says she's going to find he got a call this morning, from his son."

"How would you know that?"

"I just know."

Braddock heard it in her voice. "What is it?"

"Planned."

"What?"

"Reese said planned. That Marist planned this. I know what I saw, what's bugging me. Get over there."

. . .

Braddock had the jump on her out of Manchester Bay and she spotted him ahead of her on the H-4 and followed him, his police light flashing, siren blaring, as they made their way back down to Greyler Lake Estates and back to Marist's house.

He waited for her as she came up the driveway. "What is it?"

"Let's get inside," she replied, shaking the snow off her under the front step portico.

Inside they found Jennison. She had checked Marist's phone record. "His last call received was at 7:42 a.m. It was from his son's cell phone."

Tori offered a wan smile. "Told you."

"7:42?" Braddock replied and he radioed dispatch. "What time was it when Detective Williams radioed we'd respond to the 10-18? Uh-huh. Copy." He shook his head. "According to dispatch we responded at 7:39 a.m. That can't be right."

Tori shook her head. "It is if it *wasn't* Teddy calling."

"I'm not following."

"Reese said he planned this. If he did, where is the evidence of it, *here? Right here. In this house.*"

"What do you mean?"

"I observed some of this earlier, but it just didn't... register," Tori said angrily. "Maybe it is everyone, *everyone*, saying he wouldn't or couldn't do it. People snap but nobody thinks it possible here. The divorce was over. They settled. They haven't spoken in days. He moved on, bought a new house. Jenny Weld, Lainey Darr's attorney, said Lainey thought he was having an affair. So perhaps he'd moved on that way too. But now, *today*, he executes the plan to kill his ex-wife and run with his son?"

"But the drop vehicle." Reese ticked on his finger. "Leaving the cell phone behind. His SUV seen leaving Girard's—"

"A black SUV was seen leaving Girard's," Tori corrected. "We don't know it was his, though. We assumed it was."

"His gun is missing."

"Right, a Beretta. We have 9mm casings."

"Yeah, he shot her with it."

"Well, someone probably did," Tori replied.

"Somebody?"

"If he planned this, to kill his ex-wife and Girard, and to go on the run with his son, beyond the missing gun, where is the evidence of that in *this* house?" She led them to the master bedroom. "Look at Marist's closet. No gaps of missing clothes. His three suitcases for travel are in the closet. His shoes lined up except for a gap for one pair. One! Probably what he was wearing. If he was going on the run, he would have packed some clothes." She went to his dresser and started opening drawers. "Socks, underwear, T-shirts. No gaps, not empty, full. If you're going on the run, you're going to need clothes. Nothing is missing. No gaps."

Braddock turned and walked down the hallway to Teddy's room. "Same thing in here," he said.

"Right." Tori nodded along. "If he was planning on taking his son on the run, wouldn't he have packed clothes for him? I don't see any evidence of that. And before you ask, he certainly wouldn't have done it at Darr's house, not after having shot her and Girard. He wouldn't have had time and plus he wouldn't have needed to, Teddy had clothes *here*."

She went across the hallway to the bathroom. There was a toothbrush in a cup on the countertop. Opening the drawers she found toothpaste, floss, a comb and brush, deodorant. "Everything a boy that age needs is still here. And his toiletries were still at Girard's house as well. The wet toothbrush, remember."

Tori walked back through the kitchen to the washer and dryer room. The washer and dryer were empty. There was one cleaning basket, but it was empty. "Nothing. I mean, no evidence he packed anything. If he planned this, he'd have packed... something."

"And then here in the kitchen," she continued. "Two pieces

of toast, one full, one half-eaten. A half-cup of coffee, more in the coffee maker pot. Do you leave that behind if you're *planning* to kill your ex-wife, her boyfriend and run off with your son?"

Braddock snorted a laugh.

"So, this is what then?" Reese said.

"I don't know, yet," Tori said. "It's not as simple as we thought."

"She's holding back," Braddock said. "What she thinks is someone planned everything out this morning, step by step, and then at 7:42—"

Reese added, "They call Marist to say..."

"We have your son," Braddock said. "Marist is a patsy. He's been set up and now they want him to come for Teddy, whom they have. They called Marist on his son's phone to be sure that he would pick up the call."

"I think it's at least possible," Tori said. "But if that is the case, then the question is *why?*"

Everyone went quiet for a moment until Braddock's phone buzzed. It was Steak. He put it on speaker.

"We found a surveillance camera," Steak said. "A trail camera in the backyard of a house. They see wild animals mostly with it, wolves every so often, but in the background, it catches the parking lot where he dumped his SUV. Marist exchanged his black Suburban for a smaller gray SUV."

"It looked to be a gray SUV, maybe an old Mercury Mariner," Eggleston added. "We were able to get a partial plate, MS and we think X, no numbers, too dirty, too distant."

"They haven't made Mercury Mariners for what? Ten years," Reese said.

"At least," Steak said. "But we have it out there now."

"But get this," Eggleston started. "When he changed vehicles—"

"Teddy Marist wasn't with him," Tori blurted.

There was a moment of silence on the other end. "How did you know that?"

"That's confirmation, is it not?" Braddock said.

"It is," Tori said. "But now the question is why?"

EIGHT

"MAYBE IT'S NOT JUST ABOUT THE MONEY."

Marist exhaled a breath, snuck a look at the time in the lower right corner of the computer screen. 3:14 p.m.

He sensed the growing impatience on the other side of the table as he slow-walked the wire transfers. There were frequent checks of the watch and more annoyed, "Move it alongs," from the masked man opposite him. And he was taking his sweet time about it, double and triple checking, intentionally fat fingering the keystrokes thus requiring correction. He played it off as nervousness but that only played for so long.

He was trying to buy time. For what? The police? They were looking for him but unless they made a massive intuitive leap about the resort based on the folder in his filing cabinet at home, they weren't on the way.

"He's got a couple more after this one," said the husky one by the front door behind him, standing watch. He was communicating into a walkie-talkie, presumably with the man who had Teddy.

That would make at least four men, though as he'd listened to the man speak into the radio, it didn't *seem* like there was any more than one person. There was a fifth person, but the man across the table from him was on the phone with that person, who was monitoring the transactions.

Five people involved, four on location, three in the room with him. Given the amount of money he was transferring, and assuming all involved received an equal cut, that would leave a little over a million or so for each. He kept running that equation around in his mind as he'd made the transfers. Was that enough money to justify the risk of murdering his ex-wife, and Ed and him, and Teddy? Something about that didn't add up.

"$6.8 million, give or take, is not all that much money," he said as he tapped in an account number. "If you're spreading it amongst what? One, two, three, four—" he gestured at the phone "—maybe five people? I mean, I assume everyone is in on the cut, are they not?"

"How we handle the money amongst us is no concern of yours."

He understood that as confirmation that there were four people here. "It's just that killing two people, two innocent people, seems like a lot of trouble to incur for the amount at stake is all. I'm just trying to make sense of it."

The man simply shrugged. "Maybe it's not *just* about the money."

The man to his right chuckled at that.

Not just about the money? What else could it be about? "I imagine you thought it would be more."

"It's in the range that we'd anticipated."

He looked up. "And how would you know that?"

The man had a self-satisfied smile on his face. He indeed had an idea of what the amount would be.

"Did you have an in at the bank in Akeley? Or... in Manchester Bay?"

The man scoffed. "Move it along. The sooner you finish the sooner you get out of here."

The sooner you get out of here.

He'd spent the past several hours making the transfers and assessing whether that was a possible outcome. Initially, he had hope. Transfer the money and they would let him and Teddy go. Yes, he would have to face the music one way or another for Lainey or for the money, but Teddy would live. But as he worked that problem through, he realized there was zero chance of it. Not given the location they were at. Not if they had already killed Lainey and Ed and did so with *his* Beretta. Despite what they were saying, it was all a facade. They had a specific end game in mind and a very cavalier view of human life. Lainey and Ed were innocent and murdered. They had no compunction about taking two more lives, his and Teddy's. If you've killed two, what's two more? Why leave any living witnesses?

He'd shifted to looking for an opening to turn the tables.

Once, he'd been a high school football player, an undersized offensive guard, but a state tournament high-school wrestler. There were four men present but as of now, only three in the room. His odds, one on three, were not favorable. But those were odds he was weighing as he took care of the transactions.

He glanced to his right. The lanky man had physically sat him down earlier, but he'd been caught by surprise, not ready for the attack. As he'd replayed that in his mind, that man struck him as thin, perhaps wiry, but less imposing in the way his clothes, layered as they were given the cold, hung so loosely on his body. He had twenty, maybe thirty pounds on him. The dark-voiced man across the table was not quite so slight. He was just as tall, but thicker through the arms and shoulders. He viewed him as something of a physical equal, as he had the man over by the door who was a bit shorter but stockier.

How could he get all three?

* * *

Jared stood at the back door of the cabin, peering at the lodge, Marist hunched over at the computer, Merc pacing around behind him, Towne on a phone, Jenks keeping watch in the doorway.

He didn't know how much money there was but given how long they'd been sitting there, he assumed it must be a lot. What he didn't understand was why they had to do it this way.

The dad was a thief. Fine. You play in the dirt, you get dirty. He had no problem with that. Take his money. If he stole it to begin with, who is he going to report it to? Is he going to go to the police? No.

But why all this?

Why did they have to kill the ex-wife and the boyfriend? The boyfriend was just some rich guy, and it wasn't even his money they were taking. And the ex-wife? Yeah, she said a bunch of nasty things about Hot Rod on national television, but she was far from the only one. Did that mean they should kill her? And even so why would they have to kill the boy? Just to make a point?

Towne said it had to be done this way, that this would give them the leverage to get Marist to turn over the money, it would provide payback on the ex-wife and her sharp ignorant tongue, "And it'll keep the police occupied, investigating," he said. "Meanwhile, nobody is looking for us, nobody is even thinking about us, and we can do what we really came here to do."

That all made some sense, but killing the kid?

* * *

Marist allowed himself one more look around the room. The skinny man was the one to go after first, he could take him. He just needed to lure him in.

"I'm hitting send," Marist noted, and then leaned back from the computer.

The man on the other side listened on the other end of the phone, nodding along every so often. "Got it. Okay." He looked up to him. "There's one more."

"No."

The man scoffed, shook his head, offering a wry smile. "No?"

"No. There's $852,427 left to be moved. It's one last sizable one. Let Teddy go and I make it. All you have to do is drop him off somewhere, maybe a mile from a town and let him walk the rest of the way. Bring him in here and let me say goodbye first. You do that. I'll finish it and then you can finish me."

"I don't think so."

Marist shrugged. "I don't think so either."

"Look, I told you—"

He scoffed. "You're not going to let Teddy and I walk out of here. You want the rest, Teddy lives, that's the deal."

"I don't think so."

His eyes slid right, feeling the skinny man step toward him.

* * *

"How much longer?" Jared asked, tapping his foot nervously.

"He has one more wire transfer I think, though he's talking trash about not making it," Jenks answered with a chuckle. "He may have to be encouraged."

Jared stepped to the window at the back door.

* * *

"I only care about Teddy. Do what you're going to do to me. I've earned it. I did what I did and if this is the price I pay, I'll pay it. But not Teddy. He's ten, man. *Ten!*" Marist screamed, standing up. "He doesn't deserve to die. Let him live."

"Settle him down," Max said as Merc moved in.

"Sit your fucking ass down," Merc growled, reaching for Marist's shoulder.

Marist's eyes shifted right, as did his weight. Towne saw it a split second late. "No!"

Marist lunged at Merc, who was caught off guard. Marist drove Merc with his shoulder into the reception counter and had his left hand on the butt of Merc's gun and wrestled it loose. Merc grabbed Marist's hands and the gun as the two of them fought, crashing around the room.

Crack!

"Jenks!"

Merc pulled Marist down to the floor. The two of them rolled around, fighting for control of the gun. Marist rolled over Merc, getting ahold of the gun as they rolled over again, pulling the trigger.

Crack! Crack!

"Ahrg!" Merc yelped.

Marist rolled up with the gun.

Towne dove to his right, tipping the table as he did.

Crack! Crack! Crack!

The shots pierced the plastic table, zooming over Towne's head.

Boom! Boom! Boom!

"Towne!" Jenks called. "Towne!"

"Yeah." Towne looked up over the table to see Marist lying motionless on his side, a faint groan emanating out of him.

Jenks kicked away Merc's gun, aiming his at Marist and looking over to Towne, wordlessly asking: *Do I finish it?*

Towne nodded.

Boom!

Marist was dead.

Merc groaned loudly, grunting as he tried sitting up. "Ah fuck!" He was wounded in his left upper thigh. The outside of his jeans was moist with blood around the wound.

"How bad?" Towne said.

"Hurts like a mother."

"Towne! Brother! Brother!" Max's voice called from the cell phone.

"We're alright, though Merc's been shot. Marist is dead!"

"*What!*"

* * *

"Oh shit!" Jared blurted.

He saw Marist lunge at Merc. He saw Jenks spin around, pulling his gun. Through the lodge's picture window, he could see Merc and Marist wrestling.

Crack!

Towne dove for cover as Marist and Merc fought over the gun and then crashed out of his view. Jenks rushed inside but he could see him through the doorway, his gun up, shuffling around for position.

Crack! Crack!

The picture window was punctured.

Boom! Boom! Boom!

Those shots were from Jenks, that .45 he was carrying.

He saw Jenks step into the middle of the room as if standing over someone; his gun aimed toward the floor.

Boom!

This wasn't supposed to happen. This was not the plan. Now they couldn't make the plan work. No way.

"Jared, get over here," Jenks called over the radio. "Merc's down! Merc's down!"

"Let's just leave the kid and get out of here," Jared replied. "Let's just get out of here."

"No. Get over here. *Now!*"

"What happened! What happened to my dad!" Teddy yelped.

Jared spun around. The plan was blown. Now, they were just going to murder the boy in cold blood.

Jared looked from Teddy to the lodge back to him.

"Jared, get over here!" Jenks voice called again.

I'm not letting them kill this kid.

* * *

Towne pushed himself up from behind the table, Marist's laptop was lying on the floor, the screen cracked and partially detached from the base. He rushed over to Merc. He'd been shot on the outside of his left thigh.

"Fuck!" he groaned, blood oozing out.

"Jared, get over here. Merc's down! Merc's down!"

"Let's just leave the kid and get out of here," Jared replied. "Let's just get out of here."

"No. Get that kid down here now. *Now!*" Jenks ordered into the walkie-talkie as he rushed over to Merc.

"We need the first aid kit," Towne said.

"Jared has it in his truck," Jenks said. "Where is that motherfucker?" He called for him again. "Jared, get over here! We need that first aid kit!"

Towne inspected the thigh wound. "The bullet is still in there." He pulled a hanky out of his back pocket and applied pressure.

They heard an engine roaring to life.

"He must be driving over here," Jenks said as he turned around to see Jared's lifted pickup truck cutting through the yard, through the snow, at a forty-five-degree angle.

"Is he..."

"That fuck!" Jenks yelled, rushing out of the cabin into the yard.

Boom! Boom! Boom! Boom! Boom!

The pickup truck kept right on going.

Jenks sprinted down the driveway to the far cabin Jared had been in. He rushed inside. It was empty. "Dammit! Dammit!"

He raced back to the lodge to find Towne lifting Merc onto a sitting chair. "Give me a hand."

Towne helped get Merc's pants down to expose the wound. It was oozing blood.

"Get his coat off, get the flannel shirt off," Towne ordered, taking out his knife. Jenks helped Merc get the shirt off. Towne cut the flannel shirt into long strips. He started wrapping the wound with them.

"What's happening?" Max's voice bellowed from the cell phone.

"Jared took the kid."

"*He what!*"

"That fucking coward! Running off on me," Merc groaned. "I'm going to be the one to kill him."

"What the hell does he think he's doing?" Towne asked angrily.

Jenks closed his eyes. "I knew he was getting squeamish about this."

"You knew?" Max yelled. "You fucking knew? Why didn't you say something!"

"I should have—"

"Dammit," Towne barked as he finished wrapping the wound.

"I didn't think he'd do this. *Fuck!*" Jenks screamed, angry with himself.

"You have to get the hell out of there and right now," Max said.

"Max is right," Merc said, grimacing as he pushed himself up to stand. "That was way too much noise. Storm be damned. Someone is going to be coming and soon."

"Grab everything," Towne said.

"What about Marist?" Jenks said.

"Leave him," Max said. "No choice. Get out of there."

"Yeah. We need to put distance between ourselves and this place," Towne agreed, looking over Merc. "And we need to get a better dressing on that wound."

"And then," Max ordered, "you're going to track Jared down before someone else does."

NINE

"WE DO NOT PASS GO AND COLLECT $200."

"Where are we going?" Teddy yelped from the back seat. "Where are you taking me?"

"We have to get out of here, right now," Jared yelled and took a quick look to his back right and saw movement. It was Jenks and he noticed his posture and body movement. "Stay down! Stay down!" He ducked himself.

Boom! Boom! Boom! Boom! Boom!

Ping! Ping! Ping!

The shots pelted the back of the truck, and clipped his passenger door mirror, shattering the mirror assembly off the truck. He crashed through the gate and charged down the road.

The kid called from the back seat. "What happened to my dad?"

Jared ignored him for the moment, keeping an eye on the rearview mirror as he raced through the low-lying wetland they had crossed earlier, taking it at a much faster rate since his lifted pickup truck was able to easily clear the accumulating snow.

Five minutes clear, having made two turns he relaxed just a bit, letting out some air. He needed to think.

"You okay back there?" he asked. It had been a rough ride.

"I want my dad," he said in a meeker voice. The tone told Jared that the kid was figuring things out.

"I can't do that," Jared said as he tried smoothing out the ride a bit now that they were on a county road. He looked in his rearview mirror and saw that he was leaving a distinctive trail in the snow with his wider tires and its track.

"My dad is dead, isn't he?"

Jared closed his eyes. "I'm sorry."

He *was* sorry. This whole thing had been wrong. He knew it was wrong from the time Towne told them they were going north, but he went along with it. He always went along with it. His whole life was going along with it.

Teddy sniffled and whimpered. His parents were both dead in a matter of hours. There was nothing he could say that would help. He had no words of comfort to offer. And he wasn't good at words anyway.

For the next half-hour as he drove, Jared alternately looked at the snowy road ahead, his rearview mirror for a tail and the lump lying curled up on the bench back seat. He was now well northwest of Park Rapids. It would be fully dark very soon and with the storm building in intensity he had the roads largely to himself.

The radio was tuned to the local news station.

"KWTK radio time is 4:27 p.m. Here in Park Rapids, the temperature is eight degrees and falling with the snow now heavy. Our own gauge just out back is nine inches of snow since it started just after nine this morning. It will continue to accumulate overnight. The state patrol is recommending people not travel. Winds are now gusting at fifteen to twenty miles per hour and will increase throughout the evening hours leading to blizzard-like conditions with extremely limited visi-

bility. It is expected that by early evening roads will become undrivable as the snow and winds increase. Stay tuned to KWTK for weather updates.

"In other news, authorities remain on the hunt for ten-year-old Teddy Marist and his father, Barry Marist, aged 48. The authorities are now on the lookout for a gray SUV, perhaps a Mercury Mariner with a partial license plate of MS and possibly X..."

What now? Towne and Jenks had the money, maybe that would be enough.

Unlikely.

The money wasn't ever the ultimate goal. They needed the money for the *after*. Or at least that's what Towne always said.

Would Towne come after him?

Probably.

He, Jenks, Max were not ones to let things go. This whole endeavor was proof of that. They would hunt him; of that he was certain.

He could go to the police, right now. But he was a willing and participating accomplice to two murders, and arguably a third in Marist. Even if he turned himself and the boy in and fully cooperated, a long prison sentence likely awaited him. He would not do well caged up in a cell.

He needed to get somewhere to think and figure out what to do with the kid. A few times, as he'd approached a gas or convenience station, he'd thought of just stopping and letting the boy walk inside. But his pickup truck could or more likely would show up on a surveillance camera somewhere if he did that. He was in his actual pickup truck, with his legitimate North Carolina plates. From that, law enforcement would be able to identify him.

License plates.

That was a problem. He didn't want to give up his truck nor

was he one to just steal one, he didn't know how to do that. They made it look easy in the movies, but it was never that simple. And if he was going on the run, he didn't have the money to spare to buy a new one.

He knew a house where he might find another set or two of Minnesota license plates though. He could take them, put them on the truck and maybe slip away, put some distance between himself and Minnesota. And he could rest there in some warmth and figure out what to do. From where he was now, given the road conditions, it was less than an hour away.

* * *

They had hurriedly loaded everything into the back of Jenks's truck from the cabin. Towne drove the truck, while Jenks drove the white Tahoe. As he drove, Towne glanced back at Merc and his bloody left leg. "We'll need to stitch it up," Towne said. "Soon."

"I have a first aid kit in the RV," Merc replied, breathing heavily in pain. "Jenks can do it."

The drive to the campground north of Park Rapids took over a half-hour in the worsening conditions. The good news was that the weather was keeping most other vehicles off the roads. However, with the resort fifteen minutes in the rearview mirror, they did pass one Hubbard County Sheriff's Patrol SUV going in the opposite direction. Was it going to the resort?

Towne pulled into the campground. Were there any prying eyes?

It was mid-winter, so the campground was lightly populated to begin with, and when they'd arrived a month ago, they had carefully selected a pull through location in the middle row at the far back with the RV's side door sheltered from view from the few others there. Nevertheless, given the conditions, two vehicles pulling into the campground might draw a look or two.

Towne pulled around behind the thirty-foot long RV, parking close to the side door. Merc was able to stand on his one good leg and with Towne's and Jenks's assistance, climb up inside and hobble to his bed in the back. Towne laid out towels while Jenks fetched the first aid kit. Merc lay down on the bed. Jenks had been in the army and served a tour in Iraq and had treated battlefield wounds a few times and had watched it done many others. He retrieved the scissors and cut Merc's jeans to expose the wound on his left thigh.

Even with the ceiling lights on, it was hard to see into the wound.

"I'm going to have to dig it out," Jenks said, looking Merc in the eye. "It's gonna hurt, man."

"Gotta be done."

Jenks dowsed the wound in alcohol.

"*Ahhhhhhh*," Merc grimaced, sucking in air, his body convulsing.

"It'll hurt more," Towne said, having grabbed a bottle of whiskey and a leather belt. "Take a drink of this," he said, handing Merc the bottle. "Then bite down on this," he added, handing him the belt. "And stay still."

Merc took a long drink, bit down on the belt and nodded.

Jenks dug into the flesh with the tip of the knife, opening the wound.

Merc grunted in pain, chomping on the belt, his eyes bulging.

"Sorry, man."

The procedure, such that it was, took a half-hour. The worst of it was using a knife to open the wound and then the tweezers to first dig around, expand the wound a bit and then extract the bullet. Once Jenks had, he was able to sterilize the wound and sew it up with crude stitches. It wasn't emergency room quality but under the circumstances, it would have to do. "It's going to leave a pretty nasty scar," Jenks said. "And who knows how the tissue heals."

"BFD," Merc grunted, allowing himself another drink of whiskey, wiping sweat from his brow. Sometime down the road, a long way from here, in the warm climate they intended to go to, he might have a doctor look at it and clean it up. That was for another day. "At least it's done."

They gave Merc some time to clean up. Jenks cleaned out the back of the truck, bringing in the backpack that had Marist's laptop, flash drives, notebook, and other items. He spent a moment searching through the bag and crinkled his nose.

"What?" Towne asked, putting his hand over the phone.

"Uh... Nothing," Jenks said. "Just inventorying everything is all."

Towne was on the phone, checking in with Max. He hung up. "The money will take a day or two to clear. Just a hair under $6 million. Which we'll split four ways now."

"Speaking of four ways, what about Jared?" Jenks said. "He's out there. He has the kid. He may not know all the details, but he knows what comes next."

"Max is monitoring everything media wise. The kid hasn't turned up yet."

"Jared still has him then," Towne surmised.

"Jared's an idiot," Jenks growled.

"An idiot who has us by the balls right now. Whether he truly understands that, I don't know," Towne replied. "I see two options for us. We take the money and run. We do not pass Go and collect $200."

"The money is not why we came here," Jenks asserted angrily. "Are *you* good with that? Money? You think Max or Rod, or my dead brother or yours would be good with that?"

"It's a lot of money," Towne said.

"Fuck that. What's the other option?" asked Jenks.

"Or. The other option is for the three of us to find Jared and deal with him, and that kid." He looked at Merc. "You good with that?"

"I'll pull the fuckin' trigger," Merc declared. "He's dead to me."

"Okay," Towne said, nodding. "We don't have much time. Merc, he's going to be looking to do something with the kid. If he hasn't just dropped him off somewhere like Marist had suggested, he'll be looking to turn him over to someone he can trust to do it for him. Do you know who that might be?"

"I've got one idea."

* * *

Darkness had long set in by the time Jared reached the house. The first right turn into the driveway was barely visible. It was marked only by a narrow green post with a small blue plate on it, 9609. He stopped at the entrance, which angled back up to the right, going up a steepish rise in the woods. Snow was plowed across it over the course of the winter, three to four feet high, which created a sort of barrier. The driveway looped up and around the house and then back down, coming out a quarter mile ahead. As he rolled by the second entrance, the snow was plowed even higher and more thickly across it. The first entrance was the better option. With a run at it, he would be able to clear it. Making a U-turn, he glanced back at Teddy. "Be ready. A bit of a jump coming up."

He accelerated up the road, veered left and hit the snowbank at a bit of an angle, the front of the truck elevating and then bounding over the snow, landing, and veering right. Quickly, he jerked the steering wheel left, managing to keep the truck on the driveway, avoiding the thick mature trees pinching in on either side of the driveway and then followed the winding drive up and into a broader clearing where there was still some mature shade trees, but what he also knew in the summer would be a considerable open yard particularly to the right of the house.

It had been years since he'd been to the cabin. It had been one of his last stops to say goodbye before he'd ventured south.

His uncle Bud had looked after him as a teen after his mother died. Bud was a tough old bird who, like many of his relatives, like himself, preferred the isolation of the woods as opposed to living in town, even a small town. The cabin was a half-mile from the border to the wildlife refuge. There wasn't another house or cabin for miles in all directions. Bud and his aunt Mae lived quietly, growing what they wanted in their gardens. His uncle did his woodworking in the shop built onto the back of the two-car detached garage. It's where he'd learned woodworking himself. Bud and Mae lived south in the winter, in a trailer park in southern Texas. He had visited them once down there three years ago.

Powering through the snow he followed what he roughly thought was the driveway in a wide arc around to the back of the house, parking between it and the detached garage. Now, did they still leave a key outside? He trudged through the snow to the hose holder rack to the left of the water spigot. He reached deep underneath the rack.

Yes.

He opened the back door and stepped inside and flipped up a light switch. The power was on. Making a quick sweep of the house, he turned up the thermostat and then checked the television. His uncle didn't have cable but at least there was an antenna tower attached to the house. He would get some local stations and some access to the news. Next, he went out to the truck and retrieved Teddy. "I'm bringing you inside the house." He laid him on the living room couch and put a blanket over him. "The heat should kick in soon." To accelerate the warm up, he built a fire in the fireplace.

From a hook on the wall by the back door, he grabbed a key

ring and trudged back outside and through the snow to the garage, cycled through the key ring until he found the one to open the side door.

He stepped inside, flipped on the light and chuckled. His uncle still had the same old beat-up Chevy pickup truck he'd had six years ago. It was an old truck back then. He unscrewed the license plates from the truck and then trudged outside into the snow and put them on his own truck and put his old plates in a drawer for the workbench. That done, he went back inside and made a quick inventory of the small house. His aunt and uncle were simple folks. The interior of the house itself had hardly changed since he was a young boy, which he was counting on when he reached on top of the long hutch in the small dining room and then to his surprise, retrieved not one, but two shotguns. There was the old double-barreled Remington, a gun he shot as a child. The surprise was his uncle had also upgraded to a Beretta double barrel twelve-gauge. Shells? *Shells. Shells. Shells.* Where were they?

You'd keep them close.

He dug through the hutch and found two boxes stuffed behind some candles. Double-aught buck shells. Eighteen rounds. He set the boxes and guns on the dining room table.

The master bedroom was on the second story. His uncle wasn't going to just rely on the shotgun for protection. Not this far out in the middle of nowhere. In the master bedroom, in the bottom drawer of the dated nightstand, he found his uncle's Springfield, the old SA-35. It had a full magazine, and another stowed in the drawer.

What is down in the basement?

He hit pay dirt. Uncle Bud was one to be prepared. You never knew when the government would come for you if things went all to hell in a handbasket. If they did, he was ready with an AR-15, with a full magazine. And in a cabinet, he found more double-aught buck shells, not to mention two spare magazines for the AR-15.

On the dining room table, he laid out what he had available. He had his own truck ready to go and he had guns for protection. But what to do about the kid?

There was only one person nearby that he could call for help. But would he? He was far from his favorite nephew.

TEN

"THE FOURTH MAN."

If Marist didn't kill his ex-wife and take his son, then someone was making it look like he did. *Who? And why?* Tori wondered repeatedly.

Braddock paced in the hallway, working the phones, talking to his troops and contacts with adjoining counties and the state patrol. Tori allowed herself a peek out the window and then a quick check of her watch. It was 4:10 p.m. The snow was starting to accumulate. More was coming.

While he talked and paced, Tori continued at Marist's desk. At first, she just sat still in his swivel desk chair, trying to get a sense of Marist. As she examined the desk area, there were numerous Post-it notes attached to the stem of the desk lamp, the bottom of the computer monitor and the computer tower. Many appeared to be reminders, or passwords for this or that. The interesting thing was that they were posted... in an ordered fashion. Not cockeyed in any way but in straight lines. She laughed inwardly. She had Post-it notes all over her desk at home too. The difference being that there was just about zero order or organization as to how or why she did it. She wrote down whatever it was and stuck it somewhere. Her system was no system, whereas with Marist, her sense was, everything was systematic. So, Tori, work systematically.

She had reviewed Marist's financial records, which encompassed the left filing cabinets. It was a favorable financial picture for him. His checking account had just over $15,000 in it. He had a savings account with just under $32,000 in it. He wasn't rich by any stretch, but certainly comfortable enough. His 401k with the bank was well invested and on a good trajectory for someone of his age.

His house was brand new. He put twenty percent down, had a mortgage rate he'd probably refinance when rates dropped but he could easily handle it on his current income.

She had been through his divorce settlement and Professor Shmyr and Jenny Wells were right about the two of them fighting over nothing.

They agreed to sell the house and split the proceeds fifty-fifty. She'd seen the deposit from the sale in his savings account. He'd turned around and used a significant chunk of it to make the down payment on the new house.

Custody of Teddy would be joint, split evenly. A schedule had been worked out where Teddy would spend a week with each parent and then switch. She saw correspondence where that had been what they were doing.

While he was in a decent position financially, there was nothing in his financial records that suggested he was a target for ransom.

She was now working her way through the right side, which were bills and other family-related records.

"Do you think the reason someone would do this to him would be in the files?" Braddock asked.

She shook her head. "I don't expect to find the smoking gun if that's your question. I'm looking for hints."

"Finding any?"

Tori shook her head. "Nothing in his financials. The picture there is solid if unspectacular. He's pumped the maximum into his 401k for years and the balance is good for someone forty-eight-years old. Another ten to fifteen years of contributions and solid market returns, he'd retire, very comfortably. However, nothing that screams ransom target for money."

"Is anything missing in the files?"

"Maybe," Tori replied, opening a file drawer. "In the Rs there is an empty hanging folder."

"For?"

"I don't know," she replied. "There is a noticeable gap, like a manila folder is missing from the green hanging folder for R. Like he opened the file drawer, grabbed it, and left."

Braddock's phone buzzed. "It's Steak... Hey, what's up?" He listened for a moment and then his eyes widened. "I'm putting you on speaker." He tapped his screen. "Go."

"I've just started on my way up toward Park Rapids, actually twenty miles northwest of there. I just got a call from the Hubbard County Sheriff's Office. They found a gray Mercury Mariner and a dead Barry Marist. He was shot four times inside a cabin at an abandoned resort."

Tori's jaw dropped open, stunned. It was one thing to wonder if Marist was set up but now, they knew. "And the boy, Teddy?" Tori asked.

"No sign of him according to the deputy on scene," Steak said. "The Hubbard County Sheriff is on his way out there. The BCA will try to get someone out there. I'm on my way up right now. I assume you two will be as well."

"Yes," Braddock said, turning to leave.

"Steak, the name of the resort wouldn't have happened to be Darkwoods, would it?" Tori asked.

There was silence for a moment. "Uh... yeah. How do you know?"

Braddock gave her a look. "Yeah, how?"

Tori turned her chair and opened a drawer for the desk,

walked her fingers through folders until she pulled out a manila one.

"What's that?" Braddock said.

"A file. Darkwoods Resort," Tori said. "We better get up there."

They had the roads mostly to themselves, save the odd truck or SUV braving the conditions. And snowplows were out on the H-4, trying to get ahead of the snow.

"What's the story with this resort?" Braddock asked as he drove as fast as he dared, given the worsening conditions.

"Darkwoods Resort on Lake Caron. Or at least it was."

"Which is where?"

"Northwest of Park Rapids."

"Did Marist own it?"

"His father Otis Marist did. There's an application in the file for a loan from Lakes Community Bank."

"So, he went to his son for a loan."

"It was denied," Tori replied.

"Denied?" Braddock replied, surprised. "Why?"

"There is a copy of a loan denial letter in the file, signed by Elaine Baird. This was a little over six years ago."

"I met Baird. She's the bank president. Why was the loan denied? I'd assume someone like Barry Marist could have rubber-stamped something like that given his position."

Tori thumbed through the documents. "The resort appears to have been in a state of rather significant disrepair. It doesn't appear Marist's father did well on the upkeep, and it got rundown."

"Roger Hayes, and Steak, and anyone and everyone have all said the small resorts have been disappearing for years," Braddock noted. "It's become so expensive to operate. It was a better financial move to sell the land, or the cabins individually."

Tori nodded. "If you can. You also need to be on a good lake as well. There's a map in the file." She held it up. "This lake is kind of off on its own. And there are copies of pictures of the resort in the file."

Braddock noted her tone. "Rustic?"

"That would be one way to describe it," Tori replied with a rueful chuckle. "It reminds me of some of the mom-and-pop resorts that were on our lake when I was a kid. Small boxy cabins. Thing is, our lake is sandy with lots of nice swimming beaches plus good fishing and we're on the chain, so instead of being on one lake we're on many."

"Which is why the property taxes are through the roof."

"Darkwoods Resort appears only to have had the higher taxes but no sand. Not much of a swimming area. Looks like it was very weedy. This might have been a place more for a fisherman than a family with young kids. And then... Ew. Ick."

"What?"

"There was a bed bug outbreak eight years ago."

Braddock grimaced. "Quinn had that happen on a school retreat a few years back when they went to a camp. We had to get rid of the suitcase and all the clothes in it. My guess is that led to problems for his father."

"You could say that. The county inspected the resort and found it in a dilapidated state." She pulled another stapled document. The county inspection reports, findings and recommendations. "If I'm reading this right, they were prepared to condemn the place unless significant repairs were made."

Braddock glanced to his right, Tori running her fingers rapidly down each page.

"Geez."

"What?"

"He needed everything."

"What do you mean?"

"There were eight cabins and a lodge," Tori replied, holding up a document. "Each one needed new beds, linens, and furniture. Every unit needed new Sheetrock, flooring, and a roof. He basically had to take all the cabins down to the studs."

"Ah," Braddock murmured. "Hence the loan application."

"Yes." Tori snorted a laugh. "My guess is given the revenue the resort could generate, even with new everything, it wasn't enough to cash flow and pay the loan."

"But he had a son who was the vice president of a chain of banks. Surely, he would approve the loan. And then—"

"He didn't. Or perhaps Elaine Baird didn't. The letter denying the loan was from her." Tori turned to Braddock. "Is it odd a bank president would issue a loan denial letter. Wouldn't that just come from the loan department?"

Braddock took a moment. "This was Marist's father who was desperate and coming to him. Marist couldn't push it through. He wouldn't let the loan department issue a denial. My guess is Marist wanted Baird to write it because he needed to be able to say to his dad, he did all he could, but he couldn't get it through. His boss, the bank president, said no."

"I suspect you're right." Tori nodded.

"So, what did his father do?"

"After that, he lost the resort it appears," Tori said. "Oh. Oh no."

"What?"

She held up the newspaper clipping. "Obituary. Otis Marist died six years ago."

"Died of what?"

"Suicide. He hung himself."

"At the resort?"

"Yes."

"Hmm. The plot thickens."

"Yes, it certainly does."

. . .

The drive to Park Rapids itself, in the best of conditions, usually took ninety minutes. Given the deteriorating conditions and light, Braddock pushed it and they managed to make it in a hundred. It was then another twenty minutes to the resort northwest of town. When they arrived the Hubbard County Sheriff, Edward "Ned" Bollander, was on scene along with two deputies and Steak was waiting, having arrived just a few minutes ahead. It was getting dark, the snow coming down in waves.

"Nedward," Braddock greeted the sheriff by his nickname with a hearty handshake. "What do you have for us?"

"Well," Bollander said, waving his arm, leading them to a larger cabin on the north end of the resort. "It's an odd one, Will. Darndest thing."

"How so?"

"You'll just have to evaluate for yourself. I don't want to lead you in any direction because I'm not sure where this goes."

"Ned, how'd the call come in?" Steak asked.

"A neighbor said he heard shots fired over this way from across the lake at his house. He lives on the opposite side of the bay. Having heard the shots, he walked down to the shoreline. A few minutes after all the gunfire, he thought he saw a white SUV and black pickup truck race out of there. And then he saw part of the Mariner parked there although he didn't really know why *that* mattered. The resort had been abandoned for years and as a hunter, he knew the sound of gunfire and there was quite a bit of it, so he called it in. It took my guy about a half-hour to get here given the weather, but he saw the Mariner and matched its plate with your alert and then the body lying inside and called it in. I called Steak and drove up here myself."

As Braddock and Steak spoke, Tori looked over to the right. Despite the heavy snow, she noticed another set of deep tire tracks through the yard. "And no sign of Teddy Marist?" Tori asked.

"Not that I've seen," Bollander said. "Which is just one more reason I can't figure what went down here."

They approached the two-story cabin, the only one of that size on the property. The rest of the cabins, all boxy in structure, looked to be the same size, spaced along the bluff up from the lake.

"Now, my deputy went inside earlier to pull the wallet out of Marist's pocket to confirm his identity but did no more. He got out of there right quick, made the call and it's been undisturbed since we arrived."

"Forensics?" Braddock asked.

"They've been called but it's going to take time to get here," Bollander answered. "How hard was it for you to get up here?"

"Hard enough. It's your crime scene, Ned, but—"

Bollander nodded. "Dig in. It all started down with you anyway, plus you're looking for the boy, so have it. We'll support ya, whatever you need."

Braddock turned to Tori and Steak. "Tori and I will go in. Steak, you film with your phone. Nedward, you good observing?"

"Was planning on it."

Tori took a couple of steps inside and slipped out of her boots, as did Braddock. He handed her covers for her stocking feet. He had a pair for himself. They both were wearing leather winter gloves.

They stood in a tunnel like entryway. Tori had been in a hundred places like this when she was a kid, riding around with her sheriff father as he circuited the county. There was a familiarity of arrangement to them.

Ahead there was a built-in check-in counter running along the wall to the right with an old, weathered cork bulletin board still mounted on the wall. Along the back wall, there were two what looked to be massive stone sinks that she suspected served as fishing bait tanks. In the middle, given the markings on the old wood flooring, there was shelving and racks for other fishing supplies such as lures, ropes, fishing rods, wire, and the like. Given some of the coloring and faded outlines along the wood paneled walls to the far left, she suspected the main area contained a couple of refrigerated coolers, perhaps one for beverages and another for bait as well as a freezer for bags of ice. All remnants of those common items of a resort were long gone, likely sold off as part of whatever liquidation of the property took place. Now, the room she stood in was just an open musty area with faded and rotting paneled walls and warped wood floors. And now, inside the room more fully, they could see the front wall, with the long picture window, a bullet hole on the far end of it, the spidering of cracks from the hole.

As Braddock finished unlacing his boots, she carefully made her way twenty feet over to Marist's body and crouched. There was a light blood pool around his upper torso. "He was shot three times in the back," she said, gesturing to each wound. "The wounds are compact," she added as she slowly and carefully stepped her way around the body. "And then once here in the right temple."

"Execution," Braddock noted, leaning to examine the head wound. "And right up close given the stippling. Three in the back, *bang, bang, bang,* and one final one to finish him off."

Tori turned. "There's another small pool of blood here, smudged along the floor, like it was... dragged," she said, five feet past Marist. "And then another over here. This one is more droplets."

Braddock looked to the small blood pools and then about the room and his eyes narrowed as he examined the far wall to the left. "A bullet is in here," he said, peering at a hole in the paneling, assessing the angle of entry and then looking back to Tori.

"Then another one." Tori pointed to his left about five feet, a bit higher on the wall.

"Yeah," Braddock said, crouching.

"And then the one through the picture window."

Tori examined Marist's body again, the way he was lying on the floor, the angle of his body to the front door, versus the bullet holes in the far west wall and window.

"What are you thinking?" Braddock said.

She folded her arms. "His back wounds are in line with his spine. I'm not a forensic pathologist, but the way his legs are crumpled beneath him, I think he was shot in the back and fell right here, and probably immediately. And if so, he was shot from somewhere by the front door."

"What of these other blood pools then?"

Tori shook her head, crouching again to look at the dragged pool.

Braddock peered around the room again. "What is that?"

"Huh? What?" Tori said.

Braddock walked to the bait tanks. There was a small black box under the left tank. "Huh."

Tori squinted. "Is that a mobile—"

"Hot spot." He twirled the device in his gloved fingers. "What do you make of that?"

She walked over. "I make that it's new. Certainly not standard issue with everything else around here."

Braddock looked back to Marist, the bullet holes, and the mobile hot spot. "What happened here? What were they doing?"

Tori walked back to Marist and examined his body again, the wounds, his legs and then looked back toward Sheriff Bollander and Steak. She stood up and walked over toward Steak.

"I think I'm seeing what you're seeing," Steak said. "He was shot from over here."

"I'm seeing that too," Bollander agreed.

"But he dropped right there," Tori said.

"I agree," Braddock said. "Then this first smudge, the dragged blood smear, is it Marist's? Or... Huh." He looked back at Tori.

"The mobile hot spot," Tori said. "They brought Marist here. The Internet is the only reason you would need a mobile hot spot. To do what?"

Braddock shook his head. "To do business of some sort. Communicate with Marist? Make Marist do something they wanted? At the... bank."

"This was a set-up," Tori said, with certainty.

Braddock nodded. "Yeah, Tor, it was."

"Barry Marist did not kill Lainey Darr or Ed Girard, the people who brought him here did. They picked this resort, his father's resort, where he committed suicide. What's supposed to happen is he does whatever it is they want him to. They bring Teddy to him but then they're going to kill him and Teddy and make it look like a murder suicide, the father distraught over his divorce killing his ex-wife, son and then himself and he did it where his father had ended his life. A sad, but understandable story that would end here."

"So, you're all saying Barry Marist didn't kill his ex-wife and her boyfriend like the news has been suggesting given that he's been on the run with his son?" Bollander asked.

"That's what we're thinking," Braddock said.

"What happened in here then?"

Braddock looked at Tori. "Marist saw it coming."

"Bringing him here almost telegraphed it to him, *especially* if he knew Lainey and Girard were already murdered. He knew what this was, what he'd come into and that there was likely no escape from it."

"Why come then?" Bollander asked.

"Teddy," Steak said.

"Why not call the police?"

"He couldn't," Tori said.

"Why not?"

"He just… couldn't. He left his cell at home. Probably ordered to. Switched vehicles. I'd imagine they followed him to make sure he didn't deviate from whatever it was he was supposed to do to get here."

"As for in here," Braddock said. "They bring Marist inside to do whatever business it is they were doing and then he knows what comes next. The murder suicide part."

"How many men is he up against?" Steak said.

"Good question," Braddock said and took a moment, peered around the room again and then Marist. He walked over toward Steak and Bollander at the door. "Why shoot him from here?" He turned to the far wall and hole in the window. "This angle doesn't work for those bullet holes."

Tori looked at the blood smudge and then the other small pool. "There was a struggle," Tori offered. "Marist wasn't a small guy. Six-foot tall, two hundred ten pounds. He saw what was coming and he wasn't going down without a fight."

"When were the shots fired?"

"Three-fiftyish give or take," Nedward replied. "That's when the call came in."

"They were here for quite some time, several hours," Tori said. "While Marist was doing whatever it was he was doing, he was also looking for an opening. And finally, he saw one, or in desperation, just… fought."

"I think so," Braddock said, walking to Marist's body. "Marist and a man struggle, fight—"

"Over a gun," Tori said.

"Right," Braddock continued. "And one of the other men was… wounded. That's the other two blood pools."

"Marist got ahold of a gun," Steak said from the door. "That's the bullet holes in the far wall. He was firing at another man. And a third man fired from here." He had his gun out, holding firing position. "Marist goes down, is immobilized and he walks over and finishes him off because at that point—"

"They can't make the set-up fly."

Bollander nodded. "Okay. I can visualize that." The sheriff shook his head. "What a mess. Special Agent Hunter, you ever see anything like this before?"

Tori exhaled a sigh. "What was supposed to happen, the murder suicide part? More than once unfortunately. This? No, this—" she shook her head "—this is a new one. This is a new twist for sure. Marist is up here to do... something," Tori said, arms folded, evaluating the room. "We have a hot spot but what did they do? Sit on the floor? If he was on a computer, where is it? Where is the table and chairs?"

"Maybe they took them. Maybe they used that check-in counter," Braddock said. "Then it all went bad."

"Then the question now... is..." She rushed over to the door, slipping her boots on.

"What? What?" Braddock said.

"What happens to Teddy?"

"They took him?"

"Was it they? Or was it someone else?" she replied and looked at Bollander, her eyes wide. "You said the witness heard shots fired? Multiple, right?"

"Yes."

"If the shots were fired just in here. Does he hear them from all the way across the bay?"

"Uh... No, ma'am. Not from way over there I wouldn't think. It's possible I suppose but it wouldn't be loud and clear, and he said he heard the shot loud and clear."

"As if they were fired *outside*," Tori said.

"That's right. Rapid fire. That's what really caught his attention."

"Rapid fire." Her boots on, she grabbed a flashlight out of Steak's hand and rushed outside, everyone else following. The snow was coming down heavily, but there was that odd set of tire tracks off on its own, running diagonally through the yard, not yet fully covered by fallen snow. Those tracks came from the last small boxy cabin. She jogged toward the last cabin. At the front door there were tire tracks for a vehicle with a wide base, an SUV or pickup truck, pulled up and parked in front of the cabin. There were multiple sets of footprints in the snow, leading to the front door into the cabin. She went to the door, turned the knob and it was unlocked. As she walked inside, she got a whiff of odor, frowned, and stopped. "What am I smelling?"

"Urine," Braddock said, stepping into the bathroom. "They must have used the toilet."

There was another door on the south side of the cabin that led out to a walkway to the deck along the front of the cabin, but that wasn't what drew her attention. There was a second set of tire tracks, even wider than the first. She opened the door and stepped outside, following the tire tracks, everyone following her. The tire tracks were the ones she'd noticed earlier that went from the cabin, in a straight line through the middle of the property to the old gate.

"Those are deep tire treads to rip through there," Steak said, following the flashlight beam. "Pickup truck, big tires, maybe lifted."

"Lifted?" Tori said.

"You might say jacked up," Steak replied. "Riding high or higher than normal providing for clearance. Big and wider tires made those tracks. And they're fresh, made today I'd say, but still, what happened here?"

Braddock snorted a laugh. He saw it now. "They had Teddy in this cabin, waiting."

"Right," Tori said. "And maybe that explains the shots fired outside. The ones the neighbor heard."

"I'm not following," Steak said.

"Me either," Bollander said.

"The fourth man," Tori said. "If you assume three in the shoot-out at the main cabin with Marist. A fourth man is here with Teddy. He sees it all go down, he sees it go bad and he grabs Teddy and gets out of here."

"And the others see him racing away and they fire at him. Those are the shots the neighbor hears," Braddock said. "We need to cordon off a wider area by the murder scene. If someone was firing, we may well find shell casings somewhere in the snow."

"I'll take care of that in a minute, but why fire at him?" Bollander said. "That's the part I don't get. If he's in on it with them, why fire at him?"

"Either..." Tori started, "he wasn't in on it or... since the murder suicide wasn't going to work—"

"The fourth man wanted out," Braddock said. He looked at Tori. "And Teddy is his ticket out of this mess. Turn Teddy over, cut a deal."

"Teddy Marist may still be alive," Tori said.

ELEVEN
"DID YOU TICKLE THE LINE?"

Bollander crowbarred open the front door to another cabin to allow them all to get out of the falling and blowing snow. The sheriff had called in more resources and more men were finally arriving on scene. After opening the door, he hustled off to speak with them. The crime scene would be guarded overnight. "I pity the deputy who gets *that* assignment," Steak mumbled. "He or she better stock up. It's going to be miserable out here. It already is."

A crime scene investigator from the BCA had made it to the scene and had immediately gone to work on the main cabin.

"So, what now?" Braddock said to the group as they had gathered, standing closely together in the kitchen. They were out of the snow and wind but not the cold. It was still frigid inside, cold puffs of their breath hanging in the air as they spoke. They all kept moving and fidgeting to keep the blood flowing.

"It's dark. There has to be eight to ten inches of new snow already on the ground," Steak said. "The state patrol has closed Interstate 94 west of Alexandria due to whiteout conditions. In an hour, it's going to be the same here. If we don't want to be stuck up here, we need to get on the road back home now."

"And what about Teddy Marist?"

Steak shrugged. "Whoever has him, is thinking like I am. They're hunkering down somewhere for the night. All these guys are. This storm is going to be shutting everything down. Nobody is going to be on the roads tonight. Hardly anyone is now. You go out there tonight? You're going to end up in a ditch, freezing to death. The temp is going to go below zero. Winds at thirty, maybe forty in places, the wind-chill will be way below zero. Not a night fit for man nor beast."

Braddock looked at Tori, who leaned against the kitchen counter, her arms folded, both in deep thought and to keep warm. "You're awfully quiet."

She looked to them both. "We should find hotel rooms for the night in Park Rapids."

Steak grimaced. "I figured you'd say that."

"I'll take the hit and share a room with Braddock."

"You give and you give and you give."

"Look, I know it's going to get bad out there, but if you're right, then these guys we're looking for, if they are, as you say, hunkering down, then they aren't that far from here, are they?"

"Probably not."

"So, we stay?" Braddock said.

"We need to keep close. If we can use the time where things are shut down to figure out *who* these people are, we're ahead of the game when the roads do open sometime tomorrow."

"Well, for all of that fancy deducing you two just did as to what happened here, our killers have not yet identified themselves," Steak asserted.

"No," Tori replied. "But they've told us some things."

"Like?"

"They knew about Barry Marist's history with this place," Braddock stated. "They knew it belonged to his father. In fact, I'm betting they know his bank rejected his father's loan application to fix up and hold on to this place. That information is six, seven years old? That's not information readily available. How did they know?"

"His house?"

"Maybe," Braddock replied, folding his arms. "But how would they have known to look there to begin with? What would have identified Marist to them?" He shook his head. "There's more to it."

"I think more importantly," Tori added, "they knew Marist had something they wanted and were desperate enough to get it that they killed two people and abducted his son to lure him here. You know—"

"The bank," Braddock said.

"With the storm. Nobody is there, monitoring things."

"We are monitoring his bank accounts but that might not be the right thing to be looking at. We better call Elaine Baird again," Braddock replied. "They need to be monitoring not just his accounts, but all transactions. Maybe they had him going in the backdoor and transferring money or something."

Bollander burst inside the cabin, carrying Styrofoam cups and a Thermos. "I figure you all could use a little antifreeze."

"You're a good, good man, Nedward," Braddock bellowed thankfully, rubbing his hands together.

They all gathered around and Bollander poured them all a cup of coffee and they took immediate drinks, letting it warm their bodies.

"Would you two believe, a media truck made it out here. Shannon Murtaugh, from the television station in Manchester Bay is here."

"That's commitment to the bit," Steak quipped.

"I'll say. First thing I said to her is how did she expect to make it back?"

"You speak with her yet?" Tori asked.

"No, not on camera, but she's asked me to, and I figured I'd come in and ask you all about what the message ought to be. Why?"

"Have Darr and Girard's families been notified?"

"Yes," Braddock replied.

Tori checked her watch, then said, "I'll join you if you like, Sheriff. I've talked to Shannon before."

Braddock snapped his head in astonishment. Tori was not a fan of media appearances. She'd do it if he, or their old boss Cal Lund, or Boe asked, but only reluctantly and not until after there had been some bitching and moaning and it'll cost you, complaints. Her *volunteering* to do it was a first for him. She had something in mind.

"You're more than welcome to join me," Bollander. "I'll go out and tell her we'll give her a few minutes."

"I'll be right behind you," Tori said. After he left, she turned to Braddock and Steak. "On the bank, call, what's her name again?"

"Elaine Baird."

"Right, call her. If Marist was... compromised, that's where it likely would be based on what we know so far. That's where he had access to money, a lot of money. He's the vice president, the chief operating officer. I suspect he knew every way in and out of the system. I'm thinking we found that hot spot, that probably means laptop computer. Maybe we could extract something from the hot spot?"

"Agreed although does that tell us who these guys are?" Braddock said. "Does that help us right now?"

"We won't know until we know."

Braddock nodded. "I'll get that going."

"I'll call on hotel rooms," Steak said. "One night?"

Tori nodded. "This isn't going to go *that* long. Think about it, if we're right about what went down in that cabin over there, and that shots were fired outside, then these guys turned on each other. And one side of it has Teddy."

"Which side?"

"I'm banking on the good one because that one means Teddy Marist is alive. And if Teddy is alive, he's a bargaining chip."

Steak went to work on arranging hotel rooms for them. Braddock had his phone in hand as well but followed Tori to the back door. "A willing interview? Tori Hunter, what are you up to?"

"I'm reaching out to touch someone," she said with a twinkle in her eye.

The conditions weren't ideal for a press conference type of interview, it was cold, the snow was falling, the wind starting to blow. Bollander suggested they go inside one of the abandoned cabins but Shannon Murtaugh and Tori both objected.

"Let's do it out here. It'll take just a few minutes," Murtaugh said. "We can have a couple of these cabins in the background."

"And it'll look good, won't it?" Bollander muttered.

"Atmospherics aren't always bad," Tori said. "Makes the story a little more compelling, a little more attention grabbing, and we need all the attention we can get right now."

"Exactly," Murtaugh said, grinning, her frizzy blonde hair pulled back by her black winter wool headband. She turned to her cameraman who did a quick check and then offered a thumbs up.

"Are we going live or recorded?"

Murtaugh grinned. "Live. Then we'll rerun it, I suspect. Why? You hoping someone sees this?"

Tori shrugged.

"That's a yes."

Murtaugh started with Bollander who quickly went through the sequence of events, how they were notified to come out to the resort and that they found Barry Marist shot and killed.

"And how does this relate to the shootings earlier in Manchester Bay?" the reporter asked.

"Directly," Tori interjected.

"How?"

"We're still investigating that, but Barry Marist was found shot and killed here. We have not yet found ten-year-old Teddy Marist."

"Do you think he's still alive?" Murtaugh asked.

"We do."

The reporter's eyes went wide. "Uh, okay. Who do you think has him?"

"We're working on that," Tori replied. "But whoever that is can still do the right thing. Teddy Marist is a ten-year-old boy who has done nothing wrong. We just want his safe return. That's *all* we want."

"Did you tickle the line?" Braddock asked when Tori came back inside.

"We'll see. I took what we think we know and spoke like we knew it for certain. I wonder if I went too far." She was thinking of a later prosecution and if what she said today could be held against them if things didn't turn out just as she'd said.

Braddock was nonplussed. "We'll sort that out later."

"Murtaugh went live with the interview. She was certain it would get rerun. And she's still hanging around. She said they had rooms booked in Park Rapids." She noticed the two of them were packing up. "What are you two up to? Are you... we, leaving?"

Braddock handed her the keys to the Tahoe.

"Why?"

"We got a call from the Rapids Community Bank branch in

Akeley. To your point on the media, there is a bank teller and manager there who swore that Barry Marist was in their bank this morning before they closed early for the day, to access a safe deposit box. They saw his face on the news and called. But his safe deposit box is not under the name of Barry Marist, so we'll see."

'The R folder that was missing," Tori said. "Rapids Community Bank. That's not his chain of banks now, is it?"

"No," Braddock said. "So why have a safe deposit box elsewhere? Akeley isn't far. Those two employees live in town and are going to meet us at the bank. Steak and I are going to go and check that out, unless you want to come as well?"

Tori thought for a moment and then shook her head. "Divide and conquer. I'll stay here with the sheriff and BCA. He has his men out knocking on what doors there are around here. Maybe we'll get more than white SUV and black truck racing away." She exhaled a breath. "Did we get hotel rooms?"

"We did," Steak said. "The C'mon Inn."

"Quaint," Tori replied with an eye roll.

"It'll do for a night. It has a small restaurant and bar that *will* be open, especially after a day like this one. One reservation is under you and Braddock, the other under Williams."

"I'll meet you two there."

"Drive carefully," Braddock suggested.

"I will, I will," she replied. "Oh, hey, make sure to check Marist's body or that Mercury Mariner for the safe deposit box key."

Braddock looked over to Steak. "Not a bad idea."

"That's why I said it," Tori snarked, grinning.

"Do you ever get tired of her *thinking* she's right all the time?" Steak needled back, elbowing her good-naturedly on his way to the back door.

Braddock wrapped his arm around her, kissing her gently on the top of her head. "Not yet."

TWELVE

"JUST UNDERSTANDING MY ENEMIES."

Jenks drove Merc's truck west along the narrow county road. Towne road shotgun, while Merc rode in the back, sitting sideways, his bandaged leg elevated.

Towne hung up his call with Max.

"Can Max help us?"

He shook his head. "Not right now, not in these conditions. Too risky. Too far away. Best Max can do is continue to monitor the news and stay in touch. We're on our own."

"I hear that. I don't have a lot of experience driving in snow like this," Jenks said, an uncharacteristic nervousness in his voice. It was why they'd had Jared behind the wheel much of the day and Merc tailing Marist. They were natives, comfortable with the snowy conditions.

"You lose control when you have to brake fast," Merc grunted from the back, adjusting his body, trying to stay comfortable. He couldn't drive right now, not in these conditions with his left leg with a hole in it. "That's when you'll start skidding."

"What's the secret then?"

"Don't grip the wheel like a hammer. Grip it like you're

holding..." Merc thought for a second. "Like you're holding an egg."

"An egg?"

"If you grip an egg hard, squeeze it, it'll break. Driving with two hands, like you are, is fine but it looks like you're trying to strangle the steering wheel. Loosen your grip a bit and relax."

"Relax?" Jenks replied skeptically.

"You're so tense."

"Fuck right I am. I don't do snow!"

Merc laughed. "It's going to get worse, a lot worse if what they're saying on the radio is true."

"Fuck me," Jenks moaned.

"Pussy ass North Carolinian," Merc said through gritted teeth, sitting up so he could lean over the seat between Jenks and Towne. "I thought you mountain boys were tough. It's not like there wasn't snow in the Appalachians."

"We didn't fuckin' drive in it though."

"Okay, expert," Towne said. "Continue with the tutorial."

"Respect the weather and be cautious."

"Oh, that's keen insight," Jenks griped.

Merc patted him on the shoulder. "First, the tires on the truck are new and appropriate for the climate here, so you have a good base. Second, if you feel a little slide, don't immediately slam the brakes or rip the wheel to overcorrect. You do that and you got no shot, especially at speed. You'll lose control, start swerving and end up in the ditch," Merc explained. "Don't be in a hurry. If you're not, the snow is going to be deep enough before long that it'll actually help you slow down as long as you don't panic if you feel a little swerve in the back end. Lastly, see the road ahead of you. Keep the dashboard screen on the navigation map, keep an eye on the little side posts with the reflectors that mark the road's path for the plows. Do that and you'll see where the upcoming bends in the road are. And... relax."

"Okay," Jenks muttered, exhaling a breath, trying to loosen his muscles.

"You got this."

Towne kept working the radio, searching for news.

"There's a news station out of Park Rapids," Merc said. "It's in the hundreds. Keep going." Towne slowly advanced the stations.

"There."

"KWTK news time is 6:50 p.m. Here in Park Rapids, it is two degrees Fahrenheit. The snow continues to fall, and the snowfall estimates continue to climb as this storm has expanded, spreading from central and northern Minnesota westward back into North and South Dakota. The storm will not move out until midday tomorrow. By then, we can expect to have received as much as twenty-five to thirty inches of snow. The state patrol is recommending no travel for the night."

"That's some serious ass snow," Merc said. "That's double what they'd been predicting just this morning. Usually, the meteorologists up here overhype these storms. They predict a foot and instead you get four inches. That's obviously not the case here."

"I hear it in your voice," Towne said. "Should we get off the roads?"

Merc scratched his chin. "I'm not that worried about the snow. The truck rides high. I worry about the wind. When that kicks up…"

"Shh, hold on," Towne hushed. "I want to hear this."

"Now, as for our other top story, the statewide search continues for ten-year-old Teddy Marist. In the latest development, the Hubbard County Sheriff's Department is reporting that they

have found the body of Teddy Marist's father, Barry, at an abandoned resort northwest of Park Rapids."

"That didn't take long," Merc moaned.

"Someone heard all the gunfire," Jenks noted.

"WMB TV Reporter, Shannon Murtaugh, spoke with Hubbard County Sheriff Ned Bollander and Tori Hunter, an investigator with the Shepard County Sheriff's Department, on the status of the investigation."

There was a momentary pause and then the reporter asked the sheriff about the call to the abandoned Darkwoods Resort. The sheriff explained the sequence of events, how they were notified to come out to the resort and the report of gunfire.

"Mr. Marist was found dead upon our arrival. Nobody else was present. We continue to investigate the scene."

"And how does this relate to the shootings earlier in Manchester Bay?" the reporter asked.

"Directly," Tori Hunter interjected.

"How?" the reporter asked.

"We're still investigating that. Barry Marist was found shot and killed here. We have not yet found ten-year-old Teddy Marist, the son of Barry Marist."

"Do you think he's still alive?" the reporter asked.

"We do."

"Uh, okay. Who do you think has him?"

"We have not yet identified who is responsible for this," Hunter answered. *"We don't think Barry Marist killed his ex-wife and Ed Girard. Evidence at the scene here suggests that those responsible for the killing of Lainey Darr and Edward Girard lured Marist here to arrange a murder suicide. That plan went awry."*

"How or... why?" the reporter asked.

"We don't know—yet. The gunshots reported by the neighbor suggest to us that the killers of Darr, Girard and Marist turned on each other. We think it's possible that someone from that group has Teddy Marist. We hope to find them."

"Something like what these people pulled today doesn't just happen in a day, does it?" the reporter said.

"No," Hunter replied. *"This involved time, planning, and resources. We're going to be looking into all of that. Our investigation is ongoing as we speak, both here and in Manchester Bay and across the state, searching for Teddy Marist."*

"Sheriff," the reporter asked. *"Who should people contact with information?"*

"If anyone has any information, we ask that they contact either the Shepard or Hubbard County Sheriff's Departments." The sheriff provided the phone numbers.

The radio station switched to another story.

"The woman, she sounded pretty sharp," Jenks said.

"For good reason," Merc replied from the back seat. "I could have sworn my cousin Walter mentioned her name, and another guy, Braddock, I think."

"Your cousin Walter Dexter? That crazy guy with his place and his dogs back in the woods? That cousin?"

"Yeah, that one," Merc replied. "They came out to his place once, looking for an abducted kid and Walt's name had been mentioned by the parents as having a grudge against the family."

"He have anything to do with it?"

"Nah. Walt had had a beef with the missing girl's dad over an investment gone bad, so that's why they hassled him. He said he thought they were trespassers when they approached. He had a shotgun on them, or so he said. Like you said, he's a little crazy. But I remember him saying that one of the cops was a woman, small, tough, and also..."

"What?"

"The term he used was 'foxy.'"

"As in attractive?"

"Yeah, and on that account, I don't think Walt was crazy." Merc held up his phone with a picture of Tori Hunter standing with Will Braddock at a fundraising event from last summer. Standing a foot shorter than Braddock, she was wearing a body hugging V-necked black jumpsuit, heels, her hair up. The two of them were talking with others at the event.

"That's her?"

"It is," Merc replied and pulled up another photo, a headshot photo from the Central Minnesota State University website where she was listed as an adjunct professor. It was a flattering photo. She was smiling, her auburn hair stylishly wrapped behind her ears, falling just past shoulder length, wearing a dark blazer and three strings of pearls around her neck. Hunter had deep green eyes, a thinnish nose and with her bright smile, just the hint of an overbite.

"She's easy on the eyes," Towne agreed.

"Don't let the pretty face fool you. She's a handful."

"How do you know that?"

"Google and Max. Max told us about a special agent with the FBI who worked for the sheriff's department. You know what her specialty was?"

"What?"

"Abducted children. There is page after page on here about cases she worked, many successfully."

"Why is she here then?"

Merc flipped back to an article from over two years ago. "She's from Manchester Bay originally. Her father was the sheriff for years. Then her twin sister Jessie disappeared on the

Fourth of July before her senior year in high school. Here's a picture of the two of them."

He showed them both his phone screen. "It's grainy."

"They were identical," Towne noted. "What happened?"

"Her sister's car was found abandoned on a county road with a flat tire. They never found her sister, at least around the time she vanished. After that, it appears that Tori Hunter left home. Her bio on the university website says she has a degree from Boston College, and then she went to the FBI and had a highly decorated career."

"And she ends up back here how?" Jenks said.

"Fast forward twenty years, there was another abduction nearly identical to that of her sister's on the Fourth of July."

"On the twentieth anniversary," Towne mused. "That's what must have brought her back here. As if she was being called home."

"That's how it appears."

"And they solved it?"

"Yes," Merc said, scanning his phone. "She and Braddock, the big, tall guy from the picture at that fundraiser." He flipped back to the photo. "I'd say I know why she stayed." He turned his phone around again. "Do those two look like just co-workers the way they're standing there? It almost looks as if she's leaning into him."

Towne examined the photo, as did Jenks.

"They do not," Towne said. "What's his story?"

"A local she re-connected with?" Jenks added.

"No," Merc replied. "I saw it in one of the articles I flipped through. He was once a detective with the NYPD. I saw something about being on the Joint Terrorism Task Force. He would be no joke, either."

"How did he end up here?"

"Not sure. I could keep searching. But that's who is hunting us now."

"Really? We run into that here. Up here?" Jenks said, slowly shaking his head, staring ahead into an ever more blinding snowstorm. "And they're on it pretty good."

"Re-thinking what you said earlier?" Towne murmured.

"No. Just understanding my enemies." He looked over to Towne. "So when I face them, I know who I'm up against."

Towne took a moment and then shook his head. "They've figured out what happened, or what we wanted to have happen there," Towne said. "What they don't know is who we are and the only one who could tell them that is Jared. We find and kill him first, and that'll be the end of things."

THIRTEEN

"WHAT'S THE TALLY?"

If there was anything good about the snowstorm moving in, it was that it kept all other traffic off the roads, leaving Steak a free run. That let him make the drive to the Akeley branch of Rapids Community Bank in just over a half-hour.

As they approached the front vestibule entrance for the bank, a woman in a baggy navy-blue hoodie, black leggings, and long lace up boots, unlocked the door and let them in. "I'm Olivia Trannen, the bank manager. Which one of you is Chief Detective Braddock?"

"That's me," Braddock replied, showing his identification, and introducing Steak.

Another woman in jeans, red and black checkered flannel shirt and white stocking cap stepped out of an office. "This is Amelia Hopfen," Trannen introduced as she led them back to her office and sat down at her desk.

"Marist was here earlier you said," Braddock noted, starting the conversation.

"I was at home, lounging in my sweats, watching television when Amelia called me," Trannen said.

"Actually, my boyfriend saw it first," Hopfen started. "He had the television on, and he asked me if I'd heard about what happened in Manchester Bay. I had no idea what he was talking about. I'd just been relaxing, reading a book." She explained how her boyfriend told her about the details of the shooting, the missing boy and Barry Marist as a person of interest. "And then on the news they showed the picture of Barry Marist. My boyfriend said my jaw hit the floor."

"You'd seen him?" Steak said.

"At the bank, *this* morning, just after we'd opened. He came to the teller line and asked to access his safe deposit box. I was certain it was Marist who came in this morning."

"Except the name he gave wasn't Barry Marist," Trannen said. "And like with Amelia, you could have knocked me over with a feather because he's been coming in here for years, as Tom Nelson. The account and safe deposit box are under that name. They have been for six plus years."

"How often did he come in?" Steak asked.

"Every few months. I pulled the logs when I got back into the office. He opened a checking account here six years ago. He deposited $3,200. That account allowed him to have a safe deposit box."

"And what do you require for someone to open a safe deposit box or account in the first place?"

"On the account, an identification, a driver's license, or passport suffices, and then a deposit to open the account."

"And he had that for... Tom Nelson?" Steak asked.

"He did. There's a copy in this file." She handed the file over to Steak, who took a look at the photocopy of the ID. A Minnesota Driver's License with an address in Park Rapids. Steak did a quick check on his phone for the address. The address came up in Park Rapids. He had submitted a utility bill as proof.

"I assume the utility bill is proof the address is real?"

"Yes," Trannen replied. "It's what you probably did to open a bank account."

"I imagine my proof was my mom since I've been at the same bank since I was fourteen. Any activity on the account?"

"No. He kept just over the minimum balance needed to have the safe deposit box," Trannen said. "I have footage of him coming into the bank this morning. Amelia waited on him at the teller counter."

"And he had the Tom Nelson ID this morning?"

Trannen nodded. "He did although as I said he's been in many times. I recognized him so I just glanced at it. He had the safe deposit box key. It was all normal. The same as it had been for years."

"I'm not suggesting otherwise," Steak said. "I get it. He was a familiar customer, or at least familiar enough."

"You're saying it was normal. But was it?" Braddock asked.

Hopfen grimaced. "When he came in, he seemed impatient," she said. "When I talked to him, he was... brusque, though he immediately apologized but said he was in a hurry. I figured that was because of the storm. But he was clear: 'I need to access my safe deposit box, *right now*.' It was already snowing out, so I figured maybe it was just the weather or something that had him a little amped up."

"To Amelia's point. This is footage from this morning," Trannen said, turning her computer monitor around. 9:21 a.m. Marist charged in the front door carrying a large briefcase, paused for just a moment, and then went right to the teller window and Amelia. Amelia immediately started nodding and Braddock could have sworn he read her lips saying: *Okay, okay*.

And Amelia was right, he was agitated. As Marist waited, he rubbed his face and then frenetically circled the customer service counter, constantly checking his watch.

"He's pacing like a drug fiend that needs a fix," Steak murmured.

"He's anxious," Braddock said in agreement, seeing him check his watch constantly. Trannen came into the picture, offering a smile. "You recognized him right away?"

"Oh yes," Trannen said.

"And did he seem different?"

"Amelia told me later, when she called me at home, having seen him on television, that he had seemed agitated when he came in and when I thought back on it, I guess I noticed it as well, though he was courteous with me as he signed in and I took him back into the vault," Trannen said. "He wasn't in there more than a few minutes before he was right back out."

"And was that normal?"

"In general, yes," Trannen said and then grabbed a stapled set of sheets. "These are all his visits over the years. You'll see he's been in here thirty-one different times."

"Is that an unusual level of activity?"

Trannen nodded. "A bit, perhaps. We do have customers that will, at times, come in frequently for stretches. I have one customer who deals in trading old baseball cards, and he keeps certain ones in the safe deposit box. When he's in a buying and selling phase, he comes in and out a fair amount. For this man, Mr. Marist, he was on just a more every few months or quarterly type schedule."

"You ever ask him why he came in so often?"

"No. Or at least I don't recall doing so," she replied. "What was interesting though, when I looked through the times accessed and I kind of remembered it when I saw this, is he would come in, access the box and then usually come back a few hours later, and go in again."

"Like he was taking something out, using it and then putting it back," Braddock said. "You ever see what he took out of there?"

"Maybe," Trannen said and made a few more mouse clicks. "I'm not supposed to, of course, but on occasion, you just notice, or hear or deduce. I took the log and went through our surveillance footage we still have for those days. Sometimes customers don't hide what they've retrieved when they come out of the vault, or they don't hide it all that well." She hit play. The camera was focused on the entry into the vault. Marist came walking out, a silver-cased laptop in his right hand, and as he walked, he stuffed it into a briefcase with a shoulder strap.

"This is him three hours later."

Marist walked into the vault, pulling the laptop out of the briefcase as he walked inside and then out of view, re-emerging a few minutes later.

"Mobile hot spot," Steak whispered. Braddock nodded. "Did you ever see anything else he took out of the box?" he asked.

"No," Trannen replied, shaking her head.

"And no activity on his savings account?" Steak said.

"There was the original deposit and that's it. As I said it is not totally uncommon that people open an account just for the safe deposit box."

"We need to open the safe deposit box?" Braddock said. "I have his key."

"Without a search warrant..." Trannen hedged.

"He's dead. We're trying to find the boy. If there was something in there that could help us, we need to see it—now. We don't know how long he might have."

Trannen nodded and waved for them to follow her into the vault and safe deposit boxes. She stopped midway down the wall. The row of boxes 130-139.

Marist's was No. 134. It was a 10 x 10 x 22-inch box.

"A big one," Steak said. He filmed with his cell phone camera. Trannen put in her key, Braddock put in Marist's, and they opened the safe deposit box door.

Braddock pulled out the box and set it on the built-in counter and flipped open the top.

"Whoa!" Steak said. "Hello."

Inside the box itself were stacks of cash in $50-dollar bills increments. There were eighty-four bundles in total. The stacks were to the top of the box in the back but only one or two deep in the front. There had to be room for the laptop and whatever else Marist had in the box.

Steak counted the stacks, checking a few to make sure they were all cash.

"What's the tally?" Braddock said.

"If they're all equal, I count $420,000," Steak said, letting out a whistle. "What the hell was he into?"

"Whatever it was, it cost him his life."

FOURTEEN

"THERE ARE CONDITIONS."

Tori checked her phone. Glancing back outside, the snow was coming down steadily. They were somewhat sheltered in their location, but she knew the wind was whipping it.

Marist's body was removed from the scene by the county medical examiner an hour ago. Jody Beck, a forensic scientist with the Minnesota Bureau of Criminal Apprehension, who had traveled down from the BCA office in Bemidji, was now investigating the rest of the scene. Tori observed from the cabin doorway as Beck worked on the bullet holes in the far wall. Bollander joined her.

Tori said, "Your men find anything from knocking on doors?"

"Eh, not much," Bollander replied. "A few nearby folks remember seeing pickup trucks parked by the lodge in recent days, the road having been plowed. They didn't think much of it since the resort is abandoned and there is a for sale sign on the gate. From time to time, there have been groups interested in purchasing the property. Not *that* unusual to see someone lurking about."

"People assumed that—"

"That's what their presence signaled. Someone looking at the property."

"No calls were made to the bank to check on that?" Tori asked, knowing the answer.

"By whom?" Bollander replied with a wry smile.

"And the bank?"

"The bank had no idea anyone was out here."

Jody Beck, the forensics officer walked over, a bullet in her tweezers. "Small caliber, nine-millimeter. Based on angle of entry, those two in the far wall and through the front window were fired from somewhere along this angle." Beck walked ahead ten feet. She was firing right over where they had found the body of Marist.

Beck took three steps toward the far wall. "Right here there are fresh black scratch marks on the old wood floor and then a fresh dent here and some debris." She held up a small evidence bag. "Looks like vinyl and foam."

"Meaning?" Tori said, inspecting the shards in the bag.

"You found that mobile hot spot, so that suggests they were doing business of some kind. I doubt they sat cross-legged on the floor. I'm thinking there was a table and chairs, probably folding, right here. My guess is they made sure to pack all that and get out of here."

"That mobile hot spot," Tori said. "What could you get from that?"

Beck grimaced. "IP addresses, I suspect. Not much more but we'll give it a look."

Bollander looked outside. "I've got two men who will be out here all night," he said to Tori. "I'll await Jody finishing up here and then we'll both be driving back to Park Rapids. I just heard a prediction that the wind is going to increase significantly over the next two hours and blow like mad overnight. Why don't you head to the hotel while the getting is good?"

Tori took one last look around and nodded. "That's probably a good idea."

"I'll call you if we find anything else out here."

Tori texted Braddock that she was on her way to the C'mon Inn. He texted back a minute later: *Order me a beer.* She smiled. That sounded like a good idea. She found a radio station, looking for a weather update when she came across her own voice, the interview with Shannon Murtaugh from earlier.

She was never comfortable hearing her own voice in the media. Her voice never sounded like she thought it did. The pitch was always an octave or two lower than she expected, especially today. Probably caused by the cold weather. "Geez, Tori, it sounds like you smoked a pack and a half today," she muttered. She chuckled at the thought, never having smoked a cigarette in her life.

The other thing about the tone of her voice was that she knew that sometimes, especially when she thought she was right, she could come off as a condescending know-it-all. Once early in her career, after some successful cases had burnished her reputation in the Bureau and got her assigned to the New York City Field Office, she spoke to a *New York Times* reporter, offering a theory on a missing girl investigation well before the Bureau was convinced enough evidence had been developed to support it. Tori was certain she was right and spoke on the record without first getting the permission of her boss, Special Agent in Charge Richard Graff. The next morning, seeing her quotes in the paper, Graff was not happy. He addressed it immediately, at 5:30 a.m., in the hallway of their hotel in upstate New York.

"Special Agent Hunter, there might be a time where it makes some sense to float a theory to a reporter, to get that story out," Graff had said to her loudly enough for anyone with a room along the hallway to hear. "This was *not* that time, and it was not *your* decision to make!"

She simply stood with her head down. "Yes, sir."

"This job isn't about you. It's *never* about you. It's about the victim. And you, Special Agent Hunter, above all others, I would think would understand that."

"Yes, sir," she replied meekly.

Graff was right. She'd thought for certain she would be removed from the case, but she wasn't. She had gone to Graff a few days later to apologize and thank him for keeping her around.

"If it was about just me, you might be gone," he'd said. "But it's not about me, it's about—"

"The victim. Yes, sir."

She recovered from that lack of judgment a few weeks later when they found the missing fourteen-year-old girl, off with the kind of man Tori had theorized and later proved had abducted her. She'd been present when the cuffs were put on the abductor and the girl was reunited with her parents. When the press conference was held to announce the girl's recovery, Graff offered her a spot on the dais.

"May I respectfully decline, sir?"

"Are you sure?" Graff asked. "You know, you *were* right. And because you were, we got her back. That's no small thing."

She'd been right, yet wrong. And that she had been upbraided within earshot of their entire unit was not a secret to the reporters that had covered the case. She said to Graff that if she went on that dais, if she was made available to answer questions, she knew some of those questions would be about her and it wasn't about her, it was about the victim. "Getting the girl back is all I need today, sir."

She worked for Graff for another eight years until she left the Bureau to come back to Manchester Bay.

Ten miles northwest of Park Rapids, her phone buzzed. She answered. It was Bollander.

"Tori. You're going to get a phone call in a minute. Answer it."

"From?"

"Someone who has information on Teddy Marist. They said they would only speak with you."

"Sheriff, run the number."

"On it."

Tori hung up. She pulled to the side of the road, punched on her hazard lights, and then tapped an app on her phone and then checked the time.

8:07 p.m.

The call came thirty seconds later. It was a phone number she didn't recognize beyond the 701-area code. That was North Dakota. She set her phone on speaker and answered, "Hello?"

"Is this the Tori Hunter who I've seen on television today?" The man had a deep voice. He was calm, speaking deliberately.

"It is."

"Are you alone at the moment?"

"I am."

"How do I know that?"

"You don't, I guess. You'll have to trust that I am. I've been driving in a blizzard, trying to get to Park Rapids and a hotel from a murder scene."

"Do you want Teddy Marist?" the man asked directly.

"Of course."

"Are you willing to follow my instructions?"

"Depends. What are they?"

"Where are you right now? You said you're trying to get to Park Rapids."

"I'm maybe eight or nine miles north of town on Highway 71."

"How are the conditions?"

"Peachy."

"You're going to need to turn right in a few miles," the man said. He wasn't hiding his voice. "You, and you *alone*, need to come to Two Coves Tavern. You have approximately thirty minutes."

"Whoa. Hold on a second," Tori replied. "One, I don't know where that is. And two, why do I need to come *there*?"

"Do you want Teddy Marist back?"

"Asked and answered. My question is why *there*? And how do I know you have him?"

"I *don't*," the man replied flatly and then sighed. "I know who does. I'm calling on his behalf."

"And how do you know he has him?"

"You come here, and you'll see because I asked that very same question."

Tori exhaled a breath, thinking quickly. Was this legitimate? Was she walking into something if she went? "What does your... contact want for Teddy's return?"

"I'm not brokering that for him," the man replied. "I didn't want to make *this* call. I don't want trouble. But the boy is only ten. What's happened to him today is not right. So, if I can do something to facilitate his safe return, I'll go that far, but no further. Any deal for his return or for more information? Well, that will be between you and him. Understand?"

"Yes."

"And, Agent Hunter, one more thing."

"Which is?"

"There are conditions."

"Which are?"

"You come alone. Nobody else. No backup. No other police. And I'll be able to tell if you're alone. If you're not. That's it. It ends there."

Tori took a moment, evaluating the map on the dashboard screen. There was indeed a turn in less than a mile. "You're asking me to put an awful lot of faith in this."

"I am."

"How do I know you'll keep your word?"

"You don't," the man replied. "If you are who the news stories say you are, I simply don't think you have any other choice to make, *if* you want the boy back. Come to Two Coves Tavern. Plug it into your GPS. If you're not there in a half-hour, I'm gone and then, so is the boy."

Click.

Tori tapped the recording app and re-listened to the call.

Was it legit? She closed her eyes and listened to the voice again, his tone. His voice sounded calm enough but there was reluctance. Was that genuine or due to duress?

She sat back and thought for a moment.

If it was duress, she'd be driving into something without any backup. If it was real? Well, she was driving into something without any backup.

The man was right. There really wasn't much of a choice.

And you're not really on the line until you get there.

She tapped Two Coves Tavern into the computer GPS. The man wasn't lying. She had to turn a half-mile ahead and then double back northwest. And she was nineteen miles away from Two Coves. In this weather if she was going to go, she had to go and now.

Making the right turn she flipped on the Tahoe's police lights, though not the siren. She was in a wooded area, passing through the very lower end of a state forest so while the snow was coming down heavily, the wind was moderated to a degree. The road ahead was straight with only modest turns. She was able to see the reflector posts along the right side that the snowplows used to follow the path of the road. And there were plows out. She'd seen a couple along the way, though with the worsening conditions even the plows might be pulled off the roads. Checking the speedometer, she was going just over forty miles per hour. She was comfortable with that speed, and it would get her to Two Coves close to on time.

The route set, she exhaled a long breath and called Braddock.

"Hey there," he started. "We're finishing up at the bank. We found some—"

"That'll all have to wait," Tori interrupted. "You're not going to like what I'm about to tell you but hear me out. Is Steak there?"

"Yes."

"Put this on speaker. He should hear this too." She replayed the call and then said she had started on the way to Two Coves.

"Damn right I don't like it!" Braddock said.

"I didn't think you would."

"Yet you're going?" Steak said. "What if—"

"You think I haven't been running the what ifs through my mind from the second I took that call?" Tori snapped. "I was doing it while I was on the call. I don't think I have a choice?"

"What do you mean you don't have a choice? They could be using Teddy as bait to draw you in knowing you would come."

"For what purpose? What good am I to them?"

"A more valuable hostage than a ten-year-old boy?" Steak answered. "Maybe these guys have done some research and they realized that if there was anyone, anyone, that would come it would be you."

She took a moment. That thought had occurred to her. "That's one possible unlikely possibility," she conceded, her eyes straight ahead, her hands tight on the wheel as the wind rapidly kicked up. Suddenly there were no trees to the sides and as she checked the GPS, she was west of the state forest now. She must have driven into a more open area. *Steady.* "I get what you're thinking, I just... don't think that's what's playing out here."

"I don't think so either," Braddock replied.

"Why not?" Steak said.

"Because we don't know who any of these people are. Any

of them. Nothing we've learned here at the bank has told us that, has it?"

"Not yet," Steak agreed.

"What did you find?" Tori said.

Braddock relayed what they'd found in the safe deposit box. "Marist was into something."

"Did he double-cross these guys?"

"That might explain all this. However, if it was with these guys, we can't tell, at least not yet because we don't know who they are and there is nothing we've seen at his house, at Darkwoods Resort, or here at the bank that identifies them. Or if there is, we're not seeing it. We just found a bunch of cash and we know he left with a laptop and who knows what else. I'm guessing that was to deal with more money. But who they are? No clue yet."

"But we might get to someone who does," Tori said. "This could be a two-fer."

"Who?" Steak said.

"The one that got away is responding to Tori's call," Braddock said. "The call... suggests our theory that these guys turned on one another is right. One of them is looking for a way out."

"Her call?" Steak replied, confused. And then he got it and started nodding. "The media hit. It's playing everywhere. You were?"

"Inviting a call," Tori said.

"This man sees that we have an understanding of what he did at the resort," Braddock added. "And now, he has a bargaining chip. He's thinking he has a Get Out of Jail Free Card. This call suggests he's brought in an honest broker perhaps."

"But to go in alone? Tor, I just don't know about that," Steak said, checking his watch, and then pulled up a directions map from Akeley to Two Coves on his phone. He showed Braddock the map and shook his head.

They were a long way away from her.

Braddock looked at it and considering the weather, mouthed: *ninety minutes.*

"More," Steak whispered back. "We have to slow her down."

"Too late for that," he whispered back. Braddock knew she was doing this. The question now was how could they help her?

One of Tori's true strengths was reading people. He'd worked with the best detectives of the NYPD, and the special agents of the FBI's Joint Terrorism Task Force. Expert interrogators. Tori was as good as anyone he'd ever seen in the box, sitting across the table, looking someone in the eye, and taking the measure of them in an interview or interrogation. She could take in body language, expression, the eyes, mouth, the looking away or down, all of it, and make a read. Yet this time, all she had to work from was a voice. *What did she think she was hearing?*

"We listened to this, but you talked to him. You got the vibration of that. You think it's legit?"

"Yes," she replied. "The tone. He was calm. I heard just a hint of nervousness, which probably matched mine."

"I didn't get a sense of his identity?"

"Me neither," Tori replied. "Other than to meet him at the Two Coves Tavern. But I didn't sense desperation. It was mostly a take it, or leave it, proposition. I had thirty minutes, or he was walking and then he hung up. There was no negotiation. Come or don't, it was entirely up to me. Did you hear anything different?"

"No," Braddock said and looked over to Steak. "You?"

"No, though I noticed Tori never really said she was coming."

"He knows I'm coming," Tori replied. "And you two know I'm going."

"I don't get it," Steak said. "Why the intermediary? I mean

who is this guy? He didn't really sound like he wanted any part of it."

"I got the sense that he felt... obligated to do it. Who do you call when you're really in trouble?" Tori said. "What people are most likely to help you, despite the risk, when you call?"

"Family," Braddock replied. "This guy is family of some kind."

"Nolan. We need to put her on Two Coves Tavern. See what she can find," Steak said. "Let me call her."

"Hold on a sec, Steak. I'm going to Two Coves," Tori said. "Why is that ringing a bell with me?"

"That's where those pseudo militia guys are from, that the state had issues with a year ago," Steak answered. "All those arrests."

"The MN Partisans?" Tori said. "Those guys?"

"Yes. Now those guys went to prison, but there are more of them out that way and they are not fans of law enforcement."

"Terrific," Tori moaned. "It just keeps getting better and better."

"Two Coves makes me wonder about Lainey Darr. The MN Partisans base wasn't that far from there. Could this be some of those guys? She banged the drum pretty hard on them. Maybe we ought to be looking at them."

"It's a thought."

"That said, nutty as that group was, I don't think they're much on killing ten-year-olds," Steak continued. "They talk a big game out there but in reality, they're just a bunch of wannabe tough guys carrying assault rifles begging for someone to notice them, other than us, of course."

"All of which is why I was told to come alone," Tori replied. "They're not fans of law enforcement, especially when we come in force. How big is the town?"

"It's not a town, it's an intersection," Steak replied. "It's been a few years since I've been out that way but there's the bar, a gas station, maybe a church, and post office, I think. Might be a few other odd businesses nearby but it's basically the last town leading into the state forest and wildlife refuges northwest of there. Very unpopulated area."

"Sounds ideal."

"For an ambush," Steak warned. "Watch your back."

"What do you need from us?" Braddock said.

"Call Bollander. He was tracing the phone number. See if he found anything. And then get your asses over here."

FIFTEEN

"A PLAY IS BEING MADE HERE."

Braddock found himself checking their progress on the dashboard map every thirty seconds, as if willing them to drive faster. Steak was pushing it, police lights and siren, driving as fast as he dared given the conditions.

To keep himself occupied, he made calls. The first was to Boe, bringing her up to date with what they learned at the bank and then Tori.

"She should not be going without backup. How could you let her go without it of some kind?"

"You call her," Braddock replied. "See how far you get."

Boe audibly sighed. "Get your butts over there then."

"We're going as fast as we can."

"How bad are the conditions?"

"Just following the road is getting to be a challenge," Steak reported. "Thank the Lord for GPS is all I can say. Helps keep you on the road."

"Okay, your team all just stepped in here."

Braddock brought them all up to date and what Tori was doing. "Nolan. The Two Coves Tavern. Ownership, history, anything you can find quick."

"I'm on it. Just so you know, I just spoke with Elaine Baird again at Lakes Community Bank. They are monitoring their systems, every online transaction. She reports there has been no unusual activity. Nothing that she could trace back to Marist. But that's her report. We're not monitoring it and she hasn't been inclined to just give us access to assess for ourselves. We're going to need help from the county attorney."

"Okay. We'll get to more with the bank later. Anything forensically?"

"Not so far," Reese said. "We should get ballistics tomorrow on Darr and Girard as well as Marist. That'll matter only if we actually find a gun that was used."

"If things had gone as planned up at the resort, I suspect we'd have found the gun to match up to Darr and Girard lying next to Barry and Teddy Marist," Braddock replied. "Anything else at Marist's house?"

"Nothing beyond what you discovered earlier. He's only lived in the house for a couple of months. As you saw, not many nearby neighbors as of yet. We'll keep at it but—"

"Eggs? The Mariner? Anything?"

"We found that distant video feed of Marist switching vehicles. That was from a trail camera, and it all happened in the distance. The Mariner was placed there early this morning, before sunrise. We could see the Mariner being parked and the pick-up vehicle, what looked to be an SUV, light colored, pick up the person who dropped it off, but we can't get any more than that from it, I'm afraid. It was dark when they parked it there for Marist to pick up later. I canvassed and re-canvassed the area around that park all day. I have no other witnesses or video. Frankly, we're lucky to have what we do."

"Has anyone found anything that gives us any idea of who we're up against?"

There was silence on the other end.

"We'll keep working it," Boe said and dropped off the line.

"You worried?" Steak asked.

"She's going in blind with no backup. What do you think?"

* * *

Her father, Big Jim, the sheriff, often used the term *white knuckling* when any situation got intense. "It's white-knuckle time" he would say when a close game got to the end, or they were trying to beat a storm home while out on the lake. He used it so often she once looked it up in the dictionary. Merriam-Webster defined "White Knuckle" as: causing or experiencing tense nervousness.

This? This was definitely white-knuckle time.

First there was the drive itself. She'd had to slow her speed with the increasing winds. And while she'd rode in this Tahoe hundreds of times with Braddock it dawned on her that she'd never driven it. She was barely able to see beyond the beam of her headlights. And the high beam lights were of no use, actually making the situation even more of a whiteout than it already was.

And then there was the thought: *What are you driving into here, Tori?*

She had plenty of experience in pressure situations. But this felt different. There had always been her team with the FBI, or Braddock and his team with her. Tonight, she was truly on her own.

She squinted, slowing as she approached the small green road sign. Two Coves – 4 miles. She hadn't seen another vehicle since she'd made the turn off Highway 71. Her phone rang.

Braddock.

"Bollander says the number was for a pre-paid phone."

"Shocker," Tori said.

"The Two Coves Tavern is owned by a man named Newell DeBoer. No criminal record. Nolan, Reese and Boe are calling contacts with the Becker County Sheriff's Department to see if we can get you more. We're seeing if we can get a county deputy in position to help you if need be."

"Will, I have to go in alone. The caller was clear."

"Understood. If we can get someone, we're going to stage them in Pine Point."

"I just went through there," Tori said.

"If you just went through Pine Point, then you have to be close. How far from the tavern are you?"

"I'd say two miles now. How about you?"

Braddock sighed. "We're hustling but we've got an hour, probably more on these roads. Any way you can hold this off?"

"I don't see how. I'm pushing it on time as it is."

"Try and stall him once you get there. The roads are treacherous. It's unsafe to be out. Something."

"I'll give it a shot."

They both knew it was unlikely to work.

"Well... be careful," Braddock said. "And answer your phone."

For not the first time, the Tahoe jostled with a big wind gust, causing her to grip the steering wheel harder to steady the SUV. Leaning forward in the driver's seat, as if that and squinting would make it easier to see through the snow squall, she started to catch a glimpse of a bright light straight ahead. At first it was faint, but it became brighter, a flashing red dot. To her right she caught sight of the small green sign you found upon the entry for every Minnesota town. It read: Two Coves Township, Pop. 74. Tori slowed as she approached what looked to be a four-way intersection. The flashing red dot was a stop light, hanging on a sagging horizontal wire over the street, swaying violently with the blustery wind. There was a solitary streetlight on the left side of the road that fully illuminated the snow flying horizontally.

She stopped at the red light and took inventory. She exhaled a breath, letting some tenseness ease from her body now that she'd made at least this leg of whatever journey lay ahead.

Two Coves was just as Steak had described. There was really nothing more to it than the intersection. To the left was a small Catholic church that appeared to be abandoned, a large For Sale sign affixed over the front stone marquis. On the immediate right was a small, boxy U.S. Post Office with one postal truck parked in front, covered in a thick blanket of snow. Through the intersection to the left was a gas station and small convenience store, darkened and closed. And up ahead to the right, the Two Coves Tavern.

The sign was not alight, but she could see through the small, square windows along the front of the bar that there were lights on inside. Three large pickup trucks were parked in a line outside.

She glanced at the dashboard. It was 8:58 p.m. It had taken her nearly forty minutes.

Here goes nothing.

She drove slowly through the intersection, past the three parked pickups before turning in and parking. The front door to the tavern swung open and a burly man stepped out onto the step, peering at her. She grabbed her cell phone, patted her gun on her right hip, and opened her door, immediately hit by blowing snow. Shielding her face, she hustled to the front steps. The man who'd opened the door had his winter coat unzipped so that she could get a glimpse of his gun snapped in a shoulder holster.

"Come on in," the man said evenly when she started climbing the steps. "We've been waiting."

Show no fear, Tori. This is just a walk in the park.

She stepped inside a small boxy vestibule that immediately

turned to her left and she entered the main body of the Two Coves Tavern.

The place was on the dingy side, very much a dimly lit dive. The interior was long and narrow. To her left, there were a half-dozen small high-top tables along the front wall. At the far end was an area large enough for a pool table and two electronic dartboards mounted on the right wall. To her more immediate right was a long bar and through a swinging door with a porthole window she got a glimpse of what looked to be the kitchen in the back.

Two more men with woolly beards, wearing stocking caps and camouflage hunting coats sat at the bar, one on each end, both with beer bottles in front of them. The man on the far end stared at her, his eyes narrow, piercing, hostile. The man on the end closest to her, gave a little neutral nod though he pulled his coat back so that she could see the gun on his left hip. That was at least two of them and she was certain there would be at least one gun behind the bar and given the dirty look she was getting from the far end of the bar; he no doubt was carrying as well.

Tori shook her head and chuckled. *Okay, guys, I get it, you have guns.*

Standing in the middle, behind the bar was another man in a flannel shirt, clip on suspenders holding up his pants. He broke the ice. "Special Agent Hunter, I presume."

"Yes."

"You're late."

"Traffic," Tori replied tartly, as she walked inside, unzipping her winter coat, and taking off her stocking cap, fluffing up her hair, acting as if she had not a care in the world though her heart was racing a hundred miles an hour. She sat down on a barstool in the middle. The man gave her a puzzled look.

"Were you expecting someone else?" Tori said.

"No," the bartender replied, shaking his head. "I just

thought you'd be... taller is all, being the daughter of Big Jim Hunter."

"I got my height from my mother's side." She shook out her stocking cap and then brushed off her sleeves, ridding herself of snow remnants.

"Haven't seen it that bad out there in a good long time," the bartender said easily. "Can I offer you anything?"

"As much as I'd like a bourbon after that drive, I'd take a hot cup of coffee."

He nodded and had a pot at the ready on the back of the bar. He poured her a cup and topped off his own. Tori took a slow sip, as did the bartender.

"You know," the man started pleasantly enough, "I don't think I've ever had an FBI Special Agent in my bar." That comment told her she was speaking with Newell DeBoer.

"We don't like your type out here all that much," the man on the far end of the bar added. "Not at all."

"What? Women?" Tori said, flicking her eyebrows at him.

The man at the other end of the bar snickered a deep guttural laugh. "You walked into that one, dumbass."

"Ewell," the bartender said, exasperated. "Knock it off. She's a smart lady. I think she's already figured that much out."

"I have, Mr. DeBoer."

He met her eyes and snorted a light laugh.

"And you still haven't had a special agent in here. I'm retired from the Bureau." Tori took another sip of her coffee. "On the phone you said something about proof that whomever you're calling for has Teddy Marist."

DeBoer took a cell phone out, tapped his screen and showed her a text from 7:18 p.m. with a photo. It was Teddy Marist sitting on what looked like a couch with a dated floral pattern, his hands bound in front of him. She glanced at the top of the phone screen. "Tell me. Which family member are you doing this for?"

DeBoer let his eyes slide down to the man at the end of the bar to her right. He shrugged as if to say, what did you expect?

"Family," DeBoer said, shaking his head. "You can't say no when they ask for help, no matter how distant or dumb they may be. Kin is kin."

"That and while I know you all don't like people like me," Tori said, glancing left to Ewell for a moment before returning to DeBoer. "We're talking about an innocent ten-year-old boy here."

DeBoer looked to the man who'd opened the door to let her in. He'd come back inside and nodded his head. Tori suspected he'd remained outside to see if anyone had followed. The man stepped back into the vestibule again, the scout. Ewell, the man at the far end of the bar, got off his stool and stepped over to a front window, peering outside.

Tori looked back to DeBoer. "I'm here. I'm alone. I've done what you've asked. Where is Teddy Marist?"

"If you want him, put your gun, cell phone, and truck keys on the bar. They all stay here."

She feared this was coming. "A law enforcement officer doesn't give up their gun. Not any more than all you fellas would."

"Then eject the mag. You are not going where you're going armed. You will not be harmed, but you will not be armed. You can keep the gun. I'll keep the mag here for you, give it to you when you get back along with everything else. And you won't be driving that Tahoe either."

Tori took a moment, taking a drink of coffee, thinking it all through.

"That's the deal," DeBoer insisted. "Cut and dried. Take it or leave it."

No gun. No phone. And no keys? She took out her Glock and pulled out the magazine and ejected the chambered round, setting it all on the bar. "Since I'm getting back here, I assume

I'm driving somewhere. *What* am I driving if I'm not driving the Tahoe?"

DeBoer held up a set of keys. "My pickup truck. It's the big red one out there. She's a bit old but runs well and the tires are big and brand new. She sits high and has a wide wheelbase, so she'll get you through the snow, even in these conditions. And you'll need that where you're going."

"Where am I going?"

"It's already programmed into the navigation system. It'll take you twenty to thirty minutes to get there. My man will be waiting for you. He turns the boy over to you, and you leave and come right back here. No fuss, no muss. Round trip shouldn't take more than an hour, hour and ten tops."

"And him?"

"He gets a head start on you. My guess is he'll see how far he can get in the storm."

"That's it?"

"That's it," DeBoer said. "The dumbass got himself mixed up in something damn bad. Three murders, as I understand it. He says he didn't pull the trigger and I do believe him. But even if so, he's still an accessory, is he not?"

Tori nodded.

"Well, shit. That's on him. I'm not brokering no deal beyond getting that kid back. Now, you want to cut him a deal, that's your call. I want nothing to do with any of that. Fair?"

Tori nodded slowly. All things considered it was.

"You should go. The weather is deteriorating by the minute. When you get back here, you can ride it out here if need be. We'll be waiting for you, and we'll stick out the night. I'll fire up the kitchen when you get back," DeBoer said. "Do we have a deal?"

This was a retrieval. And while she didn't like going unarmed, this was better than she had expected. "We have a deal. One thing, though."

"What's that?"

"You have a to-go cup back there for another coffee?"

"Yes, ma'am." DeBoer poured her a large Styrofoam cup of coffee and put a lid on top and they walked out to his pickup truck. Thankfully it had a running board otherwise getting up into the cab could have proved challenging for her. DeBoer climbed inside on the passenger side and checked the navigation system, which was an old Garmin system plugged with an adapter into the lighter port. He hit start, and then looked her over in the driver's seat. She had moved the seat forward as far as she could. She was five-foot-five, about as short as you'd want to be to drive a truck like this.

"What do you drive normally?" DeBoer said. "That Tahoe?"

"No," Tori replied with a head shake, peering around the cab. "Audi Q5 SUV."

"Figures. Word to the wise. There will be some turns you have to negotiate, some sharp and you'll need to get over a snowbank at the end of the driveway to this house you're driving to. The truck has a lot of power which you'll need, but don't let it get away from you. You need to make haste given the weather but don't gun it *that* much, or she *will* get away from you."

Tori gripped the steering wheel and let out a long sigh. "I'll keep that in mind."

"Alright. I expect to see you back here in an hour or so." He offered her a wry smile. "I want my truck back."

She turned over the ignition key and the truck rumbled immediately to life. Cold inside, she turned the heater up. This reminded her of her dad's old pickup truck she used to drive when she was in high school. That old Ford wasn't lifted, but it felt just as big as this one. She could drive it well enough and had done so more than once through some heavy snow.

Same thing here, Tori.

Here goes.

She backed up and the Garmin's voice came to life: *Proceed two point one miles west on County Road 124.*

* * *

DeBoer watched as the pickup truck drove west, disappearing from his view within seconds, as if it was swallowed by the blizzard. He stepped back inside the bar.

"You think she'll make it?" Ewell said.

"I hope so, for her sake and the kid's." DeBoer took out his phone and punched the number. "Hunter is coming your way, alone, no gun, no phone."

* * *

They were starting hour three of the watch.

A light gust of wind tickled the back of his neck.

"The door must be a little open," Merc said, resting on a chair, his leg elevated, glancing to the rear of the abandoned church.

Towne walked to the back. They had pried open the back door. The door latches now no longer held and one of the doors had creaked open. He pulled it back closed and then peered out a side window. Jenks was parked in the back of the church's parking lot but with a view of the front of the bar. He had the truck running, headlights off, but ready to go at a moment's notice.

For the first hour, the lights of the bar had been fully extinguished. The only light was that of the solitary streetlamp and the flashing red of the stop sign dangling and swinging with the wind. One vehicle had been through the intersection in the past hour. It was a snowplow, coming from the west on County 124 and continued through town, plowing east.

"I'm surprised plows are out on a night like tonight. They'll move the snow, and the roads will be covered but a half-hour later," Towne murmured.

Merc chuckled. "You southern boys. Two inches of snow and you freak out and shelter like it's a Category Five hurricane. Here, we spit at it. Tell a Minnesotan not to go out and drive in this? He puts the passive aggressiveness away and says, 'Fuck you, I'm driving.'"

Towne laughed. "Tough guys, huh?"

"Hearty and stubborn for sure," Merc replied with a grin.

"Well," Towne replied. "I haven't seen too many up for the challenge so far beyond this plow driver. Maybe even this one is too much."

"Could be. This storm is pretty damn bad. Can't barely see out there."

They both watched, Towne occasionally checking in with Jenks who was in the truck, parked but hidden, ready to pick them up if need be.

"This seems like a waste of time," Towne muttered, before taking a sip of whiskey from his flask and pacing in the abandoned church's vestibule. "Nobody is there. In this weather, nobody is coming, regardless of how 'hearty' your fellow Minnesotans are."

"You sure about that," Merc said, grunting as he stood up from the chair and stepped to the side of the window, peering carefully outside. Towne joined him at the window when a large red pickup truck pulled up in front of the Two Coves Tavern. Two men jumped out of the truck and hustled inside, turning the lights on.

"Do you recognize either man?"

"Can't really tell yet," Merc said, peering through the binoculars. A moment later, a man stood in one of the front windows, peering outside, talking on a cell phone. "That's Newell DeBoer. Jared's uncle. The one that owns that place."

"You're thinking what?"

"I don't know that I'm thinking anything other than on a night where nobody is out traveling, everything is closed, he comes to open his bar at an odd hour."

Within ten minutes, two more pickup trucks arrived, and two more men were inside. Now they were interested.

It took another hour, until 8:58 p.m., when another vehicle arrived, this one with flashing grill lights.

"Now, what do we have?" Merc said, standing again, grimacing as he did, shifting his weight onto his right foot to ease the strain on the left leg.

"Leg hurt?"

"Throbbing," he said.

Towne looked out the window as the SUV pulled through the intersection. "That's an unmarked Tahoe. Johnny Law? Out here? Now?"

Merc steadied himself and observed the SUV park. A light over the front entry to the tavern came on and one of the men from inside opened the front door. He tracked the person walking to the door. "It's a woman."

"Out here? At this time of night?"

"Hearty. Remember?" Merc said. "And... Holy shit. It's..."

"Who?"

"I think that's Tori Hunter."

Jenks picked them up from the back of the abandoned church and then maneuvered their way around behind the gas station across the street and saw Hunter get into the large pickup truck she had parked her Tahoe next to.

"A play is being made here," Towne said.

Hunter backed the truck up, turned and drove west on County 124. Jenks drove west on a gravel road that ran roughly parallel with 124 for a half mile before it turned right and met 124.

"She left there alone, in the pickup truck. Why?" Jenks said.

"Jared is turning the kid over to her," Towne said. "He saw her on television and reached out, or had his uncle do it for him."

"That could be," Merc noted. "He has another older uncle who has a place out this way somewhere, way back in the woods, northwest near the Tamarac National Wildlife Refuge. I went there with Jared once, maybe ten years ago. It was the uncle that taught Jared woodworking. If Jared was going to hide out somewhere, I bet it would be there."

"Fine, but I can't get that close to follow her. I do, the jig is up," Jenks said. "How do we find it?"

"You see anyone else out here tonight?" Merc said.

"No."

He pointed to the road ahead, the tire tracks in the snow. "Just follow the breadcrumbs."

SIXTEEN

"I'LL BE RIGHT BEHIND YOU."

Jared checked his watch. It was 9:32 p.m. He'd been checking the windows out of all four sides of the house since their arrival. Twice he'd gone out to start his truck to keep the engine warmed, and the windows dusted off.

He'd been away from Minnesota seven years. In North Carolina, living and working in the mountains, the winters turned cold, but not this cold, and there was, at times, snow, but not this snow. Never storms like this. There were a few ice storms where ice wrapped tree limbs, hung on power lines, and turned roads into skating rinks, but then the temperature would spike within a day or two and the ice would be gone, and it'd be a sloppy wet mess for a day or two. This? It had been a long time since he'd seen this.

It may have been freezing outside, but the house itself had warmed in the past couple of hours, aided by the sizable fire crackling in the fireplace. He paced the house for hours, a constant loop from the living room, through the kitchen and then the dining room, often times picking up the AR-15, the shotgun or handgun, checking them, ejecting the magazines, reinserting them or checking the shotgun, fiddling with the boxes of shells and then he'd make the loop again, sometimes carrying one of the guns, checking his phone, or halting and watching the old boxy television. The local channel from Manchester Bay as well as the network channels from the Twin Cities were providing constant updates on the storm, snow accumulation, increasing wind speeds, plunging temperatures, and deteriorating roads. The northern half of the state was shut down for the night, no travel recommended. People were advised to stay sheltered and were warned that emergency personnel would be unable to respond until the storm had passed. The only vehicles likely to be out would be snowplows on the main roadways.

Then her face appeared again, standing with the sheriff.

The woman. Tori Hunter.

He'd heard her news conference on his truck radio. Uncle Newell had seen the report a few times as well. If Uncle Bud was the moody loner, Uncle Newell was the wily schemer. The smart one who could talk himself either into, if he wanted, or out of, any situation if he needed to. He called him for help. After berating him for his stupidity, Newell laid out a plan to turn over the boy to Tori Hunter.

"I've seen her on TV. Who is she?"

"An investigator of some renown," Newell said, recapping her background as he knew it. "Her career has been about returning missing children. She's your best shot."

"What are you going to do?"

"I'm thinking on it," Newell said. "Dammit, Jared, look what a mess you've made of your life here."

"I know, Uncle," he replied, his eyes moist.

"Even if we pull this off, and that's saying something, the police will figure out who you are, rapidly."

"I know, Uncle."

"So, what are you planning to do?"

"I'm going off the grid, into the mountains somewhere, and live off the land," Jared had replied. "Maybe get up to Canada."

"Well, you have that in common with Bud. If he didn't have Mae, that's what he'd have been doing his whole life, just walking around the woods."

"That and woodworking, Uncle. I wish I'd have gotten your smarts."

Newell exhaled a sigh. "Alright, son. Hold tight. I'll see what I can do."

He called two hours later to report he'd spoken with her. "She's coming to the tavern. If she comes alone, I'll send her your way."

It took over an hour until his uncle's next call just after 9:00 p.m. "Hunter is coming your way, alone, no gun, no phone."

"Alone?"

"Yes. Unarmed, with no phone and coming in *my* truck. It should take her a half-hour to get there, if not more. The storm is worsening by the minute. Turn the kid over to her and send her on her way, and then call me to tell me that it is done. Understand?"

"Yes, sir."

"And listen, Jared. You're not smart. How you got yourself into this mess—"

"I know, Uncle. I know."

"Don't screw around with her, you understand me? She was a Fed, a highly decorated one. I've looked her in the eye. She's as smart as she is fierce. Don't let her get close to you, don't let her hang around, talk, and get inside your head. You hear?"

"I understand."

"And then get the hell out of there because guaranteed once she gets back here, they'll be coming after you, storm or no storm."

Jared went to the front picture window and peered out

between the curtains to the open front yard. The house was not visible from the road, in part because the house sat up atop a hill, and in part because the property was surrounded by dense woods on all sides. However, the area around the house and garage was, in the spring, summer and fall, a wide grassy oasis cut out of the mature woods that had bled over east from the Smoky Hills State Forest, a massive tract of forest disturbed only by a loose web of gravel roads and walking paths.

He looked over to the couch and the boy, lying like a lump, curled up under the blanket. Might be time to wake him up. He walked over and leaned down. "Wake up." He pulled down his own face mask, lifted the pillowcase gently off Teddy's head.

"Who were you talking to? An uncle?" Teddy asked.

The kid didn't miss much.

"You've been listening?"

Teddy nodded.

"Hard not to, I suppose. You're just lucky you're with me and not the others," Jared said, sitting Teddy up. "They wouldn't like that you've heard some of these things today." He took the knife out of the holder at his waist and cut loose the zip tie around the boy's wrists.

"Like that your name is Jared," Teddy said as he rubbed the skin around his wrists and lower forearms, reddened from being bound.

Jared shook his head. *Yeah, exactly that,* he thought.

If the kid knew his first name and Hunter knew he was related to his Uncle Newell, they'd know they're looking for Jared Bayne soon enough.

There was no point in hiding any more. He pulled off his mask, to reveal his face and look Teddy Marist in the eye. His short blond hair, his darker beard, his blue eyes set deep under the bridge of his forehead. "I know I said it earlier but I'm sorry about your mom and dad. I am."

Teddy nodded, but his lower lip began to tremble and his eyes watered. Jared went to the bathroom and retrieved a roll of toilet paper and set it on the table next to the couch and went to the front picture window while he gave the kid a few minutes to cope.

He peered through the curtains into the storm, searching for any signs of light, but there were none. Just the falling and blowing snow. The wind wasn't as blustery, even in the clearing for the house, the dense woods all around the property breaking its ferocity. If he looked hard enough, he could see the gap where the driveway disappeared back down into the woods toward the main road. He'd been at this property at night many times, and at night you would occasionally hear the close howl of a coyote or even a wolf, or if you shined a light into the woods, you would see deer, usually many at once as they roamed about. But not tonight. Even the animals had found shelter in their dens or under the thick cover of evergreen trees.

Jared sneaked a look back at the boy. His own father had left his mother when he was three years old. Then he'd been thirteen when she was killed in the car accident coming home from Park Rapids. It was that night he avoided remembering if he could. But when he did, his recall of the details of the moment he learned about her accident, the loss of her, and instantly wondering who would look after him was always so viscerally clear.

He closed his eyes for a moment, purging the thought from his mind, before opening them and peering back out the window, just wanting to get this over with.

"What's going to happen now?" Teddy asked.

"A woman cop is coming named Tori Hunter," Jared said. "I'm turning you over to her."

"I heard her on television."

He nodded. "She should be here soon."

Teddy nodded, squirming on the couch, his feet still bound. Hunter was coming for him. He wasn't going anywhere. Jared took out his switchblade and snapped it open again, cutting loose the zip ties around his ankles.

"Are you hungry?"

"Yes."

Jared went to the dining room table and reached into his camouflaged duffel bag and retrieved two energy bars. "It's all I got."

"Thanks," Teddy said as he ripped open the wrapper. "Could I have something to drink?"

Jared went to the kitchen. The water was turned off for the winter. He hunted the shelves of the small pantry and found a can of Diet Coke. It was warm, but a soda. "My aunt and uncle have been gone for several months, so who knows," he said as he popped the top of the can. "It fizzed," he said and handed it to Teddy.

Letting the boy to the bars and soda he stuffed the Springfield in his beltline, then grabbed the Remington shotgun from the dining room and made a circuit, checking out the windows again. When he got back, the energy bars were devoured, and the soda can empty.

Jared stepped to the front picture window again.

* * *

Tori let out a long sigh, her hands tight on the steering wheel. From Two Coves the Garmin had directed her on a winding route northwest. As she peered ahead, the narrow road had been carved through forest, which was minimizing the impact of the wind to a degree. It also helped to frame the roads visually for her. Just drive down the middle. However, while the wind was neutered in the woods, the snow was coming down heavily and the windshield wipers were starting to struggle to keep the windshield cleared.

"As if this wasn't hard enough," she muttered. She stopped for a moment, halted the windshield wipers in the upright position and then leaned out the window and managed to clean the ice off, at least the driver's side wiper, with her gloved hand. Belting herself back in, she started ahead again. "That's better."

She reached for her coffee, still somewhat warm and took a long sip. *There was no way you could have done this with the Audi. Maybe not even the Tahoe.* She was literally in a part of the state that people simply did not live.

While she had her gun, there was no ammunition. Her cell phone was at the bar. The truck radio was basic, and she was struggling to dial in any station without static. *You ever heard of satellite radio?* That one made her laugh. DeBoer and his co-conspirators at the bar didn't strike her as men who had much use for technology or the modern world in general.

A few nights ago, she and Braddock watched *Leave the World Behind,* a movie about what would happen to the world were the Internet to go down, cell phones to be useless, everyone disconnected, how society would rapidly crumble. Nothing so dire as that was happening now, but in the moment, she couldn't help but think back to the movie, how dependent we all were on technology. She looked at the aged Garmin getting power from the lighter port. Such *old* technology, she thought with a light laugh. Yet old as it was, it was telling her where to go. Without it, she would have been trying to find this place with a paper map. She half wondered if the road she was on would even show up on an atlas or old fold-up state road map. Would she mind a break from her cell phone? No. Did she think the world might be a better place if people spent a lot less time on their phones and the Internet? Yes. But, at the same time, there was a comfort in knowing it was there. That if you needed to call someone, you could no matter where you were. Which on a night like tonight was a must. If she didn't negotiate a turn properly or got stuck in a snowbank, she was stranded with nowhere to go until someone found her.

The Garmin blurted: *Turn left in five-hundred feet.*

Her visibility was not but twenty to thirty yards. She slowed to a crawl, crouched forward, squinting, hunting for the turn. The bright white of the fallen snow revealed the path of the road. She slowly negotiated the left turn.

Your destination is a half-mile ahead on the right.

She could feel the road was a bit of an incline, creeping up hill, angling slightly to the left, and she could see just slight indentations ahead in the snow, tire tracks, from hours earlier she suspected given how filled in with fresh snow they were.

The road kept angling to the right.

You have reached your destination.

"I have?" she muttered.

Then she saw the track indentations going up and over the snowbank into a very narrow opening that was barely visible. The truck had a large front bumper and a black iron rack across it. She imagined DeBoer off-roading with it. *I think I can get over that if I take a run at it.* Given the angle she drove ahead a bit and turned around and then accelerated. As she hit the snowbank, there was an explosion of snow, bright white and blinding, landing with a thud on the hood and windshield, but when it dissipated she was able to see well enough to make her way up the driveway and into a clearing and she saw the house straight ahead. The front porch light came on as she approached the house, and then the front door opened. She pulled to a stop and looked over to the man at the door. No mask, but a shotgun in his hands.

Tori zipped up her coat and pulled her stocking cap down tight. She jumped down from the truck and trudged thirty feet through the snow to the front door. The man backed up inside the house, letting her come in the front door.

He was six feet tall, with shortish blond hair, a beard, holding a twelve-gauge shotgun on her.

Sitting on the dated green and yellow floral couch, a plaid wool blanket wrapped around him, looking to her with please-save-me eyes, was Teddy Marist. She gave him a little smile and then slid her eyes right to the dining room table and the weaponry spread across it. Then she turned her gaze back to the man who had stepped back from the front door and positioned himself between her and the dining room table.

"Newell DeBoer sent me," Tori started.

"I know."

"He's your uncle, eh?"

The man shrugged. He was. Figuring out his identity wouldn't take long, especially since she'd seen his face.

She looked at Teddy and offered him another smile. "I'm going to look him over."

"Yeah, sure, but make it quick."

"Teddy, I'm Tori Hunter. I'm an investigator with the Shepard County Sheriff's Office," she said as she knelt and showed him her identification.

Teddy looked at it and then her. "I think I've seen you before," he said.

"You have? Where?" Tori asked, as she checked Teddy over, noticing the red marks on his ankles and wrists but otherwise he seemed physically fine, dressed in just his hoodie, jeans and sneakers.

"School. You were there picking someone up, standing, talking to the principal."

Tori nodded and smiled. "My boyfriend has a thirteen-year-old son. His name is Quinn, Quinn Braddock. Do you know Quinn?"

Teddy nodded eagerly. "He's friends with my friend Bronson's older brother, Reiger."

"Reiger? Would that happen to be Reiger Rooney?" Tori said.

"Yeah."

"He's a good buddy of Quinn's. He's at our house *all* the time," Tori said with a warm smile. "I bet you saw me picking Quinn up one day."

Teddy nodded.

Tori massaged Teddy's wrists. "Do your wrists hurt?"

"A little. They're better now that Jared cut the ties off."

Tori smiled at Teddy and then let her eyes shift to Jared. "Jared, do you have a last name? I'll find it when I get back anyway. Especially since I've seen your face."

"My uncle said not to talk with you. That you would play mind games or something. I'm just supposed to turn him over and you can be on your way. And then I'm on my way. So, take him and go."

"In this blizz—"

There was the sound of an engine.

"What's that?" Tori said, spinning around.

"You were supposed to come alone," Jared said, rushing to the front picture window, peering through the gap in the curtains.

"I did," Tori replied, rushing to the front door, peering out the side window. "They're not with me. That's not a police vehicle." A pickup truck was parked thirty yards out. It was lifted, sitting high with a roll bar light rack on it, lighting up the front of the house. "Do you recognize *that* truck?"

"I do," Jared said with a sigh. "Trouble."

"Dammit, they must have followed me out here somehow," Tori muttered angrily. She turned to Teddy. "Get down on the floor," she said as she rushed to the dining room table.

There was the shotgun and the AR-15. She was more

comfortable with the shotgun and grabbed the twelve-gauge and cocked it. There were several Glock magazines on the table. She took one and slid it into hers and chambered a round.

"You were supposed to be unarmed," Jared said.

"Your uncle has my magazine," Tori replied. "Kill the lights."

* * *

Jenks parked. "I'm taking the big tree to the left," he said and jumped out of the truck and ran across the front.

"Can you handle the right flank?" Towne said to Merc.

Merc had his rifle and cocked it. He examined the area to their right. There were two mature trees, and then the truck Hunter had driven. All would provide good cover that would let him approach the house. "Yes. I'm hobbling so cover me."

"I will," Towne said, lowering the passenger side window before opening the door. He jumped out. "Go!"

Merc moved out to the right, hobbling, dragging his left leg to a tree.

Towne caught the eyes of Merc and then Jenks, nodding.

* * *

"What did you take from Marist? Money?" Tori asked, checking the shotgun.

"Yes."

"So, that's what this was all about?" Tori replied angrily. "Really? Money? You killed his parents and another man just for some money?"

"It's about more... than..." His voice trailed off.

"It's about more than what?"

"Oh shit!" Jared warned. "Look out!"

Bap! Bap! Bap! Bap! Crack! Crack! Crack! Crack!

Tori dove to her right into the kitchen.

Boom! Boom! Boom! Boom!

Glass, plaster, and Sheetrock filled the air with the gunfire, raining down in the living room.

Tori crawled and looked around the corner. Jared was hit. She saw him standing in the corner to the left of the window, bleeding from his lower abdomen, holding his hand over the wound.

"Teddy! Teddy!" Tori called.

"Yeah."

"Crawl to me! Crawl to me, now!"

The boy came scrambling along the floor and she grabbed his hoodie and dragged him around the corner into the kitchen. She turned and crawled through the kitchen to the other entry on the other side and peered around the corner. The two windows to the right of the front door were shot out and she could see outside.

Jared started firing. *Bap! Bap! Bap! Bap!*

There was one man using a large tree for cover, right in her line of fire. She burst around the corner.

Boom! Boom! Boom! Boom! Boom!

She spun back, scrambling on her hands and knees back to Teddy and peering around the wall to Jared. He was down on his knees. She reached up to the dining room table and grabbed shotgun shells and reloaded.

Bap! Bap! Bap! Bap! Crack! Crack! Crack! Crack!

More glass and Sheetrock filled the front of the house. She glanced at Teddy. He was terrified, covering his ears, rolled up on the floor. Tori scrambled through the kitchen to the other side, peeked around the corner, then swung the shotgun around.

Boom! Boom! Boom! Boom! Boom!

The man ducked back from firing at Jared. She carved up the tree but didn't hit him.

Dammit!

***

Jenks ducked back and looked to Towne who was reloading a mag into his rifle. Merc was hobbling but moving forward from one tree to the next, firing as he did.

He popped around the tree and fired.

***

Boom! Boom! Boom!

More debris filled the house, along with cold air and now snow was filtering in.

Not good.

Jared was loading the shotgun. "You have to go!"

"Go? Go where?" Tori said. "The truck is out front."

Jared pulled keys out of his pocket for his truck and tossed them to her. "My truck is out back. I'll hold them off. There is another driveway out the back of the property. Southeast. Go between the two big boulders and down the hill."

Boom! Boom! Bap! Bap! Bap! Crack! Crack! Boom! Crack! Bap!

Jared pulled out his handgun from his waistline, turned and fired.

Crack! Crack! Crack! Crack! Crack!

Tori scrambled on the floor to the back door. She peered out to the truck.

Boom! Boom! Bap! Bap! Bap! Crack! Crack! Boom! Crack! Bap!

Jared ducked back, breathing heavy, grimacing in pain. He'd been hit again. He ejected the magazine from his gun and pulled one from a pocket and jammed it in. Jared looked Tori in the eye and shook his head. "I don't have long. Take the kid. Go! *Now!*"

Tori scrambled to the dining room table and grabbed the AR-15. There were two more Glock magazines. She grabbed them, stuffing them in her coat pocket. She grabbed a box of shotgun shells and dumped them into another coat pocket and zipped it up. The other box she tossed toward Jared, who still had a shotgun at his feet. Jared nodded to her and started loading shells in the shotgun. She looked Teddy in the eye. "I need you to take the shotgun. Run to the truck. You have to, you understand?"

The terrified boy nodded.

"You can do it." Tori pulled the door open. "I'll be right behind you," she said, pulling out her Glock and throwing the strap around her shoulder for the AR-15.

She took one last look back at Jared. He had the shotgun again, jamming in shells. He nodded to her. She nodded back.

"*Go!*" Jared yelled then spun around and fired out the front.

Boom! Boom! Boom! Boom!

Tori shoved Teddy outside. "Run!"

* * *

Merc looked over to Towne and then Jenks who was at the big tree forty feet in front of the house. Towne nodded to him and then fired.

Merc rushed ahead, half running, hopping on his bad leg as he made for the passenger side of the big truck. At the front fender, he stopped.

"*Go!*" someone inside yelled.

Jared jumped out and fired.

Boom! Boom! Boom! Boom!

Jared didn't see that he'd moved up. Merc fired.

Crack!

The first shot stood Jared up.

Towne and Jenks opened fire on the front picture window.

Boom! Boom! Boom! Bap! Bap! Bap! Crack! Crack! Crack!

Jared fell back into the house.

Merc caught a flash of movement to his right. And then he saw another truck, Jared's rig, and two bodies running for it.

"*Hey! Hey! The back! The back!*"

* * *

Teddy ran for the truck, stepping through the deep snow, holding the shotgun in both his hands. Tori ran behind him, running with high knees for the truck as the night filled with gunfire from in and outside the house.

"*Hey! Hey!*"

That voice was to her back right.

"*The back! The back!*"

Tori spun to her right, dropping to her knee and firing.

Bap! Bap! Bap! Bap!

The man went down.

She rushed the last ten feet. Teddy had reached over and opened her door, and she jumped up inside and tossed the AR-15 into the back seat, started the truck, shifted to drive, hit the gas and wheeled around to the right.

"Keep your head down!" Tori yelled.

Ping! Ping! Ping! Ping!

The shots hit the back of the truck as she raced ahead, flipping on the headlights just in time to see the two large boulders. She raced between them and then down the hill, seeing the gap in the trees Jared said was there. At the bottom of the hill, the road ahead, there was a big snowbank.

"Hang on!"

Tori didn't brake, driving into the snowbank, snow flying. The truck lurched up and then climbed over and through it, landing hard on the road. She jerked the wheel hard right to stay on the road, the back end swerving on her, leaving her sideways and the truck stopped. She turned the wheel hard left and hit the gas and they roared down the road, trying to get her bearings and a feel for how far ahead she could see in the blowing snow. Her visibility was minimal, and her instant thought was, *I have no idea where I am.*

* * *

"Merc! Merc!" Towne yelled, rushing over to the right side of the house.

"She got me in the left shoulder," Merc moaned. "Hurts like hell. Get me up."

The two of them hobbled to the back of the house.

* * *

Jenks lost sight of the truck. He turned around and hustled to the back of the house and the back door. Towne was helping Merc to the house.

He nudged the door in. Jenks peered inside and saw the silhouette of a body in the front left corner of what looked to be the living room. He stepped inside, ducked right, shuffling through the kitchen and around the corner into the open front of the house.

Jared was sitting in the corner, two guns lying next to him, unable to move, taking rapid breaths, his body trembling.

Jenks set his feet.

"No!" Merc yelled, stumbling into the room, his gun in his right hand. Breathing heavy, his left arm limp, he looked down at Jared. "You traitorous fuck."

"You're killing... the wrong people," Jared gasped. "He was ten. His parents were innocent, they did nothing to you."

"Fuck you."

Boom!

"Fuck you!"

Boom! Boom! Boom!

Merc collapsed to his right knee.

Towne and Jenks helped Merc back to his feet and to the kitchen. Jenks flipped up a chair and sat him down. Towne turned on the lights. Merc was hit in the top left shoulder, the wound oozing blood.

Jenks quickly examined him. "The bullet went through," he said, eyeing the exit wound. He rushed to the bathroom and hunted the cabinets, finding large bandages, gauze pads and a thick ace bandage. Towne found a half-empty bottle of vodka in the kitchen.

"Pour on there."

"Give me a sip first," Merc said, taking a long slug of vodka, grimacing.

Towne poured alcohol on the wound.

"*Ahrg!*"

It wasn't a big hole. Jenks applied large bandages on the entry and exit wounds and then wrapped them in gauze and then the ace bandage. "That will have to do for now until I can sew it up."

Merc grimaced and nodded. Towne found a large bath towel and fashioned him a sling. A hole in his leg and now his shoulder. "Your left shoulder is a mess. Hell, your whole left side."

"I shoot right-handed," he replied as he looked back to Jared. "As you just saw."

"Now what?" Jenks said.

They heard a ringing sound. It was a cell phone. Jared's. The phone was in his pocket.

"We better get out of here," Towne said. "Before someone else gets here."

They got Merc into the back seat of the truck and turned to leave. At the bottom of the driveway, they could go left or right. Jenks started to turn left. "No, go right," Towne said.

"Right?"

"Yeah. If someone is coming, they'll be coming at us if we go out the way we came in. Take a right."

Jenks turned right and drove ahead. Then they saw another fresh set of tire tracks. "Hunter?"

Towne nodded. "See where they lead us."

SEVENTEEN

"OH, NOW THAT'S A BAD QUESTION."

"It hasn't moved?" Braddock asked Boe.

"No. Your Tahoe has been stationary since 8:58. It's 10:43 now. Where the heck is she?"

"I don't know. Her phone hasn't moved either."

"Maybe she's waiting at the bar."

"Then why not call back? Why no response to my texts?" Braddock said. "Something is not right."

"No, it's not," Boe replied.

"We're approaching Two Coves now," Steak said, turning off his police lights at the sight of the flashing red light of the stoplight. "The bar is up on the right."

"We're all here and we're not going anywhere," Boe said. "Let us know what you need."

"I'll call you back."

The ride through towns and along the ever-worsening county roads had been dodgy at best. They had been unable to see but fifty or sixty feet ahead most of the time, the drive taking Steak behind the wheel and Braddock's rapt attention as navigator, when he wasn't checking his phone for a message.

Braddock took his gun out and chambered a round.

"We're handling it like that, are we?"

"If she's not in there we sure as hell are."

Steak stopped at the red light for a moment. The two of them looked the outside of the bar over. They identified the Tahoe, and two other pickup trucks parked in front. Steak edged ahead and they eyed up the interior of the bar, peering in the windows. "I see at least three men, sitting at the bar."

"Four. There is one in the vestibule, peering out the window," Braddock said. "Park it. We're going in."

"Hey," Steak counseled. "Out in these parts, they don't like us too much."

"I don't care."

"Obviously. But be cool. Let them give us a reason to shoot them before we do, eh?"

Braddock nodded.

Steak parked and Braddock was out, charging up the steps. "Open the door," he ordered, holding up his badge. Steak was out, at the bottom of the steps.

The man looked at Braddock, the badge and then back into the bar.

"I said: Open. The. Fucking. Door," Braddock said, this time with extra purpose, his hand on the door handle.

The deadlock turned over and Braddock yanked the door open. "Step inside the bar," he said to the man at the door. Steak came in behind him.

"I'm Will Braddock, Chief Detective Shepard County," Braddock said. "Where is Tori Hunter?"

There were four men inside, the man from the vestibule, two men sitting at either end of the bar and the man standing in bartending position behind the bar. Nobody responded. Though three of the others shifted their eyes to the bartender.

"I asked a question," Braddock growled. "That Tahoe outside hasn't moved in nearly two hours. Her phone hasn't moved in the same amount of time, stuck right here," he said, stepping behind the bar. He looked to his left to one of the men who pulled back his coat, and quick pulled his gun.

"No, no, no. Don't even think about it," Steak said coolly from the doorway, his hand on the grip of his gun. "That's not how this is going to go down."

The man at the far end of the bar, piped up, "We don't like people like you storming in here—"

"Shut the fuck up," Braddock snapped and looked the man behind the bar in the eye. "I assume you're Newell DeBoer."

"I am."

"Where is she?"

"Who is she to you?"

"*Oh*, now that's a bad question," Steak said, shaking his head. "Not only is Tori Hunter my colleague, but she's also one of the best friends I've ever had. That's bad enough for you, but him? Well, now you're talking about the woman he loves."

"Last time I'm going to ask," Braddock snarled, his six-foot-four body looking like six-ten as he towered over DeBoer.

"She should be back by now," DeBoer said, slumping his shoulders. "I'm getting worried that she's not."

"Worried about what? What did you have her do? Where did you send her?"

"I sent her to pick up the boy, Teddy Marist." DeBoer explained it all. Jared, sending her out to his brother's place deep in the woods, that she was to pick the boy up and come back. He opened a drawer holding her cell phone, keys, and the magazine for her Glock.

"Where's her gun?"

"She had to go unarmed if she was going to get the boy. She would leave me the mag, but not the Glock," he said. "Dammit, she should be back by now, even with the weather. She should have been back here, a half-hour ago at least."

"She drove what out there?" Steak said.

"I had her take my truck," DeBoer responded. "It's good for

off-roading. It sits high, has the clearance for this. She was supposed to go out there, pick up the boy and come right back. Jared was going to turn him over, then he was going to leave and try and disappear into the storm, put distance between here and wherever he was going to go."

"Call your nephew."

"I have been," DeBoer replied. "Several times the last half-hour. No answer."

"He has," one of the men confirmed. "Repeatedly."

Braddock looked to Steak, who shook his head. *Not good.*

"My dumbass *fucking* nephew."

"Who is he messed up with?" Braddock said.

"I don't right know," DeBoer said, shaking his head. "I asked. He wouldn't tell me the names. He said that was for *my* protection."

"You buy that?" Steak asked.

"I don't know. I think one of them is Colum Mercer. The two of them went down to North Carolina together several years ago. Jared came back to Minnesota a month or so ago. It was unexpected, without an advance call, and I didn't sense it was a permanent return the few times I spoke with him before today. I've looked after Jared's old house while he's been gone. I went over to the house one day and he was in the garage, at one of the table saws in there, cutting something up. Jared was a wood worker when he lived here. In any event, that day, Colum Mercer was there with him."

"Anyone else?"

"Not that day. Jared came in here one night with Colum and two other men I did not recognize."

"You didn't go talk to them? Introduce yourself?"

"No. It was busy, I was behind the bar, and they weren't here that long. A couple rounds of beers, and they were gone. Didn't even see them leave. But he said something about getting away from them. Like I said, he wouldn't say who 'the them' was, but them is more than one."

"Let's assume Mercer is one of them. Where would we find him?"

"His family was from south of here in Menahga. I don't know if he's staying with someone down that way or not. I saw him for all of five minutes at Jared's and that night in here. That's it. I don't know anything more about *why* they came back. I don't even know everything about what he was mixed up in today, other than there were murders, and he ran off with the boy, and called me to..." DeBoer thought on the word for a moment. "He called on me to arrange the boy's return."

"In return for?"

"Nothing. I wouldn't do anything else. It was only the boy. The kid's ten. I had to help *him*, so I did. Like I said to you, Jared was supposed to call me when she left to come back. I've been calling him but no answer. She should be back by now."

"Yeah, she should," the man from the vestibule agreed. "Newell's truck could handle the snow, even all this, pretty easy if she was smart about driving it."

"It's not that," Steak muttered. "She isn't here and the nephew ain't answering the call. And you're," he said, pointing at Newell, "talking about some 'them.' I don't like it."

"Where did she go?"

DeBoer pulled a map out from behind the counter. "My brother Bud's place is northwest of here. Right up near the state park. Here." He circled a spot on the map. "Now normally it would take fifteen to twenty minutes or so to weave your way up there. Assume it takes double given the weather. It takes five minutes at the most to take custody of the boy and she comes right back here. So, an hour, maybe a bit more, round-trip given the conditions, at most. We're past two hours now."

"We have to go up there," Braddock said to Steak. "GPS work to find it?"

"Yes. I had her use my Garmin to guide her there." He gestured to the map. "This is the exact way the Garmin was going to take her. But the conditions," DeBoer said skeptically. "It could be dicey for you to get there in that Tahoe. That's why I had her take my truck."

"No choice but to try," Braddock said and gestured to Steak. "He can handle it."

"Going to have to," Steak said as he went to one of the front windows to look outside, the snow coming in horizontally, piling up, their Tahoe already covered in a light layer in just a few minutes. To the east were bright lights, approaching the town. The vehicle rolled into his view.

"Yes!" Steak ran to the front door. "Yes, yes, yes."

"Where are you going?" Braddock said.

"I got an idea."

Steak ran out into the road, waving a flashlight, holding up his badge.

A snowplow, a dingy dirty orange one, pulled to a stop.

"What the heck are you doing?" the driver called out.

"Sheriff's department," Steak said. "We need your truck."

EIGHTEEN

"YOU ALWAYS STAY WITH THE VEHICLE."

"No, no, no!" Tori yelped as she struggled to control the truck, the back end of the big truck swerving on her. "Come on!"

Tori pulled the wheel right, but that just threw the back end way left and she skidded.

"Dammit." She jerked the wheel left but that just brought the back hard around and she lost control, the truck spinning in a three-sixty.

Don't brake!

She loosened her grip, let the truck spin all the way around and let the heaviness of the snow stop them, which it did, jerking them to a halt, Tori flying into the driver's side door. She glanced to Teddy whose eyes were wide. He looked back at her.

The snow swirled about the truck and the spin around had been disorienting. She didn't know which direction she was facing. All she knew is she couldn't go back toward the house. Looking out the windshield she didn't see tire tracks. Looking back, she saw the tracks of her spin around.

She lightly hit the accelerator, kept a loose grip on the wheel and drove ahead. She checked her rearview mirror. It appeared clear.

How long since the house? Not even five minutes. Another glance at the rearview mirror. There was nobody behind her as best she could tell. Peering ahead, her visibility wasn't but thirty feet in front of her now and it wasn't much better behind, but she didn't see another set of headlights. Having shot the one man, seeing him drop, that may have given them enough time and space to get away. She allowed herself to blow out a breath, albeit a very short one.

"Are you okay?"

"Yeah," Teddy said, having been thrown around the cab.

"Help me the see the road ahead, okay."

Two sets of eyes, even if one set belonged to a ten-year-old boy, were better than one in these conditions. He took a minute and reconnoitered the interior of the cab. He'd found a wool blanket, a window scrapper, a small plastic shovel, and a flashlight. But there was no map, nor did the truck possess a GPS.

"Where are we?" he asked worriedly. "Do you know?"

"No," she replied honestly. "I don't have a map or GPS. I'd have never found that house you were at without it to begin with."

The problem was that this was a part of the state that she had next to zero familiarity with. The one thing she did know was a bad thing right now. It was an unpopulated area, like a dead zone of sorts where nobody really lived. She had no doubt the road she was trying to follow was a gravel one. Going to where? She had no idea. There hadn't been a sign of any kind since they'd been on the road.

Without a map or GPS what did she know?

The house was not far from the eastern border of Tamarac National Wildlife Refuge. She remembered seeing that on the Garmin's map display. And, testing her recall of geography, she thought the White Earth Indian Reservation was out there somewhere to the northwest.

One thing she was certain of was that the further she'd

gotten away from the house, the worse the wind and snow was. Her visibility had diminished considerably, to almost whiteout conditions. That was because it seemed as if she was now out of the deep woods and was more exposed. But without the forest to frame either side, it was far more difficult to see the path of the road.

Brilliant, Tori. You're in the middle of nowhere, no clue where you're trying to go with a monster truck and a ten-year-old in nothing but a hoodie in the middle of a biblical blizzard. No phone, no map, not even a compass. The only thing she thought she knew was when she left the house, she wasn't going east. She'd driven west, northwest to the house and when she left it, she'd gone the opposite direction of how she came out of necessity.

She had no feel for where she was going now, whether it be north, south, west, or even now east, such was the disorienting nature of the storm and the many turns. She could have gone in a circle for all she knew, though she had not yet run across another set of tire tracks in the snow. If only she had, she'd have followed them.

But other than that, how was the play, Mrs. Lincoln?

Stay on the road. It was all she could do.

It had to lead somewhere eventually, didn't it?

Her eyes focused on the road ahead, she needed some conversation, but Teddy was quiet. And why wouldn't he be given all that happened to him today. If they got out of this, he was going to need a lot of help to cope with what had happened. This was one of those days that he would think about until the day he died. It would never leave him. She knew a little something about that.

"Teddy, at some point we'll have to talk about what happened today. But for now, what I need to know is how many men are we dealing with? There was Jared. There were at least two, most likely three men who were shooting at us at that house. Are there any more than that?"

"I don't think so," Teddy said. "I only ever saw Jared. The rest of the time, I had a pillowcase over my head."

"But you think it was four. There wasn't a big group of other men or anything?"

"No. I don't think so."

Tori nodded and peered out at the road ahead, her speed fifteen miles per hour.

"Teddy, what do you do for fun? Do you play any sports?"

"Uh... yeah."

"What? Quinn plays hockey. He's obsessed with it. What do you play?"

"Flag football and basketball."

"Flag football? Do you play that before real football these days?"

"Yeah, I guess."

Tori nodded. "Do you want to play tackle football?"

"I don't know. I can't until seventh grade. That's the first year I could."

"I see," Tori said, leaning forward, the blowing snow so dense it was all she could do to keep track of the road right now. "Are you a Vikings fan?"

"Yeah. I suppose. I watched some games last season with my... dad."

Don't go there.

"How about basketball. Are you a fan of the Timberwolves?"

"*Yeah!*" he replied, a bit more enthusiastically. "I love Ant."

"Ant? Who is Ant?"

"Anthony Edwards," he replied in a tone as if to say: seriously. "You don't know who he is?"

Tori did. Quinn might play hockey, but Braddock had played

college basketball and he still liked to watch hoops and Tori, through passive attention, and an occasional glance at the television screen, had learned some of the Minnesota Timberwolves players. And Ant was a funny nickname for someone six-five. Most importantly, Teddy was animated about something. "Tell me about him."

Teddy spent the next fifteen minutes talking about Anthony Edwards and a bunch of other players for the Timberwolves, some of the names she recognized, some she didn't but Teddy was engaged about all of them, reciting their stats and talking about how well the team seemed to be doing this season. It sounded like Teddy poured over the basketball statistics like Quinn and his buddies poured over the hockey stats all the time. If it was a fifteen-minute respite from what had happened to him for the day, it was worth it.

"Will they make the playoffs?"

"For sure," Teddy said. "You're a hockey fan, huh?"

"Of Quinn, yes. I don't know much about the Wild, though Quinn follows it all closely."

"The Wild are cool. I really like their jerseys. Hockey has the best jerseys, the best logos, the best swag."

Tori smiled. "Quinn would agree." It was all he ever wore, and she often thought that if she had a nickel for every time one of Quinn's friends talked about the sweet "swag" of this NHL team or that, she could retire.

"What's going to happen to me?" Teddy asked.

This was a topic she was hoping to avoid. Tori took a moment, keeping her eyes ahead, trying to see the edges of the road. The snow was gusting in bursts, but it looked as if a soft turn to the left might be coming. "We'll figure—"

A gust blew, rocking the truck enough that it jolted her and her grip on the wheel popped loose for just a split second. "Geez!"

The windshield went white. Tori lost sight of the road and she suddenly felt the right front side start to dip.

She yanked the wheel left, hit the gas but the right rear end swung right and sank below the level of the road.

"Dammit! Dammit! Dammit!"

She hit the gas, pulling the wheel hard left.

"Come on!"

Too late. The back end kept pulling to the right, gravity and weight taking over and dragging them backward down the bank. She hit the brake, trying to stop the slide, but to no avail, the back end kept dropping until they stopped.

"Oh man."

They were caught on a steep side hill. The truck was angled to the right. She hit the gas, trying to climb the bank but she felt the rear wheels simply spinning in the snow. The tires couldn't get traction to propel them up the bank.

She reversed, thinking if she rocked back, then went forward, they could get loose. She tried that for five minutes but couldn't get any momentum back up the bank.

They were stuck.

"What do we do?" Teddy said.

Tori took a moment to think.

"You always stay with the vehicle. It's the best chance of survival in weather like this, having cover," she replied. *Would that be the case now?* It was the middle of the night. They were trapped in the middle of nowhere. The temperature was around zero with the wind howling and thick snow blowing.

"We just wait it out?"

Tori took a minute to think and then looked at Teddy. "Wrap up in that blanket, nice and tight."

Teddy nodded.

The engine was still running, and she checked the gas gauge. They had just under a half tank of gas. She left it running for now.

It was 11:30 p.m. The storm was expected to last through most of the night. It was just over seven hours until sunrise. For a road like this, it might be well beyond sunrise before a plow, or another vehicle came along to give assistance. Tori had OnStar for her Audi. She hunted around the interior cab of the truck but there was no sign Jared had that or a like service. And why would he? Being tracked was not something Jared, or his uncle and his friends, would be apt to allow to begin with.

"What do we do?"

She glanced into the back seat and eyed the small shovel.

* * *

11:22 p.m.

Steak had commandeered the truck and explained why. It didn't take much to convince Earl, the plow driver, to help them. "Get in," he'd said. "I'll drive you out there."

"I've driven a plow for the county for thirty-one years," Earl Snyder said as he rumbled through the woods, pushing the big plow at full throttle, plowing away the snow as he did. "I know every road in the county. Been by where we're going many times." His driving skills backed it up. They made far better time than they would have with the Tahoe.

Earl drove as if he was out for a Sunday drive. In twenty minutes, he had them close. The truck's massive size, weight and plowing away of the snow allowed them to move fast despite the conditions. *I'd be white knuckling this thing the whole way*, Braddock thought. He had them tracking through dense woods to the house, the map app on Braddock's phone telling him they were getting close.

There were two sets of intersecting tire tracks visible ahead of them. The two sets were of equal depth. Braddock assumed one set belonged to Tori. What worried him was the other set. There was no reason for anyone else to be out on the roads on a night like tonight.

Braddock checked his phone. "It's right up—"

"I'd say about a thousand feet," Earl said. He drove ahead to the right turn. The tire tracks leading into the snowbank. Earl plowed the snowbank away and then turned up the hill and the driveway. "I think we can make this without getting stuck." He took a run up the steep driveway.

"There we go!" Earl said as the plow rumbled up the incline of the driveway as it wound its way up to the left.

As Earl drove up the hill, Braddock and Steak both took out their guns, and their flashlights. The plow truck roared up into what looked to be a clearing. The house was up ahead to their left. There were lights on in the back of the house. There was a truck parked in the front.

"Based on his description, that's DeBoer's truck," Steak said.

"Look at the house," Braddock murmured as they approached.

The siding was shot up, as were the front windows, curtains from the front windows fluttering in the wind. So was DeBoer's truck.

"I don't like that," Steak said. "Earl stop here. Stay in the truck."

"Yes, sir."

Braddock and Steak eyed the house up quietly for a moment.

"What do you think?" Steak said in almost a whisper.

"No movement that I've seen," Braddock said after a moment and reached for the door handle. He exhaled a breath, as if steeling himself. "Let's go."

Braddock climbed out, followed by Steak, and they cautiously made their way through the deep snow to the house, guns and flashlights up.

"It's still," Steak said.

"Whatever happened out here, it's over," Braddock said nervously, fearing what he was going to find inside the house.

"Let me go," Steak said. "I'll check it."

"No." Braddock pushed ahead to the front door of the house, Steak ten feet behind, scanning with the flashlight, the wind howling, the snow blowing all about them. He opened the front door and moved inside, scanning the interior when his flashlight caught the body propped up in the front right corner. The man had been shot several times in the chest and once in the forehead, the wall bloody behind him. He had a rifle at his feet and a handgun lying by his right hand. There were ejected shell casings all around the body. Braddock looked out to the yard, trying to visualize what happened.

"Tori!" Steak called out.

Braddock joined in. "Tori!"

They quickly cleared the entire house. No Tori. No Teddy Marist.

"Is that DeBoer's nephew in the corner?" Steak asked.

"I suspect so," Braddock said, before noticing the large blood droplets around a chair in the dining room. There were stray unused shotgun shells lying about the floor, along with two empty boxes. Braddock walked through the kitchen to the opposite side. There were more ejected shotgun shells on the carpet. He looked back to Steak. "Firefight."

"All this blood here," Steak said at the chair. "Is it his? The guy in the front."

"I don't think so," Braddock replied, having knelt, picking up two bandage wrappers in his gloved fingers. "Someone did some repair work."

"Huh," Steak said and looked out the back door. "A lot of people walked out there," he said, opening the door and stepping outside. "Lots of footsteps. Different sizes and... directions." He looked to the west and saw two sets very close and crossing over one another, with one foot dragging. "Two came from the west side of the house. One guy dragging a leg."

Braddock stepped to the right, scanning with his flashlight. He looked toward the garage, and a set of tire tracks, wide base. He scanned with the flashlight, catching a flint of light in the white snow, gold. An ejected shell casing. And there were foot tracks toward the tire tracks. Smaller impressions, but two distinct sets. The tire tracks turned back to what he thought was the southwest and led away from the house. "Steak!"

He rushed over and joined Braddock who pointed to the shell casing, foot impressions and then the tire tracks leading away.

"These are pickup truck tracks, wide tires, like the ones we saw at Darkwoods. I think the truck was parked here. Someone got in it, turned around rapidly with the way the snow piled and sprayed here, and drove that way," Braddock said, gesturing to the woods past the garage.

"Tori drove DeBoer's truck parked in front," Steak said. "She comes for the kid. That second set of tracks we saw a lot of the way in, they were following. Maybe from the resort, maybe from Two Coves. She wouldn't have known. I doubt she would have seen headlights behind her. They didn't have to stay close if they were following her."

"They just followed the tire tracks, a couple of minutes behind her and then attacked the house, knowing Jared and Teddy were inside. Tori sees them coming, but it's too late. She and that Jared guy fight them off."

"Long enough that Tori and Teddy maybe got away," Braddock said, a hint of hope in his voice. "They're still out there. How far ahead of us you think?"

Steak crouched and examined the tire tracks, their freshness, checking the fresh snow depth with his right index finger. He held his snow-covered finger up. A good inch plus in fresh snow in depth. "We're getting about two inches of new snow an hour right now," Steak said. "These tracks are a half-hour, forty minutes old, I'd guess."

"We've got the plow."

Steak turned and waved. "*Earl!*"

* * *

The shovel was small, meant to be stored in the trunk of a car but to be used for this very purpose. Frantically, she dug underneath the truck, pulling out snow and hoping that if the rear tires didn't have to fight through the snow, with momentum they could climb the steep fall off from the road.

Tori had cleared out underneath the driver's side. She climbed up to the road and stopped for a moment, catching her breath, the wind abating just for a moment, allowing her the ability to evaluate where she was.

The road was cutting through what looked to be a low-lying wetland. There were cattails sticking up out of the snow five feet behind the truck bed. Along this stretch of the road there was a steep fall off to the right side of this section of road at the turn. As she evaluated it looked like a forty-five-degree incline. It was bad luck to have hit at just that moment.

She started digging out from underneath the passenger side. The one good bit of news was the snow was so new and fresh, it wasn't that compacted until she got to the bottom. She worked quickly, working from front to back. It took her a good ten minutes to dig it out and she felt the sweat on her body underneath all the layers of winter clothes. She sniffled and climbed up to the road and shoveled a small area in front of the truck.

Getting back inside, she could really feel the incline of the truck.

"You think it'll go?" Teddy said.

She was dubious. "Only one way to find out." She put the truck in gear and gunned the tires, feeling them spin in the rear, but there was little movement. Leery of backing up further, she had to get momentum. She backed up just a hair and then put it in drive and gunned it.

The engine roared as she tried to get momentum from rocking, but she couldn't get any momentum up the hill, the tires would hit the side hill and spin and she'd fall back. She tried several times and by the end, thought she might be making things worse.

"What do we do?"

Jumping out she climbed down to the rear tire and saw that it had just spun in the snow. Tori took a moment to think. It was a big truck. It had big tires, but they couldn't grip the snow coming up. What if you dug down to the actual ground? The grass or gravel under it all? That was probably another good foot or two down. The truck had rear wheel drive. If she could get to the ground and the tires could grip, that might work. She jumped back up into the truck, wanting to warm up for a second, feeling her hands and feet both getting cold.

Inside, she took her gloves off and rubbed her hands together, warming them, blowing on them. "I have to go back and dig again," she said to Teddy. He tilted his head and then gestured. "Look."

Tori turned to see headlights approaching.

"Maybe they could help us," Teddy said hopefully.

She took a good look at the lights approaching. There were headlights and then there were lights above the cab. A rack of lights.

"I don't think they're here to help."

NINETEEN
"HAUL ASS."

Earl pulled around the house and they followed the tracks. At the bottom of the hill, Earl put the plow blade down and they blew through the snowbank. Immediately, they saw the continuation of the one set of tracks, and then a second set of fresher tracks, just as before, going west.

"They're still tracking her," Braddock exclaimed. "They're chasing her."

"Earl?" Steak said.

"Haul ass. Yes, sir. Best I can," and he hit the accelerator, the engine rumbling along as he shifted gears.

"We should call for backup," Steak suggested. "Get some help out here."

"And tell them what? There might be a law enforcement officer in a pickup truck somewhere in the Tamarac National Wildlife Refuge?" Braddock said. "We don't know where she's at or going and visibility is for shit, and there's a foot and a half of snow that's fallen. Hell, only Earl is crazy enough to be out tonight."

"I've seen worse," Earl quipped.

"Not much," Steak muttered.

"No, not much. And it's getting worse. And in the wildlife refuge, there's a lot more exposure. You think the wind is bad now, give it five minutes."

Braddock tweezed out the map on his phone. "Earl, where does this road go?"

"This road goes another maybe twenty miles, winding its way through the northern end of the refuge. It eventually hits a T. If she gets there and she goes right, it leads up to County 113. That's at least a paved road. East or west, she'd hit a town—eventually."

"If she gets there and goes left?"

Earl grimaced. "There is nothing really to the south but more gravel roads, many of which dead end. A couple of roads get you all the way south to County 26. That's paved too, but get there, and again, it's a long way to a town in either direction."

"Could she find another cabin, maybe hole up there for the night?"

"There's not many structures out there, let alone cabins."

"Does anyone like actually, you know, live out here?"

"Nobody who wants to be found," Earl said with a chuckle. "You two were in Two Coves Tavern, right?"

"Yes," Steak said.

"I bet they just *loved* you two in there."

"Not exactly," Braddock said.

"You're the government. Nobody likes the government out this way, except government guys like me, of course."

"You clear the roads," Steak said.

"That's right. The rest of you they'd just soon as do without."

"There was a ruckus up this way last year. Some pseudo militia guys stirring up trouble," Steak said.

"Those Partisans guys. I wouldn't be surprised if a fella or two you ran into in the Two Coves Tavern was mixed up in all that scheming and chest puffing," Earl said with derision. "I was a soldier once, long ago, U.S. Army. I carried my rifle. Spent 1991 in the sandbox over in Kuwait. Real soldiers there. Out here? They talk tough but don't really have the balls to do anything to back it up. The state arrested all those guys and I guess I see why. Four of them might have been up to some mischief with that civil rights lawyer I suppose, though I think they just intended to scare him, not actually kill him. Though I suppose it only really takes one idiot, but those guys didn't really scare me none."

Earl steamed ahead, plowing snow along the way, following the dual sets of tracks ahead of them. "One set of tracks is fresher than the other," he said. "One is filled in a bit more, not as fresh."

"There's a gap. Time gap," Steak said.

"She got away, and they had to bandage up before they could follow," Braddock said. "She or Jared got one of them."

"They're behind her, probably ten, fifteen minutes," Steak said. "Earl."

"Yes, sir. Hauling ass."

* * *

"Man, I can barely see," Jenks said and looked back to Merc.

"We're out in the open," Merc replied. "Nothing to stop the wind. Whoa!"

A gust came up and Jenks hit the brakes. It was as if they were wrapped in a white blanket, the wind blowing, snow enveloping the truck for several seconds before the wind eased and it returned to just barely drivable.

"How do you people drive in this shit?" Jenks growled.

"We don't," Merc said.

"I thought you said—"

"Minnesotans are hearty. Not stupid. Driving in this shit *is* stupid."

Jenks continued ahead. "What the…"

"Hang on," Towne said, squinting through the snow. "Up ahead, on the right. In the ditch."

"That's Jared's truck," Merc said.

Jenks halted.

* * *

The truck held its position, not approaching.

Tori eyed up the gap as maybe thirty yards give or take. Teddy was to her right, his eyes wide in fear. She made sure a round was chambered in her Glock.

"Get in the back seat," she told him. "I want you on the floor, understand."

"Okay, okay," Teddy replied, jumping over to the back seat, and getting down between the seats. The truck was listing to the right a bit. He would be protected by the truck door, the seats and to a degree, the undercarriage. "Hand me that assault rifle."

Teddy passed up the AR-15 and she set it on the passenger seat.

She moved the front passenger seat back as far as it went, and then leaned the seat back as far back as it would go, providing Teddy a little more cover. "Stay down."

* * *

"What do you make of her there?" Towne said to Jenks.

"I make it she's stuck. Can't move but she senses trouble. She ain't getting out of that truck."

"She recognizes this one," Merc said, checking his gun. "Got a look at it at the house."

They had assault rifles, though they all were on their last full magazines. Merc couldn't use his rifle, but he could shoot a handgun. He had two of them.

Towne looked at Jenks, powering down his window. Jenks did the same.

Merc scooted to his right, lowering his window.

"Now?" Jenks said, his hand on the door handle.

"Now!" Towne replied.

* * *

There was movement, doors flew open.

"Here it comes."

Bap! Bap! Bap! Crack! Crack! Crack!

The shots pinged off the truck, the doors, and kept coming. The driver's side door and rear door glass shattered, filling the cab with cold air. She was at a vulnerable angle. She couldn't go up, but she could turn the wheel right, turn the truck all the way down into the ditch. They'd have more protection from the rear of the truck, but she had to back them off.

Tori grabbed the AR-15, raised it, and fired.

Boom! Boom! Boom! Boom! Boom!

* * *

The shots pelted off the truck's hood.

"She ain't running tame," Merc said, ducking behind the passenger seat.

* * *

Having backed them off, she had to try again. She put the truck in reverse and hit the gas hard, dropping backwards, into the cattails, stopped and she was on... flat ground. She turned the wheel hard right and drove forward and she... moved ... there was traction. She could drive.

She hammered the accelerator, the truck at first lurched into the heavy snow and then burst ahead. All she could think was: *Go!*

The truck was on more level ground, and it had enough clearance.

Go! Go! Go!

"Did you get up on the road?" Teddy called.

"No, I'm trying something else. Stay down!" She followed the bend of the road to her left, oblivious of the snow or obstructions ahead, jolting and jostling side to side, but she kept her hands on the wheel, foot on the gas and then suddenly the truck was angling up, the lower ground rising to the road. "Yes. Yes! Yes! *Yes!*"

* * *

"Let's go!" Towne yelled.

Jenks got back in behind the wheel and gave chase, forging ahead. "Where is she? Where?"

"Driving in the ditch, around the turn, paralleling the road, I think. I can't quite tell."

Easing, Jenks made the turn around the wide corner, making sure he completed it. "I think I see her up ahead. She's up on the road now."

* * *

Bless it, Tori, why didn't you think of that move sooner?

"You got on the road?"

"Yes, but stay down back there." She looked up at the rearview mirror. "They're behind us."

And with a bigger truck.

***

"Stop here!" Braddock said, peering ahead, seeing the two sets of tracks but then one set ahead appeared to go in the ditch. He jumped down out of the cab and peered down the side to the area between the road and cattails. The snow was all torn up, as if someone had been in the ditch and either tried to dig or drive themselves out, but then a set of tracks ran parallel to the road. Smart girl. Drive where you can.

"Will!" Steak called from behind the plow.

"What is it?"

"Shell casing, a .223 Remington. And it's still a little warm. Something went down here. And not long ago."

"They're not far away," Braddock exclaimed. "Let's go."

***

Hunter raced ahead of them, barely visible with the driving wind and snow, but the red taillights let them keep her in sight.

"Make it harder for her," Jenks ordered.

Towne powered his window down. Merc slid right, his window down.

Crack! Crack! Crack!
Bap! Bap! Bap!

***

A shot hit her side mirror. Tori ducked as another came through the back window and then another punctured the windshield.

"Stay down! Stay down!" Tori yelled, keeping her own head low, but when she did that it was hard to see the road and she lost speed.

Ping! Ping! Ping! Ping! Ping!
Shots rattled off the truck.

Tori raised her head just a bit more to see, trying to find the road ahead but she saw nothing but bright white snow, and then bright light glared in the rearview mirror.

She had slowed. They were closing in.

* * *

"Ram her, push her off the road!" Towne yelled. "Do it!"

Jenks veered out and pulled up along the left. Towne leaned out the window. Firing.

* * *

She felt it before she saw it, the truck pulling up on her left side.

Crack! Crack! Crack!

Shots hit the truck, one ricocheting off the dashboard, scraping her cheek.

No choice.

Tori took her right hand off the wheel, pulled her Glock, turned, and fired.

Pop! Pop! Pop! Pop!

* * *

"Whoa!" Towne howled, ducking back inside.

Jenks lost control.

The truck swerved, the back end swinging to the right. He tried to correct, jerking the wheel right but he overcorrected, sending them in a three-sixty all the way around before he finally got control and skidded to a stop in the snow.

* * *

Tori had backed him off, then looked ahead. "Ah no!"

The road turned hard to the right, she ripped the wheel right, trying to catch it.

It was too late.

She slid through the turn, the back end swinging her to the left. She careened down into the ditch.

"Dammit! Dammit!"

Tori tried pulling out, like last time, but she was in too deep. She gunned it but the truck wasn't moving, the wheels barely spinning.

Stuck.

She took quick inventory. She had the AR-15, Glock and the shotgun. Keeping a wary eye out, she took the magazine out of assault rifle. She was down on rounds, maybe fifteen, twenty left. She had seven rounds left in the Glock plus an extra magazine. Plus, there was the shotgun. That's what she had. *What did they have?*

She suspected a lot more ammunition and their truck.

Their truck.

We need their truck. That was the only way they'd survive now.

Teddy popped his head up. "What's happening?"

"I'm going to have to fight it out with them," Tori said, exhaling breath in the cold, turning the heater up to full since the truck was still running. It helped a bit but they didn't have long in these conditions. She eyed up Teddy. He was wide-eyed in fear and shivering. He needed something to focus on and she was going to need his help. "Grab that twelve-gauge."

Teddy grabbed it off the floor. She knew it was loaded. She handed Teddy the shells from her coat pocket. "Hold these. When I give you this, I'll need you to reload it."

"O-o-okay."

She ejected a shell from the shotgun. He was ten years old. He shouldn't have to learn this at his age, Tori thought. If he was going to see eleven, he had to. "It goes in like this." She quickly demonstrated how to load the gun. "Got it?"

"I-I-I think so." Was the hesitation because he was shivering and couldn't speak, or he didn't understand.

She ejected two shells. "Show me."

Teddy took the shells and properly loaded the gun.

"Good. Do that if I tell you to."

The boy nodded.

She turned to look to the road.

The truck had stopped on the road and turned so the passenger side was facing her. They were maybe eighty to a hundred feet away. Two men were out of the truck, and one stayed in the cab, in the back passenger side.

So that's how they were going to play it.

If that was it, she was a sitting duck inside.

She leaned down to make sure her jeans were tucked inside her boots and then retied them, extra tight. "Slide over to my side here. Stay very low, stay inside," she whispered as she pushed herself out the driver's side window.

"Where are you going?"

"I'm going out for some air."

* * *

Towne got out and used the rear bed as cover. Jenks used the front end. Merc stayed in the back seat of the cab.

"Now!"

Boom! Boom! Boom! Crack! Crack! Crack! Bam! Bam! Bam!

* * *

Ping! Ping! Ping!

While the shots ricocheted off the passenger side of the truck, Tori snuck to the back end.

She had to make the rounds she had count.

Eyeing up the man in the cab of the pickup, she saw maybe one way to do that.

She peered around the back end. She had the low angle for cover. She aimed for the man in the truck cab.

Pop! Pop! Pop! Pop! Pop! Pop!

Her Glock mag was done. She ejected it and jammed the other one in.

* * *

"Ahrg!" Merc moaned, the shots filling the cab.

"She's at the rear!" Jenks said, returning fire. As did Towne.

* * *

Tori pulled back, letting the return fire hit the truck or sail overhead. When the return fire stopped, she quickly peeked around the rear end and listened. She heard groaning.

Maybe we were down to two-on-one now.

Could she improve that?

She peeked around the back end again. She saw movement to the truck cab. That's what she wanted. She stepped back, grabbed the AR-15 and shuffled to the front and peeked around. The men were checking inside the cab.

Tori took a quick step left, went down on her right knee and fired.

Bap! Bap! Bap! Bap! Bap! Bap! Bap! Bap!

She'd emptied the magazine.

"Teddy!" she said. "The shotgun."

He handed it to her. She shuffled to the rear again and peered around the rear bed. She cocked the shotgun, stood and fired.

* * *

Boom! Boom! Boom!

"Shotgun!" Jenks yelled.

"Merc! Merc!" Towne said as he looked back in the cab. He'd already been hit three times and now she'd got him again. He was out of commission, barely moving, lying flat against the seat rest.

"If we don't get him help, he's a goner," Jenks said. "Son of bitch," he moaned, grabbing at his left upper arm. He'd been grazed on there. "Bitch can shoot."

"We walked into that. She wanted us to converge on him."

"I want to smoke that bitch and right now."

* * *

"Teddy?" she whispered loudly. "Are you still there."

"Yeah."

"Load the shotgun," she said.

Teddy did as he was told, though he was slow, his hands shaking. "I'm getting cold, Tori. Really cold."

She was feeling it too, the cold air getting through to her layers, feeling the sting on her ears and face. Her feet felt frozen. They didn't have that much time left.

"Me too. I'm working on it. Wrap up in that blanket."

The temperature was around zero and the wind, the wind chill well below zero. If those guys were smart, they would just wait them out. She had to force the issue.

If it was two on one now that gave her a fighting chance. The wind and snow affected her visibility, but theirs too. To her right, the ditch wrapped around the corner of the turn, providing some cover if she stayed low. The only move she had left was to try and flank them.

* * *

The snowplow rumbled down the road as Braddock and Steak peered ahead at the tracks.

"Still two sets," Steak said. "And by the way one set of tracks are weaving around the road, it's as if they were trying to avoid something."

"Or avoid getting hit by something," Braddock replied. "It was a chase."

"We're close, I'm telling you," Earl said anxiously. "Those tracks. They're fresh, you can see. Made not but five minutes ago, maybe less. She's going to veer a bit left up here."

Earl started turning to the left with a bend in the road. When his lights caught the glint of something ahead. "Is that a truck?"

* * *

"We can wait her out," Jenks said to Towne. "She can't go anywhere. They're going to freeze to death. Give it an hour. Keep her pinned down."

"We might freeze too. And Merc is dying," Towne said.

"We could charge her with the truck," Jenks suggested after a moment. "One of us up in the back firing as we come in. We have the high ground. Downward angle. Finish it off that way."

"Maybe," Towne said, and then spun around. "What's that?"

* * *

Tori grabbed the shotgun and stuffed her Glock in her waistline and shuffled back to the back end of the truck. Keeping low, she scooted around the soft corner of the road and stopped. If they'd seen her, they'd be shooting. Problem was the ditch had ended. She needed another fifty feet to have the angle on them. She raised the shotgun and set her feet to go and was about to when she heard it.

At first, it was a soft rumble. It sounded like... an engine. And the rumble was getting louder.

Then she saw it. The bright light coming around the corner and then it stopped.

* * *

"That's... a snowplow," Towne said.

"We're going to get boxed in," Jenks said, raising his gun.
Crack! Crack! Crack! Crack!

* * *

Earl eased to a stop.

Braddock swung the passenger door open, holding on to the panic bar, peering out.

"Will, do those guys have—"

"Guns!" Braddock yelled.

Boom! Boom! Boom! Boom! Boom!

Shots came in through the windshield.

"Ah fuck, I'm hit, dammit," Steak moaned, reaching for his left shoulder. "Earl get down."

"Fuck that," Earl growled, ducking but forging ahead, raising the plow blade as a shield.

"Atta boy," Steak grunted.

Braddock hung on to the panic bar with his left-hand returning fire until the plow blade raised.

* * *

She saw one of them pivot around and fire at the truck, a snowplow. She popped up with the shotgun.

Bam! Bam! Bam! Bam! Bam!

Tori dropped down and started reloading the shotgun when she realized someone from the plow was firing.

* * *

Towne spun around and fired at the plow.

Crack! Crack! Crack!

Bam! Bam! Bam! Bam! Bam!

Jenks went down, hit in the back shoulder. "Towne!"

Towne spun around and saw Jenks down on a knee. He'd been hit. "We have to go! *Now!*" He lifted Jenks and shoved him to the rear passenger door of the pickup and jumped into the driver's seat. He turned the truck right, accelerating.

"Get your head down!"

* * *

The truck turned right at her. She dropped the shotgun and pulled her Glock.

Pop! Pop! Pop! Pop! Pop!

She unloaded as the truck turned away from her, jumping out into the road, firing as the truck raced away.

Pop! Pop! Pop!

She fired until the magazine was empty.

"Tori! *Tori!*"

Braddock.

She stood still in the road as he ran up to her and embraced her, wrapping his long arms around her. "I can't believe we found you."

"Me neither," she said, burying her head in his chest for just a moment.

His right cheek brushed against hers. "My gosh. You are frozen."

"I feel that... way," she replied through chattering teeth. "Teddy."

"You have him?"

"He's in the truck. He's so cold." She turned around and her and Braddock went to the ditch and fished Teddy out of the truck. The poor kid was dressed in nothing but a hoodie, jeans, and sneakers. As Braddock carried him up onto the road, Tori grabbed the wool blanket from the back seat and hustled to wrap it around him.

The plow pulled up and Earl hustled down out of the cab.

"Detective Braddock, your man was hit."

"*Steak!*" Braddock yelled.

"Steak! Is it bad!" Tori yelped as she ran to the passenger side and climbed up inside.

"Hey!" he greeted with a groan. "Am I glad to see you."

"Right back at you," Tori said.

"Tori, your lips are blue."

"Yeah, well, it's been a couple of hours, let me tell you. Let's get a look at this." She opened up his jacket and pulled back his shirt to examine the shoulder wound.

"It hurts like a you know what. Didn't even see it coming. Never even got my gun out."

"You're getting slow on the draw in your old age," Tori quipped. The wound wasn't near anything vital, but there was no doubt some bone and tissue damage. "We need to get to a hospital."

"Closest is Park Rapids I'd think," Braddock said as he lifted Teddy up into the snowplow cab. "We're probably forty, fifty minutes away though, especially in these conditions."

"We better get going," Tori said, eyeing up Steak. "He needs help."

"Earl."

"I know, Detective Braddock. Haul ass again."

TWENTY

"SHELTER."

Braddock had his arms wrapped around a shivering Tori, rubbing her arms and torso, trying to warm her. Teddy sat to their left, wrapped in a blanket and an extra thick spare coat Earl had in the truck, then Steak, trying to stay still and Earl, who was chatting him up, keeping him awake, talking and distracted. Braddock had spent the first several minutes on the phone with the State Patrol and Becker County Sheriff's Department. He described the truck, that there were three men, it would likely have several bullet holes in it, missing windows. "And it'll be out on the roads, tonight. Nobody, *nobody*, else is out."

Not many from the State Patrol or sheriff's departments were either, given the conditions. Nevertheless, the bulletin was put out describing the truck. "And be careful," Braddock warned. "Call for backup. They'll throw down. They already have."

Braddock called Boe.

"Where are you going?"

"Park Rapids. Steak is shot in the left shoulder. Teddy and Tori are alive but are ice cubes."

"Just get there," Boe said. "I'll take care of the rest."

The calls made, they rode in silence.

"You feel so cold," Braddock whispered in her ear, his ungloved hand touching her cheek, her ear, her neck.

"I didn't realize how cold I was," Tori said, the adrenaline having worn off. Her body trembling and he held her closer, rubbing her arms and legs, trying to get some circulation going. He'd taken his coat off and wrapped her in it.

"You'll freeze now," she said.

"I'm not wet. You're soaked," he said.

With the heater on full blast, the combined body heat of five people across the single bench seat of the truck cab helped combat the cold coming in through the hole in the center of the windshield. It was a temperature standoff.

Shaking, her teeth chattering, Tori let her eyes float down to Teddy, wrapped in the blanket and old worn flannel coat. He leaned against Braddock, his eyes closed, exhausted.

"Those men went to great lengths to find him and Jared," Braddock said. "To track you in this blizzard. Why? Did Jared tell you anything?"

"I didn't get much out of him other than this was about more than money."

"More? More in what way?"

"I don't know. I barely got that out of him before those guys showed up. They got money from Marist, like we thought, but there is something else going on."

"Teddy know anything about all that?"

"I never had a chance to broach it with him. I was going to ask him those questions on the way back to Two Coves but then all the shooting started. The rest of the time was just—"

"I know, I know," Braddock said. "Survival."

"Were they lying in wait out there for us?"

"No. They picked you up somewhere, I'm thinking in Two Coves."

She thought about that for a minute. "I don't think Newell DeBoer would have set me up."

"Me neither. I think he's someone with an agenda, but that wasn't it," Braddock said. "But I'm thinking that's where they got onto you. Those guys wanted to find Jared. *Had* to find him before we did. I'm thinking they figured he might show up there looking for help from his uncle. Instead, you showed up. They made you, followed you."

"No. I checked my six the whole way there," Tori insisted. "I never saw anyone. In front or behind."

"You wouldn't have, Tor," he replied, kissing her on the head. "It was the simplicity of your tire tracks. On a night like tonight, all that fresh snow, nobody else out, it was easy. It's how we found you two. That and this big rig here."

Tori glanced over to the burly driver. "Thanks, Earl."

"My pleasure, ma'am."

"You got yourself a story to tell now, don't ya?"

Earl grinned. "I can't wait to get home and tell the war department about it."

"War department?"

He glanced at her, grinning. "My wife, of course."

"*Earl!*" Tori replied in shock, and laughter. She looked up to Braddock. "Is that how you refer to me?"

"Never. I value my life too much."

"Wait till Wanda hears about this," Earl said, still chuckling.

* * *

Towne checked the rearview mirror steadily for twenty minutes as he negotiated his way along the winding road, fighting the wind and snow, neither abating, only increasing and both filling the back of the cab, the right rear window shot out, along with the driver's side windows. Jenks was hit bad in the left shoulder and he himself was nicked in the left upper arm, along his right ribcage and something was irritating him on the back of his neck too.

Nobody had followed as he'd made his way north out of the wildlife refuge and toward County Road 113, a half mile short, he stopped and examined the dashboard GPS map. It was thirty miles to the RV.

"Jenks?"

"I'm hurting, man," he groaned in reply.

Towne turned around. Jenks was hit in the back left shoulder. He was sweating and grimacing.

"I can't barely move my left arm."

"And Merc?"

"He's dead, man. He's a corpse. Shot in the back of the head."

Towne saw a T-shirt lying on the back seat. He quickly ripped the shirt into smaller pieces. "Sit forward."

Jenks leaned forward and Towne covered up the shoulder wound to stem the bleeding with pieces of the T-shirt. He then pulled a shirt off Merc's body and fashioned a sling for Jenks to elevate the arm.

"You're hit too," Jenks said. "You're bleeding on your neck. Turn your head."

Towne turned his head.

"Yeah, got you on the back of your neck, just a grazing wound."

"My left arm and ribcage too," he said. "I'll live. And so will you."

"What do we do with him?" Jenks said.

Towne sighed. He got out of the truck and walked around the passenger side. He slipped his arms under Merc's armpits and pulled him out of the truck and tossed his body down to the bottom of the ditch and into some cattails. That done, he helped

Jenks into the front passenger seat. The windows were shot out. He needed to be closer to the heater.

"It's cold doing him like that," Jenks murmured when Towne got back in and started driving.

"What choice do we have?"

"I know, I just don't like it. Fuckin' Jared. Now what?"

"Shelter."

Fifteen minutes later, Towne had found a grouping of cabins on a lake not far off County 113. One was isolated at the end of a road. He parked short of it and took a walk all the way around. It was unoccupied, and looked closed for the winter, just a summer place but there was a fireplace inside and a woodpile along the side of the garage. He opened the side door to the attached garage with a crowbar, opened the garage door and drove them inside. Inside the cabin, he found the power and turned on the heat.

They were out of the weather.

Towne sat Jenks down in a chair in front of the fireplace and then started a big fire, the two of them warming. He searched the house and found a box of small bandages in a closet in the bathroom, a bottle of alcohol, black terry cloth bathroom towels, two larger beach towels and a bottle of gin in a cabinet in the kitchen. He was unable to find any medications. While they warmed by the fire, he did what he could with Jenks's wound, cleaning it with the alcohol, bandaging it, and then slinging him up again. He put all the wrappers into the fire.

"How's that?"

Jenks grimaced, trying to adjust to get comfortable. "It'll do for now." He sighed. "Anything to eat or drink, other than that shitty gin?"

"Nada."

"Well, we're getting warm at least."

He threw a blanket over him and then pulled up another

chair. He took off his layers of shirts and first examined the wound on his upper left arm. He was lucky. Another inch and it would have torn his bicep apart. He cleaned it with alcohol and applied two bandages. Same with the wound just under his ribcage. He cleaned the blood away. He probably needed a few stitches but a bandage would have to do for now. His neck was still bleeding. He applied coverage with a towel for a few minutes to stem it.

Jenks leaned forward and examined it. "A good scratch. Short but it took a chunk out." Towne poured some alcohol on the rag and Jenks reached over and cleaned the wound with his right hand, dried it and then managed, with Towne's help, to apply a bandage.

"What do we do now?" Jenks said, taking a drink of the cheap gin. Gazing at the fire.

"Wait out the storm," Towne replied, standing up and taking out his phone. "I need to call Max."

* * *

Even with the plow blade clearing the road all the way, it took them nearly an hour to reach the hospital in Park Rapids. Boe had called ahead, and two doctors were waiting when they pulled up in front. Two Hubbard County Sheriff's deputies were there as well as two patrol officers with the Park Rapids police. Braddock wanted plenty of security.

"Is there an imminent threat?" a trooper asked.

"I'm not taking any chances," Braddock said, mindful of what Tori had said about Jared warning this might be about more than money.

Steak was stretchered inside, one doctor examining the wound on the way into the ER.

The other doctor and a nurse took Teddy immediately to another emergency stall to examine him. There were no physical injuries, but the doctor quickly diagnosed moderate hypothermia. They moved him to hospital room, stripped him of his cold clothes, put him in a hospital bed, and immediately wrapped him in blankets. The doctor started him on a warm intravenous infusion.

"Don't you worry," Tori said to Teddy, brushing his hair out of his face. "I'm here. Braddock is here. Deputies and officers are on guard. Doctors and nurses will be checking on you. You're safe here, okay? You're safe."

Teddy nodded. "What's going to happen to me?"

"Who should we call? Do you have grandparents? Or aunts or uncles we should call?"

"My mom's brother, my uncle Tony and aunt Fi. They live in Excelsior." Excelsior was a western suburb of Minneapolis.

"Okay," Tori said. "We'll make some calls and start figuring some things out. Okay?"

"Okay."

A minute later, Teddy's eyes were closed, and he was asleep.

Tori left the room, a deputy standing guard. Braddock was waiting in the hallway.

"Steak?" she asked.

"Doc's working on him," he said.

"We have to figure out what this 'more' Jared was referring to is. And we need to call Teddy's uncle Tony."

"Yeah, we do," Braddock said, shaking his head. "But not right this minute. We need to get *you* checked out."

"I'm fine."

"You're anything but." To a nurse, he said: "Can you check her out. She was out in the cold as well. Her face is scratched."

"I'm fine, really."

"Right," Braddock replied. "She's like a block of ice."

The nurse reached for Tori's hand. "My goodness. Next door, right now with you. Doctor."

The nurse guided Tori to a hospital bed. The doctor examined her. "We need to get you out of those clothes and warm you up too."

With Braddock and the nurse's help, Tori got out of her clothes, slipped on a gown, and climbed into bed, letting the nurse wrap her in blankets. The doctor started her on a similar infusion regimen.

When the doctors and nurses left, Braddock stood over her bed. "Just rest. Everything else can wait for a few hours."

Tori nodded and a minute later, exhausted, she drifted off to sleep.

* * *

Towne peered around the right side of the front door out the narrow vertical window, the sky still dark though it looked as if it were about ready to wake up. The snow continued to blow about with the heavy wind gusts, which in a sense was good, as the blustery conditions allowed the snow to fill in and mostly cover their tire tracks leading to the garage.

He let out a long yawn. After he'd stabilized Jenks and repaired his own wounds, he'd tried sleeping but his mind wouldn't quiet down. Too much adrenaline still coursing through his body.

It wasn't much better for Jenks. Between the throbbing of his shoulder and an inability to get comfortable, there was little real rest to be had.

So, instead of sleeping, he kept a watchful eye, pacing the rooms at the front of the cabin, anxiously watching for and worrying of other vehicles, of curious neighbors wondering why there were tire tracks leading to the garage of the cabin, mostly filled in with snow as they were. In one of his later searches of the cabin, he'd found a pair of binoculars and made a circuit of all the windows, taking in their surroundings. Even in the darkness with the snow, he'd still spotted a few other nearby cabins. To his relief, none appeared occupied, they were all dark. As he'd examined maps of the area, the desolation, the lack of nearby towns, a small wave of relief washed over him. They were as safe for the time being as they could be.

With that done, he'd been careful to go back and wipe down any surfaces in the house he'd touched. He'd done the same in the garage, wiping down Merc's truck inside and out. Whatever move was next, the truck was out of commission. That done, he stepped back into the small living room and tossed another log on the fire, using the fireplace poker to stoke the flames.

"What time is it?" Jenks mumbled; his eyes closed.

"Almost six a.m. It's getting a little lighter out there."

Jenks stirred in the chair.

"Just rest. Nothing to do at the moment."

"How are you feeling?" Jenks asked.

"Sore, but I doubt as sore as you."

It was another hour when he really noticed the sky starting to brighten, despite the wind and snow. Now he started thinking: *What should they do?* And more importantly: *What did the police know of them?*

With the state being shut down from Minneapolis and St. Paul north, there was little new news to draw on that he could find on his phone.

He called Max again. They had spoken every couple of hours throughout the night.

"Anything new?"

"Not that I've heard," Max replied. "Nothing on the news and I'm monitoring everything, television, radio, Internet, social media. That said, what happened last night will break soon. The big question is what Jared told Hunter, or what Jared told the kid that he can tell the police. If they get your name, it won't take long to get mine as well." There was a pause. "What is your situation now? How is Jenks?"

"Not great," Towne replied, recapping his struggle through the night. "We're safe for now, but we're hurting bad, especially Jenks. He needs tending, more tending than I can give him here. He needs stitching and medication."

"I've mapped your location," Max said. "The snow is starting to taper off. The news said the plows are rolling but they haven't made it my way yet and it might be a few hours until they do. Once they do, I'll come for you guys but it's going to be some time yet before I can get up there. Any chance you could hold out until it's dark again?"

Towne looked over to Jenks. He was in discomfort, perspiring. They had no food or bandages. "I don't know that we can."

"Hang tight then. I'll get on the road as soon as I can."

TWENTY-ONE

"IT WAS A WOMAN."

Sometimes when you sleep, you're so tired, and the sleep is so good that you just sink into the mattress, the blankets, the pillows, and you end up in a sleeping position from which you just don't want to wake. Your mind and body at such ease you just want to stay there, comfortable, warm, resting.

That was her subconscious talking to her.

Then her olfactory senses took over. The sweet smell of coffee and vanilla wafting in her nostrils. Her eyes fluttered open to see a tall off-white cup with a brown plastic cover a few inches from her face.

A scruffy Braddock was waving the tall cup of coffee under her nose. A tan paper sack sat on her roller table. "Hey there," she said with a tired smile, stretching her arms.

"Good morning," he greeted. "How are you feeling?"

"Warmer." Tori pushed back the blankets and sat up and took the cup, taking a long drink, the hot sweet coffee swirling pleasingly down her throat, warming her body. She saw a stack of folded clothes on a counter. "Are those mine?"

"Yes. The hospital staff washed and dried them for you."

She was still in nothing but a drafty hospital gown. "Have you checked on Quinn?"

Braddock nodded. "He's with his cousins. They're outside already, building snow forts in the plowed piles along the road. He said the piles are, and I quote, epically high."

Tori laughed, took another sip of coffee, and then started eyeing up the paper sack, the hearty smell of egg and sausage calling her.

The doctor came in and checked her over, particularly her body temp and then removed the needle for the infusion from her left arm.

"How am I doing, Doc?"

"Fine," she said. "Your body temp is nearly back to normal. Just stay warm for the next few days. Maybe take it easy, get some rest."

"I'll commit to staying warm."

"I figured as much," the doctor replied with a wry smile.

"And Teddy?"

"Sleeping still," she said. "Poor kid has hardly moved. He's running a fever, so we'll be keeping an eye on him. We'll wake him soon, though. Try and get him to eat some breakfast."

The doctor left and Tori took another long drink of coffee and then unwrapped the breakfast sandwich Braddock had brought her. She realized she hadn't eaten in over twenty-four hours and was starving. "I love these even if my waistline doesn't," she said and then took a massive bite of the breakfast sandwich, savoring the egg, bacon, ham, and cheese concoction. "What time is it?" she said, chewing.

"9:15 a.m.," Braddock said, peering out the window. "The snow has almost stopped now. Roads are getting cleared. Things are starting to move a little."

"And while I was out?"

"I spoke with Lainey Darr's brother Tony. He and his wife, Fiona, are on the way up here now from the Twin Cities.

They'll be stopping in Manchester Bay and Reese will lead them up here. They already said they would look after Teddy. He said he and his wife told Lainey and Barry they'd do it years ago if something ever happened to them."

"And Steak?" She threw off her blankets. "I should go check on him."

Braddock stopped her. "He was put in an ambulance three hours ago. He's probably in surgery by now."

"What! Why the heck didn't you get me up?"

"Because he told me not to. He wanted you to rest. I did too. You needed it. I mean, after your eyes closed, I watched you shiver and shudder for another hour under all those blankets."

"Yeah?" she said with raised eyebrows.

"Yeah, but you didn't seem to notice you were so wiped out," Braddock said. "Thus, I let you sleep."

"What's Steak's prognosis?"

"Shattered clavicle and some tissue damage," Braddock said. "Doc here said he'd probably end up with a plate and a bunch of screws in his shoulder to hold things together but will be otherwise fine in time. He's okay. Pissed off he got shot, but okay."

"Is it the kind of thing where he'd have to—"

"Retire? No, I don't think so," Braddock replied and then smiled. "Though, he was threatening it when he was wheeled into the ambo. I'm going on disability, going to lead the good life, fish all day, fuck all night, blah, blah, blah. He was in good spirits, but he'll be out of commission awhile."

"Did you talk to Grace?"

"I did. And so did he. She was relieved that her husband, and you, were alright."

He sat down in a chair, leaned forward, and looked at the floor.

"What's wrong?" she asked, taking another bite.

"I was worried last night. I couldn't reach you. Couldn't

find you and then the scene at that house in the woods, the shoot-out. I wasn't there. I didn't have your back."

"The hell you didn't," she said, getting out of bed this time, walking over to him, sitting down on his lap. "You didn't sit in Park Rapids and wait. Or Two Coves. You kept searching and you found me. And just in the nick of time. I was about to rush them."

"Rush them?"

"Teddy was freezing. I was too. We didn't have long. The only way he and I were going to make it out of that alive, was to kill them and take their truck. I was trying to flank them when you showed up."

"Oh," he said, eyebrows raised. "So you didn't need me?"

Tori shook her head and murmured, "I don't think my odds of success were all that high."

"But you weren't going to sit there and freeze to death."

"No. I had one option. It was the only choice to be made and I made it but then, you were there," she said, kissing him softly on the forehead, whispering, "Thank God."

"We'd have never made it in time had Steak not had the brilliant brainstorm to flag Earl down. Without that, heck, we'd have never made it at all."

"You know Braddock, you and I may not have a dog, but you are one heck of a bloodhound." She ran her hand over his beard. "A big handsome, scruffy one."

"Speaking of dogs, Quinn has been suggesting we should get one. A friend of his, their dog just had a litter of yellow Labs. He showed me a picture. They were *awfully* cute."

"I haven't had a dog since I was a little girl," Tori replied with a laugh.

"That sounds like a yes."

"As long as I don't scoop the poop."

. . .

Tori was dressing when she heard voices next door. Braddock stuck his head in. "Tony and Fiona Darr are here."

Tori pulled her hair back into a ponytail and then hustled to the hospital room next door to see Teddy being hugged by his aunt and uncle.

"Hi, Tori," Teddy said when he saw her come in.

"Hey," she said, going to the side of his bed. "You're looking good," she said with a smile, tousling his hair, sneaking a quick touch of his forehead. He was warm, just as the doctor had said but his color looked reasonably good.

Tony Darr introduced himself, shaking Tori's hand. "Thank you for everything you did last night."

"You're welcome but it wasn't just me. It was Will here, Detective Williams and the unsung hero, a snowplow driver named Earl Snyder."

"It sounded like quite an ordeal you all went through from what Detective Braddock told us," Fiona Darr said.

"Yeah," Tori said, looking down to Teddy, tenderly clasping his hand. "That's all over now."

"Can we all step into the hallway for just a minute," Braddock suggested.

"We'll be right back," Fiona said to Teddy.

Tony Darr handed a document to Braddock. "Several years ago, Lainey and Barry asked if Fi and I would look over Teddy if anything ever happened to them. I never thought... I never thought this would ever actually come to pass. That's a copy of their will. I believe their divorce references this, but I don't have a copy of that."

"We talked with their lawyers yesterday when we were trying to find Barry and Teddy. I'm sure we can get a copy of the divorce decree, and this will all work itself out," Braddock said as he flipped through the papers.

"Do you know any more about what happened to my sister? Or to Barry?" Tony Darr asked. "I mean this is... I don't have the words." They could tell Tony Darr had not had time to truly process what had happened. That part would come when the madness of the last twenty-four hours simmered down.

"Like I said when we talked earlier, we have some bits and pieces but not a lot of it is concrete," Braddock said.

"Up until now," Tori interjected, "everything was about finding Teddy. Now that we have, we can focus on the why? We have a lot of questions. One person who can help with that is Teddy. We need to talk to him about yesterday. About what he remembers."

"Gosh. Does he have to talk about all that?" Fiona pleaded.

"I'm afraid so if we're to find the people responsible for this," Tori said. "And the sooner we do it, the better. When it's freshest in his mind."

"Tori has a lot of experience with this kind of thing, talking with kids," Braddock said, briefly explaining her career with the FBI. "There's nobody better to handle it. And I think you saw his reaction when Tori came in. There's some trust there."

"Can we be in there with him?"

"Absolutely," Tori said. "You need to hear what he's been through."

They moved to a private office with a comfortable couch and soft chairs. While Teddy, wrapped in a blanket, and his aunt and uncle got seated, Reese pulled Tori and Braddock aside.

"First things first," Reese started. "We have an identity on Jared. Jared Bayne, age thirty-one. He is the nephew of Newell DeBoer, son of Newell's late sister Pauline. He doesn't have a current Minnesota driver's license, but he does have one for North Carolina."

"DeBoer mentioned he'd been down there for several years," Braddock said. "Along with a Colum Mercer."

"North Carolina DMV records support that. It looks like he

and Mercer were down there just over six years. They both had addresses for an apartment in the town of Linville at one point but that was three years ago. Mercer also had an RV as well with North Carolina plates, so we have a bulletin out for that too."

"Where is Linville?"

"Northwest North Carolina, in the Appalachians." Reese showed them where on the map. "They were in rural North Carolina. Not all that different from Two Coves, Menahga, Arago, Park Rapids. Just that there they have mountains and better weather. We have a cell phone number for Mercer, but it is out of service, and we have no way to track it. I have files on both," he added, holding them up for them to see.

"You thought you might have killed one of them last night?" Braddock said to Tori.

"I shot one just as we were leaving that house. I saw him go down."

"We didn't find a body there, though we found blood and bandage wrappers in the dining room, so those guys may have tried to patch someone up."

Tori nodded. "When I ended up in the ditch the second time, there was one man in the pickup truck, in the back of the cab. I fired several times in there. I think I hit whoever that was. The other two converged on him. I fired at them, but I don't know if I got either of them. I couldn't tell. If I did hit them, it certainly wasn't enough to stop them from getting away when you and Steak got there."

"We have Jared who is dead, and maybe Mercer, who for now, is in the wind," Braddock said. "But there are at least two more out there somewhere."

"Jared said to me that this was about more than money."

"What did he really say," Braddock pressed. "His exact words?"

"I said: You killed his parents and another man just for

some money? And he said it was about more and then his voice trailed off."

"More? More what?"

"He didn't finish the thought. The shooters showed up."

Reese grimaced. "That seems a bit thin."

"We weren't there," Braddock admonished. "*How* did he say it?"

"The way he said it, the tone said that the 'more' wasn't a little thing, you know something minor. There was some weight to it. It was my impression that this 'more' was at least as important as the money, if not more so."

"More so?"

"My gut, intuition, whatever you want to call it, says there is something else going on here. We need to identify and find these guys. Until we do, we can't be sure this is over."

"We have a BOLO out for Mercer," Reese said. "Nolan is talking to the legal eagles down in North Carolina but neither Jared Bayne nor Colum Mercer had any trouble with the law down there. That said, inquiries about them are being made in Linville and areas nearby. Maybe we get some contacts, work from there."

"How about that house Bayne was using?" Tori asked.

"It was no picnic getting up here but thanks to your buddy Earl's guidance, Becker County is getting a crew out to that house in the woods, as is the BCA."

"I doubt they'll find much," Tori said. "But I want to talk to Newell DeBoer again. Although there's someone we need to talk to first."

* * *

Teddy sat with his uncle on one end of the couch while Tori sat at the other, facing him, relaxed, friendly, a cup of coffee in a green ceramic cup resting in both her hands.

Tori started. "Teddy, we need to talk about yesterday. If Detective Braddock and I are going to find the people responsible for all this, we need to know what you saw and heard. We need to know what you remember from yesterday up until the time that I showed up," Tori explained.

Teddy nodded nervously.

"It'll be okay," she said, patting his knee. "Let's try and start from the beginning."

Teddy ran them through the shooting at Girard's house. He heard a muffled pop from the garage and then there were three in rapid succession inside. "Then a man in a face mask rushed at me up the stairs. I ran to my bedroom, but he tackled me, put tape over my mouth, bound my wrists and feet and threw a pillowcase over my head."

He said they changed vehicles not long after they had left the house.

"Do you know how many men were in the truck?" Braddock asked.

"I think three. I heard three different voices."

"Any names?"

Teddy nodded. "There was Jared. I think he was driving. There was a man called Jenks and then the other man." Teddy shook his head. "He was called Towne. I don't think I was supposed to know that because I think Jared said their names and they got mad at him, told him to shut up, especially Towne. That man. He sat in the second row. He... he..."

"He what?"

"He... uh..." Teddy's lower lip trembled for a second and he hesitated.

"It's okay, buddy," Tori assured.

It was as if Teddy took a breath and straightened his back. "He pointed a gun at me when he called Dad. And he made me tell Dad that there was a gun pointed at me." He was defiant. *Yesterday, that would have made you cry,* Tori thought. After what he went through yesterday, all the guns, the shooting, the chase, nearly freezing to death, he'd matured ten years in a day.

"What did they want from your dad?" Braddock said.

Teddy thought for a moment. "Towne, or at least I think it was him, said they wanted that little fortune he hid from his ex-wife, from my mom."

"Fortune?"

"Yes, sir."

"That he hid from your mom?" Tori said, confirming.

"Yes," Teddy said. "He said he knew my dad had it hidden somewhere not far away. They wanted him to bring it to them."

"And what was it he was supposed to bring to them?"

Teddy thought for a moment, closing his eyes. "I remember him saying every account, password, record, things like that." Tori glanced to Braddock. This was all the contents of the safe deposit box. Interestingly, they didn't tell him to bring the money. Perhaps they didn't know about that.

"Did they say anything else about it?" Braddock said.

Teddy nodded. "It was time for Dad to... pay for his sins."

"Pay for his sins?" Uncle Tony asked, looking to Fi and then to Tori. "What are they talking about? Do you know?"

"Teddy, do you know what a safe deposit box is?" Tori asked.

He nodded. "Yeah, Dad showed me them at his bank."

"Did your dad ever take you to a bank that wasn't one of his? To open a safe deposit box?"

"No, I don't think so."

"Did he ever take you to the town of Akeley?" Braddock said.

"No, sir, I don't think so."

"After they were done talking to your dad," Tori continued. "What happened then?"

"After that he put the tape back over my mouth and the pillowcase over my head," Teddy said.

"Did they talk anymore?"

"They were quiet most of the time until we got to the resort," Teddy said. "But I still listened."

Tori smiled. "Did you now?"

"Yes," he replied proudly. "I was under a blanket, but I moved my head close to the back seat."

"I see," Tori said, again glancing to Braddock whose eyes were glued to the boy. Teddy had something he wanted to talk about. "And what else did you hear?"

"I remember we must have been on a rough road because I was bouncing around, but then I heard one of them say: Are you calling Max?"

"Hmm," Tori said. "Max? And they called him?"

"Not him. It was a woman."

"A woman," Tori said, surprised. "Really?"

"I couldn't hear everything she said, but for sure it was a woman. I heard her voice."

"Was it one you'd heard before?"

"No. I don't think so."

"Ah, I see. And what did you hear them talk about? Max and this man?"

"I heard her ask where my dad was. She said his name, Barry. I heard it."

"Barry? His first name?" Tori asked, confirming. "Not Marist, Mr. Marist, not Barry Marist, but Barry?"

"That's right."

"Anything else?"

"I remember Towne, I think it was Towne, he said Max needed to be somewhere she could watch and listen so that they could make sure my dad wasn't 'screwing' with them."

"Screwing with them?"

"Yes, although I heard this Max laugh and say something like my dad didn't have the—" He hesitated.

"Didn't what?" Tori asked.

"It's kind of a bad word," Teddy said. "I don't want to get in trouble."

"Teddy, if ever you had a free pass, it's now," his uncle Tony said.

"The woman said my dad didn't have the balls to screw with them."

"Hmm," Tori replied, her eyes drifting to Braddock. Whoever this Max was, she had some insight on Barry Marist. She *knew* him in some way. She was the connection between Marist and these men.

"What did my dad, do?" Teddy asked, his voice rising. "Why did they kill him? My mom? Ed? Why?"

"We don't know, yet," Tori replied. "We're going to start digging into that now that we got you back."

"Teddy, we don't know what your dad was mixed up in," Braddock said, pulling his chair forward. "Whatever it is, it may not have been good. But Tori and I can tell you this for certain, your father had courage yesterday when it mattered most. He fought those men in the other cabin before they killed him. We think when he did that, it gave Jared the opening to take you away from that resort before they did the same to you."

"Your dad was brave, Teddy," Tori said softly. "Whatever comes of all this, whatever it was he was doing, he stood up and fought for you when it mattered. Remember that."

"I will."

"And you had courage too. Listening how you did to those men? That was brave, and smart. And you hung in there with me last night, every step of the way. I couldn't have fought them off without your help."

Teddy nodded.

"I have a few more questions though, okay?"

"Okay."

"How long were you at the resort yesterday?"

Teddy thought for a minute. "A long time it seemed."

"Define long time for me? An hour, two hours, more?"

"More. We were there for I think five or six hours maybe."

"When Jared took you out of the cabin, was it in his truck?"

"I think so," Teddy said. "But I still had the pillowcase over my head so I can't be sure, but I know he threw me over his shoulder, and it wasn't far to the truck he drove me in."

"Did they shoot at his truck when he drove away?"

"Yes."

"And after that, what did Jared say to you?"

"He said he was sorry about my parents," Teddy replied, closing his eyes, tears welling in his eyes.

His uncle wrapped his arm around him. "It's okay, Teddy, we can be done."

"Just another question or two," Tori pressed. "Did Jared say anything else?"

"Like what?"

"Why these men did this to your father, mother, Ed? You told us about the call, the accounts, records and so forth, so your dad had something they wanted."

"What we're wondering, though," Braddock followed, "is if there was something else too?"

"Remember last night, at the house, just before all the shooting started, I asked Jared if this was just about money, and he started to say it was about—"

"More."

"Right."

"Teddy, did Jared mention anything else to you?" Braddock asked. "Anything about *what* else they were up to? What else they might have had planned?"

Teddy thought for a minute and then shook his head. "Jared didn't really talk to me beyond saying he was sorry. He kept the pillowcase on my head most of the time at that house. It was only maybe a half-hour before Tori came that he took it off my head. That was the first time I even saw his face."

"Teddy, was there a man named Colum Mercer that you heard of? Or heard a voice?"

"I heard someone say Merc a few times before we got to the resort. But I never heard that name."

"One other question," Braddock said. "The men's voices. Did they sound..." He took a moment. "Did they sound like they were from here?"

"How do you mean?"

"You know, us Minnesotans," Tori said. "We tend to say things like 'yah,' 'dontcha know,' 'for Pete's sake,' 'you betcha,' 'darn tootin,' 'uffda,' things like that. It's corny, we try not to say them, but from time to time, we all do, it's part of who we are as Minnesotans." She smiled. "We have a particular way of speaking. Did they sound like that?"

"No," Teddy said, shaking his head after a moment. "No, they didn't."

"Okay." Tori nodded. "How was it different?"

His eyes brightened and he turned to his aunt and uncle. "Uncle Tony, you remember when we went to Texas on a spring break trip."

"The resort down in Austin," Tony said. "Sure do."

"Yes. They sounded a little like that."

"A little southern *draaaaaawl*," Braddock said, mimicking one.

"Yeah, a little something like that."

"Did they ever say a state, or a city, or any geography that you remember?"

"No, not that I heard. But it was like you said, they sounded... southern."

Braddock and Tori shared a look. Teddy was tired. That was enough for now. There would be more questions in the coming days.

"Good job, Teddy," Braddock said. "Really good."

"Let's get you back to bed," Tori said.

. . .

Tony and Fi got Teddy back to his hospital room and helped him into bed. Teddy was exhausted and Tori knew the turmoil that must be going through his mind. Tony and Fiona Darr joined Tori, Braddock and Reese in the hallway.

"Was he able to help you?" Tony Darr asked.

"We learned a few things. There is a woman named Max involved," Braddock said. "That's new and important. Southern accents, which may suggest the tie to North Carolina that we're finding, given we know that's where Jared Bayne and Colum Mercer were. And they demanded Barry bring accounts, records, passwords, all that, so they had some knowledge of the safe deposit box."

"What is that about?" Tony asked.

"We don't know yet. Did you know your brother-in-law had a safe deposit box at a bank up in Akeley? It was not one of his branches. It was at a branch of Rapids Community Bank."

"No," Tony replied. He looked at Fi. "You?"

"No."

"He went there before he went out to that resort yesterday. While we don't know what he retrieved from there yesterday, video of a previous trip showed him leaving with a laptop. Yesterday, we found $420,000 in cash in the safe deposit box."

"$420,000?" Tony Darr said, shocked. "Wow."

"They didn't know or didn't ask for that, but they demanded whatever else he had in there. They knew about the resort as well and that it was Barry's father's, until he lost it."

"Otis's place, right?" Tony said. "Barry was pretty distraught back then that he couldn't help him. And then the way he died, at the resort." He shook his head. "It was pretty awful." He took a moment. "These guys knew a lot about Barry, didn't they?"

"They did," Braddock said. "Which tells us something,

maybe. We think that their plan was to kill Barry and Teddy there, make it look like a murder suicide, probably using Barry's own gun, which is also missing. Probably the same gun that killed your sister and Ed Girard."

"It was all a set-up," Tori said. "To make it look like Barry snapped."

"All for money,' Tony said, shaking his head. "Or was it as you asked, about more?"

"We don't know for sure," Tori said. "The investigation is not over. Your sister and former brother-in-law were caught up in it, but it wasn't about *just* them if I believe what Jared said to me, which I do. But there must be some tie between them, the money and whatever else they were after. Point being, we may need to speak with Teddy more. It feels like this is not done."

They spoke for another minute or two before Tony and Fi stepped back into the hospital room to check on Teddy.

"What's next?" Reese asked Tori and Braddock.

"Two Coves," Tori said. "I need to retrieve some things and we have some questions for Newell DeBoer."

TWENTY-TWO

"IT'S MORE SUBSTANTIAL WHEN YOU COMPOUND THE INTEREST OVER TIME."

The blizzard had passed through, though some stray flurries still flittered about in the late morning air. In the aftermath, the entire northern half of the state was buried in thirty inches of fresh heavy snow. The roads were jutted and icy, the plows only now out in strength, clearing the roads.

Reese drove, Braddock rode shotgun and Tori took a seat in the back, reading the files on Jared Bayne and Colum Mercer. As they drove to Two Coves, Braddock called Boe, who was at the hospital with Eggleston, waiting for Steak to come out of surgery.

"It's been a morning, let me tell you," Boe started.

"How is our boy doing?"

"He's still in surgery. The doctors told Grace that it was a straightforward procedure," Eggs said of her partner. "On his collarbone, the surgeon said he performed a similar surgery for a hockey player at the university last spring and he's played all season without an issue. So that was good to hear."

Braddock caught them up on what they learned from Teddy, adding it to what they learned yesterday.

"Teddy recalls them specifically telling his dad to bring all accounts, records, passwords. And we think he had a laptop in the safe deposit, based on what we saw yesterday. Not to mention the $420,000 in cash we found in there," Braddock said. "So, you know, nothing at all suspicious about that."

"The bank?" Boe said.

"The bank is monitoring for any suspicious withdrawals or transfers, but perhaps we need to flip that focus. This might not have been about him providing access to someone from the outside, but that perhaps this was about money that had already moved from inside the bank out."

"Embezzlement?" Boe said. "He was stealing?"

"Possibly," Braddock said. "If what Teddy heard was correct, and if what we found in that safe deposit box is a sign, I think we need to take a long look at that. The bank says no unusual electronic banking activity occurred yesterday. The money? I'm starting to think it was already gone."

"Were those accounts at Rapids Community Bank?"

"Not in his name or the name on the safe deposit box. We should investigate there. We should investigate at Lakes Community Bank. We tell Elaine Baird about this, and I can't imagine she won't start digging into every single thing that Marist did there. I mean, unless he was dealing drugs, where else does he come up with $420,000 cash plus whatever else he had. Where else would he have access to money like that?"

"And you think it leads us to who is responsible for all this?" Boe said.

"It's one avenue to pursue," Braddock said.

"What else?"

"The more," Tori said.

"Ah, what Jared Bayne alluded to. What are you all thinking that is? Do you think they planned to go after someone else?"

"We don't know," Braddock said.

"Not knowing leaves me feeling very uneasy," Tori said.

"Me too."

"Maybe it's over after the last firefight last night," Boe posited. "There's too much heat to keep hanging around. They have to get out of here."

"Do you want to bank on that?" Tori replied.

"I take it you don't."

"Jeanette, we don't know who they are. *They* had the money. Jared didn't have it. Yet these guys just kept coming and coming last night. They were not to be deterred. They must have thought Jared spilled the beans to me, or Teddy, or both of us and they had to kill us before we were able to tell anyone else. It's the only thing that makes any sense. And to go to those lengths? They could have died just as easily as Teddy and I out there. Whatever it is that Jared meant about 'more,' it sure seems to mean an awful lot to them."

"I see your point," Boe murmured warily. "We need to keep Teddy Marist protected. I'll see to that. While I do that, what are you two doing? Coming back here?"

"First, Two Coves. We need to retrieve some things, and we have some questions for Newell DeBoer," Braddock said.

With improving road conditions, they reached the Two Coves Tavern in a half-hour. Reese parked next to Braddock's Tahoe, still in the same position it had been the night before, but the snow had been dusted off it. Inside, they found DeBoer and the same three men from the night before. DeBoer was dressed again in his baggy blue jeans and suspenders, albeit with a different flannel shirt.

Tori went to the same barstool she'd taken last night. DeBoer, not missing a beat, put a warm cup of coffee in front of her. He opened a drawer behind the bar and retrieved Tori's phone, keys, and the magazine for her Glock, which she immediately slid into her gun. "I never thought I'd say this to someone in law enforcement. But truly, I'm relieved to see you."

Tori nodded. "I'm sorry about your nephew," she said softly to DeBoer, before taking a small drink of the hot coffee. "If it's any consolation at all, he died giving his life for mine and Teddy Marist. He held them off so that we could get away."

"Thank you for that," DeBoer said, nodding in resignation, leaning on the counter. "The Becker County Sheriff gave me some details of what they found out at Bud's house and what happened after. I'm glad your friends found you." He turned to Braddock. "That snowplow driver got you out there?"

"Yeah. Not sure we make it otherwise."

"I don't think you do." DeBoer shook his head.

Tori explained in general terms what happened. "I think I was followed out there to the house."

"They followed her tracks," Braddock said. "That's how *we* found her."

DeBoer and the other men all nodded, all lamenting they hadn't thought of that ahead of time.

"Those men showed up not but a few minutes behind me. Jared took the fire and covered me while I got away with Teddy Marist," Tori said quietly. "Your nephew knew he was going to die."

"Yesterday fully illustrated that he lived a life of many unwise moves," DeBoer said. "At least he went out with some shred of honor."

"Yes, a small late bit of it," Tori said.

"Had I any idea that was possible last night, I'd have never arranged all that," DeBoer said. "I'd have found another way."

"One thing I have been wondering about ever since was why he got involved with all that yesterday, an accomplice in three murders, yet then flipped, and saved Teddy Marist. I couldn't figure it. Then I read the file Detective Reese put together on him."

"And?"

"He has an eleven-year-old son, Jordan."

"Yes," DeBoer said, nodding.

"Did he have a relationship with him?"

"He tried; I have to say, he really honestly did but didn't have any idea of how to be a father. Jared was family, but he was who he was, a screw-up. Jordan's mother realized Jared's many shortcomings right quick and didn't double down on her mistake. She finished her schooling, became a nurse, married a stable guy she met in Park Rapids, and got full legal and physical custody of Jordan. To her credit, she didn't ask for a plug nickel from Jared, not that he had even that. Her husband was originally from Spokane, Washington and they moved there. Not long after that, Jared left for North Carolina."

"Why?"

"He wanted away from here, away from all his failures. He was bitter."

"At?"

"The world. The world didn't give him much to work with and he always struggled to find his place in it. He went with Colum Mercer, who had some family down that way as I recall."

"Mercer had family in North Carolina?" Braddock said.

"Yes, I think so. Distant cousins or some such thing."

Braddock nodded to Reese who took out his phone, walking away. "You were saying about Mercer?"

"As compared to Jared, Colum wasn't so much of a screw-up as he had more a screw or two loose. A bit of a *baaaaad* seed."

"Violent?"

DeBoer nodded. "He wasn't afraid of it. He got into a couple of bad fights, one happened out in the road right out there. Put a guy in the hospital, beat him so bad. He liked guns. Had run-ins with the sheriff. While you might find this hard to believe, I try and run a clean place here. I don't want trouble. As Ewell said last night, we're not big fans of people like you, we just want to be left alone, but I see no reason to pick fights with y'all either."

"Nor us with you," Braddock said.

"I might take issue with that after how you came in here all hot last night," Ewell charged.

Braddock turned to Ewell. "I had to find her. You, and the rest of ya sent her out into that shit last night with nothing. Nothing! So, fuck you!"

"Eaaaassy," Tori said quietly, turning to Braddock.

"Ewell," DeBoer groaned, shaking his head. "Read the room, would ya."

"Well, fuck. He did—"

"Enough! Last night is over."

"Fucker," Ewell griped, getting up off his stool, taking his beer, walking away.

DeBoer watched Ewell walk away. "He is particularly aggrieved by your presence."

"MN Partisans?" Tori asked.

"Yeah," DeBoer nodded. "He had some kin mixed up in all that. He has issues with how the state handled it. We all do, but I'm not telling you anything you don't already know."

Braddock, having calmed himself, shifted gears. "You mentioned Mercer last night. You also said Jared had been back for a month or so."

"Yes."

"And you saw him once at his house?"

"And once here."

"When was he here?"

"It was a month ago, a Saturday night. I think he'd just gotten back. He stopped in one night with Colum and two other men that I didn't recognize."

"Did Jared introduce the others?"

"No, he didn't but Jared doesn't really think that way. Plus, we don't wait on the tables here. If you want a drink, you come to the bar. If you order food, you come up here, order, get a number and we'll call it out when it's ready and you come pick it up."

"And Jared just came to the bar?"

"Yes."

"And how long were they here?"

"Not that long. A round of drinks, maybe two, is all. In and out."

"Do you remember what these men looked like?" Tori said.

DeBoer grimaced. "I figured you'd ask that. I just had glimpses of them, from here so my descriptions might be a bit fuzzy." He took a drink of coffee and thought for a moment. "One guy was a huskier fella, thick, with dark-black hair, woolly unkempt beard that we see a lot of these days. The other was taller. He had dark hair, rounded glasses, a full beard too, but it was trimmed up a bit more."

Braddock looked to Tori. "Ring any bells from last night?"

Tori sighed. "It was dark. I never got up close to those guys. There were three of them."

"And the other time you saw Jared?" Braddock said. "It was him and Mercer, right?"

"Yes. Despite all his troubles, Jared still owned his family's house, inherited it from his mother. It's paid for. Jared just needed to keep up with the taxes which weren't all that much. In any event, a couple times a week, I would swing by and make sure it was still standing. I went to check on the house one day and he was in the workshop in the garage."

"Workshop?" Tori said. "Doing what?"

"Woodworking. Looked like he and Colum were working on something."

"What?"

DeBoer scoffed. "I didn't look closely, or ask. Things were

still standing, they looked busy, and I needed to get to the bar here, so I wasn't there long."

Braddock took out a search warrant that Reese had brought along. "Why don't we go out and take a look. It's for the whole premises."

DeBoer read the warrant and then called to Ewell. "I need you to drive me over to Jared's."

"Why me? I don't want to go out there with... them."

"Well, you're gonna."

"Drive yourself."

"I can't. I loaned my truck out to someone last night and she didn't return it," DeBoer replied, winking at Tori.

They followed DeBoer and Ewell to the house. Ewell was also asked to drive because he had a plow blade on the front of his pickup truck. DeBoer took out a key ring and opened the side door for the garage and let them inside.

"If Jared had one reasonably good skill, it was woodworking. He had no formal training, but my brother Bud is a woodworking wizard and he taught Jared enough so that he could work at a cabinet making shop." DeBoer walked to a Miter saw on a long sturdy wood table. "Jared and Colum were working here with that wood I think."

"What were they making?" Reese asked, picking up a piece of wood.

"Colum said a box for a friend of theirs. It looked like there were a few pieces. He had the electric screwdriver and power drill out. I shot the breeze with them for a few minutes, but I didn't stay real long. I had just driven by to check on the place is all."

Braddock picked up one of the pieces of wood. "Cherry wood, right?"

"Yes," DeBoer said. "Not uncommon for cabinetry. Bud built me some shelves in my house from it some years ago."

There was a can of paint on a nearby table, along with newspaper laid out, with dark blue smears on it. "Were they painting too?" Tori asked, looking at a small can of Columbia Blue paint.

"Not that I saw. They said they were going to be an hour or two and that would be that," DeBoer said. "I remember saying take all the time they wanted, it was Jared's place. I invited them to stop by the bar after they were done."

"And did they?"

"No. I never saw him again after that and didn't talk to him again until he called me last night. You all want to take a quick run through the house?"

As they walked over to the house, Reese stepped back, holding up his phone. "Becker County Sheriff's. I should take this."

They spent just a few minutes in the small two-story boxy house. It did not appear that Jared had spent any time inside. Sheets still covered what little furniture remained. The utilities were shut off. "Has nobody lived here?"

"Off and on, I've rented the place out to either relatives or friends who needed a place for a bit. Split the money with Jared, mailing his half off to him down south. Right now, she's winterized, the water is off and such. Now, I imagine Bud and I will have to figure out what to do with it. Sell it and send the proceeds to Jordan maybe," DeBoer said. "I suspect that's what Jared would have wanted."

"Your brother Bud might need to stay here," Braddock remarked. "His house is all shot up. There's gonna be a fair amount of work required out there."

"So I've been told."

"If Jared wasn't staying here, where was he staying?" Tori said to DeBoer.

"You know, I don't know," DeBoer replied. "I never asked."

"Mercer has an RV," Braddock mused. "We should add urgency to that search."

When they stepped outside, Reese was waiting. "A Becker County deputy found a body riddled with bullet holes on the far north end of the Tamarac National Wildlife Refuge. BCA is sending someone. It looks like it's Colum Mercer. They found the body just south of County 113 and just east of Elbow Lake."

"Is that a town?" Tori said.

"No, the lake," DeBoer replied, shaking his head. "You think this area is desolate, wait until you get up there."

* * *

A plow had been through an hour ago, clearing a path on the road, pushing a large pile of snow to the left of the driveway, before it circled around and plowed the road wider on the way out. Never looked twice at the house.

Where is she? Max left home over two hours ago.

Towne paced the front of the cabin, peeking through the curtain gap, looking for any sign. His phone rang.

"Two minutes," Max said.

Finally.

He saw the black Jeep Cherokee turn down the road toward the house. He assisted Jenks up out of his chair and slowly walked him into the garage and out to the SUV, helping him up into the back seat from the passenger side, while Max had jumped over from the driver's side and helped him get comfortable. Once he was in the seat and buckled in, Max leaned in and kissed him, gently cupping his bearded face in her hands. "How are you?"

"I need some tending to, Maxie, honey."

Carefully, she pulled back his winter coat and shirt, examining the crude blood-soaked bandaging job. "We best get you home."

She got back into the driver's seat and leaned over and hugged her brother. "Sorry I couldn't get here sooner. There is a cooler with sandwiches and drinks back there and a couple of ice packs," Max said as she drove away from the house and down the road.

Sore as he was, Jenks flipped open the cooler with his right hand and handed up a soda and sandwich, before grabbing ones for himself, as well as a soft ice pack, which he gently positioned on his shoulder. "That actually feels kinda good."

Max turned left and they could see the county road up ahead, that road visibly cleared. She handed a small pill bottle to Towne. "Vicodin."

"Give me that fucking Vicodin," Jenks said.

Towne opened the bottle, took a pill for himself and then handed it back.

"Oh shit," Max squeaked, jamming on the brakes.

"What?" Towne yelped, turning around.

Coming from the east were two sets of flashing police lights. Two sheriff's Chevy Tahoe's with grill lights roared past, heading west, not having even given them a look.

Towne looked back to Jenks. "Merc?"

"Could be."

"Merc?" Max said. "What? They found his body?"

"Maybe," Towne said, explaining where they dumped the body. "I figured the snow would cover him and he wouldn't be found until we were long gone."

Max shook her head. "You should have made damn sure, brother. Damn sure!"

"Easy, Maxie," Jenks said.

Towne turned to his sister. "You weren't there last night. You weren't out here. We didn't have the time to shovel a fuckin' hole and bury him."

"I know, I know," Maxie said, sighing. "Sorry. It's just that we're so close is all. So close."

* * *

The drive took twenty minutes in the daylight on ever more cleared roads, Braddock following Reese. When they arrived, two sheriff's deputies were parked along the side of a partially plowed road. Braddock evaluated the map and then shook his head. "Earl, he's a savant."

"What?" Tori asked.

Braddock tweezed the map a little smaller and pointed to the lower right corner. "We found you there. Last night Earl said you would have reached a T a few miles ahead, if you went right, you'd eventually get to County 113. When those guys got away, what do you bet they hit that T, turned north, and dumped the body just before they reached the main road."

Tori and Braddock peered to the bottom of the ditch and a small area of cattails where two legs were sticking out. "Any identification?" Braddock asked.

"No wallet but he was shot several times and we've heard all about the shoot-out south of here," the deputy said. "And we have this photo, and it looks like a match." It was the North Carolina driver's license photo.

Reese, wearing thick winter boots, carefully made his way down with the deputy and from a few feet away, examined the body and a photo on his phone for confirmation. "It's him alright. Shot, several times. Once in his left leg, several in his upper torso and once in the head, just above his left ear." He looked up to Tori. "Nice shooting."

"Might have been Braddock," Tori replied and glanced back to see two vans coming down the road. It was forensics and the medical examiner. "They just dumped him," she muttered. "Like they were tossing garbage."

"He was one of the men trying to kill you and Teddy," Braddock murmured.

"I'm not saying he didn't get what was coming to him. But the ones who dumped him?" Tori said. "The ones who killed Jared, killed Teddy's parents, Ed Girard, certainly didn't give two hoots about their man down there."

"Two hoots?" Reese needled.

"Fine. Two shits if you like," Tori retorted. "Point is, they just coldly dumped his body and moved on. These guys have no regard for human life."

"You expected a burial? He was dead with that head shot," Braddock replied, nonplussed. "These guys were in survival mode but, your broader point is right, these guys are killers."

* * *

The drive south to Max's house took nearly three hours because of a stop at the RV. They wiped it down, got everything they needed, and would not return. While Towne drove the white Tahoe, Max drove her Jeep Cherokee, Jenks uncomfortably riding in the back.

The roads may have been plowed but they remained treacherous with hardened snow and ice that made for a less than smooth ride that required an abundance of driving caution. She had her hands at two and ten on the wheel for the whole drive. More than once she'd felt the back end of her Jeep Cherokee wiggle enough to cause discomfort. *Keep it on the road*, especially with the cargo under the big blanket in the back.

Max took the exit off the H-4 just south of Holmstrand and then drove two miles east on the icy county road before turning onto a winding but roughly plowed road and then into the narrow driveway to her one-story ranch-style house. She hit the garage door opener as she came up the driveway and pulled into the empty space, Towne parking in the driveway behind her.

She and Towne helped Jenks inside the house and sat him down in a chair at the kitchen table. While Towne helped Jenks shed his jacket and shirt, Max grabbed a desk lamp with an extended arm. She adjusted the light to hang over Jenks's left shoulder and then carefully pulled the blood-soaked bandages away from the wound.

"*Grrrraaaah*," Jenks growled. "Fucking hurts."

Max and Towne inspected the bullet wound under the bright light.

"It doesn't look infected, though I worry," Max said, getting close, sliding on her reading glasses, touching around the wound, Jenks wincing in pain as she did.

"Can you sew him closed?"

"Going to have to." She looked Jenks in the eye, cupping his chin firmly in her left hand. "It's going to hurt, more than a bit. You need to sit still."

"I'm on the Vicodin. Just get it done."

Towne poured himself a whiskey and one for Jenks, while Max organized new bandages, sterilized a sturdy needle, and then threaded it.

Jenks held his glass out and Towne filled it with whiskey.

"He's on the pain meds," Max protested. "That's enough."

"Fuck it," Jenks replied, slamming the whiskey. "Battlefield anesthesia."

She sat down at the table and examined the wound again under the bright light, pulling on thin rubber gloves from her first aid kit.

"Sew me up."

Max went to work on the wound, plunging the needle into the skin just to the left of the wound and Jenks immediately seized up.

"Sit still."

"You sit still!"

She looked to Towne. "Stand behind him. Hold him still."

Towne took position and Max put the needle in for another stitch.

Jenks sucked air in as the needle dug in.

"The money is safe?" He grunted through gritted teeth as she pushed and then pulled the needle through. He might have been hopped up on Vicodin mixed with whiskey, but he was still feeling the penetration of the needle through the inflamed skin and tissue around the wound.

"Yes, and half of the transactions have cleared now. The rest will clear by Monday I should think. It's accessible from anywhere, which works with our timeline," Max said as she pulled the needle and then plunged it in again.

"Ouch. Fuck!"

"Sorry. I'm not a nurse. I'm doing my best," she replied, grabbing his chin, eyeing him. "Sit very still and we'll get done a little sooner. Quit flinching, you big baby."

"Man up," Towne half-teased.

"Yeah, yeah. I don't see no big holes in you, pussy." Jenks took another drink of whiskey.

"And that's enough of that!" Max charged, before looking to Towne, who reached out his hand for the bottle. Jenks reluctantly handed it to him.

Max got back to work, pushing the needle in. "The question, now is," Max said as she pulled the needle through for another stitch, "I know I said earlier we're so close, but I think we have to talk about our situation. The money, do we take it and run for good. Or do we stay and finish this."

"We finish it!" Jenks growled. "This was never about the money. It wasn't that much money to begin with."

"Maybe not when you were splitting it five ways," Max replied as she threaded another stitch, the wound now starting to close. "We've got two fewer mouths to feed now. It's more substantial when you compound the interest over time."

"You'd know all about that," Towne remarked.

"Well, I don't give a damn about any of that," Jenks said and then turned Max's face to his. "Do you?"

"I want to gut Cooper Farrow like a fish," she said, taking a moment to inspect the wound, assessing if she should keep the stitches a bit closer together before she dug the needle in again. "The question is can we after all this. After losing Jared and Merc. What do you think, brother?"

"I feel like you do."

"That's not the question. The question is do you want to walk or finish it?" Jenks asserted.

"You know what I want."

"Rephrase. Are we going to finish it?"

Max pulled the needle through one last time and then knotted it off before cutting the thread. She cleaned the wound with a cotton ball soaked in alcohol, and they then covered it with gauze and a large bandage.

"I asked a fuckin' question," Jenks railed after she'd finished. "I want a fuckin' answer."

Max turned to her brother. "What do you think?"

"They, this Braddock and Hunter, must still be looking for us. If we do this, I want to succeed. I want to make a statement. I'm not afraid of dying, but I'm not on a suicide mission either."

"I never said you were," Jenks replied.

"Any reason to believe the law back home can connect Mercer and Jared to you two? And you two to me?" Max said, now pouring herself a whiskey, her doctoring complete.

"No, I don't think so," Towne answered.

"They *were* both at the farm that day," Jenks warned.

"Yeah, but way up the mountain from us. They were never apprehended, remember. They stayed up the mountain for a week before they dared even come down. They never got caught up in the dragnet of all that."

"Still." Jenks sighed. "The sheriff or state police back home could start poking around, asking questions, making connections for these guys here. If they talked with some of our old friends, one of them could put them with us."

"Any reason to believe they would?" Max said.

"Anything is possible, but... no," Towne said. "I don't think so. First off, we all kind of went our separate ways. I'm not sure where a lot of the guys from back then are. Now, a few might still be hanging around Linville and Boone but I've heard nothing so far and if the law came poking around, you and I would have heard, and we haven't."

"Well then—" Max started.

"Well then what?"

"They have to know *who* you are before they can look for, let alone find you. I've seen nothing to suggest that they know *who* you are."

"She has a point," Jenks asserted.

Towne took a moment, sipping his whiskey before nodding. "She does at that."

TWENTY-THREE

"THE SMART ALECK STUFF IS YOUR DOING."

Five minutes into the drive back to Manchester Bay from Elbow Lake, Tori laid her head against Braddock's shoulder and her eyes drifted closed. When she woke, it was almost an hour later. She caught sight of a green road sign that said Pine River – 10 miles.

She took in the broad expanse of land in the late afternoon sunlight, letting mile after mile of the pure bright white landscape go by. This road was particularly picturesque in that it alternately cut through wide open fields and then dense forests of pine trees.

"It's pretty."

"Ansel Adams could take pictures of this for days," Braddock said. "Amazing that you can find beauty in something that was so miserable last night. But I see it now, and it makes me wish I had found my way up into the Adirondack Mountains in the winter when I lived back east. It must be beautiful up there."

"Really? You're a native New Yorker and you never went up to Lake Placid?"

"I had great parents, but they were not explorers. I bet they flew less than five times in their lives. They literally lived their entire life in their little universe on Long Island. They were city through and through. You and I were in the middle of all this last night, and it was awful. But to look at it now."

"It's almost tranquil."

"*Not* like in New York City. We'd get a Nor'easter every so often, dump a foot, eighteen inches of snow on us, but it never looked like this."

Tori laughed. "In Manhattan a big snow looked good for about two hours and then it was a sloppy and dirty hellscape until it all melted."

She sat up and stretched her arms, yawning. "I took a nap."

"You were out cold."

"The world went away for a little bit," she replied, moving her neck side to side, unkinking it. "Where are we at?"

"While you napped, I've been thinking."

"About?"

"North Carolina."

"Jared Bayne and Colum Mercer going down there."

"Yeah. Something happened down there that brought them up here. What's odd is while you napped, I called Tony Darr. He said neither his sister nor Marist had any ties to North Carolina."

Tori thought for a moment. "Mercer and Jared Bayne do but that begs the question as to what their connection to Ed Girard, Lainey Darr or Barry Marist is?"

"Perhaps they're not the ones with the connection," Braddock said. "Towne was on the phone with this Max. I get the sense that Mercer and Bayne were the help and this Towne and this Max, are the brains behind the whole operation."

She agreed with that insight. "Which begs the question still, what's the North Carolina connection?"

"Boe, Reese, and Nolan, are going to try and rustle up some assistance in North Carolina. See if we can attack this problem from there. Get to whatever family Mercer has down there and see if they know who Mercer and Bayne were running with. I'm not sure what else to do. And... I'm completely fried from the last thirty-six hours."

"I hear that."

Tori re-situated herself as they came into the small town of Pine River. Braddock turned south onto the H-4. A half-hour to home.

"What is Quinn doing tonight?"

"Sleepover at a friend's house. It's been planned all week, so he won't be back until about noon tomorrow. Our night is free. Dinner somewhere?" The sun was nearly gone for the day.

She thought for a moment. "I just want to go home and be warm. How about some easy takeout?"

"You choose."

Tori called their favored Chinese place. "Should be ready right as you pull into town."

Quinn was home packing his overnight bag when they got home, and they got to spend a few minutes with him. Tori held the hug from him for an extra couple of seconds. She laughed inwardly. Quinn was in seventh grade and was a couple of inches taller than her now.

"I heard you got Teddy Marist back," he said to Tori.

"We did."

"But, man. His parents."

"He has an aunt and uncle who seem like good people who are already with him. He'll be in good hands."

"Still, though," Quinn said.

"Be grateful you have this guy," Tori said, smiling at Braddock.

"I am," Quinn said, giving his dad knuckles. "I gotta bounce."

"You gotta *bounce*?" Braddock said, while Tori laughed.

"It's a new one for you, Dad. You guys working tomorrow?"

"Probably have to some," Braddock said. "Uncle Drew will pick you and Pete up tomorrow and we'll go from there."

"Gotcha."

A car horn honked outside and just like that he was out the door.

While Tori set out their takeout Chinese food, grabbing plates and spoons, Braddock made quick work of opening a bottle of white wine for her and extracting a Corona from the refrigerator for himself.

They relaxed at the center island in the kitchen, eating and talking about Quinn.

"I only got five minutes with him," Braddock mused. "I should say 'we' only got five minutes with him."

"*We* better get used to it," Tori said with a sly grin. "He's thirteen. A teenager. For the next several years, your child is not going to listen to you. He might listen to me, but he'll think you're an idiot."

Braddock laughed. "We'll see."

"Uh-huh. Just you wait," Tori needled.

"How awful were you as a teen?"

"I beg your pardon," Tori replied in mock offense.

"This is me you're talking to. Confess."

Tori thought for a second. "I was like any other teen girl, at times a complete hormonal emotional terror, although Jessie was worse, she had a lot more drama to her than me. Big Jim was a single parent, like you. He had his hands full with her and me, but especially Jess. She was the one to push the rules."

"And you were the rule follower?"

"I colored inside the lines, and she was more free form."

"Hah! The contrast of identical twins."

"I was the ying to Jessie's yang, I suppose. Jessie would

decide what we were doing a lot of the time, and I was there with her."

"Participating."

"Yep. The sheriff knew all this. He sat us down when we were sophomores in high school. We were both invited to a party where there might be alcohol. He told us to have our fun, but don't do anything stupid, and he defined what that was."

"Which was?"

"Anything that would embarrass him as sheriff," Tori said.

"I'll probably have to have that kind of talk with Quinn at some point?"

"I know you'll have to have it. But that's okay. He has been well raised and has a good head on his shoulders. That's your doing."

Braddock nodded. "Thanks."

Tori nodded, taking a long sip of her wine, finishing off her glass.

He stood up and walked to her, picking up the wine bottle, pouring her another glass. "There is one difference between me and your father."

"What's that?"

"I'm not alone. I have you now."

"I'm not his—"

"Mother? You don't have to be. What matters is he thinks the world of you. I've heard you two tell each other you love one another."

"You've heard that, huh?"

"Yes. I can't tell you what a comfort it is just having you here to even have *this* talk."

"Well, I do love the kid. Smart aleck that he is."

"The smart aleck stuff is your doing."

"Is not!"

"*Right*," Braddock said, kissing her. "Different subject, you met with Professor Silby the other day. How did that go?"

Tori took a sip of her wine. She had been thinking they needed to talk about this. "He offered me a full-time teaching gig." She recapped the conversation. "I was surprised."

"I'm not."

"Really."

"I could see it coming a mile away. They'd be *crazy* not to want you. You already were a prized get for them, just to teach one class, but to have you a full member of the faculty? That's a big hire for them."

"You think?"

"I know. The university has grown leaps and bounds towards becoming a major university. Division I sports, discussions of a law school, the symbiotic relationship with Mannion Companies, this political event on Tuesday, is all part of that long-term growth plan. You're a little piece of that too. Your career with the Bureau. The cases you've worked. The people you know and have access to, with the Bureau and locally."

"Locally?"

"Come on, Tor. You think hiring you would go unnoticed by Kyle Mannion? Or that the university doesn't know how good a friends you are with him and his brother Eddie? This isn't just about teaching a couple of classes. You're more than just a professor for them. You bring unique cachet that they will, in time, no doubt want to leverage."

"I hadn't thought of it like that. How did you get so smart?"

"I have the superpower of observation. But the question is, do you want to do it? Teach more. Is that where you think you're heading?"

She took a moment, before nodding. "I like it. I like the students, seeing them get it. That's fun."

"Then I say do it. Can I still call you when I need you?"

"I told Silby I wouldn't even consider it if I couldn't."

"And he said great, right?"

"Yeah."

"I figured as much. It's because of what you've done, what you do, is why they want more of you. I totally get it."

"So," Tori started. "You'd be okay with that?"

Braddock grinned. "Absolutely. If it's what you want to do, I'll back your play all the way. But—"

"But?"

"Promise me you're not going to start dressing like an academic."

Tori smiled. "You still want the fashionista?"

"I love the fashionista. She's a total smoke show."

"Ha!" Tori giggled. "I kind of think the university likes that part of me too."

"I bet they do," Braddock said, leaning down and kissing her again. "I'll clean up."

"I'm going to go upstairs and take a very warm, very long bath," Tori said, grabbing her wine glass and bottle, looking back to him, catching his eye as she slowly walked up the stairs.

Tori drew the bath in the large whirlpool tub, and lit a couple of candles, dimming the lights. She swirled her hair up in a tie and dropped herself down into the tub. Lying against one end, two of the tub's jets massaging the sore muscles of her mid back. She took a long drink of her white wine and let her eyes drift closed, leaning her head back against a soft white towel, the warm water soothing her aching body. Marlena Shaw's *California Soul* played lightly from her songs from movies playlist.

Relaxing.

The events of the last twenty-four hours still swirled in her mind. But however recent they were, they were in the past. And if she had become better at anything through all the therapy, it was letting the past be the past, whether distant or recent. You can't go back in time to fix things, so handle what's coming, and forget about what already happened.

Life wasn't just that simple, of course. She was who she was, with a hard-wired difficulty letting certain things go, but it was a healthy way of thinking that she was trying to live by. And she wasn't doing it on her own. If she was a comfort to Braddock when it came to raising Quinn, he was a comfort to her when it came to coping with her past. He was the master at putting something in the file drawer and forgetting about it. She envied that about him and strived to emulate it and not without some small success along the way.

She exhaled a breath as Dusty Springfield's "Son of a Preacher Man" filled the room. She loved the song, having added it to the playlist after she'd heard it recently when she and Braddock re-watched *Pulp Fiction*.

It was a great scene where Vincent goes to pick Mia up for their arranged date. Mia tells Vincent to mix a drink while she finishes getting ready. "Story of my life," Braddock had quipped. "Having a drink, waiting for you to get ready."

"Oh, you're so aggrieved."

There was a light splash into the other end of the tub, and she allowed herself a smile.

Braddock.

She opened her eyes to see him dropping his long, lean, and fully naked body into the other end of the bathtub, a fresh bottle of Corona in his hand. "Mind if I join?"

Tori smiled and took another drink of her wine. "I was rather hoping you would."

"Why don't you come down my way," Braddock suggested.

"What did you have in mind?"

"Rubbing your shoulders and back."

"I was rather hoping you would do that too. They are very much in need of your attention."

Tori handed him her wine glass and made her way to him, turning around and sliding between his legs.

"Wow," he said as he started lightly rubbing her shoulders.

"What?"

"Your shoulders, the muscles, are so tight, they're like rocks."

"It's been a day, or two," she replied, taking a drink of wine.

"That it has," he said, leaning down and kissing her neck, whispering, "Let's see if we can do something about that."

"I do rather like it when you tend to me like this."

"You've earned it," he said. "In light of recent events." He kissed her neck again, wrapping his long arms around her, pulling her close. "As I lay here with you, I must admit at times you do amaze me."

"And how might that be?" she asked, turning to her left, glancing back.

He whispered into her ear, "That someone so small, such a pretty fashionista, can be yet... so fierce."

Tori offered a little smile. "An irresistible package."

"Mmm, it is," he said, easing her away just enough to massage her shoulders and back.

There were many things she loved about her big lug of a man, one of which was despite his big bear paw like hands and long fingers, he possessed a remarkably tender touch.

They talked and laughed, the music playing softly as she sipped her wine and he gently rubbed her neck, shoulders, and arms, occasionally stopping to take a drink of his beer.

And he was right, she must have been knotted up because as he slowly kneaded her neck and shoulders, she could feel her muscles releasing, the tension fading, her mind clearing. Her light moans of approval only served to further encourage his continued attention to every inch of her shoulders, neck, back and then she laid back against his chest and he lightly caressed her temples, and she felt the warmth and safety of his long body beneath her.

She felt herself drifting into an almost light trance-like state, as if she was floating. He brushed her neck with his lips as his hands gradually explored the rest of her body, his hands gently touching and caressing her breasts, ribs, and stomach before his left hand slid lower.

"Hmmm," she purred at his touch. "That feels so good."

Her eyes closed, she leaned back into him, arching her back, her hips moving to his now rhythmic touch, slowly reaching her left arm back around his neck, turning her face to him, drawing his mouth to hers, her lips and tongue soft to his, letting her body go.

"Ooooh, mmm," she moaned breathily, savoring in the feel of her trembling body.

Letting out a long breath, her body calming and completely at ease, she slowly turned and let him pull her forward to straddle him. She leaned in for a soft kiss as she lowered herself to him.

* * *

Jenks, for all his bravado, was weary and they helped him to bed so that he could rest. Towne and Max returned to the kitchen and sat down with beers.

"If we're going to do this, you're going to have to go in with me," Towne said to his sister.

"Me?"

"He can't. It's a two-person job."

"Then you better show me."

Towne and Max emptied her Jeep, and he laid all their materials out on the workbench in the garage. To complete Jenks's earlier metaphor, as the surgeon he ran through what he needed Max to do to help him be as efficient as possible.

"All the pieces are pre-cut, and pre-drilled," he said. "They're stained and painted and should be a match."

"And you're sure it'll take the weight?"

Towne nodded confidently. "We tested it."

"And the explosives?" she said, examining the gray blocks of C-4. "That'll all fit in there?"

"Yes, the bricks, blasting caps, timer. And we'll use this—" he held up a small black device that looked like a small cell phone "—to trigger the timer."

Max nodded. "I see."

"It'll take me fifteen to twenty minutes to disassemble and then reassemble the podium. We just have to get in there with enough time to work without anyone seeing us. While I'm working, you'll be keeping an eye out. And if Jenks is up to it, we'll have him as a second set of remote eyes."

Max nodded. "Do you set the timer then?"

"No. We'll do that the day of. And I'll need to be close to activate it. Once our window opens, I'll set it for fifteen minutes. That'll leave enough time to get far enough away, yet be close enough to see it all go down."

Towne packed everything up, wrapping the individual wood pieces in fabric. The rest he put in a backpack, and he checked their coveralls. Max was tall enough to wear the coverall, but it would hang a little loose.

When he came back inside the house, he found his sister standing in the living room, peering out of a small vertical gap in the curtains for the front picture window, a glass of whiskey in her hand. He poured a drink of his own and joined her, peering outside on a clear night. Even in the darkness, the fresh snow, bright white, framed the length and width of her property.

She had a wide lot. Three acres she'd said when he and Jenks stayed when they first had arrived. He leaned forward a bit. Scattered specks of rectangular and squared interior lights for distant houses were visible through the otherwise dense woods to the left and the right. No doubt you wouldn't be able see the other houses in the peak of summer when all the leaves and ground vegetation filled in.

"The view reminds me of home, you know," Towne

observed. "No mountains here and more snow for sure, but the woods, the peace and quiet, nobody bugging you out here. None of that crazy fascist city communist shit. At least not that I've seen."

"This isn't Minneapolis or St. Paul but don't kid yourself, it's *all* making its way here," Max said. "It creeps in like an invasive weed. It comes with the money and there is a lot of money here and more people like that Girard guy come here every year, scooping up prime land on all the best lakes, tearing down modest cabins or homes, replacing them with million-dollar monstrosities and pricing out all the locals or working-class folks."

Towne nodded. "All that shit sure seems to follow, doesn't it? I've talked to some friends out in Montana. All those wealthy west-coast types moving into the Bozeman area, buying up all the land, talking about how they want to be away from the city but what they really want is the city for a cheaper price." He took a drink of Scotch. "They don't want to adjust to live there, they want life in Montana to adjust to them."

"But when people like us push back? Like the Partisans here last year. Like Rod and Warrick, some bureaucrat in some big city says we have to comply with this law or that. And we fight for our freedoms and what do they do? They send in the sheriffs and the state police types or the Feds to come after us. Us! The ones who live there." She exhaled a breath. "We were standing for our freedoms, for our way of life and they killed us for it. And Lainey Darr? She got what she had coming for all that crap she spewed about Rod, Warrick, all our friends all those years ago, all that stuff she'd go on television and say about people like us. I was here, brother. I was here and had to listen to that shit. And I had to see her, often. Yes, Mrs. Darr, no Mrs. Darr, of course, Mrs. Darr, whatever you need, so glad to help."

"I'm sorry for that."

"I just wish I could have been there when Jenks shot her. I wish I could have been the one to pull the trigger."

"Think you could have done it?"

Max turned to her brother, her eyes cold. "I know I could have."

"Well, sis, we're fighting back now. Just a couple more days is all," he said, clinking his sister's drink. "Finish your drink."

"Why?"

"I want to take a drive."

"Where?"

"Let's do a little late-night scouting."

TWENTY-FOUR

"FOLLOW THE MONEY."

Tori's eyes drifted open. The small clock on her nightstand said 9:43 a.m. That was late for her no matter what time she went to bed. She rolled over to find Braddock's side of the bed empty. Rolling onto her back, she stretched out under the blankets of their bed, naked yet comfortable and warm, the satisfying feelings of her bath and, all that went with it, still lightly percolating through her body. She turned her head to his pillow, breathing in the smell of him, when she heard the crashing of a pan down in the kitchen.

A few minutes later she made her way down the steps in her thick bathrobe and found him taking a carton of eggs out of the refrigerator. The kitchen smelled warmly of toast, coffee, and bacon. The newspaper spread out on the kitchen island. "Good morning."

"Good morning," he said, wrapping an arm around her as she moved in for a hug "Hungry?"

"Starved," she said.

A few minutes later, over easy eggs made, they sat down at the table with coffee and ate their breakfast. Braddock had pulled the shades for the windows and patio door open.

Northern Pine Lake was the brightest of whites, almost blinding, the new fresh blanket of white snow set against the deep greens of the pines and the crystal-clear blue sky above.

"Looks beautiful out there, doesn't it?"

"This is why you would never sell this place. The view is just so good. It amazes me sometimes how often I look out these windows and see just a perfect picture postcard," Tori replied, her legs pulled up under her even though sitting on the chair, sipping her coffee. She reached for her phone and took a couple of quick snaps. "I'm not sure an artist could do it justice, but I should have Lizzy try." Her friend Lizzy was an art history teacher at the university and an accomplished painter, particularly of landscapes. Tori had ruminated on having her paint the same view from their deck for the spring, summer, winter, and fall.

Vroom!

"That snowmobile is hauling ass," Tori blurted with a laugh.

"I already heard about a dozen of them zooming across the lake," Braddock said. "Those guys will be in heaven with all the new powder. And the skiers too, over at the ski slope, will be happy."

"Probably added another month of business," Tori said, but now a bit glumly. "It's February twenty-fifth. It'll be a while before it all melts. Spring could be very late."

"Good thing we have a spring break trip then." They had rented a house on Marco Island in Florida for school spring break in a month with his brother-in-law Drew and his family. It was becoming an annual trip. "This will make that warm weather feel all the sweeter."

They ate their breakfast, cleaned the plates, and then sat around the kitchen island, having another cup of coffee. She'd have liked nothing more than to just lounge around all day under a blanket and maybe read a book by the fire. But they were in the middle of it and there were far too many questions that needed answers.

"Did you check on Teddy?"

"Yes. He's being discharged from the hospital this morning. He'll have a police escort all the way down and while they're in town, until we give the all-clear."

Tori nodded. "He won't be truly safe until this is all over. We need to find the people he identified. We need to figure out what that 'more' is that Jared talked about."

Braddock checked his watch. "You hit the over."

"The over?"

"I set 11:00 a.m. as the betting line of when you'd bring this up. It's 11:20. I owe Reese ten bucks."

"Very funny."

"It was kind of funny," he said.

"Until you lost."

"I didn't factor you sleeping in so long. It must have been the lingering impact of all the sex."

"Please. It wasn't *that* great," Tori deadpanned.

"I kind of think it was," Braddock retorted.

Try as she might, she couldn't hold back a grin.

"That's what I thought. Tell you what. Let's get dressed, go see our boy at the hospital and then, after that, we'll head into the office and start puzzling it out."

* * *

Max's eyes flitted open, the morning light filtering in around the edges of the thick window curtains. She rolled over onto her left elbow. Jenks lay on his back, still sleeping, though he was sweaty, drops of perspiration on his brow.

She'd known him for twenty years, ever since her brothers started bringing him around the house in Boone. He was the handsome wild man with the flowing black locks and leather jacket riding a motorcycle who'd caught her eye when she'd looked up from her high school math assignment. Not long after, he was her first when she was just barely sixteen and he was twenty-one. Then he was gone, along with her brothers, to live their nomadic lives up in the mountains and she found her way off to college, and then marriage and then moving away. They'd run into each other a few times in passing over the years, usually around holiday times back home in North Carolina when she had come home to visit family, and he was tagging along with her brothers. After the incident at the farm, she had gone home for her brother Rodney's funeral. She remembered the night after Rod had been buried, the three of them sitting in the bar in Boone, talking about the thirst for payback.

"We'll have to be patient," Towne had said. "Jenks and I need to keep a very low profile as it is. After all this, the law will be keeping an eye on us. But someday, a chance will present itself and Farrow will pay."

Then the event at the university was announced. Cooper Farrow was coming to town. "This might be your chance up here in our little sleepy vacation area when their guard is down. And we can make it a real two-fer."

"How so?"

She explained it to him. They'd get Darr and Marist and then Farrow.

"It is at that," Towne had said, and she could hear the interest in his voice. "My little sis, the criminal mastermind."

"What do you think?"

"I think if we do all that, we all can *never* come back. That includes you, Max. We'd all have to leave for good. There will be no coming back from that. The government? They'll hunt for us forever."

"Well, that's why it's a two-fer. I have a way we can all go away in comfort if we're willing to get a little extra dirty first with Darr and Marist."

Towne came up for a look. He brought Jenks along, who took a long look at the opportunity and then another long look at Max. He and Towne were staying in the guest rooms in the basement. It wasn't long before there was a little late-night knock on her door. She didn't totally love the big woolly beard, but the rest of him sure felt nice.

Her brother liked the broad outlines of her plan and thought they had enough time to execute it. Jenks did as well but if they were going to do it, they needed some woodwork done. "I know just the men for it."

That's when Jared and Merc arrived. Two local guys. "And they'll both do whatever Jenks and I tell them, no questions asked. They always have. And they were both there *that* day. They'll want what we want and won't have any issue with what it takes."

She understood why they were needed, and it wasn't just because of Jared's skill around a saw. It would take at least three, and perhaps four men to pull off the deal with Darr, Girard and Marist and his kid. Nevertheless, she thought them both meatheads, an impression she shared with Jenks during pillow talk.

Jenks didn't disagree. "We need them. For now. After? We'll see how it all shakes out. Maybe we don't travel with five. The herd can always be culled."

The takedown of Marist went just as she'd planned it, with the storm an unexpected gift.

Then Marist threw a curveball.

She wouldn't say it to her brother, or to Jenks lying by her side all shot up, but she knew full well they got caught with their knickers down for Marist to get ahold of that gun.

Jenks stirred, taking in a breath, running his tongue over his lips. His eyes opened.

"You're a sweaty mop," Max said, leaning down to kiss him on the forehead. She thought the sweat had more to do with the heat being cranked up in her house than his wounds, which she had checked repeatedly overnight. "How are you feeling?"

"I'll live," he said, grimacing as he sat up. Despite his left arm being in a sling and the thick bandages, he was able to grunt his way through rotating his shoulder. It was a good thing he was right-handed. It would be a while before he was doing a lot with his left one. "Ain't gonna be nothing but another scar, Maxie." He'd had plenty to begin with.

There was a knock on the door. "Are you two up in there?"

She helped Jenks out of bed and the three of them gathered around her kitchen table. The weather had cleared, the sky a crisp blue, the sun bright and the temperature rising.

"I've been listening to the radio, watching television and searching the Internet," Towne said. He'd been at it for some time it appeared.

"And?" Jenks said.

"The media has Jared's name and Merc's now. There are stories about the kid, Teddy Marist, about how he was rescued. And the police are looking for two more men seen with Jared and Merc."

"Who would have seen you with the two of them?" Max asked.

"Maybe people at that bar out in Two Coves," Towne said. "I knew we shouldn't have gone there."

Jenks nodded. "It's why we left after just a couple of beers."

"The only other place might be the RV park. People could maybe give a general description, but no names," Towne replied.

"Unless they took down license plates," Max said.

Towne grimaced. "If someone did that, then that could be a problem, but who does that?"

"Nobody," Jenks said. "I ain't worried."

"You might want to be about this sheriff's detective, or his former FBI agent girlfriend."

"Tori Hunter." Max nodded. "I told you she might end up involved when we went down this path. Her and Will Braddock."

"There you go again sounding like you admire them," Jenks moaned. This was not their first discussion of the people who might investigate what they had set in motion.

"I could never admire people like them, what they think of and do to people like us. Never. But that doesn't mean I'm not wary of them. I've seen and read about what they're capable of."

"She's not wrong," Towne said. "Hunter got the best of us the other night."

Jenks waved dismissively. "We'd have taken her down had her friends not shown up."

Towne wasn't so sure. "She hit us. Unless it hasn't been reported, we never hit her."

"She's a smaller target." Jenks was not going to concede the point.

"Fine, you don't want to accept their danger to us, so I will. I've been reading up on them. Hunter specialized in missing children with the FBI. She was as decorated as any agent could be with the Bureau, man or woman. Braddock was NYPD, a detective who worked terrorism cases. Together, they've taken some people down and I have no doubt they're looking to do the same to us." He took a drink of coffee. "They're hunting us, probably as we speak."

"Hunting us how?"

"Some connection to Marist, or Jared or Merc."

"Or the kid," Max said. "You don't know what he knows."

"I think that if they had our names," Towne said, gesturing to Jenks. "Those names would be public by now, everyone would have them."

"But nothing?" Max said.

"Not that I've seen," Towne replied. "But I'm sure they're wondering why we tried so hard to track him and Jared down."

"They'll think we thought they knew something."

"Right," Towne said. "And while we never said anything to the kid, he probably heard a few things we wouldn't have wanted him to, but we only talked about his father, about where we were going, the resort and so forth."

"You called me," Max said.

"Yeah, but we never uttered your real name, sis. And we never talked about why we're *really* here." He looked to Jenks. "Did we?"

"No. Hell, Jared and Merc didn't know all the details, although they knew what the ultimate goal was."

"How is that possible?" Max asked.

"We kept that shit close," Jenks said. "The overall plan wouldn't have fazed Merc. But we didn't tell Merc everything because he would have told Jared, and he wasn't as… dependable."

Max frowned. "If you thought that, why did you bring him here?"

"We needed that base built," Towne said. "He built it—perfectly."

"And didn't he ask why you had him build it?"

"Jared and Merc knew in general what we were up here to accomplish, but they didn't know *all* the specifics."

"But they knew the target, right?"

"Yes."

"If Jared said anything about that?"

"It's like Maxie said last night, they have to know who they're looking for before they can find us. I think we'd know if they had identified us. Our names would be out there to the public. The event would be cancelled. I don't think they have any idea what's coming."

"That, and while you were resting last night, Towne and I went over to the university and drove around," Max said.

"And?"

"It was quiet. No sign of any extra security."

Jenks looked over to Towne. "We keep going?"

"Until they give us a reason not to."

* * *

They stopped and bought four good coffees, and then made for the hospital.

Steak was awake, propped up in the hospital bed, his left shoulder and arm heavily bandaged and restrained. His wife Grace was helping him eat some lunch when Tori and Braddock came in.

"Gracie," Braddock greeted, walking over to her, giving her a quick hug, and then handing her a coffee.

"Thank you," she said, taking a drink of a latte. "The hospital means well," then she lowered her voice to a whisper, "but their coffee is for crap."

"Ah, man, you're the last two people I want to see me like this," Steak moaned, albeit with a welcoming smile.

"Nah, buddy," Tori said, kissing her lifelong friend on the forehead. "We're the ones who understand best. Although," she said, a mischievous smile forming, "seeing Grace feeding you was a nice little treat. I should have had my phone out, taken a picture."

"You kiss me and then you blackmail me in my weakened state."

"Works every time," Grace said with a wink.

"How's our boy, here?" Braddock said, gently clasping Steak's good right shoulder.

"Hey, boss."

"He's a terrible patient," Grace said wryly. "Grumpy, groaning, pissed about the shoulder, snapping at nurses."

"Hey!" Steak defended. "I haven't snapped at a nurse."

"He's going to be a total sourpuss for the next few months," Grace said. "But I'm certainly relieved it wasn't worse."

"I'll live. But I'm out of the game for a bit, boss."

"Not completely. We thought we'd bring you up to speed, get your thoughts on a few things."

"You two are going to make him work?" Grace said, playfully shaking her head.

"Just a smidge," Tori said with a grin. "He didn't suffer a head injury, or at least a new one."

"Let me tell you what else we now know," Braddock said and spent a few minutes recapping what they'd learned from Teddy Marist, DeBoer, going to the house, and what they'd learned about Jared Bayne and Colum Mercer. "Teddy said the men had southern accents," Braddock noted. "Mercer and Bayne are locals but were in North Carolina for several years. We're having inquiries made down there but nothing has come of it yet."

"Could Teddy identify them?" Steak asked.

"By voice maybe, but not physically."

"But did *they* know that?" Steak said, closing his eyes, thinking.

"Clearly not because they kept coming after us. They obviously felt they couldn't risk us capturing Jared," Tori said. "He knew something that made them keep after him. Something that made them risk killing a cop, and a ten-year-old boy and chase us all in a whiteout blizzard. And they did this when they already had the money. Probably a lot of money. That suggests to me their broader motive is something *beyond* money."

"Beyond money?" Steak said.

"That's the part that gnaws at me," Braddock said. "The more I think about it, the more I think Tori is right about that."

"That might well be true. But here's what I keep coming back to. How did they all know about the money Marist had to begin with?" Steak said. "You have these four guys, two meatheads from Minnesota who haven't been here in years, and the other two who sound southern, maybe North Carolinian, and the woman. If Marist had an account or accounts of money beyond what we saw in that safe deposit box, how do these five know about any of that? How?"

Steak reached with his good hand and took a sip of the coffee, savoring it. "Say I buy all that you two are telling me about Jared, about something else being up, that all may be true, but you still only truly know one thing. One."

"We know about the money," Braddock said, nodding.

"What is it Deep Throat once said?"

"Deep Throat?" Tori looked at him quizzically. "Wait, are we talking Watergate?"

"Yes," Braddock said. "In the movie *All the President's Men*, Deep Throat said to Woodward in the parking garage: 'Follow the money.'"

Steak nodded. "That's right. Follow the money."

TWENTY-FIVE

"I'M GETTING ALL TINGLING INSIDE JUST THINKING ABOUT IT."

Tori had never seen *All the President's Men*. The movie was released a decade before she was even born, and she wasn't one to watch what she viewed as *old* movies. Braddock on the other hand, had, several times. "We should watch it some night. It must be on one of our streaming services."

As they drove to the government center Tori pulled up YouTube and found the movie clip of Hal Holbrook, who played Deep Throat in the movie. "Follow the money" was uttered as part of a longer soliloquy about campaign staff in the Nixon White House not being too bright and things getting out of hand.

"This is what all the mythology is about?" Tori asked.

Braddock smiled. "In real life, Deep Throat existed, his name was Mark Felt."

"I know that. He was Deputy Director of the FBI, in fact."

"Correct. But he didn't actually say: Follow the money. It is not in the book. But in the movie, it makes sense. Woodward and Bernstein learned much about the Watergate break-in and the broader conspiracy from tracking down the illicit use of campaign funds."

"You've read the book?"

"I have. In fact, I wrote a thesis paper about Watergate in college."

"What was your thesis?"

"That Nixon's approach to the campaign, the dirty tricks they called rat-fucking, the Muskie Letter, the DNC break-in, the fundraising, the slush money, all marked a significant change in modern political campaigning, or so I theorized. I think the years have suggested there was merit to my view."

"How very Poli Sci of you. Do you still have the paper?"

"I might, in a box somewhere with all my college stuff. Longest paper I ever wrote. Got a B+ for it as I recall," he said proudly. "We should watch the movie. I think you'd like it. Jason Robards played Ben Bradlee brilliantly."

"Do you still have the book?"

"It's on a shelf in my office."

Braddock pulled into a parking slot in front of the government center. They walked inside to find the building quiet on an early Sunday afternoon, though there was some bustle of activity in the sheriff's department offices. They found Boe in her office along with two sergeants. "What are you two doing here?" she asked.

"Following up on some things," Braddock said as he and Tori chatted up the sergeants and Boe, giving them the update on Steak. Boe had a map of the university campus spread out on her desk, marked up and color coded. "More plans for Tuesday?"

"Just going over personnel and where our people need to be per the State Patrol and Marshals Service, who has security for the commerce secretary. No big thing," Boe said and did a quick review of the arrangements. "What are you two doing here?"

"Digging into the who and *why* of the Marist case," Braddock said. "Special Agent Starling here—"

"Hey now," Tori protested, slapping him on the arm.

"Clarice is thinking that our killers' motivation was about more than money. I'm inclined to agree."

"What we know for sure is there are still two other men and this Max still out there," Tori insisted. "They need to be found."

"Aren't they gone by now?" Boe said.

"Would that stop a U.S. Marshal from still hunting for them?"

Boe smiled. "No it would not."

"They murdered three people," Tori said. "You're right, logic says they're all long gone by now, but... I'm not so sure."

"Call us ill at ease," Braddock said. "If we figure out who they are, we can find them. And if they're not here, we can call on your marshal friends to track them down."

Boe's phone rang, and she quickly answered. Braddock and Tori turned to leave.

"Hold on you two."

"What?"

"Ned Bollander on the line," Boe said, hitting speaker. "Ned, go."

"We found an RV owned by Colum Mercer at a local campground. Now, before you get too excited, the BCA is already here, and they tell me it's been wiped down and cleaned out. No prints of any kind. No garbage of any kind. They're going to work it, but on that front don't get your hopes up."

"Do you have any good news?"

"Descriptions of four men. Two are Bayne and Mercer based upon descriptions from the manager here, who called it in when he saw Mercer's picture on television. The two others, one was a huskier fellow, big bushy beard. The other was taller, bearded and wore rounded glasses. He saw them a few times. We're going to see if we can sit him down with a sketch artist, get you a little more on them."

"How about vehicles?"

"A couple of pickup trucks, one with a light rack, and he

said he saw a white SUV at one point but didn't recall what brand or model, just white."

"How long had they been there?"

"Almost five weeks."

"Ned, you need any help up there?" Braddock asked. "I can send people up."

"There aren't but a few others at the campsite, being winter and all. We got it covered but if we find something of interest, you're my first call."

Braddock opened a conference room, and they collected the files from Eggs, Reese, and Nolan's work areas. They had documents from all three victims, at least what existed in each of the homes, as well as all evidence thus far accumulated in the investigation.

They dug in.

It dawned on them that given how the case unfolded, they had spent little, if any, time on Lainey Darr or Ed Girard, or Barry Marist, for that matter. For the next several hours they worked through the boxes of personal documents.

"Your friend, Lainey," Braddock started. "She wasn't uncontroversial."

"I assume you're referencing all her media time from last year on that MN Partisans stuff."

"Yeah."

"She didn't mind media attention."

Braddock nodded. "She'd warned about the Partisans, or at least that kind of movement, for many years. I mean, she's been doing television hits for what, eight, ten years. The cable networks would all call her on fringe group type stuff."

"That and guns," Tori said. "She worried about the sociology, psychology, and the weaponry of those kinds of movements. A toxic stew was her term. She studied them for years and wrote a couple of books on the topic, which is why she would get those calls to go on television I suspect."

"She probably experienced a nice little spike in book royalty income every time she went on television too."

"You're such a cynic."

"Pot meet kettle."

"In any event, she raised the alarm when the MN Partisan stuff started percolating around here, or at least northwest of here. She had the kind of profile that people had to take her seriously when she spoke."

"The governor took her seriously, especially after the thwarted attempt on that attorney. The state moved on those guys, shut them down before anything more serious happened."

"You think it would have?"

Braddock took a moment. "I know those four guys were found in that van with guns so you can't just dismiss that. That was real. That was a legitimate threat."

"But?"

"For the most part, I think Ole Earl Snyder had it right. They talked tough but in reality, the MN Partisans were just a bunch of guys who wanted their picture taken holding a gun. They wanted 'acknowledgment' and 'validation.' To be heard."

"And your air quotes are why guys like Newell DeBoer and Ewell don't like our type, because they perceive us as looking down on them," Tori said. "Beyond that need for acknowledgment and validation lie real fears in rural areas of a world that is passing them by and leaving them behind socially and economically."

"Perhaps. Still, your friend—"

"We weren't really friends."

"I know but, she was assassinated."

"To make it look like Marist snapped."

"But we know he didn't. We know it wasn't him. It was

someone capable of killing. In that family, she was the one with exposure to that. Not Barry Marist."

Tori thought for a minute. "You might assume that because of what she did, what she spoke and wrote on, but I'm not aware of any threats against her. The university president, Berman, and Gene Norwich said there were no known threats."

"None?"

"Well, they said a few times in the past there were some troubling messages, emails, and such that they reported to the police but nothing recently. She had not mentioned anything like that in quite some time."

"Still, makes me wonder," Braddock said, flipping through a folder, and then he stopped. "Huh."

"What?"

"Your colleague kept a separate cell phone," Braddock said, holding up records from Verizon. She had a phone under a family plan with T-Mobile. "I'd imagine for communicating with Girard."

"Not the first time we've heard of that," Tori said. "There was Mitch Arnold, remember?"

Braddock threw his head back in laughter. "What a dumbass."

Mitch Arnold was a married sheriff's deputy with a wandering eye for the ladies. His wife found his second phone in his aptly named pickup truck. When he was asleep one night, she used the facial ID to unlock the phone. Mitch was on multiple dating apps and there wasn't just one woman. There were regular calls and messages to three different cell phones, his regular dates. Mitch had an open marriage; he just didn't tell his wife.

"What was it his now ex-wife called him?" Braddock asked.

"Sewer dick," Tori replied with a laugh, flipping open a box of records from Marist's house that Reese had collected. "It was rather apt." She gestured to another stack of documents. "Those are for Marist too. And that's his laptop from home. There is a sticky note with login information there."

Braddock pulled the stack and laptop over. "How much longer you want to work?"

It was approaching five o'clock. "Let's get through the Marist stuff."

Braddock nodded and flipped open the laptop and began poking around. A half-hour in he paused. "Would you look at that."

"What?" Tori said, not looking up.

"I'm in his email, his personal account. The login was saved so I got right in. He was interviewing for new jobs."

"Really?"

"Yeah. Last few months and..." He tapped through another couple of emails. "He was talking salary and title with Manchester Bay State Bank. He had a follow-up meeting with Oren Fulton on Tuesday. He's the bank president." He took out his phone and placed a quick call.

"Who are you calling?"

"Boe," he said. "Hey, do you have a phone number for Oren Fulton? ... I thought you might, campaign donations and all. ... Yeah, yeah, yeah, it wasn't a cheap shot, Jeanette. Can you call him and have him call me? It's about Barry Marist. Why?" He gave her a quick thumbnail. "Just following up."

Fulton called five minutes later. "I wondered if this might all come to light."

"What's that?" Braddock said.

"Our interest in bringing Barry on board."

"What would have been the position?"

"Senior vice president, which would have given him a title bump and we were going to bump his salary nicely as well."

"He give you any indication as to why he was interested in making a move?"

"Well, he said he was going through some life changes on a

personal basis and thought a professional change would be in order as well. He said something to the effect that life had gotten stale, and he wanted something new. We were looking to bring someone on in a senior leadership position to help upgrade our operations and he fit what we were looking for and he was already here and familiar with the community. I was terribly saddened by what happened to him."

"How was his relationship with Lakes Community Bank?"

Fulton paused. "It seemed… fine."

"Seemed?" Tori murmured to Braddock.

"Explain what you mean by seemed fine?" Braddock said.

"He didn't say anything bad about it really. I asked about his relationship with Elaine, and he said it was good, no… issues."

"You say that like there were."

"He was cautious, Will. You don't impress a future employer by trashing your current one. He went out of his way to not say anything negative, but I think your insight serves you well. I suspected there was some tension there for some reason. In the end, Barry just said he wanted and needed a change. I could understand that, and I was willing to benefit from it."

"Were you hiring him?"

Fulton sighed. "We'd had those discussions. We'd talked about fit, responsibilities, time horizons, salary, benefits, title, and things of that nature. We were supposed to sit down again this week and I was thinking I wanted to try and close that deal and get him onboard. Alas, we're starting over, given what's happened."

Braddock spoke with Fulton for a few more minutes and then hung up. "Was it me, or did Fulton seem to be holding back?"

"He was certainly guarded about Marist being cautious talking about Lakes Community Bank. There was something going on there."

"I got $420,000 in safe deposit box in Akeley at Rapids Community Bank that supports that notion."

"Did Fulton dodge a bullet?"

"Oh, I think he might have."

They continued to work through the material on Marist. An hour later, Tori looked at her watch, stretched and went to the small refrigerator and retrieved a bottle of water. Braddock looked engrossed in a stack of records. She took out the last file from the box. It was a file for a credit card. It was in a file marked Lakes Community Bank, but it was found in Marist's file drawer at home.

She flipped it open. It looked to be another corporate credit card for the bank.

Or... was it?

The statements went back over two years. The interesting thing was the credit card was in Marist's name but the address for the account was listed as Lakes Community Bank in Manchester Bay. However, the bank wasn't paying the balance. Marist was, in an electronic funds transfer from an account at the bank.

"Weird."

"What?" Braddock said.

"This account. It's a credit card. It's in Marist's name with the mailing address being the bank."

"Corporate card."

"I don't think it is. The bank isn't paying the balance. Marist is," Tori said as she started flipping through the statements, examining the charges. "See." She traced the payments on the statements from an electronic account at the bank. Braddock took the bill and examined it. She started flipping through the other statements. There were not a lot of charges each month but there was a similarity to them. "Check this out."

"What?"

"What he was paying with this card." She flipped through

the months of charges. "Strictly hotels, up until a few months ago."

Braddock leaned over her shoulder. There were four hotels. Regular stops.

"I know these places," Braddock said and pulled up a map on a laptop. "The Northern Star Casino is here, halfway between Detroit Lakes and Thief River Falls. DL House is in Detroit Lakes. Miners Inn is in Virginia. The Lumberjack is in Bemidji."

"Jenny Weld, Lainey Darr's divorce attorney, told me that Lainey suspected Barry was fooling around too. She didn't care that much because she had already decided she was leaving him for Ed. I bet—"

"He was hooking up with his paramour at these hotels," Braddock said. He looked at the map and then reached across the table for another folder and retrieved a pamphlet. "This shows all the Lakes Community Bank locations." There were eighteen branch locations. He took a red marker and marked all the bank and hotel locations. "Right along the roads to all these banks."

"Was it someone he worked with?" Tori wondered.

"There might be one way to find out." He started scrolling through his contacts. "You always keep a phone number because you just never know. Chay. Chay Tobias."

"Who is that?"

"Director of Security at Northern Star Casino. I did him a favor a few months back and had Reese track someone down for him. He said if I ever needed anything or wanted a free night's stay, just give him a call. Seemed like a good dude."

Braddock gave Tobias call. He answered right away. "Will Braddock! You've been in the news, my man, doing the good work. To what do I owe the pleasure?"

"Chay, if I give you the dates someone checked into the

casino hotel," Braddock replied. "Can you get me video of him? I want to see if he met up with someone and who that is."

"Hell yeah. Give me the parameters and I'll get on it."

"Like... now."

"Like first thing in the morning. This wouldn't happen to have something to do with that Marist thing."

"The guy you're looking for on the tape *is* Barry Marist."

"Ahh," Tobias replied, and Tori could hear the enthusiastic *what could this be all about* curiosity in his voice. "I'm getting all tingling inside just thinking about it. Very titillating."

"It is," Braddock replied. "I'll email you the dates and times here in five minutes. It'll be waiting for you."

"On it, my man," Tobias replied.

Tori was the faster typist, so Braddock read off the dates while she typed up the email and then sent it. The email gone and receipt quickly acknowledged by Tobias, Braddock sat back in his chair with a faraway look. He was thinking of something.

"What is it?"

"What does this really get us?" he said.

"Who he was having an affair with perhaps."

"And that tells us what exactly?"

Tori shrugged. "Maybe someone else to talk to. Maybe she saw something or knows something. Maybe she could explain all the money he had in the safe deposit box. He went to great lengths to hide the expenditures. Maybe..."

"What?"

"For all we know it could be Max. Whoever it is, is definitely worth talking to."

"True enough." Braddock checked his watch. "You know, Quinn is over at Roger and Mary's, and she texted a while ago that they were having a late dinner. I'm famished. You?"

"A home-cooked meal sounds great. Let's go."

TWENTY-SIX

"SHE'S OPENING THE DOOR."

"How are you doing back there?" Towne said, looking back to Jenks, who was sitting in the back seat of the Tahoe, his black stocking cap pulled low and his left arm in a sling inside his heavy winter coat.

"Fine," he grumbled back, suggesting he was anything but. "Let's do this."

Max looked over to Towne, who nodded. She drove ahead, pulled into the parking lot, and then backed into the parking space. "How's that?"

Jenks raised the binoculars to his eyes with his right hand and made a full scan of the building. The few visible windows on the upper levels were dark. The main level had a wide and open atrium along the front that led into more narrow-windowed hallways on either side that hugged the building. Interior night lights providing some small amount of illumination, enough for Jenks to see if anyone was about late on a Sunday night. "I've got a good view of three sides. I see nobody. All is quiet. I'd say now is as good a time as any you're going to get."

Towne and Max got out and they each pulled duffel bags

and threw them over their shoulders, and walked up a set of stairs to the right of the row of dumpsters and then inside the maintenance building. Inside they found two cleaning carts and stowed their duffel bags underneath. Towne took out his phone and pulled up the building and tunnel map. Max leaned in and with his finger he traced their path.

The two of them made their way to a freight elevator and took it down to the underground tunnel level. The tunnel system webbed its way underneath all the buildings on campus, allowing students to make their way to classes, the student union, the sports facilities, and dorms without necessarily having to go outside in the winter months. It was a lengthy walk, both pushing their cleaning carts, occasionally stopping along the way to dump the contents of a garbage can into their larger one to look the part.

Following the overhead signs, ten minutes later they found the right turn they were looking for, and then took an elevator up two levels. When they emerged, they pushed their carts out into a windowed hallway.

"I see you both," Jenks said, his voice in their EarPods. "You're clear so far."

"Any unfriendlies about?"

"Negative."

The two of them made their way ahead. Max broomed the long length of the hallway, while Towne made a good show of it as he made a circuit and emptied garbage cans and picked up scraps of paper, until he reached their target door and tried the handle. As he'd expected, the door was locked. He extracted the key ring from his pocket, sifted through the keys and picked the one with the black dash marked on it. He opened the door and then pushed his cart inside, followed by Max. Along a bank of light switches, he flipped on and then off until he found the one he was looking for.

They pushed their cleaning carts across the backstage area to the podium.

"That's it?" Max murmured.

"That's it," Towne said as he wheeled it away from the wall a few feet. He and Jenks had examined, measured, and taken photos of it a month ago on a night much like this one. This was all a theoretical exercise back then. Something they *might* do.

They took out the two duffel bags and laid the contents out on the floor and went to work.

* * *

Jenks felt the chill starting to seep into the SUV. Over the phone, he could hear a whirring sound. The electric screwdriver. "How's it going?"

"Halfway," Max said.

He checked his watch. It was 12:35 a.m.

Raising the binoculars, he scanned the area again. To his left—south—there was a four-story building. He'd observed random lights going on and then off after a few seconds along each of the floors, and it was happening on the first floor now. There was an open glass entryway into the building. That's when he saw her, a security guard, exit the front of the building, locking the door behind her.

The security guard walked ahead on the shoveled sidewalks until she came to an intersection. The sidewalks of the campus grounds were an interconnected web and they had all been cleared. At the intersection, she could go any of eight directions.

"You there?" he asked.

"Yeah," Towne replied. "What is it?"

"Possible unfriendly. Hold a second."

The security guard turned to her right, walking parallel to the auditorium, and then turned right into another building, extracting her keys and entering it from the side.

He exhaled in relief. "False alarm."

"Who was it?" Towne asked.

"There is a security guard lurking about, checking buildings. She just went into a different building to the north. How much longer?"

"Ten minutes."

* * *

He locked the wheels in place.

"Okay, sis," Towne said. "Help me lift it back onto the base here."

The two of them lifted the top and stem of the podium onto the base.

"It's heavy," Max complained through gritted teeth.

"We have to make sure the screw holes line up." It took them three attempts before Towne thought he had the alignment they needed.

The edges appeared aligned, and Towne set the first screw, using the electric screwdriver.

* * *

Jenks reached down for his tumbler of coffee and took a long sip.

Shit!

She must have come out of the western end of the building. The security guard was opening a door to the back of the auditorium.

"Heads-up! Heads-up!"

* * *

"What is it?" Max replied in a whisper, her eyes locked on Towne's, who pulled up the screwdriver. He'd been driving in the third screw.

"Security guard is coming inside the auditorium."

Towne rushed over to the light switch bank and killed the lights. Max tossed their tools and bags into the garbage can of one of the custodial carts. He rushed back and grabbed Max by the arm and dragged her back behind a gathering of curtains the opposite side from the door.

"She's in the same hallway you were, checking doors. Did you lock yours?"

Towne grimaced and looked at Max, who was suddenly shaking. He held his finger to his lips.

"She's at your door."

Towne peered around the edge of the curtain.

"She's opening the door."

They heard the click of the door handle and then the door opened, a dull beam of light fanned out across the backstage area. The security guard was a woman, maybe five foot seven or eight, wearing a uniform with a winter coat, boots, and stocking cap.

Towne looked back to a terrified Max.

The security guard was slowly scanning the backstage area with the flashlight.

Stay still, Towne mouthed to Max as his hand slipped down behind his back and he pulled his gun.

Max's eyes went wide. She knew he would not hesitate if he had to.

The light beam from the flashlight swept across the backstage area as footsteps moved closer. The beam focused on the podium, scanning it from top to bottom.

The guard was maybe fifteen feet away.

Towne let his right index finger slide to the trigger.

* * *

Jenks felt the sweat beading on his forehead, and his body.

He had the binoculars tight to his eyes.

The side door to the backstage area was open. The guard had been inside there for what seemed like an eternity, with the flashes of intermittent light sweeping around.

Her flashlight. They'd had time to kill the lights.

He didn't dare speak, not with the guard in there. He could hear Max's nervous breathing. She wasn't supposed to be in there to begin with, doing his job.

This is taking too long.

Come on. *Come on.*

He let out a long breath and exhaled a slow whistle.

The security guard stepped outside and pulled the door closed, locking it, and she moved breezily on, twirling her keys, strolling toward the large atrium lobby at the front of the building, casually checking other doors.

"Is she gone?" Max whispered.

"She's doing a walk around the front atrium," he replied. "Where are you?"

"Hidden behind the stage curtains."

"Stay put."

The guard slowly worked her way around the auditorium. Eventually, her circuit complete, she zipped up her winter coat to her chin and exited the other side of the auditorium.

"She's gone."

"Anyone else lurking about?"

Jenks made a scan of the broader area but didn't see anyone. "No. How much more time do you need?"

"Five minutes."

He scanned the area around the auditorium and then even further out, but with the time approaching 1:00 a.m., there was little to no other foot traffic about the campus grounds. Amped up now, he anxiously waited for them to finish.

"We're done."

"You're clear."

He watched as they both emerged from the side door, pushing their carts, making their way to the elevator. Ten minutes later the two of them exited from the back of the building and made their way to the SUV.

"And?" Jenks said when they were both inside.

"We're set."

TWENTY-SEVEN

"BE NICE AND A LITTLE LESS INSUBORDINATE."

Braddock and Tori were up early with Quinn. After a quick breakfast, they dropped him and his cousin Peter off at middle school. There was a stop for good coffees after that and as they drove the last few blocks to the government center, Braddock's phone rang. The dashboard screen showed the caller: Chay Tobias.

"Here we go," Braddock said. "Chay."

There was no preamble. "Braddock my man, I think, no wait, I know, *I know*, I found what you're looking for," Tobias said excitedly. "He definitely was there with a woman. Who? You'll have to suss that out, I don't have an identification there but if she's someone from Marist's life you ought to be able to find her. Email coming shortly. I'm sending you video packages of his last four visits. I have him checking in and videos of him going to his room. And an interesting note for you."

"Which is?"

"He always requested a room at the end of a hallway. It was a note on the reservations. Every time he called, that was the request that was made."

"Any insight as to why?"

"Yes, but I'll just let you see it for yourself," Tobias replied. "Your boy checks in and... well, you two just watch the rest. I've sent you four videos, but I'd grab some popcorn and watch the third one all the way through. It's the best, most... vivid one, shall we say and, in the end, gives you the best and longest look at his lady friend. Enjoy!" Tobias clicked off.

"That was quite the teaser," Tori mused.

At the government center, they went into the conference room, closed the door, and opened the email from Tobias.

"Play the third one first," Tori said. "Let's see what he was all excited about."

Braddock clicked on the third video link, dated September 19th.

"A Tuesday," Tori noted, consulting the calendar on her phone.

Marist checked-in just past 2:00 p.m., sunbeam streaks through windows visible in the background, on what must have been a bright sunny day. Marist was wearing sunglasses, a black suit coat and white button-down dress shirt as he went through check-in.

"Hmm," Braddock murmured. "Notice how he keeps looking back toward the sunlight."

"Yeah... I do. As if he's checking for someone."

Marist slid his credit card to the front desk attendant. After he'd signed the necessary paperwork, he held up two fingers.

"Two keys," Tori said. "And there we go," she added as the desk clerk put two key cards in a small sleeve. Marist turned and left the front desk, and the video went black for a moment. The next snippet had him stepping off the elevator and then walking down a hotel corridor toward them.

"Room 502 is the reservation," Braddock reported. "No luggage," he added. "Just a duffel bag."

"Marist always wanted a room at the end of the hallway,"

Tori said. "He probably didn't realize that's where the security cameras often are located."

"Maybe that wasn't his concern."

He reached the door and reached in his pant pocket for his room key.

"Whoa! *Hello!*"

A woman burst from the stairway to the right, rushed across the hallway and into Marist's arms, kissing him, and with verve.

"She's frisky!" Tori said, the woman's left leg wrapping around Marist's right leg, her hands inside his suit coat before she wrapped her arms around his neck. "That's quite the kiss she's giving him." Marist reached down and aggressively cupped her butt in his right hand, raising her leg higher. "And he's... definitely reciprocating."

"But who is she?" Braddock said.

The two of them finally eased the embrace and Marist turned with his key card, while the woman wrapped her arms around the front of his chest and then turned her head away from the camera, as Marist stepped inside the room and she followed, the door slamming.

"I might need a shower," Tori quipped.

"Who is it though?" Braddock said.

The clip advanced to 8:10 p.m. "Five hours. Quite the session."

"You sound almost impressed."

"I'm just noting the lengthy passage of time," Tori said lightly. "Okay, who do we got?"

The hotel room door opened, and Marist stepped into the hallway, his duffel bag on his right shoulder. Then the woman came out into the hallway, her head down, digging in her large shoulder bag, now dressed in athleisure, black yoga pants and a sky-blue zip-up hoodie. The woman looked up and they saw her face. Her black hair, down when she arrived, was now swirled up in a messy bun and she had slipped on dark-framed glasses. Nevertheless, her face was plainly visible.

"Holy shit," Braddock muttered.

"Who is that?"

"I did not see this one coming. Not after the call with Oren Fulton."

"*Who* is it?"

"She and him? Wow!"

"*Who?*"

"The President of Lakes Community Bank, Elaine Baird."

Tori's eyes went wide. "Hold on. You're telling me he was hitting it with the boss!"

"Yep," Braddock replied. "That never ends well."

"I'm hitting it with the boss," Tori snarked.

"And everybody knows it." He stared at the monitor for a moment. "You don't think..."

"Yeah, I'm thinking," Tori said as she went to a stack of documents and started looking through the hotel and phone records again. "The last hotel visit, which was in Detroit Lakes, was a little over three months ago, late November, right? It looks like just after Thanksgiving is the last time."

"Yes."

"And it was pretty consistent before that I think, right?"

Braddock sifted through the credit card records again. "Yeah, almost always once a week, sometimes twice. There were periods where there are two weeks between charges, but overall, there is a consistent pattern for... two years, give or take. Then the credit charges just end."

"Because *they* ended."

"What do his cell records show?"

Tori reviewed Marist's cell phone records. "A lot of calls between them for months going back, though not unexpected, given they were two executives that worked together, probably had to talk a lot of business from time to time. Think of all the calls between you and me, you and Steak, you and Eggs, you and Boe, etc. especially when we're on a case."

"Sure, I get that, but what after the end of the hotel stays, what then?"

Tori realized what Braddock was asking and reviewed the phone records again, highlighting the ones between Marist and Elaine Baird. She had the September through December records in one pile and then the January and February bills in another.

"Look at the records before December," Tori said, tracing with her yellow highlighter. "Lots of calls between them. Some he initiates, some are incoming from her, a healthy back and forth. But look at December forward."

Braddock examined the records. "Late night calls, well after business hours, sometimes multiples on the same night."

"All initiated by—"

"Her."

"It goes for a good three weeks, maybe a month and then…"

"Starts petering out. It's over." Braddock flipped through the records again. "The subordinate dumps the boss. Not sure I've seen that one before."

Tori sat back in her chair and thought for a minute. "Hell hath no fury like—"

"A woman scorned," Braddock finished. He took a chair and kicked his feet up on the table, his hands behind his head. "What evidence do we have of that?"

Tori waved at all the documents.

"Circumstantial. But it's you and me, so speculate away."

"They have had an ongoing affair for perhaps two years based on the credit card records, slinking around to hotels. A year ago, Lainey filed for divorce, while the two of them are carrying on," Tori posited. "Now, Marist's really available to her and the affair keeps going on. Maybe she starts thinking the two of them have a possible future together."

"Might be tough with her the boss and him the subordinate."

"He was interviewing for jobs as we've seen. He could have gotten a new one. But before he starts hunting for something new, what's he do?"

"Breaks it off," Braddock asserted.

"It's over. I mean we saw her jump him in that hallway not but a few months before it ended."

"You're saying she was in love with him."

"Let's assume for the sake of argument, she was. He breaks it off."

"She's devastated," Braddock said.

"Not only that," Tori urged, "she's embarrassed, and worse, trapped."

"Trapped?" Braddock queried. "How?"

"She has to see him every day," Tori said. "It's not like she could fire him. If she did—"

"He outs her as sleeping with a subordinate," Braddock replied, seeing it. "He claims sexual harassment. That could destroy her. Instead, she has to just sit there and take it. Of course, he *was* looking for a new job."

"You think she knew?" Tori said skeptically. "He wouldn't tell her that. And then there's—"

"The money," Braddock finished.

Tori leaned back in her chair rubbing her temples. "We've asked the question before, where did the money come from and the only place it makes any sense is the bank. Did she know about it? Did she somehow know about the money?"

"That's a thought now, isn't it?"

"Were they in on it together and then he took it all? If he did, what's she going to do? Report him? Who is she going to go to? If she goes to us, she—"

"Implicates herself," Braddock declared. "She's going to

look bad, bank president, used, abused, discarded. Her career will be in ruins if she reports him."

"So instead, she what?" Tori said. "Brings in four goons to help her get it back?" She scrunched her nose, not necessarily buying the conclusion she just reached.

He paused for a minute, scratching the back of his head. "Well, it's a... theory that would explain all this. It's about more as Jared said. The money and her revenge."

There was a knock on the door. Eggs, with Reese and Nolan behind her, stuck her head inside. "What's going on?"

Braddock smiled. "Come on in and take a look."

He ran them through the video clip. Then they reviewed the other three that Tobias had forwarded and were able to confirm, it was Elaine Baird.

"Well, well, well, ain't all that some shit," Reese mused with a big smile, before taking a bite of an apple.

"Scandalous," Nolan said, a rabid consumer of mindless trashy drama TV to begin with.

"I'm envisioning a *Watch What Happens Live* with all of this," Eggleston quipped and then more seriously. "What's the play here?"

"That's the million-dollar question now, isn't it?" Braddock said. He looked to Tori. "What do you think?"

"It's what we've got. See where it leads."

Braddock checked his watch. "It's 9:50 a.m. Ninety minutes. Everything we can get on Elaine Baird."

The group reconvened at 11:30.

Reese was able to track down video footage from two of the other locations where Marist and Baird met up. "The footage isn't as salacious as what you saw from the casino, but nonetheless, it is the same kind of arrangement. He checked into the hotel and then she would arrive later. I will say, when they were up in Virginia, she did spend the night, twice."

Nolan reported that Elaine Mackenzie Baird, age forty-seven, was born in Wilmington, North Carolina.

"North Carolina," Braddock said. "Interesting."

Baird attended the University of North Carolina, Asheville, and graduated with a degree in finance. She had been working in the banking industry since her graduation, having worked at two banks in Lexington, Kentucky, before moving to Louisville, where at her second position she was a vice president of a local community bank system. She parlayed her rise in Louisville to a move to Memphis, where she took a bank vice president position with a larger local bank. It was also in Memphis where she married and then later divorced Simon Fitzmorris.

"She didn't take his name?" Braddock asked.

"She'd built her career on her own," Tori noted and then asked, "Does that offend you, Braddock?"

"Not in the least," he said defensively. "Just asking a question, sheesh. Reese, what do we know about Fitzmorris?"

"He's still in Memphis. He works for an investment firm."

Eggleston reported that Elaine was one of seven children in the Baird family, and she had five brothers, two older and three that were younger. They all resided in either North or South Carolina. One, an older brother, had brushed up against the law a time or two, although he'd never gone to prison. It appeared he tended to get drunk and get in fights and that was many years ago. Nothing recent there and he was living in Charleston, South Carolina. Two of her younger brothers had enlisted in the army out of high school, though both had been honorably discharged and were working, married, with children living in the Wilmington area.

"Her brothers seem unlikely candidates to have hooked up with Jared Bayne and Colum Mercer," Tori muttered.

"She wouldn't have had to use family members for this," Braddock said. "If she did it. We certainly haven't seen any paper or electronic connection between her and Bayne and Mercer."

"She could have hired it out," Tori said. "If we assume the reason they were out at that resort was for some sort of financial transaction. There was that hot spot we found. Marist had a laptop with him."

Braddock nodded. "As to that hot spot, I haven't seen that the BCA has found anything there yet." He flipped through some papers. "Still, we have what we have."

"You interviewed her. What did you think?"

"Her biggest concern at the time seemed to be the negative publicity Marist's suspected actions would bring on the bank. The other two, Nora and Joan, her aides, seemed far more concerned about Marist the person when I think on it." He thought for a minute. "At the time, I just thought she was kind of obtuse, focusing on the business, about how Marist killing his ex-wife and running away with his son would look for the bank. It was a PR issue. Now, knowing what we know, I'm not sure what to make of the interaction." He took a moment. "What do you think?"

"Maybe she was masking her feelings for Marist in a way. I haven't met her, but I saw her... passion for Marist in the video clips. That wasn't just casual hooking up, at least for her. That was desire."

"I agree based on what I saw on the other videos," Reese said. "It wasn't like the one you showed us but the way she touched him. One time, when they left the hotel room, she basically hugged his right arm as they walked down the hallway. My girlfriend does that sometimes."

"Oh, she's a girlfriend now?" Tori asked.

"Don't sound so surprised."

"Things are getting serious?"

Reese shrugged. "Could be."

"So where does that leave us?" Braddock said, getting them back on task.

"We know about the affair. We have video of it. We know it happened and we strongly suspect it ended," Tori said and then pondered for a moment. "What we don't know is why it ended and how she dealt with the aftermath of it? So, there's that, and there is all this money we found in that safe deposit box. There is what he was doing with this laptop. Was she aware of any financial misfeasance at the bank? Who do we talk to about all that?"

Braddock thought for a moment and checked his watch. It was almost lunchtime. "Eggs, Nolan, Reese, here is what I want you to do."

He explained his plan.

"Tori and I will cover the other."

As he drove, Braddock called Boe and filled her in on Elaine Baird. There was a long pause and then a sigh. "Tread carefully, huh. The affair is one thing, but murder? That's a whole other matter."

"Are you suggesting I not pursue it?"

"*Nooooo*. Just that, you know, she's the president of a large local bank and a named sponsor of the event at the university tomorrow where more than three thousand people and many of our mutual friends will be in attendance. Elaine Baird is a known, respected, and well-regarded business leader in Manchester Bay, the county, and the region."

Braddock knew what that was all code for. "And, of course, a campaign donor? Is she a potential one or a previous one?"

"Be nice and a little less insubordinate," Boe replied tartly. "You know what I'm saying."

"I do, and I hear you." And Braddock did but the two of

them often did this dance when someone who wrote campaign checks was in his investigational crosshairs. She had never asked for special treatment but did always ask for caution and discretion and for him to be sure. And with a bunch of politicos coming to town on Tuesday, she didn't want anything to distract from that. He knew she'd rather he waited until, say, Wednesday. He had no such intentions, and she wouldn't order him too. "We're not starting with her anyway. To your point, we know about the affair. We need to learn about whether she had motive beyond that."

"That's better."

Braddock had Eggs, Nolan and Reese pick up Nora Bartness and Joan Wills over the lunch hour. Both women had left the bank premises. Bartness was picked up making a stop at a drug store, while Wills was stopped while getting lunch. Both were asked to appear voluntarily, though neither of them was left with the impression that they had much of a choice. Each was placed in an interview room. Braddock and Tori took Bartness, while Eggs, Reese and Nolan took Wills.

"Detective Braddock," Nora Bartness said warily when he and Tori stepped into the interrogation room. "Is something... wrong?"

"Well, the vice president and chief operating officer of your bank was murdered, along with his ex-wife and boyfriend," Braddock said. "That investigation is not over." He gestured to Tori. "This is Tori Hunter. She's an investigator working with me."

"Did I do something wrong?"

"I don't know, Nora," Tori said. "Did you?"

"I... I... don't know," Bartness replied, flustered. "It was unsettling to come out of the pharmacy and your people were waiting at my car, is all. Is this about Barry? I was so thankful to see that you were able to rescue his son. Is he okay?"

"He's safe," Braddock said. And he was, with his aunt and uncle as well as a police guard watching him that would also escort them down to the Twin Cities, and there would be a patrol around his aunt and uncle's house for a time. "And to your question, yes, we have some questions about Barry Marist and the bank."

He hit record and made some notations for the record about the date and time, the case file number and Bartness's name. Once done he nodded to Tori. Given the initial topic they were handling, it was thought she would be best to lead.

"You've been the assistant to Elaine Baird for how long?" Tori asked.

"Seven plus years now," Bartness said guardedly.

"I recall her saying she couldn't run the bank without you," Braddock said.

"Elaine is very kind."

"That suggests to me you work with her very closely," Tori continued.

"Yes, I suppose so. I mean if she's there, I'm there. If she calls, I answer. That's the job of an assistant, I guess."

"Late night calls?"

"Yes."

"Weekends?"

"If needed."

"So, are you more or less like her personal assistant?"

"I wouldn't go that far," Bartness said. "She doesn't make me get her dry-cleaning or get the oil changed on her car or things like that. But at the bank, I'm with her all the time, at least here in Manchester Bay."

"Do you travel around with her?"

"Rarely."

"But you'd know what her social calendar looks like?"

"It's busy, I know that much," Bartness said. "At least there are lots of social events where she appears. I think that's expected given her position. And not just around here—"

"There are what? Eighteen branches after all," Tori said. "She must have to go to places like Detroit Lakes, Thief River Falls, Park Rapids, Hibbing, Virginia, all those places."

"Yes." Bartness nodded but she caught Tori's leading tone.

"Would it be fair to say you have more contact with her on a day-to-day basis than anyone else?"

"Probably so. I don't know who else would. She works a lot. Her job is demanding."

"As is yours."

"It can be at times. What does all that have to do with Barry?"

Tori and Braddock shared a look and Braddock nodded.

"What?" Bartness said.

Tori thought for a second about how she wanted to pose the question. Her quick assessment of Bartness was she didn't need to beat around the bush. "Did you know Elaine and Barry Marist were… hooking up?"

Bartness's head dropped. "I thought they might be."

"A woman knows," said Tori.

"How do you know?"

"Hotel receipts, schedules, *video*," Braddock replied.

"Video?"

"Yes. And the video does not lie."

"I see," Bartness replied, slowly shaking her head, sitting back.

"You know, yet you seem… surprised," Tori said.

"My suspicions were always intuitive, if you will. I never

saw anything to, you know, confirm it. Just little signs here and there."

"Like?"

"I've worked for Elaine for seven years. She's not an unattractive woman. Elaine has always dressed nicely but professionally. But the last year or two, there was a little additional self-care, with her hair, nails, and clothes. She was going to the gym and trimmed up. I know Elaine. I knew Barry. I don't know how long they were sneaking around before I caught on, but I caught on."

"Did you and Elaine ever discuss it?"

"No," Bartness replied with a shake of the head. "No, no, no. We are not... confidants, not in that sense. Our relationship was always on a boss and employee level. I'm always aware of where that line is."

"No girl, girl talk?"

"No."

"Never?"

Bartness shook her head. "Had she confided, I certainly would have kept it in confidence, if she'd needed to talk about it, but... I'd never say anything to her without her first raising it. Never, never, never. She's the boss and I really like my job."

"Never discussed it?"

"No," Bartness replied emphatically. "Ms. Hunter, I make really good money without having finished college because Elaine has looked after me and treated me well. It wasn't any of my business. They were two consenting adults. What they did on their time was their business."

"Did she know you knew?"

Bartness took a moment. "I would think, yes. That said, I didn't really know *for sure*. She and Barry were careful about it, though I guess not careful enough."

"Did you ever ask Marist about it?"

"No, that would have likely been the same as asking Elaine. No good would have come of it. It was none of my business."

"Did anyone else know?"

"You know, I don't think so," Bartness said after a minute. "If someone suspected, say Joan, or any other vice president, anyone on the bank board, they would have probably asked me about it because I spend more time with her than anyone else."

"Nobody ever said a word?"

"No. Never."

"There was no: Hey, Elaine and Barry seem kind of cozy with one another. You think they could be fooling around?"

"No."

"But you understand the issue with it?"

Bartness dropped her head into her hands, rubbing her face, nodding. "Oh, I do. I'm probably going to lose my job over it now."

"Why would you lose your job?"

"Come on," Bartness said. "This is going to come out, the relationship and that I knew, or at least suspected. If Elaine gets fired over it, so do I. Can't you see that? The powers that be will say that if I knew or even suspected, I should have said something. Or they'll say if I didn't know, I *should* have known and said something. I didn't. That makes me as guilty as them. That's how this will all go down. Unless," she said hopefully, "you can keep my name out of this."

"Hey, we're just talking right now," Tori said, leaning back.

"Let me ask you this. If you knew or suspected the relationship, I then suspect you also knew it was over," Braddock asserted.

After a moment, Bartness nodded. "I figured as much."

"How did you figure?"

"Again, just some little signs. There was her mood, or mood swings so to speak. It had been very light. The mood a woman is in when she's got someone in her life. You can just see it, another level of satisfaction, happiness, confidence. I don't believe you have to have someone in your life to be complete but if you do have someone who makes you feel good, it can be that much better."

Tori looked over to Braddock. "It can at that."

"And that changed. I noticed. And it was…"

"Abrupt?"

"Yeah," Bartness said after a moment, nodding. "It resonated with me in a way."

"How so?" Tori asked.

"That change was me a year ago when I got divorced. My ex-husband and I moved here ten years ago from St. Louis. I really liked it, the small-town feel, the lakes, and woods. He was in sales and took a job up here with Mannion Companies. I thought we were happy here, but then all of a sudden, he's like, I want to move back to St. Louis. I didn't. We argued about it. Then boom, a few months later he says he wants a divorce, the next day I get papers and two days later he'd moved out of the house and had taken a job down in Missouri."

"That had to be rough."

"It hit like a ton of bricks."

"When did you first notice Elaine's change?"

"A few months ago. And it wasn't just her either."

"Him too?"

"Yes."

"Describe what you were seeing?"

"Her and Barry became very… cool with each other. Before they were comfortable in each other's space, they would go to each other's office, they'd chit-chat and laugh, maybe even occasionally light touch or brush one another. There was rarely a cross word between them."

"Were there cross words?"

"There wasn't any sort of open hostility or anything, they kept that locked down. It was just… a coldness. Yes or no questions, passing in the hallway and not even acknowledging one another, stuff like that. Not loud but noticeable *if* you were looking."

* * *

"I had no idea, my gosh," Wills said, her eyes wide, her mouth agape, when shown the video proof of the affair between Baird and Marist.

"Really?" Eggs said skeptically. "Come on. You worked closely with him every day. You had to have at least an inkling?"

"No, I swear, I didn't. Barry never said a word to me. He was not one to talk about things like that. I mean, he rarely, if ever, uttered a word about his divorce. We knew it was going on, knew it had some contentious moments, knew Lainey up and left him for another man who lived in big house on the lake and was some California business big shot with a ton of dough. We knew all that, but I didn't know about this. I mean, what a frickin' fraud."

"Barry?"

"Yeah, Barry. He spent weeks trashing Lainey for doing the same shit he was. And on top of that, it's a real problem, the two most senior people at the bank carrying on an affair." Wills shook her head. "This will look very, very bad when it comes out. I mean what was Elaine thinking?"

"Elaine?" Eggs pressed. "She never said anything?"

"No," Wills said with a vigorous head shake. "I mean, I didn't know about any of that."

"Seeing all this, I find it hard to believe."

"I don't deny what you're showing me, but I didn't know," Wills said, bewildered. "Maybe I should have but I didn't. God." She put her face into her hands. "This so isn't what I thought you were going to ask me about."

Eggs sat back in her chair, her arms folded, glancing quickly to Reese and Nolan. "Well, Joan, what *were* you expecting?"

* * *

"Who seemed to show the most..." Tori thought for a second. "Anger towards the other after the break-up?"

Bartness grimaced.

"Nora?"

"Elaine. She's been terse for the past few months, particularly toward Barry. And that is not her... normal way. She's the smiling face, setting the tone and there was still plenty of that in public, in the common areas of the bank with the rank and file, but behind closed doors, or after hours, I saw it. The ire. Things had changed."

"And how did Marist react?"

"He just rolled with it and let the little barbs and shots go. It was as if he was... checked out, you know." She paused for a moment, closing her eyes for a moment. "That's why Friday threw me for such a loop."

She was leading somewhere. "In what way?" Tori said.

"I wondered if Barry was maybe looking for a new job. He finalized his divorce, bought a new house. All those signs point to a fresh start of some kind. I thought about that a little bit after my divorce. But then Friday happened, and I thought, well, maybe he snapped over what happened with Elaine, and what happened with his divorce. I wondered if I'd been reading the whole situation wrong, you know. Like maybe Elaine dumped him, and with that, you add in his divorce and he just... blew and went postal."

"He didn't," Tori explained. "He was set up for money and maybe more."

"More?"

The was a knock on the door. Tori looked away from Bartness, annoyed. Braddock spun around. It was Eggs. "Sorry, but I need you two for a minute out here in the hallway."

Braddock closed the door.

"Sheryl, what the hell!" Tori charged. "We're right in the middle of it."

"I know, I know, never interrupt you two when you're doing your thing, but you need to hear this." Eggs led them back into the interview room with Wills. "Mrs. Wills, you need to tell them what you just told us."

"Barry was responsible for all our internal controls. He's been with the bank for a long time, long before we all got here. I mean, nobody knew the bank inside and out like Barry did. He literally wrote every procedure, protocol, authentication, verification, all of it. We're very secure, or, at least I thought so."

"Explain," Braddock demanded.

"I was reviewing our unclaimed money account procedures a few months back. Those procedures were rewritten years ago by Barry. Under the new procedures, if there is no activity on an account for five years, we escheat that money to the state as unclaimed property. The state puts it on its unclaimed property site."

"You've heard of that right?" Eggs said. "Someone is out there searching the unclaimed property site and says they saw your name."

"I know I have," Nolan said.

"Fine. Get to the point," Braddock pressed.

"I remember Barry explaining our new procedure on escheating to the state a few years ago. He said at the time that we hadn't been doing that and we had some really old accounts that we needed to get rid of. Made sense and he drafted the procedures and protocols and so forth because that was his strength. He just understood the step by step of procedures and internal control. What I didn't realize at the time was how much there had been in unclaimed money."

"How much?"

"At the time of the rewrite, Barry said it was just under $200,000 when you added it all up. For a bank system of our size, that seemed like a lot."

"Did all that money go to the state?"

Wills grimaced. "I think *that* money did. I was reviewing that policy change back in December, the history of it because that process was made part of my group's responsibility under an internal reorganization. When we redid the policy like four years ago, we escheated a little under $200,000. However, when I looked at the amount of unclaimed money accounts from six years ago, the amount was a little over $600,000."

"What happened to the other $400,000 plus?" Tori said.

"I don't know. I couldn't find a record of that."

"Did it just disappear?"

Wills shrugged. "I don't know."

"And did you ask Barry Marist about it?"

"I did."

"And?"

"He said he couldn't recall but said they must have reconciled some accounts determining where the unclaimed money belonged, or that people had come in and made claims for it. He said the money would fluctuate over time. He asked if I'd checked the annual audit."

"Had you?"

"I did," Wills replied. "And it didn't detect any problems and his explanation made some sense. And who was I to question Barry. I mean, he wrote the book. But then, the more I thought about it, despite what the audit said, I thought his explanation was kind of... unsound. I hunted around in our system, and I couldn't find any documentation of that reconciliation taking place. That money seemed to disappear into a hole somewhere and I couldn't find that hole."

"So, what did you do?"

"I raised it to Elaine. I asked her if she wanted me to... investigate it further. Revisit the issue with the auditors."

"When?"

"Back in December, just before New Year."

"And what was her reaction?"

"She asked me if I was sure, and I said I wasn't, other than I didn't see anything about how those unclaimed accounts were reconciled."

"Did you say you thought the money was stolen?"

"I didn't phrase it that way."

"But the implication was..."

"We might have a math problem. Money *might* be missing."

"And did she do anything with this information?"

"I honestly don't know. She said she'd think about what to do. I didn't follow-up with her. But now, with everything that's happened," her voice trailed off. "With it turning out Barry was being set-up, I guess some hard questions need asking."

"And these unclaimed accounts, was Marist the only one dealing with them?"

"Yes."

"What do you think happened?"

Wills sighed. "I don't know."

"I think you do," Braddock asserted. "He's dead. His ex-wife and boyfriend are dead. Two people responsible for the killing of those three are dead. His son is scarred for life. Cough it up."

"What I fear," Wills started, closing her eyes, "is that if someone looks into it, they might find that some accounts escheated to the state, and some didn't. For those accounts that didn't, that money ended up somewhere else. And by somewhere else, I think somewhere outside the bank."

* * *

Tori and Braddock burst back into the interview room and to Bartness.

"How badly did Elaine take the break-up?" Tori said, leaning on the table. "Be straight with us."

"What are you saying?"

"Barry Marist was set-up," Tori said. "The killing of his ex-wife and boyfriend, was part of a broader scheme, that was due, at least in part, to money."

"Money from where?"

"Well, you all were working at a bank," Braddock asserted, hands on hips.

"We've been monitoring everything since Friday," Bartness said. "There has been no unusual withdrawal activity. We are checking constantly. Our IT people are monitoring everything. It's been clean."

"What if the withdrawal had already happened?" Braddock said.

"What do you mean by that?"

"What do you think?"

Bartness looked at him for a moment and then her eyes went wide. "Oh, God. Are you saying Barry and Elaine were stealing money from the bank?"

"We're aware of something suspicious," he said, knowing what Wills had said was yet to be vetted. That didn't matter right now. They were interested in her reaction.

"You are? What? What is suspicious?"

"Tell us this," Tori pressed, leaning on the table. "Did Barry Marist oversee bank financial operations?"

"Uh, those were his duties," Bartness said, nodding nervously. "It's why he was the chief operating officer."

"Then it would be safe to say that nobody knew the bank's operations better, did they?"

Bartness froze and then slowly nodded her head. "He wrote the book on it all."

Tori played the video for Bartness of Baird embracing and kissing Marist in the hallway. Bartness's eyes went wide, seeing the affair in its reality. "What do you see there, Nora?"

"I see a woman very much in love," Bartness replied bluntly.

"Ms. Hunter here asked you a question a few minutes ago," Braddock said. "How badly did she take the break-up?"

Bartness closed her eyes. "I think she took it really hard."

TWENTY-EIGHT

"SOMETIMES ONE PLUS TWO ACTUALLY EQUALS THREE."

Heeding Boe's earlier request for caution, Braddock called Elaine Baird and asked her if she'd be willing to come over to the government center. Voluntary rather than mandatory.

"When?"

"It's approaching six p.m. which is closing time, is it not?"

"It is."

"Then come over after close of business," Braddock had said evenly, sitting back in his office chair, one leg crossed over the other, Tori listening in.

"What is this about?"

"Barry Marist. There are three murders still needing to be solved. We think Marist is the linchpin of that investigation so we're digging in on him and his history and obviously you're integral to developing that history. I thought, given it's the end of the day, it would be better if you came to us rather than us coming to you. It stays out of the public eye that way."

"I certainly appreciate your discretion. I'll be there in a half-hour."

The minute Braddock hung up, Tori asked, "Are you sure we do this now? All we have is a theory."

"I know. But the next step is a search warrant for the bank, bringing in forensic accountants and exposing their relationship. She'll lawyer up. This might be our one free unobstructed run at her."

"Better hope she doesn't lawyer up now."

She didn't.

"Here she comes," Tori said a half-hour later, watching Baird walking in along the front sidewalk into the government center.

"You take the lead," Braddock said. "She hasn't met you yet. You can go over all the territory I covered and take it from there."

Tori nodded. "Two professional ladies getting to know one another?" she said.

"Something like that."

Reese met Baird out front. Just as Tori and Braddock were going to the interview room, Eggs stopped them. "I found this." She held up a folder. "Might be relevant."

Braddock opened the folder and read the document and then handed it to Tori. "Interesting," he said.

Tori read it and nodded. "It kind of fits, doesn't it?"

Reese brought Baird down the hallway, and they met her outside the interview room. Braddock opened the door and Tori led them all inside. "Thank you for coming in," Tori said, gesturing to a chair for her to sit.

"Of course," Baird replied pleasantly enough, sitting down, though Tori caught a hint of wariness. "You know, Elaine, I wasn't with Detective Braddock when he first spoke with you," Tori started, a notepad in front of her. "So, if some of my questions are redundant, I apologize but there is some ground I need to cover."

"I understand."

"How well did you know Barry Marist?"

For the next fifteen minutes Tori sat relaxed, one leg over

the other, getting Baird to talk about her history at the bank and working with Marist, taking some notes, or at least making a show of it. It was all being recorded. And while Braddock faded into the background, Tori turned it into a conversation between the two of them as Braddock had alluded to, as if they were chatting over a cup of coffee or glass of wine.

"Elaine Mackenzie Baird," Tori noted. "Was Baird your maiden or married name?"

"Maiden. Mackenzie was my mother's maiden name. Ella Mary Mackenzie."

"Mackenzie. You know, one of my good friends in college, she had the last name of Mackenzie," Tori fibbed. "I called her Mac; others called her Max? Those were her nicknames. Anyone ever use that for you, or your mom?"

"No, not that I ever recall," Baird replied, nonplussed.

"Well, with a name like Mackenzie, not to mention Baird, you have to be Scottish."

"Aye."

Tori smiled. "Is there a family tartan?"

"Blue, green, and purple plaid. How about for Hunter? That's got Scottish roots. Are you Scottish?"

"I am," Tori replied eagerly. "On my father's side, and I recently learned there is in fact a tartan for Hunter. It's green and black with orange and white pinstripes. I bought a blanket in that pattern for our bed." She looked over to Braddock.

"Our? So, you two?"

"Yes," Braddock replied.

"So, you're Scottish," Tori continued. "Where are you from originally?"

"I was born and raised in Wilmington, North Carolina." She talked about going to UNC Asheville before moving to Lexington, Louisville, and later Memphis as she worked her way up in the banking industry that led to the job in Manchester Bay.

"Lexington to Louisville, to Memphis to Manchester Bay is quite the change, geographically and culturally."

"Oh, I don't know. Manchester Bay reminded me so much of Asheville and Wilmington. College towns with growing business cultures. Just in my time here I'm amazed at how the area has grown. It's been good for business. Plus, I love the lakes. And—" she nodded "—I wanted to put some distance between me and my divorce. My ex-husband and I met through work. After the divorce, I found myself running into him far too often and I wanted nothing more than to *avoid* him."

There was anger there. Tori probed. "I suspect all divorces are difficult but was yours particularly so?"

"He remarried a month after our divorce papers were signed."

"Oh my. An affair?"

"Yes, with someone else he met at work. Someone I also ran into frequently. So, yes," Baird declared with some salt, "it was difficult."

"I can only imagine."

"I needed a change, a big change. Moving here was a totally fresh start, a thousand miles away from him."

"Let's leave that behind then," Tori said. "Let's talk about Barry Marist."

"That would be... *fine*."

Tori let her eyes slide to Braddock. That too was a sore subject.

At the encouragement of the bank board, Baird had retained him when she was hired as bank president. While his duties as vice president and then for the last two years, as vice president and chief operating officer, were wide ranging and encompassed every component of the bank, his bread and butter was operations. "For lack of a better way of putting it, he kept the trains running on time," Baird explained.

"Processes, procedures, internal controls, things of that

nature?" Tori said, before taking a casual drink of her Diet Coke.

"Yes. For the whole bank system, that's what he did. He developed it, implemented it, taught it. More than almost anyone I've ever met, he understood, truly understood, not only how a bank operated, but how it had to operate."

"He understood every nook and cranny of the bank then?"

"Very much so, yes."

"And he traveled a fair amount for that I imagine?"

"He did," Baird said. "He went to all the branches often. He was on the road weekly."

"I suppose you are as well?"

"Of course," Baird replied. "Manchester Bay is our home bank as we call it, but I like to get out as well each week. That's part of the job, to be seen by the troops. We're all one big bank."

"I see."

"You undoubtedly knew Barry well professionally, but how about personally?" Tori asked.

Baird took a drink of soda, a long drink. "Professionally, I knew him well as you said, but not very well on a personal level. I mean we were certainly friendly and cordial and professional with one another."

"In fact," Braddock said, piping up, flipping to a page in his notebook, "you said on Friday: And I quote: 'I was his boss, and we worked well together but we weren't necessarily close friends outside of work.'"

"That's sounds right, yes."

Tori paused for a moment before slowly shaking her head. "You were doing so well."

Baird furrowed her brow. "I'm not sure I'm following."

Tori eyed Baird up for a moment before leaning forward, clasping her hands. "When I learned interrogation techniques, one of the things my instructor at Quantico taught me was to always keep this thought in the back of my mind: why is this person lying to me? Elaine, you're now lying to me. Why?"

"I'm not—"

"You weren't close outside of work?" Tori said, eye to eye with Baird. "You didn't really know him personally?"

Braddock stepped forward and spun his laptop around and pushed play on the video. It was the clip of her charging across the hallway and embracing Marist. "Seems kind of close to me."

"I mean that's one... passionate kiss," Tori said, having stood up. "Hooking the leg around him like that. I mean... wow."

Baird's eyes bulged, but she then took a moment, maintaining her composure, though her eyes were moist now. "Turn it off... please."

Braddock shut it off before asking, "We're wondering why it is you didn't tell me about this when he was murdered?"

"Well," Baird started indignantly, "I hardly think I have to justify myself to you two. You work together and are together."

Tori shrugged. "With two rather big differences being, one, he and I are not a secret. We're not sneaking around to hotel rooms and using off-the-books credit cards. And, two, we're *both* alive."

Baird snorted in annoyance, offering a dismissive wave. "Barry and I were two consenting adults."

"Until he broke it off," Braddock said.

"It was a mutual parting—"

"You're lying again," Tori needled. "I suggest you stop."

"It wasn't mutual." Braddock laid out the cell phone, credit card and hotel records in front of Baird. He started with the hotel records. "You two were pretty regular, once or twice a week for nearly two years, just based upon the credit card and hotel charges we've confirmed thus far."

"He didn't want Lainey to know, did he?" Tori said.

"Of course not. They were getting divorced. She looked bad, running off with Ed Girard. He wanted to keep it that way.

He wanted the best financial and custodial settlement he could get."

"That, and it certainly wouldn't look good, the bank president caught up in an affair with a subordinate," said Tori. "That's why he had the credit card with the bank as an address, and a direct payment from a separate account he kept at the bank. And the only other deposits into that account?"

"Were transfers from one of your accounts," Braddock said, noting the entries he'd highlighted in orange.

"Then it all stops in November," Tori said, leaning on the table. "And as we examined his phone records for November and December, for a good month there were a lot of calls between the two of you."

"We worked togeth—"

Tori plowed through. "The calls were mostly at night, *late* at night." She held up the phone records. She paused for a moment before speaking softly. "Elaine, we've all been there at one time or another. Someone we care about, maybe love, breaks it off. The one who is dumped? They didn't see it coming. It's like a left hook out of nowhere. At first, they're stunned. Then there's denial and finally anger. It's just human nature. They can't understand why the person they cared for left them. So, they try to hang on, calling, thinking if we can just talk it through, if I can just convince them that we still love each other, we can get back to the way things were."

Braddock held up the phone records. "It's all right here."

"How dare you!" Baird charged. "We talked work at night all the time."

Tori shook her head, sitting on the edge of the table. "Come on, Elaine. They were almost all initiated by you. There were only a few calls from Barry and they were daytime calls. *Those* may have been work related. But calls at 10:33 p.m., 11:04 p.m., 10:50 p.m., 12:34 a.m., 9:40 p.m., night after night after night. It all culminates with the night of December eleventh. Three calls between 10:30 p.m. and 12:30 a.m. And then after the third call, Barry called the police."

Braddock held up a different record, the one Eggs handed them. "Manchester Bay PD paid a welfare call that night to your address. Barry called out of concern and, I think mindful of your place in the community, requested a *very* discreet check be made to make sure you were okay."

"After that, there was one call the next night and then they pretty much trail off from there," Tori noted. "It was over."

Baird shook her head and looked away.

"Or was it?" Braddock asserted.

Baird's head snapped back. "What the hell does that mean?"

"Well, Marist was murdered. And we think we know at least one of the reasons why." Braddock laid another set of evidence photos out on the table.

"What's all this?"

"That building is the Rapids Community Bank branch in Akeley," he replied, regarding the first photo. "Marist had a large safe deposit box there for going on six years under the name Tom Nelson. This is a photo of at least part of the contents of the safe deposit box."

Tori whistled. "That's a lot of cash."

"$420,000 in fact." Braddock took out another photo. "This is Marist walking out of the safe deposit box area of the vault on Friday." He reached for his laptop and hit a video clip. "This is him walking out of the vault another time, sliding a silver-cased laptop computer into his shoulder bag. This is him returning about three hours later, pulling the laptop out of the same shoulder bag as he heads back to the safe deposit boxes. If you look closely at the safe deposit box, the cash is stacked to the top in the back, but in the front, there is enough room to put the laptop inside."

"Safe deposit box, under an alias, stacks of cash, a laptop, and who knows what else," Tori said whimsically. "Nothing at all suspicious about that for a bank vice president and chief operating officer."

Tori and Braddock shared a look as a shocked Baird took in the photos. It was time to see if she would go on tilt and tell them the rest of the story.

"We had Joan Wills in earlier today," Braddock said. "Wills said she came to you in January about a concern she had regarding your unclaimed accounts procedures. That there had been over $600,000 in unclaimed accounts but that a little less than $200,000 escheated to the state."

Baird looked up.

"Where did that extra money go?"

"How would I know?"

"You sure you want *that* to be your answer? You're the bank president," Tori asserted. "It's your job to know."

"I have this safe deposit box with all this cash in it," Braddock asserted. "I've got Marist appearing at the bank in Akeley on Friday morning to retrieve, not the cash, but the laptop computer. Then he ends up at his father's old resort, a resort for which you rejected his request for a loan to save it."

"Justifiably so."

"That may be. But that was Barry Marist's father. You rejected the loan. His dad had nowhere else to go. He lost everything and committed suicide, at the resort. He hung himself."

"If you say so," Baird flippantly replied.

"You *know* so," Braddock shot back. "And I find it incredibly interesting that that was where we found Marist dead. It was all a set-up. Barry Marist was being framed for the murder suicide of his ex-wife, boyfriend, and ten-year-old son. And it all happened after his divorce, at his father's resort that he lost because he couldn't get a loan through for him."

"It's a compelling set of facts," Tori said. "Who wouldn't have bought that?"

"And who would know that whole picture better than... you," Braddock alleged.

"Now hold on—"

"But then the set-up went bad," Tori posited. "Barry, staring down at least three other men, figuring he and his son were going to be killed, fought back."

"And the men who killed his ex-wife and boyfriend, who killed him, who intended to kill his ten-year-old son, then had some sort of falling out of their own."

"Thank God," Braddock said. "Teddy Marist is alive because of it."

"Which is a relief," Baird said.

"Is it?" Tori asked.

"How could you say such—"

"A thing?"

"Let's see," Braddock started. "I have a bank president who was dumped by her subordinate. The video and phone records show us you were hurt when he broke it off. After that, it's reported to you by Joan Wills that there is missing unclaimed account balances. So not only did he dump you, but—"

"He's been stealing from you. And given just the cash in the safe deposit box, probably for years and a lot of money."

"Maybe you figured that out after Wills brought it to you. You found that, *and more*. Or perhaps—"

"You knew it already," Tori speculated. "Maybe a little pillow talk along the way. Or perhaps you two were in on it all along but he had control of it all, on the laptop, in the safe deposit box in Akeley."

"And you wanted it all. You wanted the money. You wanted to get back at him for dumping you."

"Teddy Marist is a smart kid with exceptional hearing. He

overheard one of the men who had taken him talking to a woman on the phone. He heard the woman say: *Barry* doesn't have the balls to screw with you. Not he, or Marist, but *Barry*."

"Who would know whether he had the balls to do something better than... you?"

"I would never!" Baird howled.

"What's on that laptop he had?" Braddock continued. "I'm thinking it's banks, balances, accounts and he was dragged up to that resort to transfer the money from his accounts to the kidnappers."

"The kidnappers you hired," Tori alleged.

"And it was all going to plan until—"

"Barry Marist, fighting for his son's life, showed he in fact had, despite what you said, the balls to screw with them."

"It's electronic banking," Braddock noted. "Surely a president of a growing bank chain that offers such banking services, would know how to guide the transfer of those dollars. Hire four thugs to pull it off, pay them, you get the rest, and nobody asks any questions about things at the bank or if they do, Barry can't tell the tale, and he just gets blamed for it all."

"And hey. There was a storm on Friday. You closed all the bank branches for the day. That left you the whole day to be free to handle it all."

"Until it all went bad."

Elaine Baird shook her head. "No. I didn't do that. I didn't do any of that."

"Come on!" Braddock barked.

"No. I'm guilty of having an affair with my subordinate. That's going to get me fired. And the worst of it is, he never told me why he broke it off. Those calls you pointed to on that night, three calls, the night the officer showed up at my house late, that's why I was calling. I wanted an answer. I deserved an answer."

"Him not giving you one, must have made you angry," Tori said. "It would anger me to no end. Especially if it's out of the blue like that. Did it do that to you, Elaine? Were you angry?"

Baird sat back. "Was I angry with him? Yes, of course. I loved him. I thought he was a second chance at love in my life with him getting divorced. I worried about the work part of this, he and I. We could have worked that out. Even after it was over, I still loved him. I still held out hope. Would I hurt him like this? Kill his son and his ex-wife who had moved on? What kind of monster do you think I am?"

"You tell me?" Tori said. "I know what I'm seeing here. He not only left you, but with all this money, he could have ruined you professionally. What more motivation does someone need?"

"No," Baird said, shaking her head. She took a moment, calming herself, before turning to Braddock. "Detective Braddock, am I under arrest?"

She was calling their bluff.

Braddock shook his head slowly. "No, at this point, you are not. You remain, however, a person of interest to us. Stick around town. And, Elaine, I don't think I'm going to have any problem getting a warrant for the bank, all the records, any of it. Whatever was going on there, we're going to find it. This is your one chance to get ahead of it."

She stood up. "You want to speak to me again, it'll be through my lawyer. But I'm telling you, both of you, this right now. I don't know what Barry was or wasn't up to. But how dare you think I'd do something like this. I loved him, I still loved him, and I would have never hurt him or his son like that. Ever."

Braddock and Tori watched as Elaine Baird walked out of the building into the darkened night, her cell phone to her ear.

Eggs, Nolan, and Reese watched with them. It was late, a long day.

"Eggs?" Braddock said.

"Two deputies in plain clothes are on her. Does Boe know?"

"She does," Braddock replied, nodding. "That's enough for today. We'll hit it first thing. We'll start going back through everything. Through the interviews with Wills, Bartness and Baird, Marist's history, and think about who else we need to talk to. And we'll sit down with the county attorney about getting into the bank and maybe even Baird's house and life."

"Just FYI, boss, I have to be up at the university later in the morning," Reese said.

"Me too," Nolan added. "Extra security for that big shindig."

"No worries. We'll work around all that. Get your rest, come in early and we'll put together a game plan."

They rode home in silence. When they arrived, Braddock immediately went to the small beverage refrigerator and grabbed himself a beer. From the wine fridge, Tori took out and reopened a half-bottle of Chardonnay, giving herself a healthy pour. They sat at the kitchen island, sipping their drinks, silently pondering.

Braddock took another long swig from his beer, exhaling and then wiping his mouth with the back of his hand and broke the ice. "Did she do it?"

Tori took a sip of wine. "I don't know. Usually, I know. I can tell. Here, I don't know. Maybe I just need to sleep on it."

Braddock shook his head in a role reversal. Usually, Tori was the one to keep at it. "Let's... flesh it out."

Tori closed her eyes for a moment.

"What do we know?" he asked.

She opened her eyes. "That her feelings for Marist were genuine, both the love and the hurt," she said, taking a quick sip of her wine before gesturing with her wine glass. "And she'd been shivved before, by her ex-husband."

Braddock shook his head. "That's her side of it."

"What matters is what *she* thinks. What matters is what's going through *her* mind. Maybe," Tori posited, "this time, instead of moving on, she shattered. Marist, her subordinate, dumps her." She took another drink. "And the last time this happened with her ex-husband, it was with someone she would see all the time, so she moved, here. This time she says, no, no, no. I'm not moving. He's the one who has got to go."

"But Marist has Teddy. No way he's leaving town."

"Except in a body bag."

Braddock nodded before taking a drink.

"Sometimes one plus two actually equals three. It *could* be that simple."

"Maybe."

"Maybe." Tori nodded.

"We would have to *prove* that. We'd have to prove that Elaine Baird, local bank president, respected member of the community, arranged the murders of not one, but *four* people, Tori. That she killed not only Marist, but Darr, Girard, that she would kill Teddy all because Marist dumped her. Is she really *that* monster?"

Tori winced before taking a long drink of wine. "Well, there is the money. He dumped her *and* he was stealing from her."

"We think."

"I don't know about the how, but I feel certain we'll find, eventually, that money, a lot of money, is missing," she concluded. "So, not only did he hurt her, but now he's going to steal from her and torpedo her career?" She shook her head. "She said no way, not this time."

"You don't sound so convinced, though," Braddock said.

"Neither do you."

Braddock nodded. "No, I'm not. Is it having to prove it?"

"No... I'm not sure it's that."

"Then what?"

"You tell me your doubts first."

"It's easy to get lost in the silo of that interview," Braddock said and took a drink of beer and then went to the refrigerator. "Take the wider lens to this thing." He grabbed leftover Chinese out of the refrigerator and then two plates. "I could argue that having been through it before, says you can get through it again. After that night, the welfare call, she stopped calling him. It was over. Moving on takes time but she may have been moving on." He put a plate of leftovers in the microwave.

"She said she still loved him."

"Sure. That doesn't end just like that," he said, snapping his fingers. "That wound takes time to heal."

"Or fester," Tori replied. "Maybe that's when she transitioned from getting him back to getting even."

"She has motive but... I just found myself open to the idea it wasn't her. But that's a gut reaction that cuts against some of what we think we know." He took the plate out of the microwave and set it in front of her and put his in to reheat. "You don't believe her?"

Tori crinkled her nose. "I just don't know." She took a bite and then gestured with her fork. "I'll fully admit, she held it together despite all we threw at her. I mean we pressed her hard, we had to. We had to on that."

"I have no problem with what we did," he replied. The microwave beeped and he took his plate out and took the stool kitty-corner from her.

"We showed our cards and went for it, even on the Max or Mac thing. She didn't bite on that, did she?"

"No. Not even a little."

"And she was perceptive enough to know we were theorizing as to what happened between the two of them, and what happened at the resort or even where the money came from," Tori said, pouring herself a little more wine. "Does that mean she'd thought about it ahead of time and was ready for it, or simply thought quickly on her feet. She thought herself through it enough to know we didn't have it. At least yet."

"Not yet we don't," Braddock said, with a nod.

"On motive alone she looks good for it. I mean, who could be more motivated to hurt him? She was a woman scorned and as we found out, it wasn't—"

"The first time."

"Yet."

"Yet?"

Tori shook her head. "It's not just what you said about proving four murders, three accomplished, one attempted on Teddy. Would she really go *that* far? Is she *that* monster?"

"Depends on how badly she wanted to hurt him," Braddock said, before taking another bite.

"Now I'm confused. Which side are you arguing?"

"I'm just trying to see all the angles. I haven't picked a side, yet," Braddock said, and then took a sip of his beer, eyeing her up. "Something else is eating at you. What?"

"You said take a wider lens. Ask yourself this. Is all this what Jared was referring to about this being about more than just money?"

"He said it to you. Not me, so I didn't get the tone of that like you did," Braddock replied. "You tell me."

She grimaced. "I don't know. Her hurt over the loss of the relationship, and then this missing money... is that what this is really all about? I mean if this is about her anger, just kill Marist. Go over to his house, shoot him. Why all the cloak and dagger stuff?"

"To hurt him, to gut him like she'd been gutted," Braddock theorized. "How do you do that? Set him up for the murder of his ex-wife and lover? Kill his ten-year-old son, make sure he knows who killed him in the end plus recover all the money. In that scenario, it is about a *lot* more than money."

Tori scrunched her face.

"You don't buy it?"

"It still feels..."

"Unsatisfying?"

"Insufficient." She shook her head in doubt. "Maybe it was just the fact I was caught up in it. It could just be the way these guys hunted Jared Bayne and Teddy and even me. They kept coming and coming and coming after us. I mean, in that blizzard, they kept after us after the shoot-out at that house. They were no more likely to survive out there than we were if they ended up in a ditch or stuck. Between the temp and the snow and the remoteness. I mean *why*? Just to get the money and save Elaine Baird's position at the bank? These guys risked it all for... *that*."

"Because they thought Bayne would talk and identify them all," Braddock said. "They'd committed three murders, Tori. Dead men, or women, tell no tales. Did Teddy hear something? Did you? Did Jared tell you who the killers were or who Max was? I mean, she didn't bite on the reference, but that doesn't mean Elaine isn't Max."

"Say she is. Is protecting her worth all that happened? Worth the chase? They had the money. Marist was dead."

"If that's what Marist provided them."

"Assume it was. Whatever the amount was, they had it. They most certainly had a plan to disappear a long way from here. So take the money and run. Yet..."

"Yet."

"They stayed. And chased. Relentlessly. I'm still asking why."

"You think it's not related to Elaine?"

Tori took a moment, a drink of wine and then nodded. "I

think Elaine has a role in all this. She's a player in it. But I've thought for two days that it feels like there is something else, something we haven't seen or thought of yet. You said you were trying to see all the angles. I worry there's one we're not seeing, yet."

TWENTY-NINE

"MAKE ALL WE WENT THROUGH ON FRIDAY NIGHT TO SURVIVE WORTH IT."

When Tori and Braddock arrived at work, there were a couple of surprises awaiting them in the reception area.

"What in the heck are you doing here?" Tori said to Steak, who was leaning against the wall, his left arm wrapped in a tight sling underneath his jacket.

"I called Eggs this morning and she said you guys might have something cooking."

"I don't know what we got, if anything, but... shouldn't you be home resting?"

"I will be," he said. "But I just can't sit around and do nothing. I can't do it. I'm already going nuts. I'm already driving Grace crazy and it's what? Three days. She said I should come for a few hours this morning and then go back home and rest. Besides, if I didn't come in, I might not have seen that guy," he said, gesturing behind Tori.

She turned to see Teddy Marist sitting with Tony and Fiona. "Hey, what are you guys doing here?"

"We're on our way down to the Twin Cities," Tony said. "We wanted to get home for a few days, get Teddy settled there. He insisted we stop by and see you," Tony said and then tipped his head. He wanted a private word. While Braddock and the others huddled around Teddy, Tony and Tori stepped away.

"Fi and I also wanted to stop in. I know you're very busy, but I was kind of hoping you could sit down with him for a few minutes. He's had a very rough few days."

"And there will be more to come. He's going to need some help to process all this."

"My wife and I completely agree. We'll get him with someone. But in the meantime, I hate to impose, but I read up on you after watching you with him on Saturday. You've been through something like this as a teen, and it seems you've come out all right."

"If you only knew the truth," Tori said.

"Right now," Darr said, "I know it's only been a few days, but he needs some encouragement that things *will* get better. Fiona and I can say it will get better with time but what credibility do we have on that with him? The answer is not much. And, as you've seen, he's a pretty perceptive kid for his age. Lainey and Barry were very smart people. The apple didn't fall far from the tree."

"No, it didn't," Tori said. "Let's sit down for a few minutes. I can tell him my story and how it's come out." They walked back to the group and Tori approached Teddy. "Why don't you and I, and Tony and Fi, go talk for a few minutes before you head home. Would that be okay?"

"Yes," Teddy replied.

The question was where to go. Tori didn't want a conference room. Too sterile. She wanted comfort but Braddock wanted to hold a meeting in his office. Boe walked into the reception area, dressed in her full uniform, and stopped, seeing Steak and greeting him and then recognizing Teddy Marist. Tori introduced her to the Darrs and then Teddy.

Boe knelt to Teddy. "My name is Jeanette Boe. I'm the

Shepard County Sheriff." She held out her hand to shake Teddy's. "You're going to sit and chat with Tori for a little bit?"

Teddy nodded.

"We just need a good comfortable place," Tori said.

"My office," Boe said, her hand gently on Teddy's shoulder. "It's got a big comfortable couch. Take all the time you need."

"Hey," Nolan said, busting into the reception area. "These just came in from Ned Bollander." She handed out photos to everyone. They were facial sketches. "The sketches are based on the description given to a BCA sketch artist by the manager of the campsite where they found the RV."

"Let's give those a look," Braddock said.

Sketches in hand, and with Tony and Fi following along, Tori held Teddy's hand, guiding him down the hallway, stopping along the way a few times to show him offices or interview rooms and even her little cubby.

"This is yours?" Teddy asked, perplexed, looking at her small cubicle.

"Well, I only work part-time for the sheriff's department when they need help. I spend more time at the university these days, teaching. I have my own office there."

"You work at the university?"

"I do. I'm what they call an adjunct professor."

"Did you know my mom?"

Tori nodded. "I did, a little. I liked her."

She led him into Boe's office and showed him around for a minute, spending some time on Boe's ego wall filled with pictures of some prominent politicians such as the governor, Minnesota's two United States Senators, a few basketball and football players that Teddy recognized, before leading him over to the couch. "I'll be right back," she said, returning a minute later with a laptop and notebook. Teddy noticed them but didn't say anything when Tori set them on the coffee table in front of the couch.

Even with the warm-up of the office tour and look at the photos, Teddy sat straight on the couch, his eyes looking vacantly ahead. Tori knew that look, that feeling of stunned shock, as if you were paralyzed, unable to even process what had happened. She was like that for weeks after Jessie disappeared. It took a long time for the fog to clear. She sat down and turned her body toward him, her legs curled up underneath her.

"Your aunt and uncle say you've been pretty quiet."

Teddy just looked straight ahead.

"You miss your mom and dad."

Teddy looked down, not responding but his eyes were moist, and he nodded slightly.

Tori scooted a bit closer and leaned in, almost whispering, "I know you do. I know what this is all like."

He didn't move.

"I know what you're feeling. How much it hurts, way deep down inside. It's like an ache down in the pit of your stomach, isn't it?"

He simply nodded, not looking up.

"I know, *I know*. I've been through it myself. Almost the exact same thing."

"You have?" Teddy said, his eyes lifting to hers.

"I lost all of the people I loved before I was twenty years old," Tori replied, talking quietly. "When I was six, my mom died of cancer." She took out her phone and swiped through her photos and then shared the phone with Teddy. "That's her. Her, me and my twin sister, Jessie."

"Your sister. She's a twin?"

"Identical, it was quite difficult to tell us apart, especially at that age."

He held her phone.

"I don't remember that much about my mom, but I know

I've missed her all my life. After she died, it was just Jessie, me, and my dad. My dad was the sheriff. This—" she gestured around the room "—was his office. I was here all the time as a little girl with Jessie. Running the halls. We knew everybody in the department, heck everybody in the town, the county it felt like. My dad. Well, he is kind of a legend in these parts, Big Jim Hunter." She swiped to another photo of her and her dad. Tori was in her soccer uniform. "That's him."

"That was your dad?"

"You bet."

"He was a big guy."

"Larger than life," Tori said with a smile, looking at the mountain of a man her father was. "Jessie and I were much more like our mom physically, so it made for funny family photos. Jessie..." She halted for a moment. She could talk about it these days, but it still would hit her, choke her up some when it veered to her disappearance and murder. "She was my sister, my best friend, my... everything. We were rarely apart. We did everything together." She swiped to another photo. "We were both seventeen in that picture." They were in their prom dresses, both dressed in dark blue matching dresses. "And then she was gone."

"What happened to her?"

"A few months after that picture, her car was found abandoned north of town in the middle of the night with a flat tire. My dad and all his men searched and searched for her, but they couldn't find her. She had just disappeared, vanished into thin air without a sign of where she went. It was the Fourth of July. We were together earlier that night and that was the last time I ever saw her. Nobody knew what happened to her, not for twenty years."

Teddy looked at the picture.

"It was really hard on my dad," Tori said. "He was the sheriff. He sat in this office when his daughter disappeared on his watch." She sighed. "He was never the same after that. He died eighteen months later of a heart attack when I was away at college in Boston. So, I was nineteen, a freshman in college and had no family left."

"None."

"None. No aunts or uncles. No other siblings or cousins." She reached over and, with her left index finger, lightly turned Teddy's face to hers. "But I went through all that and I'm okay. I mean, don't I look okay?" She offered up a wide smile.

Teddy nodded.

"I was older than you when I lost my sister and my dad, but I know what you're feeling. What this is all like. What these first few days are like. I know what's ahead. And this is all going to really hurt for a good long while, but it will get better."

Teddy nodded, but his head went down again.

"I want you to look at me now," Tori said softly, tipping his chin back up again. "Look at me."

He raised his eyes to her.

"Did the sun come up this morning?"

Teddy looked at her for a moment and then nodded.

"The world hasn't ended. It keeps right on going. And we have to keep going with it even though those we loved are no longer here. You can't stop thinking about your mom and dad, right?"

"No," he said, tears in his eyes. "Or when we were being chased."

"Yeah, well, it'll be a long time before I stop thinking of that too, but you and me? Together, we made it. We're here, right?"

"Yes."

"And your mom and dad, you shouldn't stop thinking of them. What happened Friday, all of it, you'll think about it probably every day for the rest of your life and you know what I've learned?"

"What?"

"That that's okay."

He closed his eyes. "I just want it to go away. I want my mom and dad back."

"I know, buddy," she said, throwing her arm around him, looking to Tony and Fi, both of them teary eyed, and she knew what the last few days must have been like for all of them. With the focus on Teddy, it was easy to forget what they had both lost in this as well.

"Didn't you want your sister back, Tori?" Teddy said. "Your dad?"

"Yeah, Teddy, every day. I think about my sister, my mom and dad all the time. But they're not coming back, are they?"

"No," he said, sniffling, wiping his nose with the back of his hand. "How do you get over it?"

"Oh, you don't, buddy, you don't," she said, reaching for his hand. He should hear the truth, she thought, even at his age. Get it out there. "It never goes away but... in time, you get used to them being gone physically, but I think about my sister, my father, my mom, every day. They're always with me."

"How?"

She looked him in the eye. "It's hard to explain, but I feel their presence."

"Like they're ghosts or something?"

"I don't know about that, but I do feel as if they're looking in on me, checking on me, guiding me. I feel them here." She touched his heart. "And here." She touched his head. "I believe that if you remember them then they are never truly gone. They are always with you." She smiled even though holding back tears of her own. "I think they would be proud of me, what I've done with my life," she said, surprised at the degree she was choked up. "Do you want your mom and dad to be proud of you?"

He nodded.

"I truly believe they'll always be watching over you. Make

them proud," she said. "Make *me* proud. Make all we went through on Friday night to survive worth it. Can you do that for them? For me?"

"I'll try," Teddy replied softly.

"Good."

She gave him a hug, holding him close while he cried a bit. Tony handed her some Kleenex and she let Teddy wipe his eyes and nose.

"Did you figure out who did this to my mom and dad?" Teddy asked.

"You know, we're working on it." She reached for the sketches. "Do either of these men look familiar to you in any way?" One sketch was of a man with a large head and a longish bushy beard. The other man too had a beard, more trimmed and round glasses. They loosely matched the descriptions Newell DeBoer had provided of two men he'd seen in his bar. These were the men they were still after.

Teddy examined the photos and shook his head. "I don't recognize them. I only saw the one man with a mask and then Jared. I never saw their faces."

"Okay," Tori said, setting the sketches aside. "Now, you said you heard a woman's voice when you were in the back of the SUV, right?"

"Yes," Teddy said, nodding. "Her name was Max."

"You're sure?"

Teddy nodded.

"Could it have been Mac?"

Teddy took a moment. "No, I heard the voice clear. Max." He was firm, and she believed that was what he heard. She reached for the laptop, opened it, and pulled up an audio file. "I want you to listen to this."

Teddy listened for twenty to thirty seconds, Elaine Baird talking about her history with the bank.

"Does that sound like Max?"

"No, that wasn't the voice I heard," Teddy said emphatically. "I've heard that voice before, that sounds like Ms. Baird from the bank."

"You're sure," Tori pressed. "Absolutely sure."

"Yes. That voice is kind of..."

"High pitched."

"Yes," Teddy said. "That's not the voice I heard. The voice I heard was, I wouldn't say man like, but it was lower."

Tori nodded. "Like mine?"

"I'd say even lower than yours."

"Okay."

Tori pondered that response for a moment. The fact he'd identified Elaine quickly but then said she wasn't Max fed her theory—or was it fear—that they were still missing something.

Tony Darr snapped her out of her trance. "You probably have work to get to."

"Ahh, yes, I do," Tori said, but then looked back to Teddy. "Your aunt and uncle have my phone number. If you want to talk, just call. I always have time to talk. Okay? Especially for you."

For the first time all morning, Teddy offered a real smile, not a forced one.

As they slowly walked down the hallway, they went by a conference room. The door was open, and Tori could hear the voices of Eggs, Nolan, and Reese. They were listening to a recording of an interview from yesterday, Marist's name being mentioned.

Tori took a couple of quick steps ahead to pull the door closed. She turned around. "I'm sorry... about..."

Teddy's eyes were wide open, his eyebrows raised. At first, she thought because he'd heard his father's name, but then she realized that wasn't it. She looked at the door and then back to Teddy. "What is it?"

Tony looked down to his nephew and saw the look in his eyes. "Teddy?'

Tori knelt to him. "What is it, Teddy? Did you see or—" she looked to the conference room door "—hear something. You heard something? Didn't you? Tell me."

"That woman's voice before you closed the door."

"Yeah?"

"That's the voice I heard when I was in the SUV."

"Max?"

Teddy nodded.

Tori pushed open the door to the conference room, pulling Teddy inside by the hand.

Nolan stopped the voice. "Sorry, Tori, we were just reviewing—"

"Let it play. Let him hear it."

"O-o-okay," she said and hit play and let the interview run. Observing Teddy as he listened to the woman's voice as she answered questions from Braddock. Teddy looked at Tori and nodded. "That's her."

"You're sure?"

"I'm sure. That's Max."

Tori looked to Eggleston. "Go get Braddock. Now."

Eggleston rushed out of the conference room. Tori led Teddy, along with Tony and Fiona Darr, to the reception area.

"What was that? Was that important?" Tony Darr asked.

"Yes," Tori said, kneeling to give Teddy a quick embrace, holding his face gently in her hands. "You did good. You did so good." She looked up to Tony and Fi. "He did good. I... have to go."

She rushed back down the hallway to find Braddock in the conference room listening to the voice. "That's her?"

"Max is Nora Bartness."

THIRTY

"IT'S RIGHT THERE IN BLACK AND WHITE."

Braddock called the bank and spoke with Joan Wills. "Is Nora Bartness there today?"

"Nora? No, she's not. She called in and took a PTO day. She said she wasn't feeling well."

"Is that unusual?"

"Kind of. It isn't something that happens often," Wills replied. "I was thinking maybe yesterday unsettled her and she just needed some time. It's a bit tense around here this morning."

"I imagine so. I need to speak with her. If she comes in or contacts you, let me know." Braddock hung up. "Nolan."

"I'm supposed to be going up to the university on crowd control. Me and Reese."

"Not now."

"On it." Nolan nodded. "Everything I can find on Bartness."

To everyone else, he ordered, "Let's go."

Braddock and Tori, followed by Eggleston and Reese and two deputies, with lights and sirens, made the speed run north on the H-4 to Holmstrand, taking a right off the freeway, just south of town. He made a right turn off the county road, turned off his siren but left his lights flashing.

"It's the third one up on the left," Tori said, examining the map.

Braddock turned left and accelerated up the long driveway, the house sitting on a wide multi-acre lot. He skidded to a stop twenty yards short of the garage. Reese pulled up right behind, followed by one of the deputies, the other blocking the end of the driveway.

He and Tori made their way to the front door. Braddock knocked and hit the doorbell but after waiting a few seconds, there was no response. He turned and gestured to Reese and Eggleston, who each took a side of the house while he pounded on the door again. Tori drifted from the front door toward the garage, standing on her tippy toes to peer in the small horizontal windows. "Black Jeep Cherokee inside," she hollered.

Braddock hustled over for a look. "No answer and it doesn't feel like anyone is home. That and as I look, the shades and curtains are all pulled."

"They are," Eggs said. "Along the back and sides too. Can't see a damn thing inside, not even the window over what I suspect is the kitchen sink, blinds are closed shut."

Braddock walked around to the side of the garage and tried the knob for the side door. It was locked but there was a rectangular window, high on the side. He peered inside. "Pretty empty other than the Cherokee."

He walked around to the front and called a deputy over. "You park your ass at the end of the driveway, understand. Anyone shows up, you hold them and call it in."

"Yes, sir," the deputy replied.

He turned to Eggs and Reese. "Let's get a bulletin out for Nora Bartness."

"On it," Reese said.

"The bank?" Tori said.

"Yes."

Braddock raced back to Manchester Bay but this time, as he pulled into the parking lot, he didn't have his police lights on. Inside, they found Joan Wills and Elaine Baird.

Baird was smart enough to lead them back to her office and close the door. "I'm calling my lawyer."

"We're not here about you," Braddock said.

"I don't care. I'm not saying a word—"

"Nora Bartness," Tori said, looking to Wills and then to Baird. "What do you know about her?"

"Nora?" Baird said, sharing a look with Wills. "She's worked as my assistant for, gosh, seven years, maybe more. She had been at the bank when I got here, in—" she pondered for a moment "—it was in electronic banking when I got here. She was—"

"Electronic banking?" Braddock said.

"Yes, why?"

"Tell us more about her?"

"Why?"

"Answer the question. She was in electronic banking, you hired her as your assistant."

"Umm, I'd been here a few months when the person who was originally assisting me left unexpectedly. I remember going to Barry and asking him for anyone he thought could step in and help until I replaced the person. He said Nora almost immediately. Nora, he said, was whip-smart, reliable and would be able to help. I didn't know her, but she came to work for me and after about a week, well, I realized I had who I needed. She's a whiz. Heck, she'd be one of our vice presidents if she'd have finished college. She's three semesters short of her college degree. Her credits from Appalachian State all would transfer to the university here. I've encouraged her repeatedly to finish."

"Appalachian State?" Tori said. "That's North Carolina, right?"

"Yes," Wills said. "Some town up in the mountains, I think. Bone, Boone, or something like that. Always made me think of the Boonies. Nora would often say she was from the Boonies."

"Why are you asking?" Baird said.

"We're investigating. We learned something we're following up on. I need a copy of her personnel file."

"We can't just—" Baird started.

"Yes, you can," Tori said. "Barry Marist might not be the only one who was set-up here."

Baird's eyes locked on Tori's for a moment. "Joan, go get them her file."

"But, but..."

"Just get it."

Braddock's phone buzzed. It was Nolan. "Nolan, what do you got?"

"Boss, you need to get back here. Right now!"

* * *

Nora drove the white Tahoe through the maze of apartment buildings and old houses north of the campus, mindful of her rearview mirror as the SUV climbed a gentle incline and then turned right into a parking lot and looped around behind a three-story apartment complex.

They were here. It was time. It had her thinking back to last night when she'd gotten home. She'd found Towne and Jenks sitting in the kitchen, beers in front of them, laughing until they saw her expression.

"What is it?" Jenks asked.

"Well," she said as she walked to the refrigerator and retrieved a beer for herself. "I spent the whole afternoon being interrogated by the police. By Will Braddock and Tori Hunter."

Towne had immediately rushed to the front windows of the house, peering outside, his gun drawn.

"Calm down. I wasn't followed. They weren't interested in me that way."

"How do you know?" he replied, carefully pulling the curtain back. "How can you be sure?"

"Because I'm not under suspicion," she replied. "Elaine is. They're warming to the thought that she was behind everything."

Towne peered back. "Really?"

"They know about the relationship between her and Marist. They had evidence of it, hotel records, even video, which amazed the hell out of me. And then they had Joan Wills in at the same time I was, and she told them about the unclaimed account money that was missing. And as I've told you two, that was just the tip of the iceberg. They also know about the safe deposit box up in Akeley."

"Just like you did," Towne said.

"That's right. They're onto all of that so, now, they're focused on the bank and Elaine and that she did all this to punish Barry."

Her brother's eyes brightened. "Just like you thought they might."

"Exactly," she had replied, raising her beer to her smiling lips. "And I didn't even have to be the one to tell them. They came to me. They'll spend all day chasing that lead tomorrow while we're doing our thing and—" she smiled "—then just slipping away."

Now, Nora sat still, her hands on the wheel, the top of the auditorium with the clock tower spire rising from it visible in the distance. To their left was an open field, though several backstops were visible. A large green sign fifty yards away had an arrow toward a gap in the fencing. It read: CMSU Intramural Fields. She reached for a set of binoculars. With the expected security around the university, and the auditorium in particular, they knew they couldn't risk getting too close to the campus.

From their perch atop the rise, they had a clear view. The main body of Central Minnesota State University was in the shape of two long east to west rectangles. The south side of the campus had residence halls around a broad lawn. The north side of the campus was shaped much the same, with the lecture halls and administration buildings running on the north and south sides of a long mall of intersecting sidewalks. Located in a small north south box of its own, was the Riley Auditorium, the top half of which was visible in the distance to the southwest, a bit over five hundred yards away.

"When did you find this spot?" Jenks inquired.

"Saturday night," Nora answered, scanning the area. "Towne and I did a drive around the campus."

"It's an easy walk-in on foot from here," Towne said. Fifty feet to their right was a walking path that led down the hill to a sidewalk that would take him south right into the northwest corner of the campus grounds. Towne pulled his gun from his shoulder holster, checked it, and then snapped it back in and zipped his black winter jacket up tight.

"I'll hoof it in. I just need to set the timer and then it'll all be over but the shouting."

"We'll be listening," Nora said, the radio tuned to the campus radio station that would be carrying live audio of the event.

Towne climbed out of the SUV, tugged his coat down and started walking toward the path.

* * *

The drive back took three minutes. Nolan was waiting in the conference room. "Boss, this is not good." She was projecting her laptop screen on the flat-screen. "Nora Bartness, née Meade, has an interesting background, first of which is Bartness is her married name. She married a man named Delvin Bartness, eighteen years ago when she was twenty-one, down in Boone, North Carolina. They had both been students at Appalachian State University. He was two years her senior. He graduated, she did not."

"That jibes with what Wills and Baird just told us. She's from North Carolina. Where Bayne and Mercer were living, that same general area."

"Right. Bartness and her husband moved to St. Louis and then here. Delvin apparently used to work for Mannion Companies."

"That perhaps explains why she didn't finish college," Tori noted, explaining what they learned at the bank. "She married early, moved to St. Louis and for whatever reason, never finished school."

"Perhaps. Her and Delvin divorced a little over a year ago," Nolan said. "Just like she said last night, but that's not what matters. What matters is Nora's true birth name was Nora *Maxine* Meade."

"Maxine," Tori said. "Max."

"Possibly," Nolan said. "I did a quick family history. The name Maxine I suspect comes from her father's mother, who was named Maxine Meade. Nora got it as a middle name. But there is more, maybe a lot more. Max matters but so does the last name, Meade. These are her brothers Rodney and Townsend."

"Towne," Tori murmured. Townsend Meade had a tight beard, wore glasses and looked a bit like the man in one of the sketches. "You don't suppose?"

"Yeah," Braddock muttered, nodding. "He's one of our guys."

Nolan continued. "Rodney is dead, Townsend is still alive.

Those two have had themselves some issues with law enforcement down in North Carolina and Tennessee."

"Like what?" Braddock asked.

"The oldest brother was Rodney. He led a loosely affiliated group of anti-government activists who lived up in the mountains of North Carolina."

"Militia?"

"They didn't call themselves that. It was a pretty small informal group that didn't have any sort of a name or manifesto or any of that, but Rodney Meade, had some pretty extreme and inflammatory views he was putting out there. I've been skimming from summaries, but early on he mostly railed against federal and state land management but as time went on, he was posting anti-immigration stuff as well, but again, nothing *that* unusual. Lots of that out there the last decade. We've seen it around here from time to time, you know, the MN Partisans thing last year."

"In any event, Meade lived on this farm up in the mountains outside Boone, North Carolina." She pulled up a photo array.

"I've seen that photo before?" Tori blurted. Then it hit her. "Meade? Meade? The Meade Farm Standoff?"

"The standoff in... North Carolina," Braddock said, closing his eyes. "Shit. Not good."

"I think *that's* the tie here," Nolan replied. "This farm in the photo was a meeting spot for Rodney Meade and his like-minded followers, like younger brother Townsend." She switched to an aerial map. "This was in the middle of nowhere northwest North Carolina. Very rural, very isolated. Lots of room to roam and do whatever you want, assuming you don't draw any attention to yourself."

"Which they did," Braddock said. "Reminds me of Two Coves and environs west of there, especially the area where

Bayne's Uncle Bud lived. People who live out there usually just want to be left alone."

Tori nodded along. "Remember, they don't like our kind."

"That said," Nolan continued, "Rodney Meade wasn't on anyone's radar until someone inside the group had loose lips one night at a bar in the small town of Stony Gap, population 207. This guy, a few too many beers in, thought he was amongst like-minded friends. He talked big about Rodney Meade and his guys wanting to make a point and were looking at a pro-immigration rally in Knoxville, Tennessee, at the university, as the place to make it. Problem was, one of the guys within earshot was concerned about what he heard. His brother was an officer with the North Carolina Department of Natural and Cultural Resources. Meade's guy said it wasn't going to be a counter protest, or some guy driving a truck into the crowd, or roughing a few folks up. It would be something that would be *loud*."

"Ahh, that's why this is ringing all kinds of alarms," Braddock said.

"The DNR officer looked up Rodney Meade, read some of his rantings online and reported what he heard to his boss, and within a few days the report made it all the way up the chain of command of the North Carolina State Police. But by the time it made it to the top the scramble was on as it was the day of the actual event in Knoxville. Four men from Meade's group were already in a small roadside motel in Knoxville, ready to make their move on the rally."

Nolan switched to another photo.

"In coordination with authorities in Tennessee, the motel was raided, and the North Carolina Governor ordered a simultaneous raid on the Meade Farm up in the mountains."

"There were two incidents, right?" Tori said. "The first was at the motel. They arrested three men who were outside, getting into a truck, but the other one still inside—"

"Didn't go quietly," Nolan said. She pulled up a photo of

four men. "These are the four involved. The supposed leader of this quartet was Warrick Jenkins, second from the right." Jenkins had wide shoulders and a full beard. "Jenkins was the man still inside the motel room. The police showed and he just started shooting. Two officers were severely wounded. Jenkins ended up dead, shot five times. In the motel room they found explosives and several other weapons. In fact, it looked like the plan was similar to the Boston Marathon. The four of them were going to the event in Knoxville and were going to drop backpacks at strategic points with bombs on timers and well..."

"Knoxville was the appetizer," Braddock said, now sitting in front of the computer. "The main course is what happened at the farm in North Carolina."

"That's right." Nolan nodded and hit a few more keystrokes, flipping back to the mountain location. "The state police were on the phone with the North Carolina Governor's office, after all that happened in Knoxville. The governor himself ordered the state police to immediately move on the farm before anything else happened. It was a mistake."

"Why?" Braddock asked.

"Unbeknownst to the governor and the state police, before he went down in his blaze of glory, Warrick Jenkins made one last phone call to his best buddy Rodney Meade. Meade and six other men in the house with him were ready and spoiling for a fight when the North Carolina State Police came charging up his driveway literally a minute after the call from Jenkins. There was a big firefight. One state police officer died, and two others were wounded. Meade and four of his other men were killed. Meade and two others in the house were fatally shot, the other two died in an explosion of the farmhouse, two others in a barn were severely wounded."

"It was far more complicated than that though," Tori said, jogging her memory when the shoot-out was part of the national news for a few days. "If I remember right, the state police got there, took position and called out to Meade and his men to surrender." She reached over and took over the mouse from Nolan and scrolled down the page. "Meade responded he would do no such thing. Then there was movement in a barn that was behind the police. There were armed men inside. Two officers turned to confront them. Someone fired. And then all hell broke loose with dual firefights, the state police caught in the middle, Meade's men firing from the house and the barn."

"Who fired first?" Eggs asked.

"It was unclear *that* day. The FBI and the U.S. Attorney's office were brought in to investigate," Tori said. "There was some stonewalling, some lawyering, but eventually a state police officer fessed up and said he fired first. He was in an exposed position and saw a move from inside the barn and thought he was going to be fired upon. He said in his mind, knowing what had happened in Knoxville already, it was kill or be killed."

"Did that officer face criminal charges?"

"No. The U.S. Attorney declined to charge. That decision was controversial, at least in that part of North Carolina," Tori said, reading through the report. "It was a tense situation."

"It was a powder keg," Braddock observed. "The state police had no idea what they were driving into."

"That's all of interest, but not as much as this is right now," Nolan said. "There were other men who were also arrested that day. Six men were found higher up the mountain behind the farm. They were heavily armed and had high ground positions. It could have gotten that much uglier but by then, more support had arrived and the force in place was overwhelming. Those men up the mountain eventually stood down. Two of them were Townsend Meade, who I showed you, and Wayne Jenkins, brother of Warrick."

"Jenks," Tori said.

"Looks a bit like this sketch does he not, with the big beard?" Braddock said.

"He does. I think we've identified Towne and Jenks. These are the guys that DeBoer described. These are our guys from Friday."

"I think they are," Braddock said. "Townsend Meade witnesses his brother Rodney go down."

"And Wayne Jenkins knew his brother Warrick had died in Knoxville," Nolan said.

"I'm surprised they did stand down," Eggs observed.

"It's like Nolan said, after the initial firefight, sheriff's departments from every surrounding county responded, along with a SWAT Team from Boone," Tori explained. "They went from not enough force to overwhelming force. Despite the high ground it would have been suicide to fight it out."

Reese blurted out a laugh. "Why weren't they part of this from the get-go?"

Tori nodded in agreement. "Why a SWAT team wasn't part of the initial move on the farm is just one more part of the total clusterfuck this thing ended up being. The governor gave the order to move immediately. The state police went in all hot and aggressive on the governor's orders without fully knowing who or what they were up against or where they were all positioned. They drove themselves right into being surrounded and ambushed."

"In retrospect, the authorities in Tennessee or North Carolina didn't truly understand what they were dealing with that day," Braddock said. "Meade's group was unknown but turned out to be far more violent, extreme and committed than anyone could have anticipated."

* * *

Friday and Saturday had been a whiteout blizzard, temperatures hovering around zero. Now, it was glorious, not a cloud in the sky, the sun brilliant against the deep-blue cloudless sky, the air fresh and clean, the temperature in the low-thirties. You could already see the effect of the bright sun working on the large snow piles, the slow melt beginning, pools of water gathering in the low spots on the sidewalks and crosswalks.

In his fully zipped black puffer winter coat, his stocking cap low on his forehead, sunglasses tight to his face, Towne walked with his hands in his coat pockets. He crossed a street and stepped onto the campus and veered at a forty-five-degree angle to his right on a sidewalk leading down a slight incline between two academic buildings. As he emerged from between the two buildings, he found himself on the eastern end of the long open lawn that dissected the middle of the academic part of the campus, where he saw more pedestrians strolling about over the noon hour on a bustling Tuesday, the university alive, students everywhere.

Ahead a hundred yards, on the far side of the lawn, the last of the crowd was filing into the Riley Auditorium, security scanning tickets and checking people as they walked inside, police officers and sheriff's deputies visible and walking about. The seating capacity of the auditorium was 2,800. It would be an overflow crowd.

So much the better.

Fifty yards short of the auditorium he spotted an empty bench on the right side of the sidewalk. He sat down, crossed his right leg over the left and relaxed, and took out the detonator that looked much like an old cell phone. The signal from the receiver was strong.

He slipped it back into his pocket and checked his watch. The program would start in five minutes.

Now it was all a matter of timing.

* * *

"Were Jared Bayne and Colum Mercer caught up in this?" Eggs said, bringing it back to the case.

"No," Nolan replied. "At least not in any official record. It would have showed up when we dug into them. Given what we know of them, that they eventually found their way to guys like this, if they did, shouldn't be all that surprising."

"What happened to Townsend Meade and Wayne Jenkins and the others found on the mountain?"

"They didn't engage in the gun battle. They surrendered without firing a shot. Given how the investigation shook out, that the police *initiated* the gunfight, they were charged but got probation. No prison time," Tori said, continuing to slowly scroll through the file projected on the screen. "The final outcome was political so everyone would just walk away."

"Well," Eggleston started. "This is all very interesting. But how does all that relate to us? Nora is Max. Does she call up her brother Townsend, and maybe Wayne Jenkins, plus perhaps Bayne and Mercer, and they do the Marist thing for the *money*? And their plan is to just walk away."

"No, there's more to this," Tori said as she scrolled through the file on the computer. "There's something else."

"Stop!" Braddock said to Tori, grabbing her right arm. "Scroll back up. Now. *Now!*"

Tori reversed course with the mouse. "What? What is it?"

"No, higher. Higher!"

She slowly scrolled up.

"Oh shit!" Braddock exclaimed. "Shit. Shit. *Shit!*"

"What!" Eggs said.

"We have to roll and right now."

"What? Why?" Tori said.

"There's the more that Jared talked about. It's right there in black and white," Braddock said, his eyes wide. "The Governor of North Carolina was the one who made the call to rush the Meade farm. The governor was Cooper Farrow."

"Farrow?" Tori's eyes went wide in recognition. "Cooper Farrow, the Secretary of Commerce. The university." She looked at her watch. "What time does the event start?"

"It already has," Braddock said, grabbing his phone and police radio. "Nolan. Get pictures of Meade and Jenkins out with Nora Bartness and any other known associates. Everyone else, come on!"

* * *

He checked his watch again. Farrow was scheduled to speak at 12:25, after the university president, a local businessman named Kyle Mannion, and the Minnesota governor had finished their remarks. His cell phone buzzed in his pocket. It was Nora.

"Where are we at?"

"They're right on schedule. Farrow is next."

Towne hung up and stuffed his phone in his left coat pocket. He pulled the transmitter out of his right pocket, checked the signal again and then activated it, the clock on the display screen flashing.

15:00… 14:59… 14:58…

THIRTY-ONE

"WHICH WAY DO YOU WANT TO BE WRONG?"

They all raced out of the building, and Braddock tossed Tori the keys as he was on his phone trying to reach Boe. "She isn't answering," he said as they got in the Tahoe. "The program has started. She was invited to sit with them on the stage with the governor, the senators, state, and federal representatives. She can't answer her phone sitting there, and she definitely doesn't want to get off that stage."

"Text her."

"Text her what?"

"We're coming. There may be an attack."

"Yeah, but what kind? And when? From where? We have the who. We don't know the how."

"We'll fill in the details when we get there. Just text her."

Tori drove, turning on the lights and racing away from the government center and through downtown, clearing traffic with the siren. Reese and Eggleston were right behind. As they crossed under the H-4 and raced up the hill toward campus, Braddock killed the siren.

"The state police in North Carolina had no idea what they

were driving themselves into. Neither do we. Let's not announce too much presence."

The flashing police lights were enough to clear any traffic. Knowing the campus road grid, Tori took the road framing the south of the main campus and then took a left, a service road that threaded between two dorms and past a physical plant building and came in behind the auditorium, where they were met by two Minnesota State Patrol officers, Deputy Sheriff Cole Lamb and a man in a U.S. Marshal's jacket holding a radio.

"Will, what's going on?" Lamb asked.

"Cole, there might be an attack, we think on the secretary of commerce among others," Braddock said as Tori led everyone to a back door to the auditorium.

"Detective Braddock, I'm Marshal Jackson," the stocky man in the marshals jacket said. He was responsible for the secretary's security. "You said an attack on the secretary. What kind of an attack?"

"We're not sure," Tori said. "But it ties in with our triple murder last Friday which I suspect Sheriff Boe has mentioned."

"She has," Jackson retorted. "How does that relate to the secretary?"

"There's not a lot of time, but if there is a threat, it'll be directed at the secretary," Braddock said, giving the marshal a rundown as they made their way through hallways to the back of the stage. "I know it's not much but we're looking for this woman and this man we think. Nora Bartness, maiden name Meade," Braddock said, holding up his phone. "Townsend Meade is her older brother. And maybe this man." He swiped to another photo. "Wayne Jenkins, a known associate of Meade. These photos are going out to my people. The troopers, marshals, campus police and security all need to be on the lookout."

* * *

7:07... 7:06... 7:05...

Towne rested on the bench, making a show of casually reading his phone, feeling the warmth of the sun on his face. Students were flowing by, chatting with classmates or with their eyes glued to their phones, paying him no attention.

He caught the distant sound of a siren to the west from town for a few seconds, but then it was gone. A minute later he caught a glimpse in the distance of what he thought were flashing police lights which in and of itself wasn't alarming, there were police vehicles spread about that had their lights on, a loose sort of security for the event.

Between the buildings to the south, he caught hints of it and then two black Tahoe's with their grill lights flashing zoomed in along the same narrow service road they had taken on Sunday night. He saw Braddock get out of the lead Tahoe and then the smaller Hunter from the driver's side and they were met by others and then hustled to the back of the auditorium. He took out his phone and called Nora. "Something is up. Braddock and Hunter just rolled in here in a big old hurry, police lights flashing. Do they know?"

"The kid? Maybe those uncles of Bayne?" Nora said.

"Or the bank," Jenks said, looking at Nora. "You thought they were all over Elaine. What if?"

"They looked deeper into me," Nora said. "Saw my maiden name. Did a little digging."

"That could be," Jenks said. "Assume they've identified us. We have to get out of here."

"Get back here," Nora said to her brother.

"On my way," Towne said, standing up. He was about to start walking when he saw more police vehicles approaching the campus. And suddenly the campus mall was flooded with police officers, deputies, and troopers. They were stopping people, checking on them. He looked to his left and the sidewalk he walked into the mall. Officers had the gap cut off between buildings, stopping people. Turning to his right, it was the same between buildings. They were cordoning off the mall area. They were putting resources in position rapidly as if they were expecting some sort of attack, or to ward it off. Either way. He was trapped.

He checked the transmitter.

3:22... 3:21... 3:20...

"I have to hold position."

* * *

"We need to pick a side. Which way should I go?" Nolan exclaimed as she reached the top of the hill and campus in her department Explorer. It was either go left, right or hold position.

"Go left, swing around the north side of the campus," Steak suggested.

"Why that way?"

"The motorcade, such that it is for the secretary and governor are set up to leave through the north side of campus. If they were going to attack that, they would position themselves in that direction."

Nolan turned left, while Steak peered into the campus, glancing from the blown-up pictures of Meade, Bartness, and Jenkins and into the campus.

She took one look at Steak. "You should not be here."

"Yet I am," he said. "Hand me the radio."

* * *

"Check the motorcade exit route," Steak's voice called from the radio. "Check that route, it's the most likely area of attack."

"Copy," Braddock replied.

"Meade? Meade?" Marshal Jackson said, squinting at them. "Why does that name ring a bell."

"The Meade Farm Standoff down in North Carolina. The secretary was the governor of North Carolina back then and ordered the state police to hit the Meade Farm."

The Marshal nodded. "Okay. And you're saying Meade and Jenkins are here."

"We think it's possible."

"But we don't know what we're dealing with. Or what kind of attack?"

"No, we don't," Braddock said as he and Tori, along with Jackson and Lamb walked towards the door to the backstage area. Braddock looked to Lamb. "It's most of our guys and troopers around here, right?"

Lamb nodded.

"They've been texted photos of Meade, Jenkins, and Bartness. They need to keep their eyes open for one of them. They could be lurking about. Check vehicles. Eyes, and ears open. And check that exit route and clear it."

Lamb rushed off.

Braddock opened the door, and he, Tori and Jackson stepped inside and then made their way along the left wall of the stage, invisible to the audience behind curtains, but they were able to get a fuller view of the stage. The Minnesota governor was currently speaking, the audience laughing at a comment.

Jackson and Lamb were looking out at the audience, particularly up front. Four men in uniform, two campus security and two Manchester Bay police officers were now visible in the back. Two more entered from side doors, taking place along the wall.

Braddock glimpsed Boe who was peering out to the audience, and he could see that she had noticed the sudden increase in security. She turned to her left and caught the motion of Braddock waving and glared at him. He waved for her to come over. He could tell she didn't want to leave her seat. Braddock mouthed: *Get over here. Now!*

Boe took one last look around, then slinked out of her chair and to the side of the stage.

"What the hell?"

"There may be an attack," Tori said.

"May?"

Tori explained what they found on Nora Bartness and Meade. "They're here. The secretary is here. It's a seemingly innocuous event where he's bestowing money on the university. It's a chance."

"When does he speak?" Braddock asked.

"Uh, next," Boe said, showing Braddock the program. "The governor is wrapping up, getting ready to introduce the secretary. What kind of an attack?"

"We don't know. They had guns and explosives in North Carolina," Tori whispered.

Braddock scanned the auditorium and then the stage area, looking to the governor. "Oh no."

"What?" Boe said.

"Tori, the podium."

Tori checked out the podium, the cherry wood, the decorative Columbia Blue stripe painted around the base. "You don't suppose."

"The wood in Bayne's garage, the pieces by the table saw were exactly like that wood. *Exactly*. They were the width of the base of it. The blue paint, the *Columbia Blue* paint. CMSU Blue."

"They were going to bomb that immigration rally in Knoxville," Tori said. "They were going to use C-4 in backpacks and set them off with remote detonators."

"Bomb squad?" Boe said.

"No time right now," Braddock replied and turned to Jackson. "We need to clear it out."

Jackson contemplated the move, starting to nod.

"If we're wrong," Boe said.

"We overreacted," Tori said. "And Braddock and I take all the blame."

"But what if we're not, Jeanette!" Braddock said. "There's three thousand people plus in here. More outside. A lot of our friends are in here. Which way do you want to be wrong?"

"But if we start evacuating, don't they trigger the bomb?"

"They trigger if we don't."

"We gotta move on this," Jackson asserted. "It's my call on the secretary." Into the radio, he ordered: "This is Jackson. We have a potential bomb threat. Evacuate the auditorium. Evacuate the entire area. Now!"

He stepped out onto the stage with Boe, approaching the governor and secretary. "Mr. Secretary, Governor, everyone, we have a possible threat. Come with us."

* * *

"This is Jackson. We have a potential bomb threat. Evacuate the auditorium. Evacuate the entire area. Now!"

"Bomb!" Nolan blurted. "Holy shit."

"Keep driving," Steak said. "Eyes open for these guys."

"They could be miles away and blow that thing."

"Nah," Steak said, shaking his head. "Not these guys. This is about revenge. They're going to want to see it for themselves. No way they miss this. Not now. Not this close."

* * *

Boe guided the dignitaries off the main stage. Braddock and Tori made their way down the side wall and through a door into the auditorium seating area. "Come on," he said waving to everyone in the front row of the audience. "We're evacuating. Now."

People looked at Braddock in a mix of confusion and apprehension. "Now! Come on! Out the exits! Out the exits! Evacuate! *Move!*"

Tori rushed up the side aisle, waving for people to move. "Come on, let's go. Let's go! Go! Go! Go! Out the emergency exits. Come on!" Thankfully there were numerous exits along the side walls and some of the attendees were professors and recognized and knew Tori. If she was saying go, this had to be serious, and they encouraged people to move along. "Let's go! Let's go!" a professor urged.

"Come on! Come on!" Tori waved. "Go, go, go. Hustle, hustle, hustle."

She worked her way up the aisle, people now frantically rushing by. She quickly looked back to see Braddock waving people to the side door near the front, attendees rushing out both sides of the auditorium. She saw him move to the door itself, holding it open.

* * *

Meade checked the transmitter.

:27... :26... :25...

People rushed out of the auditorium, from the front atrium, out the side doors, running away in all directions.

:17...:16...15...

He stood up and started walking east, blending in with the crowd rushing away from the auditorium.

* * *

"Turn the corner," Steak ordered. "Go ahead, stop just after the building. We can see all the way down the mall."

"Copy that," Nolan said, pulling to a stop.

* * *

Tori looked back at the stage, Jackson, Boe and Lamb had cleared everyone away.

People were moving rapidly out of the auditorium, people rushing up the center aisle out the back or fleeing via the side exits. She held the door open and then stepped into the exterior hallway and moved to another exit door, holding it open. "Let's go! Let's go!" she urged, windmilling her left arm. "Come on. Come on!"

Where was Braddock?

* * *

Towne looked back as he walked, people still rushing out of the auditorium and out onto the mall, rushing in every direction. He looked down at the transmitter.

:09... :08... :07...

* * *

Tori held the door open, people still rushing by. She looked back toward the door nearest the stage. Braddock, where are you?

"Braddock! Braddock!" she yelled.

And then she saw him, following the last of the people out of the auditorium. He caught her eye. "*Get out! Go!*"

* * *

Towne looked down to his right hand.

:04... :03... :02...

He walked faster.

* * *

BOOOOOOOOOOOOM!

* * *

"Oh my God!" Nolan exclaimed at the towering fireball.

"Dear God," Steak murmured.

"Did they all get out? Did they get out?"

"Will! Tori!" Steak called over the radio. "*Will!*"

There was silence, Nolan and Steak staring at one another in horror.

"Oh God," Steak murmured.

The two of them sat still, barely able to breathe.

"*Will! Will!*" Steak screamed into the radio.

Come on, answer. Answer.

THIRTY-TWO

"IT'S TOTAL CHAOS RIGHT NOW."

"Whoa!" Jenks bellowed. "Yeah! Yeah! *Yeah!*"

"Did we get them?" Nora asked. "Where is Towne? Brother?" she called into the phone.

"I'm fleeing with the crowd," Towne replied, keeping up the brisk walking pace. He planned to walk out the same way he'd come into campus but as he looked ahead to his left there were police between the buildings on the sidewalk, still checking people as they walked by. If the police had figured out the bomb before it happened, they likely knew who he was.

"Where are you now?" Nora called in his EarPod.

"I'm walking to the northeast corner of campus. There are cops everywhere," he muttered as he kept straight ahead, now flowing with the crowd toward the east end of the campus. The problem was that now people were sensing they were safe and were stopping and looking back toward the rubble of the bombed-out auditorium. The crowd around him was thinning out. He was more exposed.

* * *

"Will! Copy!" Nolan called into her radio. "Will! Come on, Will!"

"Nolan?" Steak said, snapping out of his shock, gesturing with his right hand.

"Yeah?"

"Take a look at something. That guy in the black jacket and stocking cap," Steak said. "See him?"

"Uh, yeah, I do now," Nolan said. "What about him?"

"He has a look about him." He held up the photo of Townsend Meade. "The beard is shorter, but he's tall, has the beard, is older, and..."

"And what?"

"Nolan, he's calm. He caught my eye just after the explosion and he was... calm. Walking, not running, not frantic, just... walking."

"He's angling away from us," Nolan said putting the Explorer in reverse, zooming backward.

* * *

There was a slight incline in the sidewalk up to the northeast corner of the campus. Towne rushed up the sidewalk now largely on his own, isolated and there were no cops. The sidewalk led to an intersection. He looked up the hill in the distance and he could see the white Tahoe up on the bluff in the parking lot. Two minutes and he'd be with them.

There was a squeal of tires.

A black Explorer backed up right into the middle of the intersection, grill lights flashing.

* * *

"That's him," Steak said as Nolan backed up into the middle of the intersection, skidding to a stop.

They both locked eyes with the man.

"That's Meade!" Nolan exclaimed.

"We got eyes on Meade!" Steak exclaimed. "Northwest corner of campus."

* * *

Towne stared at the two officers. One raised his radio up.

* * *

"Oh shit," Nora blurted. "Towne, get out of there!"

Towne pivoted to the right and sprinted.

* * *

"Nolan!" Steak exclaimed.

Nolan put the SUV in drive and tried cutting him off but was too late.

"We got a runner! Follow him!"

"I am. I am."

"Will! Will! Are you out there dammit?" Steak called into the radio.

* * *

The shockwave propelled Tori forward off her feet, driving her hard into a large snowbank, glass and debris landing all around her.

"Oof," she moaned as she rolled onto her back, dazed, her eyes blurred by smoke and flames, her body jarred and searing from the blast and then her impact into the snowbank. She squinted, her ears ringing. A massive hole had been blown in the middle of the auditorium, the glass obliterated, the bricking and structure collapsed. Smoke and flames, and now she felt the heat of it.

Someone shook her. "Are you okay! Hey, are you okay!"

She tried to focus.

"*Tori!*"

It was Braddock, his face dirtied from smoke and cuts, blood running down the side of his face. "Tori, are you okay!"

"Yeah," she groaned. "I'm... okay." She shook herself to attention, checking all her limbs. "You're bleeding."

"I'm okay," he said, as he inspected her head and scalp. "You're bleeding too but not badly."

Braddock helped Tori onto her feet, her legs a little wobbly. "I can stand," she said and exhaled a breath, and then looked about. People were lying on the ground, groaning. "All these people."

Sirens filled the air.

"Will! Will!" Steak called over the radio. "Dammit, Will! Answer!"

"Steak, I'm here, I'm here," Braddock said.

"And Tori?"

"Her too. We're... we're okay."

"Then start running east."

"What? Why?"

"Because Nolan and I have a bead on Townsend Meade," Steak exclaimed as Nolan raced ahead before turning hard left, her lights and siren blaring. "He's on the run, east of campus, into the University East neighborhood, he just ran between two houses."

"Get after him!" Braddock replied. There was no time to go back and get the Tahoe. It was on the other side of all the rubble. "Fuck it." He took off in a sprint east, down the center sidewalk of the campus mall.

Tori hesitated and then took off after him, slowly at first, shaking the disorientation of the blast, her head still pounding.

Braddock, with his long strides, covered ground rapidly. He glanced back and saw her coming.

"Don't wait! Go!" she said, picking up the pace, her head clearing.

"This is Braddock," he barked into the radio. "Any units still mobile, move to the University East Neighborhood. Suspect Townsend Meade is on foot. He's likely armed. Approach with caution."

* * *

Towne reached the front side of the house and peered around back up the street. It was clear. He took off, running between two parked cars on the west side of the street and then up a driveway. He glanced right at the sound of an engine and caught the pulsing of a flashing light.

* * *

"Where did he go? Where did he go? We need more people," Nolan exclaimed anxiously.

"It's total chaos right now," Steak said, getting more than he'd bargained for when he came in to see what was going on. The neighborhood was all to their left. "Turn in."

Nolan turned left onto a long boulevard, motoring ahead.

"There! Ahead. On the next block. Running across the street." Nolan accelerated.

"We see Meade," Steak radioed. "University East Parkway north of Brainerd Avenue!"

Nolan raced ahead.

"It's that house, that one up there! He went right behind… Oh shit, there he is. Get down! Get down!"

Nolan slammed the brakes.

Crack! Crack! Crack! Crack!
Bullets pelted the truck.
Crack! Crack!

The right front of the Tahoe suddenly dropped. The tires.

"You hit?" Nolan asked, sneaking a peek over the dashboard.

"Ahrg," Steak groaned. "No, but I jarred my shoulder good. Can you see him?"

"No," she replied, her gun out.

* * *

Crack! Crack! Crack! Crack!

"Shots fired, to the east! To the east!" Braddock called on the radio as he rushed across the street and between two houses, glancing back to check for Tori.

Tori waved for Braddock to go as she reached the street in time to see him run between two houses and into the middle of the neighborhood. As she crossed the street, she glanced to her right and saw a Manchester Bay patrol car and sheriff's deputy Explorer approaching from the south, though they were still several blocks away. What she knew of the neighborhood though was the only way into it was from the west and the south. All support, when it arrived, would come from those directions. She ran between the same two houses as Braddock and pulled her gun, slowing for a moment.

If the support was all coming from the south. That would drive Meade east or north. What was east or north?

She thought for a moment.

School. An elementary school. She'd watched Quinn play baseball there.

She veered to the left and ran straight north, pulling her gun.

"What the heck is going on!" a woman yelled from her front stoop.

"Sheriff's department, ma'am. Get inside and lock the door!" Tori yelled as she sprinted by and through the intersection before turning right and sprinting east along the far sidewalk, using the piled snowbanks for cover.

* * *

Braddock ran through a gap between two houses and turned left, seeing the Tahoe sideways in the street, Nolan out. He sprinted to her.

"Are you okay?"

"I'm fine," Nolan answered. "Steak's not shot, but he's hurting."

"Stay with him," Braddock ordered. "Which way did Meade go?"

"East, we think," Nolan said. "He hit us, and then we lost sight, but he went between the houses, right side of the street."

"This is Braddock. Suspect is running east northeast through University Park. He is armed and has fired on officers." He started running down the sidewalk. "We need units to come in from the northeast."

"Will!" Steak grunted. "Will!"

"Will!" Nolan yelled.

"What?"

"There's an elementary school at the northeast end of the development," Steak muttered, grimacing.

"University East Elementary," Nolan yelled.

Braddock's eyes went wide and raised the radio, turned, and sprinted. "This is Braddock. We need that support from the east. Contact University East Elementary. Put the school on lockdown!"

* * *

"Can you see him?" Nora asked Jenks.

"No. No, I lost sight of him," he replied. "We're too low now that we're down the hill. The trees and houses are blocking the view. Keep looping around to here, behind that elementary school, go to the convenience store. That path comes out there."

"Towne? Where are you?" Nora called.

* * *

"I'm in the neighborhood east of the university," Towne said, running between houses, trying to stay out of sight. "I'm running between the houses."

"I saw you a second ago and then lost sight. Keep going northeast, that's away from all the police," Jenks said, looking at the map on the dashboard screen. "There is a treeline, you should be able to see to the northeast. It's behind the last street and row of houses. There's a gas station on the other side of the treeline near the elementary school. Get there."

Towne saw his target destination in the distance. Sirens were audible behind him. They were coming but they weren't here yet. They were all tied up at the university, the people and traffic snarling everything up. There was still a chance. "I see the treeline."

"There is trail path by the elementary school, get to it. We'll be waiting at the end of it."

He saw a man and woman across the street, standing in their driveway. They saw him and the gun in his hand. They turned and scrambled back to their own house.

Towne ran up their driveway, past their back door and through their backyard, keeping his eyes on the distant treeline. *Keep moving that way.* The quickest way was to run the streets, but he couldn't risk getting into the open. Not yet. Not with all the sirens and shouting he heard behind him.

* * *

Braddock made it to the end of the street and caught sight of the line of tall trees that was the far corner of the development. The elementary school was back there. He angled right and ran down the middle of the street, radio in his left hand, gun in the right, peering left down the backyards of the houses.

What was that? He saw a black blur.

He sprinted ahead to the next corner and looked left. There he was, running across the street, mid-block, working northeast.

"This is Braddock. Meade is two blocks from the school, weaving northeast through the houses."

He'd never catch up to him if he followed. Instead, he ran straight ahead another block. At the corner he sprinted across the street and then turned left and ran north up the sidewalk on the other side. He should come out somewhere up ahead.

Where is he?

* * *

Towne ran up a driveway and behind the house veered left, around a homemade backyard hockey rink and then through a small grouping of short spruce trees before emerging into another backyard. He ran around the right side of the house and to the driveway.

And right into three women standing there.

* * *

Tori reached the last street to the north of the neighborhood. She reached the corner and ran across the street and onto the sidewalk. The elementary school was three blocks ahead. Using the mailbox rows and scattered parked cars for cover she sprinted ahead, her gun hanging low in her right hand. It dawned on her as she ran along that she wasn't geared up. No vest.

Be careful.

Looking ahead to her right, she heard screams.

"No! No! Get away! Get away!"

* * *

The elementary school was a block ahead. Braddock could see the main entrance underneath the portico. Three people were standing at the main doors peering pensively outside.

Screams.

"No! No! Get away! Get away!"

That sounded like it was back to his left a block.

* * *

Towne ran past the scurrying women, looked left and saw the trail path through the houses and the trees. The white Tahoe was just pulling into the convenience store parking lot.

"I see you!" he exclaimed.

"We see you," Jenks replied. "Run!"

Towne burst into the open, in a full sprint, running down the middle of the street, heading for the path.

* * *

The screams were up to her right. Careful, Tori crouched down while jogging ahead, both hands on her gun. To the right, a half-block ahead, she saw a flash of black between two houses: a man running in her direction.

Meade.

There was a parked car just ahead. She hopped the snowbank, and crouched at the front fender, using the engine block for cover, her feet set as Meade ran into the street a half-block ahead.

"*Meade!*"

He raised his right arm. She fired.

Pop! Pop!

She ducked down behind the front of the car.

Crack! Crack! Crack!

Shots pinged off the car.

She peeked up. Meade wasn't breaking stride, charging down the trail path. She readied to fire, then stopped.

The school was in her background.

"Dammit!"

* * *

Braddock heard "*Meade!*"

That was Tori, to his left, to the north.

Pop! Pop!

Crack! Crack! Crack!

He reached the corner and saw Meade run between two houses on a running path. Tori ran out from behind a car a half-block back.

"Tori!"

"Go!" She waved for him to run around the far side of the elementary school.

* * *

Pumping his arms, Towne ran through the narrow opening of the treeline. The blaring of sirens filled the air now, no longer so distant, moving closer.

"Come on!" Jenks yelled, his window down. "Come on! Come on!"

* * *

The sound of the sirens told Tori that help was getting closer.

She hurried up the front sidewalk of the house just before the path, and then veered right and around the front corner, peeking around to see Meade sprinting along the path. Then she saw the white SUV, the exhaust from the tailpipe. Waiting. For Meade.

Scrambling down the side hill of the yard, she reached the path and ran. Meade was almost to the SUV.

She scanned her background again and then set her feet. Now or never.

* * *

Braddock, in full gallop, hustled around the east side of the elementary school and saw why Tori told him to. Through the small rear playground, he could see the end of a treeline that led to the back of a small strip mall. He saw Meade nearing a white SUV, then further back he saw Tori setting her feet to fire.

Pop! Pop! Pop! Pop! Pop!

He ran through the playground, jumped down a small embankment and into the parking lot.

* * *

Jenks opened the back-passenger door. Towne dove for the back seat.

Pop! Pop! Pop! Pop! Pop!

"Ahrg!" Towne groaned loudly, his legs hanging out the door. He'd been hit in the back of his left thigh.

"Get in here!" Jenks shouted, using his good right arm, grabbing the back of Towne's jeans to drag him in. He looked up and saw the woman, Hunter, coming. He turned to Max. "Go! Go!"

Max was looking straight ahead. Frozen.

Jenks turned.

Braddock was right there, a hundred feet ahead, gun up. He looked left. A Minnesota State Patrol cruiser skidded to a stop, the trooper quickly getting out. The sound of more sirens suddenly flooding the air. He looked ahead and saw flashing lights coming up the road.

"What do we do?" Max shrieked. "What!"

"We gotta go! We gotta go!" Towne exclaimed. "Now! Go for it!"

"Run that son of a bitch!" Jenks yelled. *"Run him now! Go!"*

She hit the gas.

* * *

Braddock heard the first bit of gravel when the tires spun. He depressed the trigger, firing at the driver.

Boom! Boom! Boom!

The SUV was coming right at him.

Boom! Boom! Boom!

Braddock dove to his left as the SUV zoomed by him.

Pop! Pop! Pop! Pop! Pop!

Bap! Bap! Bap! Bap! Bap!

Tori and the trooper were both firing.

He rolled onto his back. The SUV jerked hard left, hit a cement parking block, and flipped into the air and then over, and then again.

On the third roll, it burst into flames.

The SUV came to a rest upside down in the parking lot, engulfed in fire.

"Are you alright?" Tori called, running to him, her gun up, her eyes fixed on the burning SUV.

She helped him up and they slowly approached the mangled, fiery SUV. The state trooper approached first, shielding his face from the flames. Another trooper pulled into the lot and was immediately out with his fire extinguisher.

"Don't bother," Braddock said, the SUV fully aflame. If they weren't already dead from the gunfire, they were dead from the flames. "They got what they deserved."

A fire department truck arrived five minutes later and quickly put out the fire of the SUV. There were three bodies inside. They knew one was Meade. They were certain that when the smoke cleared and IDs were made by the medical examiner's office, the other two would be Nora Bartness and Wayne Jenkins.

The SUV scene secured, Braddock and Tori made their back to check on Steak. A state trooper had arrived and said he'd transport Steak to the hospital. Tori helped ease Steak down into the back of a state trooper's cruiser. She leaned in and helped him with the seat belt. Tori wasn't sure what Steak was dreading more; that he'd done more damage to the shoulder or the reaming he was in for from Grace.

"Tell her the truth. Paint yourself as the hero that you are. You're the one who identified Meade running away from the blast," Tori said. "We caught up to him, Bartness, and Jenkins because you spotted him. That ought to account for something."

"Maybe you should tell her."

"I will if you want me to, buddy," Tori said. "Just say the word. I'll call Grace for ya."

"Nah," Steak replied, sitting back with a pained yet wry smile. "I'll take my beating. I shouldn't have been here to begin with."

"I'm damn glad you were though," Tori said, tenderly grasping him on his good right shoulder, the two of them sharing a relieved look and laugh before she closed the door and pounded on the roof. The trooper pulled away.

Reese and Eggs drove them back to the auditorium. The fire department continued to douse the smoldering fire, though the smoke had now largely cleared. They could now see more clearly that the Riley Auditorium was a hollowed mass of rubble with only some segments of the exterior walls still standing. Shattered glass, mangled steel, and shards of brick, cement and stone made for a massive debris field in the middle of the campus. Meade had used enough explosive to put a hole in the world.

Emergency personnel continued to tend to victims of the blast. Those who remained appeared to be suffering from cuts and bruises and more minor injuries, though additional ambulances continued to arrive.

"The truly critical have already been transported," Boe said, her own clothes bloodied from helping the injured. "I know of no deaths, at least so far," she added, "which borders on a miracle." She stunned Braddock, embracing him and then Tori. "To get that building cleared was..." Boe had to compose herself, shaking her head. "I'm just grateful."

"Agreed," Jackson said, walking up, shaking hands with them. He had returned with the governor and commerce secretary; both wanting to assess the situation. "The secretary is on the phone with the president right now," Jackson said. "I just have to say hell of a job you two."

"It wasn't just us. It was our whole team," Braddock said.

"And we need to thank Teddy Marist," Tori said, and related how he'd put them onto Nora Bartness when he heard her voice playing in the conference room. "If Teddy didn't hear that, well..." Her voice trailed off. "God, I don't even want to think about it."

"You got Meade, and his compatriots?" Boe said.

"They're barbequing," Tori said. "Let's just say they'll be extra crispy."

"Good. Is there anyone else?"

"As of right now," Braddock started, "I don't think so. We thought there were four men, we got Meade, Jenkins, and Mercer, plus Jared Bayne. Max we knew about and now identified as Nora Bartness. That makes five. We got them all."

THIRTY-THREE
"A DRIVEN PERSON WHO NEEDS A PURPOSE."

In the days following the bombing, surveillance video from inside the auditorium showed that the bomb emanated from the base of the podium. In culling through the university's security surveillance system between when the event was first announced and the day of the bombing, Townsend Meade, disguised as a custodian, paid three different late-night visits to the Riley Auditorium. The first time was on his own. The second time was three nights later with Wayne Jenkins five weeks before the bombing, and the final time with Bartness two nights before the event, when it was thought they set the bomb in the podium base.

That left the money to chase.

Marist had in fact been embezzling money. The FBI brought in a forensic accounting team to scour Marist's work at the bank for the past sixteen years. It took three months, but the FBI determined the theft occurred in a period from six years to a year ago.

Wills had been correct. The first embezzlement involved abandoned accounts. One of the forensic accountants told Braddock, "I won't bore you with the jargon but what he did was very well hidden and papered over so you wouldn't see anything missing on the surface or even a layer or two below the surface. You had to dig in and peel back many layers but once we did, we found money was missing that you can't tie out anywhere. It wasn't just the abandoned accounts either. That was his first scheme, and it ties back to when the loan for his father was denied. He started on the abandoned accounts a few weeks later."

Beyond the abandoned accounts, Marist had gone on to create fake customer bank accounts and used them to transfer money in a variety of ways. The transactions all looked normal to the naked eye of any bank employee, the bank's auditors and even at first and second blush, to the forensic accountants. It took time to find the accounts and understand all that Marist had done to hide his tracks. The same forensic accountant explained to Braddock, "I'm telling you; he knew all the holes in the systems and internal controls and exploited them before he closed them. It's brilliant really. He would identify a vulnerability, take advantage of it in small unnoticeable daily or weekly amounts, drip, drip, drip, for a period, funnel the money into the accounts, transfer it out of the bank to other banks and then in the name of efficiency and security would review the procedures, point out the risk they were exposed to and then plug the hole he'd actually been exploiting so you could never know what he had been doing. And in the process, everyone thought he was this brilliant employee because he discovered the problem and provided the solution, ostensibly *before* it became a problem. He traveled around giving presentations on it. And nobody, given his position, and supposed expertise, ever questioned him. It was one heck of a cover. Nobody saw it."

"Someone did," Braddock said. "Nora Bartness."

Bartness's college transcripts revealed she was a solid student with a particular aptitude for math and accounting, courses for which she had straight As. The same forensic accounting team also reviewed Bartness's computer activity. Nora Bartness had, for eighteen months, been stealthily investigating Barry Marist using Elaine Baird's passwords to access all corners of the bank's systems.

"She didn't finish college, but she was whip-smart," Braddock said to Tori as they ate dinner one night after the investigation at the bank was completed. "And likely underemployed."

"For some reason, she developed suspicions about Marist," Tori said. "But her first inclination wasn't to report it to Elaine Baird."

"Or maybe when she started it was, but then somewhere along the way she figures out Elaine and Marist are sleeping together. If she reports it, Elaine might start asking all kinds of awkward questions about how Nora figured it out, how she got access, all those sorts of things. My guess is she was sitting on it, wondering what to do with it."

"And then opportunity knocks," Tori said. "Secretary of Commerce Cooper Farrow, the man who ordered the attack on their brother, whom she held responsible for his death, is coming to town. Coming to *her* town. He'd be right here."

Braddock nodded. "We now know from their phone records that Nora and her brother were in regular contact. Nora says to her brother, we can get what we've always wanted. Farrow's going to be here, at the university, at an event that will have some security, but it'll be light, just the local yokels and a few U.S. Marshals. It's the secretary of commerce. Who goes after somebody like that? Oh, and by the way, do you remember that woman, Lainey Darr, who said all those nasty things on cable news about Rodney? Thanks to Marist, we get her too."

"So, Townsend Meade and Wayne Jenkins come up here, walk the university, get into the auditorium, view the podium and they see their opportunity.

"But if they pull it off, they have to go away, forever. And in Marist, what does she have? The golden parachute. They just have to find a way to take it and do it in a way that everyone looks at Marist and nobody looks at them. So, use his divorce, kill Lainey, Girard, take his son, set him up. It was a good plan. If Marist doesn't mess up their plan at that resort?" His voice trailed off.

Tori shook her head. "Man, we were lucky."

"Yeah, we were," Braddock said, and then paused. "But we also put ourselves in a position to be lucky. I think we did our jobs quite well."

"We did."

The question after that was where all the money went.

"What did you find on that Wi-Fi hot spot we recovered?" Braddock had asked the FBI's forensic accountant.

"IP addresses for banks in Bermuda. Is six million dollars worth the battle with banks that consider privacy of their clientele vital to their success? That's a decision well above my pay grade."

"I heard the White House is interested because of the domestic terrorism angle to this thing. And an attack on a cabinet officer. Someone close to the president."

"That might be enough to tip the scales for these banks," the FBI accountant noted. "Is it worth making an enemy of the U.S. Government over a few million dollars?"

Braddock and Tori discussed the money angle over dinner one night at Mannion's on the Lake.

"What's odd to me about all this," Tori noted. "Is that there is no evidence Marist ever spent any of it. Embezzlers always spend their ill-gotten gains. They live large. A lot of the time that's how they get caught, living beyond their means. Lavish trips, sports cars, fancy watches. But Marist? His house was nice but certainly easily affordable given his income. His bank balances well in line. The only investments in his files at home were for his 401k with the bank and some small individual IRAs. He didn't have to give up any of those balances as part of his divorce settlement, so he was quite comfortable financially without all of this. I suspect he originally stole the money to give to his dad, but when he died, why not put it back? Or why keep going with the risk? Why take on more if you didn't need it?"

Braddock had a theory. "I've investigated embezzlement once or twice. It always seems to start with doing something small once. Maybe they needed money at that point and saw a way to get it, so they took it. And then they don't get caught."

"And if I got away with it once," Tori said.

"I could do it again. It all started after the bank refused to approve the loan," Braddock noted. "The first thing he stole were those unclaimed account dollars. They were just sitting there, abandoned. He stole that money and planned to give it to his dad to allow him to rebuild. If the bank wouldn't loan him the money, then Marist said fine, I'll just take it."

"But then his dad committed suicide," Tori said, seeing it. "So now he has the money but rather than put it back..."

"He kept it," Braddock said. "And then once he'd stolen that, and nobody noticed, he found another way to skim some money. And then another. He just kept helping himself a little at a time, then covered the problem and then went looking for another one. Until it started to add up to some real money that he would have eventually spent some way somehow in time. He robbed the bank fifty dollars at a time from the inside and nobody ever noticed, other than Nora Bartness."

And because nobody other than Nora Bartness had ever noticed, a few months after the bombing, Lakes Community Bank quietly announced that Elaine Baird would be moving on.

Tori had stayed in regular communication with Tony and Fiona Darr, in part to check in on Teddy, and in part to warn them of what was coming. Three months after the bombing, she and Braddock drove down to the Twin Cities on a Saturday morning. On the following Monday the FBI would hold a press conference on the investigation and they were going to address Barry Marist and his embezzlement from the bank and how it factored in. Tori wanted Teddy to hear about it from her first.

"My dad was a thief," Teddy said sadly, his eyes moist. "He stole all that money. And that's why Mom is dead, isn't it?"

"Your dad didn't want that to happen to your mom," Tori said. "He could have never foreseen that. I'm not excusing what he did, what he did was wrong, it was a crime, but he was not responsible for your mom's death. That wasn't his fault. Don't hold him responsible for that."

"But he was a thief."

"There was good and bad to your dad," Tori said. "He committed a crime. If he were alive, he would go to prison for several years. That's the bad. The good? He fought for you. He sacrificed himself and did everything he could to protect and save you that awful day. I think you should remember that too."

"I will," Teddy replied.

That night after speaking with Teddy, Tori needed wine. A lot of wine. She and Braddock watched a movie and then as they often did, they opened a second bottle and just talked about any number of topics. Eventually, Braddock asked: "So, is it going to be Professor Hunter full time?"

"How would you feel about it if I did?"

"My only question would be, is that what you want?"

She took a slow drink of her wine. "I have financial security. And from time to time, you bring me into an investigation, so I still get to scratch that itch. And I know I could work more regularly for the sheriff's department but—"

"It'd be too mundane."

"Your words, not mine," Tori said.

"It's okay," he said, smiling. "Can I make an observation?"

"When have you ever needed my permission?"

"I don't," he replied, before tenderly reaching for her hand. "You've been back here nearly three years. In that time, you've given up your FBI career, healed, made peace with your past, gotten into a good place mentally, fallen in love, at least I think you have."

"You know I have."

"But you're still Tori Hunter. A person who needs a purpose. You need something to get you up and going every day. Amirite?"

"I think I do."

"Taking your experiences and becoming a teacher?" He smiled. "What could be more rewarding."

"I do like it, much more than I ever thought I would."

"Then I say go for it," Braddock said. "Although I do have one question."

"Which is?"

"Will Professor Victoria Hunter still want to help out Will Braddock from time to time?"

Tori leaned over and kissed him softly. "From time to time she will."

THIRTY-FOUR

"HOW 'BOUT THEM APPLES."

June 22nd

Braddock poked at the ribeye's sizzling over the searing heat of the grill.

"They're looking pretty, pretty good," Steak said, handing Braddock another cold beer with his left hand, pleased that he could use it again. He was still a few months away from returning to work, but he was getting some functionality back. They clinked bottles and looked out to the lake, the sun setting behind them on a pleasant mid-June evening.

"What a night," Steak mused. It was seventy-five degrees, not a cloud in the sky, a light breeze keeping the bugs away.

"This is why people have lake places," Braddock agreed. "Nights like this."

"This right here is as good as it gets. Can't improve on perfection."

"Oh, we'll see about that."

"What?"

"Nothing," Braddock said as he spun around. Laughter emanated from the other side of the deck where Tori, Steak's wife Grace, Eggs and her husband Bruce, Reese and his girlfriend and Nolan talked, relaxed, and laughed along with Boe and her husband, who Braddock had added to the invite list at the last minute. All of them were taking turns with the puppy, the yellow Lab Quinn had named Boomer.

"How long?" Tori asked, Boomer climbing on her, his tail wagging.

"Not long."

Ten minutes later and a few more pokes with his long grilling fork, he declared, "They're done."

He hoisted the thick, perfectly cooked steaks onto the massive serving plate and walked them over to the long deck table, setting it in the middle, the aroma wafting into the warm night air. Tori and all the others brought out the salads, corn on the cob and potatoes and everyone dug in, enjoying a barbeque on a beautiful Minnesota summer night.

After dinner was finished, dessert was served, and Braddock made sure everyone had a fresh libation. Boe clinked her wine glass. "Can I have everyone's attention." She looked over to Braddock. "If you would do the honors."

Braddock stood up and handed out envelopes to Tori, Steak, Eggleston, Reese, and Nolan. He kept one for himself.

"You'll notice that the envelopes are from the White House," Boe said with a big grin.

Braddock and Tori smiled for they already knew what was inside. Boe had informed them yesterday and Braddock invited everyone over for the barbecue and reveal. With pride he and Tori watched the eyes of their friends slowly widen in shock reading the letter from the White House.

"Holy shit," Reese blurted.

"You've got to be kidding," Eggs said in wonder.

Nolan shook her head. "No way."

"Is this for real?" Steak said, looking up, his wife Grace's jaw dropping as she read the letter.

"As real as it gets, my friend," Braddock said, smiling.

Boe stood up and raised her glass. "It is my distinct honor to inform you that because of your bravery in the line of duty on that day in February, yes, on August fifteenth in a ceremony at the White House, you will all be awarded the Medal of Valor by the President of the United States."

Tori smiled. "How 'bout them apples."

The Public Safety Officer Medal of Valor is the highest national award for valor by a public safety officer. The medal is awarded annually by the President of the United States to public safety officers who have exhibited exceptional courage, regardless of personal safety, in the attempt to save or protect human life.

Braddock, Tori, Steak, Eggs, Reese and Nolan were part of a group of sixteen law enforcement officers from across the country to receive medals. Tori smiled as she received her award, shaking the president's hand, posing for a photo and then winking at Quinn, who sat with his grandparents in the audience, all of them beaming at her and Braddock.

After the ceremony, everyone moved to the East Room for a reception. A presidential aide asked Braddock and Tori if they would follow her. She led them over to the West Wing and the Oval Office. She left them inside alone for a few minutes, awaiting the president.

Tori had turned to Braddock. "What are we doing here?"

"I don't know, but this is kind of amazing," Braddock said in wonder, shaking his head. "I never ever thought I'd do something like this."

"I didn't think you got starstruck."

"This is something entirely different. This is something special to soak in."

"Yeah," she replied, wrapping her arms around Braddock.

The door was opened by a secret service agent and the president, and the presidential photographer, arrived and another photo of the three of them was taken standing in front of the Resolute desk.

After the photographer left, the president said, "As I understand it, you two in particular were responsible for saving Secretary Farrow's life, among all the others. Coop is one of my oldest and dearest friends. We go back forty plus years to college. I'm so very grateful to you both. Thank you. Truly, I thank you."

"You're welcome, Mr. President," Braddock said.

"As you know, I'll be coming to Minnesota in October when ground is broken for a new auditorium at Central Minnesota State University. Coop will be there as well and we're going to celebrate the courage of you and your fellow detectives, of course. But for the two of you, for my friend Coop, is there anything else I could do for you?" the president said, smiling. "I do have some pull."

"Mr. President," Braddock replied, holding his medal, and then gazing around the Oval Office. "I think you've done enough, sir."

"Not so fast there, Detective Braddock," Tori said, and the president smiled broadly. "Mr. President, I can think of one request I have if you were so inclined. It's not for us though, but for someone else."

"Ask away."

"Chief Detective Braddock and I, Detectives Williams, Eggleston, Reese, and Nolan, we did all lay it on the line that day and we were all extremely fortunate to walk away from it, but we wouldn't even have had the chance if it weren't for a ten-year-old boy named Teddy Marist. His wits and bravery were every bit as responsible as we were."

Tori quickly explained what Teddy had been through, how he had learned of the existence of Max, the chase and then hearing Nora Bartness's voice. "Mr. President, you have a unique capacity, born of your own life experiences, to relate to people who have suffered from tragedy. Teddy has had a rough go, losing both his parents. When you do come to Minnesota, if you could spend just a minute or two with him, shake his hand, offer a few kind words of encouragement, take a photo like this, I can only imagine what that might mean for him."

The president smiled. "Tori, Will, I think we can squeeze in more than a minute or two. Do you think Teddy might like to fly on Air Force One?"

A LETTER FROM ROGER

As always, I truly appreciate that you've chosen to spend some of your hard-earned money and free time reading *Taken in the Cold*. I hope you enjoyed it. If you did, I'd like to keep you up to date with all my latest releases, just sign up at the following link. Your email address will never be shared, and you can unsubscribe at any time.

www.bookouture.com/roger-stelljes

It is you, the reader, that I always have in mind as I work. For me, the fun of writing this series is that I get to create this world of Tori, Braddock, Manchester Bay and all the characters in it. Every book, I am provided the opportunity to think about my characters and what little character quirk I can add and what little piece of backstory could build their legend. And the setting of Manchester Bay, of Minnesota lakes country, provides the ideal visual canvas to tell a new and interesting story I've never told before. As readers, please know that every day I wake up thinking about this world I've created and what is next for Tori, Braddock, Steak and all the rest of the gang. I truly hope you enjoy reading their adventures every bit as much as I do the process of crafting them.

One of the best parts of being an author is seeing the reaction from readers, both those who have read all my books and those new to the scene. My goal every time I write is to give you, the reader, what I have always looked for in a book myself. An exciting story that draws you in, puts you on edge, makes you think, on occasion pulls at the heartstrings, and always, *always*, makes you want to read just one more page, one more chapter, because you just couldn't put it down. That is my litmus test for a good book. It is my credo as a writer. I endeavor to deliver it to you, the reader, every time.

If you enjoyed the story, I would greatly appreciate it if you could leave a short review. Receiving feedback from readers like you is important to me in developing and writing my stories, but is also vital in helping to persuade others to pick up one of my books for the first time.

If you enjoyed *Taken in the Cold*, and it's your first time with Tori, Braddock, and their friends, they can also be found in *Silenced Girls, The Winter Girls, The Hidden Girl, Missing Angel, The Snow Graves* and *Their Lost Souls* and in more stories to come.

Thank you,

Roger

www.RogerStelljes.com

facebook.com/rogerstelljesbooks
x.com/RogerStelljes
instagram.com/rogerstelljes

PUBLISHING TEAM

Turning a manuscript into a book requires the efforts of many people. The publishing team at Bookouture would like to acknowledge everyone who contributed to this publication.

Audio
Alba Proko
Sinead O'Connor
Melissa Tran

Commercial
Lauren Morrissette
Hannah Richmond
Imogen Allport

Cover design
Ghost

Data and analysis
Mark Alder
Mohamed Bussuri

Editorial
Ellen Gleeson
Nadia Michael

Copyeditor
Jane Eastgate

Proofreader
Shirley Khan

Marketing
Alex Crow
Melanie Price
Occy Carr
Cíara Rosney
Martyna Młynarska

Operations and distribution
Marina Valles
Stephanie Straub
Joe Morris

Production
Hannah Snetsinger
Mandy Kullar
Jen Shannon
Ria Clare

Publicity
Kim Nash
Noelle Holten
Jess Readett
Sarah Hardy

Rights and contracts
Peta Nightingale
Richard King
Saidah Graham

Milton Keynes UK
Ingram Content Group UK Ltd.
UKHW020153241024
450133UK00005B/276